OBOE

CAL ROGAN MYSTERIES BOOK 2

ROBERT P. FRENCH

FOREWORD

Thank you so much for choosing Oboe. For more on Cal Rogan, there is information at the end of the book where you can sign up to get free copies of upcoming books.

Enjoy!

ACKNOWLEDGMENTS

My very special thanks go to Lisa Rector-Maass of Third Draft Editing in New York, who supported and mentored me from day one through all the drafts.

Also many thanks to a marvellous employee of RSA who explained some of the intricacies of encryption. He asked to remain anonymous. I apologize for anything I may have got wrong.

I would also like to thank the Vancouver Public Library for providing the perfect working location for any writer.

To my wonderful wife Penny who believed in me when I had stopped believing in myself.

ALSO BY ROBERT P. FRENCH

Junkie (Cal Rogan Mysteries Book 1)

Lockstep (Cal Rogan Mysteries Book 3)

Three (Cal Rogan Mysteries Book 4)

Cabal (Cal Rogan Mysteries Book 5)

Captive (Cal Rogan Mysteries Book 6)

Jailed (Cal Rogan Mysteries Book 7)

They are all available in large print from Amazon

1

CAL
MONDAY

The thought of crossing this line fills me with dread. I feel rooted to the ground; I know that once I move, I will be changed forever and not for the better.

Steeling myself—or am I just delaying the inevitable?—I look up at the trees. They are old growth, moss covered monsters that have stood here for centuries. The enmity with which they glare down at me, through the forbidding early light, seeks to warn me off; they know I am a member of the species that has just profaned their woods. Although the thought skips through my mind, I know I cannot turn back.

I lift the yellow tape and stoop under.

At twenty paces, facing away and clad, like me, in crime-scene clothing, heads tilted forward, they look like alien prisoners about to be executed by a bullet in the back. Five of them are standing in a semicircle looking down at the sixth, a man, crouching over something on the ground. Cops at a murder scene often indulge in gallows humour, a futile mechanism to try and erase the horror of the brutal theft of a human life, but as I approach, I note they are silent.

I take my place beside my minder, at the left-hand end of the group; the outsider. He doesn't bother to acknowledge my presence but a distant peal of thunder announces my arrival. Or is it a warning of what this case might do to me? Nothing has prepared me for this, the crime scene every cop dreads, especially a cop with a child he once failed to protect. But it is also the crime every cop wants to solve, especially the outsider who wants back in.

In an effort to delay the inevitable, I exchange looks and nods with the others present. There are no smiles today. Glad of the excuse, they fix their eyes on me. Waiting for the reaction, I suppose.

With no other option, I force myself to look down.

The grey light filtering through the forest canopy is just enough to illuminate the body in the mud. He is wearing funky yellow and green sneakers and grey sweat pants bearing the red Nike swoosh. They are muddied and ripped. He is naked above the waist and is drenched in blood. He looks to be about nine or ten years old, forcing other unwanted images into my mind. I struggle to banish them... and only partly succeed.

There seem to be five wounds in an approximate circle with his belly button at its centre As if this were not enough, on his face there are two knife slashes forming an X. Each slash starts on one cheek and finishes on the opposite jaw line, with the centre of the X over his mouth.

The eyes are bloody, damaged in some way. There is not a lot of blood on his face and I am praying that the facial wounds were inflicted after he was dead.

I look up. I survived but I was right. I know exactly how this crime has already changed me and, God help me, I embrace the change. The shiver that runs through me has nothing to do with the cold February morning and I can feel burning rage building inside. A good rage. A rage to consume me until I find the monster who did this.

"We'll know more later but I estimate time of death at about eight or nine PM yesterday," says a voice in a Québécois accent. I turn back and see that the coroner is on his feet and I am grateful that I do not have to look down again. "Cause is almost certainly the wound to 'is solar plexus. The facial wounds were *post mortem* and there is no obvious sign of sexual assault." At this last, there is a sigh of relief from everyone but me. Not even that abomination could make me more determined to find this child's killer. He nods toward Steve, my boss, "We should 'ave more for you later."

I force my jaw to relax. "Was there any ID on the body?" I ask. He shakes his head.

It is time for the removal of the body and then the Forensic Services techs can take over. Before I clear the scene, I make myself take a good look around the area. About five feet from the body is what I guess to be the remains of a green t-shirt and a yellow winter jacket—it's the exact shade of yellow that is my daughter Ellie's favourite colour A part of me screams to call Ellie, just to hear her voice and know she's OK, but right now I need to move heaven and earth to get my hands on the monster who did this.

Nothing else on the forest floor seems to be out of place but, if anything is, Forensics will find it; unless the firemen, typically first at the scene, have trampled it out of existence.

I somehow bring myself to take a final look at the body. Three lone rain drops fall from the leaves above and I watch them spatter on the child's bloody torso. Claudius' words spring into my mind, *Is there not rain enough in the sweet heavens to wash it white as snow?*

No, Claudius. There isn't.

I head down the trail, back to where the cars are parked, and the not-so-sweet heavens open, baptizing us all into the select cult of those who have looked upon the body of a murdered child.

As badly as this day has started, I know it is going to get worse. By the time it draws to its close, I pray the images of this particular morning will keep my rage alive and keep at bay the longing for the sweet release only heroin can bring.

2

CAL

And now another line to cross. One I have crossed before. But this time will be a thousand times worse. I am angry at my minder's curt "you handle this, Rogan," but am glad too, because I will do this so much better than he ever could.

The door is snatched open.

She sees us and casts a desperate look around and behind us. I know what, or rather whom she is looking for. I hold up my badge, "Mrs. Wright? I'm Detective Rogan and this is Detective Stammo. May we come in, please?"

Her eyes settle on mine, switch to Stammo and then back to me. She knows to a certainty why we are here.

"Nooooooooo!" she collapses against the door post.

Stammo springs forward to stop her from falling but a man appears and puts both arms around her. He looks at Stammo. "Is it... Terry?" he asks.

"Yes, sir. I'm afraid so." There is a catch in Stammo's voice. My minder *is* human after all.

"Oh God, no." He half carries his wife into the house. "Come in," he throws back over his shoulder.

We follow him through the tiny entranceway and into the tiny living room. It feels familiar but not in a good way. I was brought up in houses like this.

He helps her onto the couch and sits beside her with his arm around her shoulders, steadying her. I try to imagine the pain that is coursing through them. If it were me being told by two strangers that Ellie... I need to stop myself going there. Too much empathy is a dangerous thing in a murder investigation.

I sit in the worn chair opposite them and they turn their faces toward me. Stricken: his, wide-eyed and haunted; hers, awash in tears, no hope in them, not wanting to hear what I have to tell them... but needing to.

The ticking of a clock somewhere in the room seems loud.

I dry swallow. "I'm so sorry to have to tell you

but we've found the body of a child. We believe it could be your missing son, Terry."

"You're not sure?" Elizabeth Wright clutches at a desperate straw.

"I'm afraid we will need you to come and identify the body to be certain." I tell them. "But he was dressed as you described in the missing person report and the photo matches. I can't tell you how sorry I am."

As his wife sobs in his arms, Wright asks the question, the answer to which will haunt them forever. "How did he...?"

There is no way I can sugar-coat the answer with the empty phrases *I'm afraid that* or *I'm sorry to have to tell you,* so I just and say, "His body was found in the UBC Endowment Lands. He was murdered."

Elizabeth Wright's sobbing has become a wail and her husband buries his shocked face in her hair.

I look up at Stammo and even he is blinking his eyes and looking at the ceiling. I see a real pain inside him. The shock makes me forget my anger at the cruel departmental joke that, given our history, made *him* of all people my minder, the supervisor of my probationary period.

The clock ticks in rhythm to Elizabeth Wright's sobs.

To distract myself I look around the room. It is a

small living/dining room and, through a hatch in the wall at the back of the dining area, I can see a kitchen. On the far end of the formica dining-room table there are the remains of an abandoned breakfast. Sharing the table are three very large computer monitors each displaying a writhing screen-saver. The monitors are connected to two tower PCs located under the table. It looks like a very expensive setup to my untrained eye and is at odds with the low-cost, rather shabby look of the rest of the house. The computer makes a pinging noise and the screen savers vanish. The screens fill with what looks like gobbledygook to me.

"Why would someone murder my son?" Mark Wright asks suddenly, drawing my attention away from the screens. "He was just a kid. Everybody loved Terry. It doesn't make any sense."

I turn to him. His eyes flick toward the computer screens. Why? His eyes pan back to mine and I try to read what's in them. Is he trying to hide something? Guilt?

I turn back to the monitors and try to make sense of what I see. I can feel the awkward silence behind me. On the middle one there are words, numbers and symbols... lots of parentheses, but on the right hand one, just long lines of letters and numbers without spaces.

"Do you know why Terry went missing?" I ask.

"Rogan!" As I turn, Stammo's eyes drill into mine for a moment. Then they soften. "We don't know why someone would murder your son, sir," Stammo says, his voice more gentle than it has ever been with me, or with anyone else for that matter, "but believe me, I promise you we will do *everything* in our power to find out who killed him and bring that person to justice."

An image springs into my mind: Stammo and I in an alley, armed with baseball bats, administering justice to this particular killer. The thought feels better than it should.

Elizabeth Wright ignores him but looks at me and brushes away the tears with her fingertips. "Was he... you know..."

She cannot say it. Before I can speak, Stammo supplies the word. "Molested?" She shudders. "At this point we don't think so but we won't be sure until after the autopsy."

She nods her head and buries her face in her husband's shoulder.

Stammo gives me a half nod. I stand up. "We have to ask you to come downtown to identify the body." I tell them. "I am going to send in two uniformed officers; they'll drive you there and bring you back home afterward."

They both look up and nod vaguely in my direction.

Stammo and I make our own way out and signal the patrols to go in.

"Very sensitive, Rogan." The old Stammo has returned. "Your job was to help them through this, not stick your nose into the man's computer programs and definitely not to start questioning him. What the hell were you thinking?"

I don't know which surprises me more: the fact that he knew the stuff on the monitors was a computer program or that he did a better job in there than I did.

As we walk to the car, the rain redoubles its efforts but does nothing to wash away my feeling of isolation.

3

CAL

lack! My child is dead; And with my child my joys are buried.

The Wrights embody the Bard's word. From the moment they identified the mutilated face, they have become like zombies. The loss of their son Terry has sucked their life force and left them husks, sitting together on the elderly couch, holding hands, forlorn. Elizabeth Wright is a striking woman with thick, curly, straw-coloured hair tied behind her head in a scrunchie. She looks like she has cried all the moisture out of her system. Her husband Mark looks disheveled, curly hair awry, two days growth of black stubble, his eyes focused on some distant point.

"We're sorry to have to ask you all these questions so soon after the loss of your son," Stammo is saying, "but the faster we pursue the investigation, the more likely we are to get an outcome. And we will do everything we can to find who did this to your boy."

They both just nod.

It bugs me that Stammo is taking the lead. After some training to update me, I'm back in the Vancouver Police Department, thanks to the influence of the Mayor and the Deputy Chief, and I am on a kind of probation with Stammo supervising me. But we both know I am the better detective, which irks him. Pairing me with Stammo of all people was probably the result of someone's resentment at my return, most likely Superintendent Cathcart, head of Investigations Division.

Or maybe someone wants to punish Stammo.

However, at least I am in the Homicide Unit. If I hadn't solved Kevin Wallace's murder last year, I'd probably be handing out parking tickets in Kerrisdale.

So Stammo will ask the questions. On the drive over here, he said, "I don't want you screwing up like you did earlier, Rogan. You take notes; make use of that Master's degree in literature." He never misses a chance to take a shot.

"Can you tell us about when Terry went missing?" he asks.

They look at each other and something passes

between them. I can't quite identify what it is but my gut says she is signalling that she wants to take the lead on answering the questions. She looks at Stammo and her husband looks down at his hands. I try to imagine what would happen between Sam and me if Ellie were murdered when she was with me. I can't.

"I came home from work at eight and he wasn't here," she hesitates, cutting a look at her husband. "I checked with the neighbours and called his friend Michael's family. But no-one had seen him. Mark got on his bike and went round the local streets looking for him while I called 9-1-1 and re-ported him missing."

"Yesterday was a Sunday. You were at work?" Stammo asks.

"Yes, I'm a nurse at VGH. I was pulling a twelve hour shift."

Before Stammo can ask his next question, Mark Wright groans, "It was my fault." He leans forward and puts his head in his hands. "I should have been watching him better but I was working on the com-puter. I kinda lost track of time and he must have run off."

His wife cuts him a look.

"When was the last time you saw him?" I ask, drawing a scowl from Stammo for interrupting his flow.

"It was about five-thirty." Tears are coursing down his cheeks. "We had just got back from a play date at his friend Michael's house. I needed to do some stuff on my computer and so I sent him to his room to play. Next thing I know, it's eight o'clock and he's gone."

"So he disappeared sometime between five-thirty and eight," says Stammo, re-establishing his position as lead interviewer with a redundant question.

They both nod.

Instead of asking one of the questions struggling to get themselves off my tongue, Stammo says, "OK, Mr. Wright tell us about Terry's day yesterday. Starting from when your wife went to work."

"Sure. Elizabeth left at about six-thirty in the morning. Terry and I got up at about eight. I made his favourite breakfast, dollar pancakes with maple syrup. I let him play on his computer while I did the dishes and then I took him out. I practically had to drag him away from his game."

I'm watching him like a hawk for any tells that would indicate that he is lying. I can't think why he would but it's a habit.

"We went to Best Buy," he continues. "I needed to buy some stuff. Then we drove down to the airport. Terry loved to watch the planes land. We parked in that area right under the flight path." He looks at his wife and again something passes between them. Something feels wrong here.

"Did anything unusual happen at the store or at the airport? Did you see anyone you know or talk to anyone?" Stammo asks, sticking with the pedestrian questions.

"Not really. Terry had a major meltdown in the store; he wanted to stay there and play with one of the Wii games. But apart from that, nothing out of the ordinary." For the third time, the look at his wife.

"So what did you do after the airport?"

"We went over to his friend Michael's house for lunch and a play date. Dave and Grace, Michael's parents, are good friends of ours and we often visit each other. We stayed there for the afternoon and then got back here at about five-thirty, like I said."

"And nothing unusual happened at all?" Stammo is reaching the end of his limited repertoire.

"No nothing." Wright shakes his head.

Stammo looks at me. At last, permission to speak. In the momentary silence, I notice that the clock I could hear this morning is no longer ticking.

"Could you show me his room, please?" I ask.

Elizabeth Wright rises to her feet. "Sure," she says. I follow her back into the entranceway. Stammo does not bother to come.

I look down the hallway which bisects the house. There are two closed doors on the right hand side of the corridor, an open door to a bathroom at the far end and a door on the left that I guess leads into the kitchen. She opens the second door on the right and ushers me into the tiny bedroom; there is barely enough room for us both. My first impression is that it is not a typical kid's room. On the walls are large sheets of white paperboard covered in intricate, colourful designs. They are not the work of the average kid of that age.

"How old was Terry?" I ask.

"Ten, last month."

"My daughter, Ellie, was eight a couple of months ago," I volunteer.

Ellie loves to draw and is, I think, pretty good—she is going through what I call her Grandma Moses phase—but Terry's pictures are quite different. Each one is made up of tiny geometrical shapes, of different colours, like microscopic tesserae. As I look at one, I let my eyes defocus and, with a shock, I see that I am looking at a huge, futuristic motorcycle made up of the tiny bright colours

"Wow," I say.

"Yes, Terry's a wonderful artist," she says with pride which holds for a moment and then deflates. "Was," she amends.

As I study each picture, a different image springs

to life from out of the chaos of the tiny shapes: a fire engine; a plane; what looks like a Mustang convertible. These are amazing. The kid was a *bona fide* genius with an unbelievable attention to detail.

I drag my eyes away from the pictures and take in the rest of the room, not sure what I am looking for. There is something odd about it. There is a desktop computer with a clunky old monitor, an X-Box, a PlayStation, an electronic keyboard and hundreds of Lego cars, trucks, aircraft and spaceships, all on shelves, all meticulously aligned. There is an untidy array of clothes on the floor but the bed is made with military precision. It reminds me of my own room when I was a kid because it is so different.

"Terry was very... organized," I say.

"Well yes..." she replies. For a moment I think she is going to say more but she doesn't.

I turn to leave but Elizabeth Wright does not move and I have to squeeze past her. Her eyes hold mine like magnets. I am very aware of her beauty and catch an alluring hint of perfume, Coco Chanel, the same as Sam wears. Although she is a mess right now, she seems to look into my soul and stirs in me an unexpected, almost animal attraction. I cannot stop the wildly inappropriate thoughts that tumble through my mind and affect my body; I want to slip my hands into my pockets for fear of what they might do. And throughout my struggle she just looks into my eyes, her thoughts un-readable.

Breathing a little faster, I force myself to move. I think of Terry's corpse in order to avoid any visible reaction to what just happened. Across the hall I find that the door on the other side of the hallway does indeed lead into the kitchen. It is small and the kitchen cabinets look like they were built in the six-ties. This house dredges up uncomfortable memo-ries: everything in it reminds me of several of the many run-down houses that I lived in as a child. I may have had a crappy childhood but unlike Terry, I survived it.

The back door is locked but an old fashioned key is still in the keyhole. I turn it with difficulty. Years of Vancouver rain have warped the frame and rusted the hinges so I have to pull hard to open the door, which protests with a loud creaking noise.

The garden is somber under the heavy grey clouds. Everything looks run down and decayed. A rusty Schwinn bike sits in the middle of an ne-glected lawn.

I close and lock the back door and take the door which leads into the living/dining room.

Stammo is talking to Mark Wright, reviewing the details of his last day with Terry. While I was in the kitchen, Elizabeth has rejoined her husband on the couch.

Stammo rises as if to leave.

I flip open my note pad. "Mr. Wright," I ask, "you said that you were on your computer when you got back from Michael's house at five-thirty, until your wife arrived home at eight."

"Yes."

"That computer right there on the dining table?" For the first time I notice that on this visit the computer's monitors are powered off.

"Yes."

"So how could Terry have left without you knowing? The back door creaks when it's opened and the front door is right there behind you."

Elizabeth answers for her husband. "Terry was always sneaking out through the window in his room. Ever since he was a child he was very active. He first climbed out of his bedroom window when he was seven."

The explanation doesn't ring true to me. I look from her to him. There's something they are not telling me. There was another question I wanted to ask. I open my notebook to see what it was.

"Mr. Wright, you said that when you were in Best Buy, Terry had a meltdown. What exactly did you mean by that?"

I hear Stammo sigh.

"Well he became kinda angry when I told him—"

"Oh, for heaven's sake Mark," Elizabeth interrupts him with a flare of anger. "You act like you are embarrassed by Terry's condition." She turns to me. "My son was autistic, detective."

Mark shakes his head and takes to looking at his hands again. But at least Stammo is not sighing anymore. I realize I don't really know much about autism other than it's some sort of mental disorder. Yet what I saw on the wall of Terry's room was more the work of a genius than of someone who is mentally ill.

"From childhood he was always physically active," Elizabeth Wright is explaining. "He had to be moving all the time. He would climb and jump on furniture, even climb bookcases. Several times he climbed out his bedroom window. We thought about putting up bars but we just felt we couldn't cage him in like that..." She starts to cry and the sound breaks my heart. I try to imagine what I would do if it had been Ellie lying dead in the woods and, for a second, I can feel a small fraction of what the Wright's are suffering. It is a real physical pain. "But now... I wish that... we had." She buries her head in her husband's chest and I feel a strong desire to reach out and touch her, comfort her.

"He's... in the hands... of the Great... One," she says between sobs.

He puts both arms around her and holds her tight. He looks up at me; the hurt in his eyes is raw. I know the guilt he must be feeling. Terry disappeared on his watch. It is quite likely that his guilt, stirred with her blame, will be the recipe that kills their marriage. I was wrong about the looks passing between them; they were expressing her blame and his shame.

"Autistic children can be very rigid in their behaviour, they have difficulty regulating themselves." he says quietly. "He was playing with a Wii game in Best Buy while I was doing my shopping. When I told him it was time to go, he refused and when I took the controller away from him, he started screaming and kicking at me. That's what I mean by a meltdown. He didn't stop until we got to the airport. It was why I took him there. He liked it. He would put in earplugs and watch the planes; it always calmed him."

I do not know what to say, a rare occurrence. I look over at Stammo and he shrugs.

"I don't think we need bother you anymore today, Mr. and Mrs. Wright. Just one last thing, can you give me the names and address of Terry's friend Michael's parents."

They know I need to contact them to verify Mark's story but neither of them seems offended. I write down the information they give me.

"Terry was very open and trusting," Elizabeth says. "He couldn't read facial expressions. He couldn't tell if someone had bad intentions."

"There's one other thing," I add. "I would like to take Terry's computer with me and have our forensic techs look at it. Check the email, internet browsing history and so on."

"We really tried hard to give Terry his privacy," Wright says. "I'm not completely comfortable giving you his computer."

"Well, it could—"

"Oh for heaven's sake Mark." Elizabeth Wright's words cut me off. "If it will help find who did this to Terry... Of course, detective, take it."

Carrying the computer, we take our leave and trudge through the easing rain back to the car.

I'm doing the driving as we head back to Gravely Street, the VPD's nice new office building, built while I was away from the job. Stammo asks, "Did you ever work a child homicide before, Cal?"

I am shocked. Not at the question but at the use of my first name. He always calls me by my last name, never Rocky, never Cal. I want to believe that it's a breach in the wall that has always separated us but I don't think it is. I think this case has made a big crack in that tough shell of his.

"No, Nick. I haven't."

"Me neither." Silence. "Those poor people."

Longer silence. "And what that little kid had to go through. Jesus!"

"We'll nail the bastard who did this." I make the promise to myself as much as to him. And, on another level, I realize I am making the promise to Ellie. It's a promise to take one sick bastard off the streets and make the world a tiny bit safer for her.

"You better believe it."

We lapse into silence.

I think back over the interview. I cannot get out of my mind the physical reaction that I had to Elizabeth Wright as we were leaving Terry's bedroom. It was a feeling of raw sexuality. I felt that if we had been alone in the house we would have been tearing off each others' clothes, right there and then. I sensed that she felt the same way. I can feel my body reacting to the thought. It feels good but so, so wrong. I shake my head to clear out the thoughts.

After I had been using heroin for three or four years, it blunted my libido; sex rarely entered my mind. Since I quit, the stirrings have returned but never so strongly. Not even for Sam... Oh, Sam... God, I want you back.

I turn left on to Renfrew.

"Earlier on, I had an image come into my head. You and me in an alley beating the crap out of whoever did this. When we catch him, the justice system is not going to give him what he deserves."

"Yeah, I know what you mean. I would feel good while you were doing it but you know what Rogan? You can't become a vigilante. It leaves you feeling too dirty."

It sounds like the voice of bitter experience and I know he's right. But I still want to do it. I cannot help savouring the thought.

Stammo breaks into my reverie. "What do you think she meant when she said, 'He's in the hands of the Great One'?"

"Well, I'm guessing she's not talking about Wayne Gretsky. I expect she means in God's hands."

"So why didn't she say that then?" he asks. I shrug.

We are silent again for several minutes. I cannot keep the thoughts of the child's almost ritualistic murder out of my mind. Rather than fight it, I mentally reexamine the crime scene.

"You know we could have a crazy here, maybe even a serial killer," he says, just at the very moment I was thinking it. It's not often Stammo and I are on the same page.

4

CAL

Conflict. I cannot get the images out of my mind: the half-naked child's body in the mud of the woods; the bloody wounds; the cross carved over his mouth; the stricken parents. I try focusing on one of the other cases that we are working but nothing can purge those images. They revolve in my head without surcease. I see Ellie as the victim, I see the blame in Sam's eyes. I don't want this case. I know that it will haunt me until it's solved and for long after. I fantasize about asking for a transfer. Maybe writing traffic tickets in Kerrisdale *is* a better option.

But I know that's BS. This case is has my name written all over it. The fate that I don't believe in has placed it firmly in my hands. Outrageous as it may seem, being partnered with Stammo is somehow going to be the key to solving it... if I can just keep the images at bay.

One of my rehab counsellors used to say that the craving for heroin will always be less than half a step behind you. Right now it is standing in front of me, screaming in my face. The thought of the peace that a hit would provide is seductive; in fact, orders of magnitude more than merely seductive.

I sweep up my car keys and head for the door. I am less that ten minutes drive from the downtown east side, the hub of Vancouver's drug trade. To just wash away, just for half an hour, the images and thoughts of Terry Wright's murder will indeed be bliss.

I stop, grasping the front door handle. I am sweating. The Bard's words fill my ears: *A sick man's appetite, who desires most that which would increase his evil.*

Not today. Not today. If I can just get through today...

I takes all my will to let the keys fall from my hand onto the tile and force my feet to take me back to the living room.

On my balcony, a sparrow is perched on the feeder, nibbling from the seed bell hanging there. He's sheltered from the rain by the balcony above but he looks cold and wet. Cold and wet... a flashback to life on the streets. I think of Roy and wish he were here in my nice warm condo drinking a beer and chuckling at life's ironies.

I can't get through this alone.

Time to use one of my lifelines. I grab the phone and dial. I can feel my heart beat faster as my antici-pation rises. One ring... two rings... thr—

"*Hello, Ca—, Rocky.*" She laughs. "*I still can't get used to calling you Rocky.*"

"Hi, Sam." I can feel the big smile on my face, straining the sides of my jaws. "Don't sweat it, call me Cal if you want."

"*No. It's OK. I know why you want to be called Rocky and I really respect it.*" It's wonderful to hear that voice. She sounds happy; bubbly even. She sounds happier than I have heard in a long time, in fact, since the split with her former fiancé. "*How's work?*"

Sam will know exactly the right thing to say to help banish the images of Terry Wright's corpse; I just have to open up to her about the case.

But "Good," is all I can say.

"*I'm happy you're back doing what you love. Did you want to speak to Ellie?*" she asks.

"Yeah, of course. But I uh... wanted to speak to you first."

"*Sure, what's up?*"

She's got me there. What can I say to her? Can I tell her that I still love her and that I want us to be back together? Her, Ellie and me, a real family again. Can I tell her that I'll never use heroin again; that I'll never put her through the hell of living with an addict and with the lies, evasions and stealing that go with it. She put up with all of that and more as I spiralled into addiction. My habit cost us our savings, our condo and my income. Can I beg her forgiveness for all of those things? Do I have any right to even ask her for forgiveness? No, no and no to all of the above.

I'm going to do it anyway. I have to tell her.

But the words that come out of my mouth betray my resolve. "Nothing, I just wanted to see how you were doing," I say, kicking myself.

"Pretty good, actually," she says. *"Over the last few months, I've kind of got back on my feet. Work's going well, I got a commission from a huge downtown law firm to do the photographs for their website and their annual calendar. Ellie's happy at her new school and with you taking her a couple of evenings a week and every other weekend, I feel a lot less stressed. I think I'm in a bit of a remission phase. I only seem to need my stick toward the evening when I start to get tired."*

Sam has MS.

"That's good news, Sam. Maybe it will stay stable for a while." I take a deep breath for courage and jump in with both feet, "Sam, there *is* something I have to tell you."

"Fire away."

"Sam, I... I want to say... Listen," I cave, "do you want to grab dinner one night?"

There is a moment of hesitation, then, *"Sure. There was something that I wanted to talk to you about too. How about Friday evening when you come to pick up Ellie for the weekend? The three of us could go to Earl's. Ellie always likes it there."*

That was not exactly what I had in mind. I need to just tell her. "I was thinking—"

"Hang on." I hear her muffled voice talking to Ellie.

"Ellie is dying to talk to you. Just quickly, are you still on for her staying at your place on Wednesday?"

"Of course, I wouldn't miss it for the world. I'll pick her up from after-school care." Deep breath. "Sam, I just wanted to say—"

"Good. Phew. That's great, thanks." I wonder what she is so relieved about. *"Anyway, she is standing patiently beside me waiting to speak to you. See you Friday, Rocky."*

Desperate, I force out the words. "I love you. I love you so much."

"I love you too, Daddy. Hey, you'll never guess what happened at school today. We made Valentine's cards for all the kids in the class and do you know what Dugan said..."

Her lovely little voice, always laced with her

hallmark enthusiasm, lifts my soul but her timing crushes my heart. I try to console myself with the thought that I will see Sam at the end of the week. What is it that Sam wants to talk to me about? I push the possibilities out of my mind.

As Ellie prattles on, I imagine her and her classmates enjoying their Valentine's Day. Bright, shiny, laughing faces. Terry Wright should have had a Valentine's Day party at his school today. It seals my determination to nail the monster that stole it from him. I'll use the picture of those bright shiny faces to keep the other images at bay.

Hell, if I can do that, winning Sam back will be easy by comparison.

5

CAL
TUESDAY

I resent being here.

I am in South Langley on a new case, the hit and run killing of a Mrs. Marguerite Varga on Sunday night. Hit and run is not normally the province of the Major Case Squad but the victim and her husband are friends of Superintendent Cathcart, the head of Investigative Services, so her death is getting the red carpet treatment, which is unusual, to say the least. Stammo, with a sickening show of magnanimity, told me I could do this one 'unsupervised'. As nice as it is to be on a case without him, an element of paranoia whispers that he's trying to hog Terry Wright's murder investigation; maybe even trying to get me reassigned.

I need to get this over and done with quickly and off my back.

"Hello there, young fella. Come on in out of the rain and tell me what can I do you for?" This wiry old man with a big smile is not what I expected. I follow him into the house, putting my umbrella in the copper bin beside the front door. He leads me through the house to a cozy farm kitchen, smelling of freshly baked bread, where a plump elderly woman is standing at the sink doing dishes.

Surely these people can't be— Maybe they have a son.

He indicates a chair at a big wooden table that looks like it pre-dates Shakespeare.

"Sit down, son." He raises his voice, "Florrie, pour this young man a cup of coffee," then to me, "How do you like it?" he asks.

"Black, please," I say, a bit bewildered.

He plumps himself down opposite me, takes a pipe and a pouch of tobacco out of his cardigan pocket. "So what can we do for you?" He gives me a big smile.

I take out my ID. "I'm Detective Rogan of the Vancouver Police Department. Are you Mr. Philip Franks?"

"Sure am and this here's my wife, Florrie." He turns to her and goes up a few decibels. "This young fella's a policeman, Flo. What have you been up to?"

This is surreal. I expected to be talking to some twenty-something yahoo, not this nice old couple.

33

I need to hurry this along.

She chuckles as she brings me the mug she has just filled from the largest percolator I have ever seen. "Here you are, dear," she says in a voice that sounds like she just got off a boat from England, "made the good, old fashioned way."

I thank her and gratefully take a long sip.

It is the worst coffee I have ever tasted. I suppress the gag reflex rising in my gorge and smile at her as I put it carefully on the table in front of me. "Mr. Franks, are you the owner of a Ford F150 license plate ZOA 1645?"

"Had her fer twenty years and she stills runs like a charm. The Ford that is. Florrie I've had a lot longer, eh Flo?" He tamps the tobacco in the pipe.

"Can you tell me where you were at seven-thirty last night?"

He gives me a look, eyes narrowed. Surprise or something else?

"Sure can. We were here watching the Canucks get hammered by the Kings." No smile now.

"And where was your truck?"

"Why, it was parked out back. Just like always."

"Does anyone else have keys to your truck? Could anyone have used it while you were watching?"

"Only our daughter has a spare set of keys. She lives in Winnipeg, so I'm guessing it's not her." He fixes me with a beady eye and lights his pipe. "I think you'd better tell us what this is all about, son."

"Do you have a son or anyone who works for you who might have used the truck?"

"No way."

I decide to level with them. "Your truck was involved in a hit and run on Granville Street in Vancouver at seven thirty-three last night. A woman was killed."

Florrie takes a quick breath in and covers her mouth with the fingertips of both hands. "Our truck?" she says. Is her shock a tell that she knows something? Something unpleasant that she doesn't want to face?

"Couldn't be. There must be some mistake." Franks is adamant. He looks over at his wife. There is an involuntary twitch in his left eye.

"There were two eye-witnesses, one of whom got a partial license plate and it was confirmed by a traffic camera at 49th Avenue," I tell them.

They both shake their heads.

"Where is the truck now?" I ask.

He pulls himself to his feet. "Right out back here. Come and take a look fer yerself."

He leads me out onto the back porch and Florrie follows in our wake. A baby blue F150 is parked on the gravel facing us, not ten feet away. For a twenty year old farm vehicle, it is in mint condition. I step off the porch and examine the front carefully: fenders, grill, bumper. There are no dents, no scratches, no signs of blood, no bits of fabric, nothing. Unless it has been in a body shop overnight, this cannot be the vehicle that slammed into the body of Mrs. Marguerite Varga and snuffed out her life in an instant. The vehicle is immaculate, except for the filthy license plate, DIA 7410. I crouch down and examine it. It is grimy everywhere except around the screws holding it in place.

My resentment at being here vanishes.

I call back to Mr. Franks. "Are you sure that this is your truck, sir?"

"Hell, son, I drove it down to the store this morning to buy milk. I know my own truck." There is irritation in his voice.

I go back to the porch out of the rain and take out my phone. Two minutes later I know that the license plate currently on the Franks' truck is from a Jeep Cherokee, stolen in Surrey on Sunday morning, and I'm guessing that the Franks' license plate is on the truck that hit Mrs. Varga that night. The hit and run was a hit. This is a real case. Superintendent Cathcart unknowingly did a smart thing assigning it to the Homicide Unit.

Someone planned this hit well and I'm going to enjoy finding out who.

"Did you take the truck out at all yesterday?" I ask.

"Of course we did. We go to church in Surrey every Sunday morning then we go have fish and chips for lunch in White Rock."

I tell them that they must not touch their truck until I can get a forensic team out here to examine the license plate and surrounding area. I tell them why.

Philip Franks is stunned into silence.

"Well, I never," says Florrie.

I thank them and tell them I have to rush off to follow up this lead, sidestepping any further contact with the toxic waste that Florrie blithely calls coffee.

6

STAMMO

The Chan family live in this fucking monster house in Kerrisdale. It don't seem to bother Cal 'call-me-Rocky' Rogan that Chinese immigrants are slowly taking over the city, driving up the house prices. But why should he care? He's got some sort of trust fund, money given to him by his best friend's dad before he died.

Rogan is being a pain in the ass, as always. He's so full of himself because he has discovered that the Varga woman's death was a murder. Like anyone else couldn't have worked it out. Another murder we've got to solve. I used to look forward to a nice new challenge but now I'm getting too old for this shit. Still, I can get Rogan to do the legwork and at least it will mean some overtime. God knows I could do with the money.

I've got a bastard of a hangover. I couldn't get the thought of that poor kid's body out of my mind last night. No kid should die like that. It made me think of my own kids back in Toronto; then I couldn't get *them* out of my mind. I could only get to sleep with the help of my good old buddy, Jim Beam. I told Rogan he could do the interview today.

He's been through the whole Sunday with Grace and Dave Chan, the parents of Terry Wright's friend Michael, and it looks like Mark Wright was telling the truth about his day with Terry. They have even verified that the Wrights were worried about Terry always climbing out his bedroom window. Christ, it's hard enough bringing up kids without them doing shit like that.

Rogan's about to wrap up with them when their kid walks in. He's a funny looking kid and he doesn't look at us. That's a bit odd. Two strangers in your living room and you don't look at 'em.

He starts walking in circles in the middle of the room. "JGK 8315," he says. That's odd. I'm pretty sure that that's the license plate of our Crown Vic. He's more observant than most adults. He'd be a great witness.

He says it three times, stops and then points at me, doesn't look, just points. "He smells funny." He says. Cheeky little shit. If I was his father I'd—

"I'm really sorry Detective Stammo," the father,

39

says. "Autistic children are sometimes..." He sighs.

Oh, he's autistic too, like Terry Wright. Poor little kid. My anger disappears faster than it came. I know what it's like to have a kid who's different. My kid Matt for one. Kid could read before he was three. His teachers said he was gifted, put him in a special program and everything. And he did real well. Got scholarships for college, the whole nine yards. But being a fuckin' genius didn't stop him from doing some drug dealing on the side. Made him better at it in fact, 'cause he's a thousand times smarter that the other scum-ball dealers. But he still got caught. Killed his chances of college. No-one saw it coming. All they could see was the genius kid.

Maybe if I'd been there when he was growing up... At least this kid's got a father who cares enough to stick around.

Oh crap. I feel a prickling in my eyes. I have to look away and think of something else. Anything. Good thing they're all looking at the kid. I get up and walk over to the window; stand with the light behind me. That's better.

"Michael, remember about keeping thoughts like that inside," the mother tells him. She draws the kid onto the couch beside her. "Michael," she says, "these gentlemen are policemen. They're here to ask about Terry."

The kid's looking at the fingers of his right hand,

which he's waggling like he's playing a riff on the guitar. "Terry is my friend," he says.

"Hi, Michael," says Rogan.

"Terry is my friend," he repeats.

"Yes, I know he is. Do you remember playing with him on Sunday."

"We played. Terry is my friend." The kid is still looking at his fingers. What's that about?

"What did you play, Michael?"

"X-Box." The kid does a lightening quick glance up at Rogan, then back to his fingers.

"You and Terry played X-Box. That must have been fun." I'm starting to wonder what Rogan is getting at. But he's clever. One of the sharpest in the Department, despite all the drugs. Trouble is sometimes he's too sharp for his own good; he pisses off a lot of other members who ain't quite as quick as him.

"I played X-Box. Not Terry."

"What did Terry play?" Rogan is starting to piss *me* off now. Who cares what the kids played?

"Terry played Lego."

Now the kid's father chimes in. "Terry could make amazing things with Lego. They were like these complex sculptures. You should have seen his art work." The mother's starting to cry now but the kid is still just waggling his fingers and staring at them.

"I did," Rogan says. "I saw his bedroom. His art was amazing." He looks back at the kid again. "Michael, did Terry say anything to you? Anything unusual?"

The mother is about to say something when the kid says, "O – B – O – E ssshhhh!" in a loud whisper.

"Did Terry say that, Michael?" Rogan asks.

"O – B – O – E ssshhhh!" the kid repeats, a bit louder this time. "O – B – O – E ssshhhh!"

"Michael, what did Terry mean?"

"O – B – O – E ssshhhh! O – B – O – E ssshhhh! O – B – O – E ssshhhh!" his voice is getting louder each time he says it. "O – B – O – E ssshhhh! O – B – O – E ssshhhh! O – B – O – E ssshhhh! O – B – O – E ssshhhh!" He keeps repeating the same gibberish and he is starting to rock back and forward in his chair. Now he's shouting it.

His mother pulls him onto her lap and holds him real tight but he still keeps shouting it. She picks him up and takes him, wriggling, out of the room.

"I'm so sorry if I upset him," Rogan says to the father. The kid's shouts have turned into screams.

"It's not your fault, Detective," the father says. "It happens with autism."

"Do you have any idea what it was about? O – B – O – E. Oboe. Did Terry or Michael play the oboe?"

"No. They're both musical. Terry had perfect

pitch and he played a keyboard. But as far as I know he never played the oboe. When Michael calms down, I'll ask him what it means and see if I can make any sense out of it... I doubt it will mean anything."

I don't know why Rogan is wasting his time with all this but it has triggered something in my memory. "There's another thing I'd like to ask you Mr. Chan," I say. "Mrs. Wright said something like, 'he's in the hands of the Great One.' Any idea what that might mean?"

"Well Elizabeth is quite a religious woman. She often says things like that. I suppose she means that he's in God's hands."

I look over at Rogan and he shrugs. I guess even the great junkie has run out of questions.

We say our thanks to David Chan and he shows us out. Somewhere upstairs we can still hear the kid screaming. "O – B – O – E ssshhhh!" Thank God they didn't try and blame us for setting their kid off like that. What a nightmare. How do those parents manage?

And the poor little kid. All you see is the weirdness, the difference, not what he's like inside. How's he ever gonna make friends if he can't look people in the eye and can't stop himself saying the first thing that comes into his head?

7

CAL

I do not want to go in. I hate it in there. Despite the fact that the rain has not stopped and the temperature is dropping fast, I am perfectly happy to stay out here and delay the inevitable while Stammo finishes his after-lunch cigarette.

As he takes a deep drag, I cannot help taunting him, "So we all have our addictions, eh Nick?"

"What d'you mean?"

I nod toward the cigarette in his hand.

"Fuck off, Rogan. It's just a cigarette. I'm not like some scum-ball junkie. Cigarettes are legal."

"What if they weren't?"

He takes another drag and I get the feeling that I've spoiled his enjoyment of it.

He changes the subject. "I keep thinking about that kid, Michael. Weird, huh?"

44

I shrug. "I suppose."

"How's your kid?" he says.

It is the first time that he has asked me about my life outside work. "She's great. She's eight."

"What's her name again?"

"Ellie."

"Nice name, Ellie." He takes another drag of his cigarette and stares off into the distance. He looks at me for a while before deciding to speak. "I got kids, too. Two of 'em. A boy, Matt and a girl, Lucy." Another deep drag. "I never see 'em, though." I am stunned. I had no idea he has kids; we have never been close but we have known each other since he moved here from back East, nine years ago.

I want to ask him more about his kids but before I can say anything, he drops the butt and grinds it out with his foot.

"Let's do it," he says as he pushes open the door.

The first thing I hate about this place is the odour It's different from the rest of the hospital. It's more chemical: a mixture of heavy duty cleaning liquids, formaldehyde and something else indefinable but unpleasant.

"Where's Dr. Marcus?" I ask the girl at the desk. She and I do not get along. Never have.

"Doing an autopsy." She makes a point of speaking without looking up at me.

Crap! There goes any chance of talking to the pathologist in her office.

Stammo leads the way up the corridor and through the double doors into the autopsy room. We know the drill in here. We have to stay at least six feet away from the corpses to avoid any possibility of contaminating them.

Dr. Kaye Marcus, the pathologist, is bent over, working on the body of a middle aged woman. It makes me feel uncomfortable, voyeur-like. How would this woman feel if she knew she was lying here naked, for all to see. I make the effort to look anywhere but at the corpse.

Stammo does not seem to share my sensibility in this area. "Hiya, Doc," he says. "What you got for us on the kid who was killed in the Endowment Lands?"

She looks up. "Hi Nick, Rocky." She is new in the job so she never knew me before, never knew me as Cal. She peels off her gloves and throws them in the trash, then grabs a new pair from the box beside the autopsy table and snaps them on.

"The first wound was to the heart, via the solar plexus," she says. "It was delivered either from the front by a lefty or from behind by a righty. It didn't immediately stop the heart but I'm guessing it did a lot of damage to the aorta, hence the blood. The other four body wounds were delivered *post mortem* as was the cross on the mouth and the wounds to the eyes."

I cannot shake the image of someone doing this to Ellie. I know I won't sleep properly until I have this killer off the street.

We follow her across the room to the drawers that hold the bodies.

"By the pattern of the blood on the body, I think that the heart wound was made first while he was standing up. The killer kept him upright for a minute, pumping blood, and then laid him down to deliver the other four wounds and the cut across his mouth." Stammo swears and I imagine the terror that Terry must have felt as he watched the blood spurting from his chest. His brain must have still been working as the killer laid him down and delivered the other four stab wounds. He must have known that he was going to die right there in the woods. I feel a rage bubbling up inside me. I don't just want to catch this killer, I want to hurt him. I have always abhorred vigilantism but a tiny part of me wants to kill him.

She stops and looks at me. There is puzzlement written on her face.

"It's an odd murder," she says. "I've seen a lot of rage killings and this wasn't one. It was done slowly with a great deal of precision and care. The five body wounds are very symmetrical and even the cross on the mouth is done carefully; the arms of the X are meticulously done by either a very sharp knife or an old open razor. It was all very clinical and extremely creepy, if you ask me."

Her habitual humour is on hiatus as she undoes the padlock and pulls open the drawer containing the body of Terry Wright. The cold air releases smells of chemicals and putrefaction. I really didn't want to see this body again. I was hoping for a nice chat in her office, maybe with photographs.

"TOD?" I ask.

"Eight or nine Sunday night."

I look into the drawer and see that the body is covered by a sheet but my relief is dissipated as she pulls it down to his waist, revealing what she wants us to see.

I feel my stomach churn. Not from the unusual marks on Terry's body and not from the distinctive Y-shaped autopsy scar. It is because he was a child, not much older than Ellie. My mind sees her like this. How would I face myself ever again if I let something like this happen to Ellie. I feel a wave of sympathy for what Mark Wright must be going through. In my mind I can see him sitting at the untidy table in their tiny house, bent over his expensive computers while someone did this to his only child, the child it was his duty to protect. How will he be able to spend the rest of his life knowing this.

"What the...?" Stammo's exclamation brings my mind back into the room.

"I didn't notice it at first," Dr. Marcus tells us, "because his torso was covered in blood. The first thing that was odd was that the five knife wounds form a perfect circle and are evenly spaced. Then, when I washed the blood off..." She leaves the sentence hanging.

The five knife wounds are connected by five lines, shallow cuts into the skin. The lines form a five-pointed star with one of the wounds at each point.

Stammo shakes his head and looks away. "Jesus! Why would anyone want to carve a star on the body of a kid?"

"Maybe it's a pentacle." Dr. Marcus and I say exactly the same words at exactly the same time.

"What, one of those symbols they use in witchcraft?" Stammo breathes.

Dr. Marcus covers Terry's body with the sheet and slides the drawer closed. "The pentacle is a very old symbol," she says. "It is still used by the Wicca religion today."

Stammo turns to me. "Remember what the mother said? 'He's in the hands of the Great One.' That's been bothering me ever since she said it. Normally you'd say, 'he's in God's hands' or something like that. I wonder if she's in some weirdo religion and this is some sort of ritual killing?"

My overcharged imagination sees a circle of hooded celebrants holding black candles and chanting as a robed priest slaughters Terry like the sacrificial lamb. I must check the crime scene reports for footprints.

I pull myself back to the body. "What about the cross on his lips?" I ask.

"That too was *post mortem*, almost certainly done with the same blade that carved the star. His eyeballs were crushed. It looks like someone pushed his or her thumbs into the sockets. Fortunately also *post*."

"Anything else?" Stammo wants to know.

"Nothing too unusual. I've posted my report on the system, so if you have any questions let me know." She covers Terry's body with the sheet, then closes and locks the drawer.

On a hunch, I ask, "Do you know anything about autism, Doctor?" I wonder if Terry's death is connected to the fact that he was autistic.

She's caught by the change of subject. "Yes, as a matter of fact, I do. Why?"

"Terry was autistic and his friend Michael is too."

Stammo chimes in with, "That poor little kid's just so weird. What chance..." He shakes his head.

There is an unusual gentleness in his voice which, for some reason, makes me angry.

Dr. Marcus cuts him a sharp look. "Children on the autism spectrum," she says, "have a great deal of difficulty handling social situations. If you interpret that as weirdness, that's your problem, not the child's." Stammo's hurt look changes to one of anger.

She turns to me. "Did you have a question about it, Rocky?"

"Yes. Terry's friend Michael kept saying 'O – B – O – E ssshhhhh!' over and over again. Does that mean anything to you?"

She shrugs. "Not the letters, other than that they spell 'oboe', but sometimes autistic people get obsessive about something and repeat it continuously."

"Michael didn't seem, I don't know the word, what we used to call retarded." I don't like using the word; it feels cruel somehow.

"Delayed," she corrects me. "Many autistic children are delayed but there are some who are geniuses or are highly skilled in a very narrow field, like engineering or computer science. Remember the movie *Rain Man*?"

I nod. "Terry was like that. He was an amazing artist. I saw some artwork in his bedroom. It was way more sophisticated than an average ten year old's."

I'm surprised that Dr. Marcus knows so much about autism, it seems out of scope for a pathologist.

Stammo has turned away. "We'd better get going," he says without turning to face us. There is a catch in his voice. This case has got to him too. I shouldn't be surprised... but I am.

"Hang on Nick." While I'm here I might was well get an update on my other case. But Stammo doesn't hang on. He heads out, letting the doors slam behind him.

Dr. Marcus sighs. "Everyone reacts differently to the death of a child," she says.

Glad to be able to change the subject, I ask, "Are you also doing the autopsy on Mrs. Varga, the hit and run?"

"Yes. That's her on the table." She walks back to the autopsy table and goes through the ritual of changing gloves. "Pretty straightforward. Her neck was broken when she was hit by the vehicle. Death was pretty much instantaneous."

"Anything unusual?" I ask. I want there to be something unusual. I want there to be something to puzzle over, to become engrossed with. Something that I can turn to when I want to distract my mind from Terry.

"Not yet but I'm only about half way through. If anything odd shows up, I'll call you."

We say our goodbyes and I head out. I am not looking forward to the drive to the Bentall Centre. I just know that Stammo is going to be exploring his killed-by-witchcraft theory, making us *companions that do converse and waste the time together.*

Thank heavens it's a short drive. I want to get this next interview over quickly.

8

CAL

Stammo's hard shell is back in place and he is pissing me off again. Yesterday he assigned me the hit and run killing of Mrs. Marguerite Varga and told me that it was my case to handle as I wanted. "I think you're ready Rogan," he said. Smug bastard. The fact of the matter is that he probably didn't want to drive all the way out to Langley to interview Philip and Florrie Franks. But now that I have discovered that it was almost certainly murder, he wants in on the action. "You should handle the interview," he says, "but I just need to be there to supervise."

As if that wasn't enough, I feel out of place in these plush surroundings and I don't like the feeling. For some reason I have always been intimidated both by banks and by high powered executive types and here we are at the offices of Toronto National Bank, about to interview the Senior Regional Vice President of Private Banking. My only consolation is that Stammo, his wrinkled suit hanging on his skinny frame and stinking of cigarette smoke, looks very much my junior in rank, if not in age, and is completely out of place.

A secretary, as plush and as lush as the surroundings, leads us into the office of Harold Varga. Mr. Varga is in a suit that would cost a month of my detective's salary and I wonder what his annual bonus might be as a senior VP at one of Canada's largest banks. We show him our IDs, offer condolences at the loss of his wife and he leads us graciously to a corner grouping of leather furniture I would love to have in my apartment.

On the drive here, while Stammo expounded what I must admit is a pretty convincing theory that Terry Wright's killing was connected to the black arts, I planned out my interview with Mr. Varga. In Vancouver, most murders are drug related—of which I have seen more than my fair share, both as a cop and as a junkie living on the streets—or spousal. So when a woman not involved in drugs, is murdered the first suspect is the husband. I need to come at this obliquely.

"I appreciate your visit, detectives," Varga is saying, "my good friend Superintendent Cathcart said that he would put his best men on my wife's hit and run."

The combination of name dropping and the implied flattery of us as Major Crime Squad's best men makes me suspicious of this man. We will see how he answers my first question.

"Well I'm sorry to tell you, sir," Stammo is in there before I can open my mouth, "but I think we should be honest here, we have discovered that your wife's death was probably murder."

It is all I can do not to shout at him. Within three minutes of telling me I should handle the interview, he has butted in and completely blown the line of questioning I have prepared, probably in an attempt to ingratiate himself with a friend of the most senior detective in the VPD. He has compounded the sin by revealing what we know so early in the interview. It is a fundamental tactical error.

With a supreme effort, I avoid turning toward Stammo and maintain my focus on Harold Varga. There is an initial flicker in his eyes that gives way to a puzzled frown. "Murder?" he echoes, the disbelief strong in his voice.

"I'm afraid so, sir," Stammo says. "I think—"

I need to get this interview back on track. "Can

you tell me sir, exactly what happened last night?" I interrupt. "Where was your wife going?"

"She was walking to her church." He is talking like a man in a daze, as one might expect. "On Monday evenings at seven o'clock they have a committee meeting that she attends. She is very involved in the church." he says. "Or was." Genuine grief is evident on his face and I feel sorry for the guy. A wife's death is bad enough, but murder...

"The incident was at 49th and Granville. Was it the church on the corner there?"

"No, her church was on Oak. She enjoyed the little walk." The sadness is evident in his voice. I never imagined that I would feel sorry for a rich banker... but I do.

"May I ask the name of the church please sir?"

There is an instant change in his demeanour

"I have no idea. I don't share my wife's uh... religious interests." He says this in a snide manner, banishing my feelings of sympathy for him.

The answer to my next question will likely be shaded by the knowledge that his wife's death was murder. He must know that he is *de facto* a suspect. It may make him harder to read.

"Where were you at the time of your wife's death sir?"

"I was on my way home from work." He shows none of the signs of dissembling. "I arrived at about six forty-five, microwaved some frozen lasagna, ate and was watching CNN when the uniformed officers arrived to tell me of my wife's death at around eight-thirty."

"Is there anyone who can corroborate that?"

He cuts me a look. The frustration in me bubbles up; this would have been so much easier if Stammo hadn't told him it was murder.

"No."

"No phone calls?"

"Uh... No."

Why the hesitation?

"Are you sure?" I ask.

"Quite sure."

I need to do a bit of bridge building. "I'm truly sorry to have to ask you these questions but I'm sure you realize it is just routine. We are obliged to ask."

He nods and gives a wan smile of understanding. It is not the look of a man who killed his wife.

"Did your wife have any enemies?"

"Of course not. She was just a housewife." Now he's switched to a pompous ass again. It's like the good guy and the insufferable one are jockeying for position. He stands up and walks to the window, looking north toward the mountains. His hands are clasped behind his back and he is rotating the wedding ring with the thumb and middle finger of his right hand.

I sense that he will soon be asking us to leave.

"How about you sir? Do you have any enemies. Someone who might want to hurt you by killing your wife?"

He shrugs, his back still toward us. I can't see his face as he says, "These days there are a lot of people who don't like bankers, but I can't imagine..." He sighs. His shoulders sag and he looks somehow diminished. Not at all the imposing executive whom a scant fifteen minutes ago I felt intimidated to meet. I wonder where that feeling of intimidation came from in the first place.

"Would it be possible to come over to your house and look through your wife's papers and computer records please sir?"

He turns and fixes his eyes on mine. "I'll need to discuss that with my lawyer first. Now detectives, unless there is something specific that you want to ask me, there are things that I need to do."

"One last thing sir; do you have a recent photograph of your wife?"

He strides over to his desk and removes an eight by ten black and white photo from a gilt frame. He holds it in his hands staring at it for a moment. He touches the image of his wife's face and gives the slightest of smiles, his thoughts unreadable, then hands it to me. It seems familiar. Not the people but the pose; it is unusual and quite different from the standard husband and wife shot. I turn it over and stamped on the back is 'Samantha Cullen Studios'. As I thought, my ex-wife took this picture; it is her style for sure.

We rise and I decide to suppress the one other question I really want to ask.

9

CAL

As angry as I am at Stammo for screwing up the start of the interview with Varga, I have to hold it all in. If I blow my top about his interference while I am on probation in the department, it will be reported upwards as 'unstable behaviour' One slip up and I could lose the job I live for. For the second time. There would be no going back. A worm of fear crawls through my gut.

This time I'm driving the black unmarked Crown Victoria—a vehicle that a blind man would recognize as a cop car—and he is looking out the window at the North Shore Mountains. My knuckles are white as I grip the wheel, suppressing my anger at him.

"Didn't you think is was funny," he asks, "that he was at work today, the day after his wife's death."

"Yeah, I did," I reply. "I wanted to ask him why at the end of the interview but I didn't want to antagonize him."

"Me too... Sorry about jumping in at the beginning there, by the way. I just wanted to spring the idea of murder on him and see how he reacted."

I am stunned. Stammo is not one to apologize to people, especially to me. Suddenly all my anger seems petty and it drains away fast.

"S'OK," I say. "Did you see that flicker in his eye?"

"Yeah. Difficult to read but I think he knows something. More than he's telling us anyway. What d'you think?"

Stammo is full of surprises today. We are right on the same page. Maybe his instinct to jump in was the right one.

"You were married, right Nick?"

He grunts.

"If your wife went to a church meeting every Monday, don't you think you'd know the name of the church?"

He snorts. "The only reason my ex would go to a church is if they gave away free booze. But I know what you mean. There's a lot of weirdo churches on Oak; we should get a patrol car to go visit them all with that photo and see if anyone recognizes her."

He is staring out the window again, deep in his own thoughts.

As we pull up in front of the Wright's house, he looks at his watch. "Do you really want to do it?" he asks.

"What, question them about the wife's religion?"

"No, not that. I'm asking do you really want to be back in the VPD?"

The question is out of left field and floors me. What is he getting at?

"I gotta tell you Rogan, there's a whole lot of people resent the fact that you got parachuted back in by the Mayor and the Deputy Chief. Especially the young guys coming up. Why risk having a junkie back in the department is what they're saying. People feel they can't trust you; what happens if you start using again? You could put a lot of people at risk."

He can see the flush that has risen to my face in counterpoint to the white knuckles which are again clamped on the steering wheel, for fear of what they might do. I try to calm myself by focusing on my hands but become aware that I no longer have a wedding ring; it was sold long ago to buy drugs.

Although my former partner Steve and his boss Inspector Vance—a popular, street-smart cop and shrewd politician who heads up the Major Crime Squad—genuinely welcomed me back, I have sometimes felt that some others were wary around me. But nobody has spoken up like this before. I don't know which is greater, my anger or my humiliation.

"What do *you* think, Nick?" I ask.

"Truth?"

"Yeah."

"All I'm saying is that I'm not a hundred percent comfortable knowing that right this very minute you're the one who's got my back."

He gets out the car, leaving me awash in shame.

Somehow I have to put this behind me for now, so I get out and follow him up to the front door.

The door opens before Stammo reaches the top step. Elizabeth Wright looks like she has not slept in days; she is wearing the same clothes that she wore yesterday. Her curly blonde hair is no longer tied back; it gives her a wanton look. Her puffy eyes are ignoring Stammo and are riveted on me. Again I feel the overt sexuality in that gaze.

Stammo looks at me and then turns back to her. He can see it too.

"Can we have a word with you and your husband, Mrs. Wright?" he asks in a tone that makes the question a demand.

She turns and leads us into the same room as before. Mark Wright is sitting at the computer on the dining table, absorbed in the figures on his screens.

"They're here again," his wife announces and with a mouse click, the windows vanish from all three monitors leaving a plain blue desktop devoid of icons. Is he hiding something from prying eyes?

Wright gets up from his computer and sits on a chair signalling us to sit on the sofa. I comply and sit at the end farthest from him but Stammo elects to stay standing. Elizabeth Wright stands staring out the front window.

"Mrs. Wright," Stammo says, "we have some things that we would like to discuss with you and your husband. Would you come and sit down, please."

She turns, recognizing his presence for the first time, and I am sure that she is going to refuse. She holds his gaze for a long moment then sweeps around her husband's chair and sits at the other end of the sofa from me.

Stammo stands waiting, until he has got their full attention. "I'm sorry to have to discuss these details with you," he says with minimal sincerity, "but your son's body was mutilated after his death. Carved on his chest was a five pointed star…"

There is a sharp indrawn breath from Elizabeth. Her husband's eyes widen as he looks at her.

"It looks like a pentacle," I add. She looks at me and shakes her head hard. Three times.

Stammo and I exchange a glance and remain

silent. Although the room is buzzing with tension, neither of the Wrights speak.

"There was a cross, like an X carved over his mouth and his eyes had been damaged," he tells them.

"It seemed symbolic of wishing to silence him for something he had seen or heard," I add, earning a glare from Stammo for putting in my ten cent's worth.

Elizabeth Wright makes a choking sound and rushes from the room. A door slams and we can hear her muted sobs. I cannot suppress the uncharitable question that springs into my mind. Is it the natural anguish of a mother at hearing the details of her only child's death or is it something else?

Wright doesn't follow her but leans forward in his chair with his elbows on his knees; he massages his temples with his fingertips.

"Mr. Wright," Stammo says, "given that these marks on your son's body look like they might be, uh, religious in nature, I have to ask you about you and your wife's religious affiliations."

There is no movement from the chair other than from his fingertips. He is not wearing a wedding ring either.

"Mr. Wright?"

"Uh?" Mark Wright looks up at Stammo as if

seeing him for the first time. "Sorry officer, what was that?"

Stammo cuts me a quick glance and repeats his question. It takes Wright a moment to absorb what he has been asked. "Well, I don't—"

"Mark!" Elizabeth Wright's voice is strident. She is standing in the doorway from the hall and her hair is in greater disarray than when she opened the front door. She turns to me and the look in her tear-reddened eyes is wilder than her hair. "Shouldn't you be out looking for my Terry's murderer rather than infringing our rights by asking about our religion?"

Stammo says "We have—"

"I was asking him!" she says, pointing at me. Her voice has risen a half octave and several decibels.

Stammo nods at me. Permission to speak.

"We have several detectives and forensic technicians on the case, Mrs. Wright," I tell her. "I can assure you that we are doing everything possible. It's just that given the nature of your son's injuries we need to investigate any religious or mystical angle. Perhaps there's someone at your church who wants to harm you or your husband by killing your son."

"That's ridiculous and I refuse to answer your questions." She turns back to the bedroom door but does not move toward it. She stands stock still for a moment and then turns slowly back. The quaver in her voice makes her sound like she is on the very edge of descent into madness. "If you are suggesting that Terry was killed by someone in order to hurt us, ask my husband about that."

She stalks off, banging the bedroom door behind her.

Mark Wright sits staring at the space where she was standing, shaking his head.

"What did your wife mean by that Mr. Wright?" asks Stammo.

Wright looks up at him and takes a deep breath which comes out as a sigh. "I don't have any idea detective. She's obviously very distraught." He stands up. "I must go and comfort her."

But Stammo is not going to give up that easily. "Just one thing before we go, sir. You didn't answer my question about you and your wife's religious affiliations."

With what looks like a great sadness in his face, Wright turns to him. "Go away detective and please call before you come back again." He walks into the hallway and opens the front door.

Stammo shrugs and leads the way out the door. I follow him and, as I pass in front of Wright, I stop and ask on impulse, "Can you tell me, what does 'O – B – O – E' mean?"

He looks at me. No expression. His eyes are

voids. Nothing. After a moment, "Oboe. It's a musical instrument, like a clarinet," he says.

Stammo has turned back. He gives an angry signal for me to follow him.

But I don't.

I look back into the house, into the living/dining room. I see the shabby furniture, bland modern art prints on the walls, the dining table and the hatch through to the kitchen which looks particularly messy now. Messy, just like this case is about to become.

I snap back my head and look into Mark Wrights eyes. And behind the cold blank stare held carefully in place, I can sense a primal fear.

10

CAL

The building looks creepy. It is hemmed in by trees which give it a dark aspect and it is more like a house than a church; a house from the nineteen-fifties that would fit well in a Hitchcock movie. Despite the Wright's unwilling-ness to reveal the name of Elizabeth's church, one call to Michael Chan's mother revealed the name; Elizabeth Wright had at one time persuaded Grace Chan to attend an introductory service here.

This is our last call of the day. Stammo didn't want to drive back to Gravely Street after this inter-view so we checked in the Crown Vic and I am parked outside in my own car, getting impatient while waiting for my minder. Stammo gave me strict orders to wait for him and I suspect that he is taking his time just to annoy me. I am itching to go ahead and interview the Reverend Morgan Harris by myself but I have to learn to obey orders—never my long suit. *I am to wait, though waiting so be hell* as the Bard said.

However, waiting for Stammo gives me time to make a quick but important call to Sam and then to examine the place. The sign on the lawn, carved into a rustic-looking piece of wood and painted a muddy brown, reads *The Church of the Transcended Masters*. Oak Street is the home of a lot of alternate churches. The house itself is stucco, painted the same colour as the sign, and has dark green, peeling, wooden window frames. Dismal is the word. Attached to each side of the house are the ends of a seven feet high, industrial-grade, chain-link fence topped with a single coil of razor wire. There are no gates in the front wall of the fence, the only ingress is through the house itself. Forbidding. There is nothing welcoming about this church.

It is too dark to see what is in the area behind the fence but I think I see what looks like playground equipment. Nothing on earth would persuade me to let Ellie play in there.

I am blinded by the lights of an SUV pulling up behind me as they reflect off my mirror. It is Stammo in his beloved Buick Enclave; heaven only knows how he affords it on a cop's salary.

I get out of my fifty year-old Austin Healey 3000:

my one extravagance. Stammo comes and stands beside me while he finishes his cigarette. "I had one of the new guys do some research on her 'Great One' remark. Once he'd excluded all the references to Gretzky, he discovered that the 'Great One' is a way of referring to Satan."

Stammo is really keen on this religious angle and I have to admit that a lot of things point in that direction.

"Have you had anyone looking into similar murders?" I ask.

"Yeah. I talked to Steve and he's having someone check all of Canada and the Pacific Northwest of the US too."

"How do you want to handle the interview?" I ask.

"Watch and learn."

Smug bastard.

He drops his cigarette and grinds it out on the sidewalk. "Come on, Rogan. Let's do it," he says. We head for the front door. "I don't want to spend too much time here on our first visit; I got stuff to do this eve—"

We are halted in our tracks by the deep rumble of growling, coming from behind the fence. If it's a dog, it is a giant of a dog. Stammo looks at me uneasily and I am reminded of his comments about not being happy that it is me who has got his back.

But now my emotion is anger rather than shame. I step forward and hear him follow me.

A sign on the front porch informs us that there is a service at six tonight, less than an hour away. The double doors look new, out of step with the rest of the house. Stammo grabs the lion's-head knocker on the right-hand one and raps it twice. For no reason, I look up and see, two feet above the doors, a diagram painted in red on a white disk. It features five-pointed stars and crescent moons of difference sizes. I nudge Stammo and indicate with my eyes. He takes it in and gives me a smile that borders on the feral.

The city property records indicate that the house is owned by the Church of the Transcended Masters, the Chief Executive of which is the Reverend Morgan Harris. I am dying to know if the mental image that I have of the Reverend Harris—crafted in my mind on the way over here—tall, dark and saturnine, will resemble the man in the flesh.

As Stammo reaches up to knock a second time, the left-hand door opens part way revealing a figure in a hooded, white surplice. Five feet three inches maximum and of slight build with long blonde hair, she has a timeless beauty and looks to be in her mid-teens. The Reverend Harris has a taste for beautiful, possibly underage, acolytes.

Stammo badges her. "I'm Detective Stammo and

this is Detective Rogan. We are here to see the Reverend Morgan Harris."

A slim and elegant hand reaches out and takes Stammo's ID wallet. She scrutinizes the photograph with infinite care and compares it to his face before handing it back; it is something I have never seen anyone do before. She turns her attention to me and I feel sure that she is also going to ask to see my ID too but, after a long moment's hesitation, she gives a secret smile and opens the door wide enough for us to enter. Why do *I* get the walk to first base?

The interior is larger than I imagined. The ground floor is one open area except for a small room off to the right which looks like a kitchen. On the far right-hand wall, stairs lead up to the next floor. There are curved rows of folding chairs facing the back wall, in the middle of which is an altar covered in white cloth and bearing hundreds of white candles of varying sizes, all of them lit in readiness for the upcoming service, I presume. Immediately behind the altar are black drapes; so close to the candles, I cannot help but think about the fire hazard they pose.

The other walls are all draped in pairs of curtains, alternating black pair with white. Each pair of curtains is held back with heavy, braided, golden ties and between each pair is a picture. The pictures framed by the white curtains are of beatific-looking men and women, some surrounded by halos of white light, whereas the pictures framed by the black curtains look like they were painted by Hieronymus Bosch on a bad day... a very bad day. They feature strange birds, ravening dogs and tortured men and women. The net effect makes me uneasy.

Before I can examine them in more detail, the child-woman who opened the door glides down the centre aisle between the chairs and stands facing us with her back to the altar. "Please detectives, come and be seated," she says. Her voice is deep and sensuous and sends a small but pleasant shiver down my spine.

Stammo and I exchange glances, make our way forward and sit in the front row on opposite sides of the aisle. Immediately I sit down, I realize, with some discomfort, that we have both obeyed her without question and thus put ourselves in a disadvantaged position to conduct our interview. When Reverend Harris shows up, I will make a point of standing to shake his hand and will not sit down after.

"How may I help you, detectives?" she says. The mellow tones of her voice makes me revise her age upward; no teenager could sound like this.

"As I said, miss," Stammo replies, "we would like to speak with the Reverend Harris."

Her laugh is a kid's laugh and I can see that it pushes all kinds of buttons for Stammo but before he can react, she says, "*I* am Morgan Harris, Detective Stammo," which leaves us both speechless.

"I was elevated to the ministry on the death of my father, so I repeat, how may I help you?"

I recover more quickly than Stammo and, forgetting his stricture against my leading the questioning, I say, "We are here investigating the murder of Terry Wright. I believe his parents are your parishioners."

"Elizabeth is. I am afraid that Mark no longer attends. I hope that he will return; he may find some comfort after the loss of Terry."

"Does she come here regularly?" Stammo asks, glaring at me.

"Several times a week. Sometimes she would bring Terry. Her beliefs are very strong." Her responses are even and measured. For someone who appears so young she exhibits a great deal of self-assurance.

"And what exactly are those beliefs, Miss Harris?" Stammo asks.

"That's *Reverend* Harris, detective," she chides him gently then she laughs again; her humour seems genuine. "And that very short question will require a very long answer I'm afraid. We hardly have time before the service at six o'clock."

Stammo checks his watch and takes a different tack. "Mrs. Wright said to us that Terry was in the hands of 'the Great One'. Does that phrase mean anything to you?"

"Ah," she smiles, "you probably misheard her. I suspect that what she in fact said was in the hands of the Great Ones, plural. She would have been referring to the Transcended Masters whom we revere as role models for humanity's highest ideals and who have gone before us to prepare a place for us. Terry is certainly with them now."

I search my mind but I can't be certain whether Elizabeth Wright used the plural form. However, this interview is not going well; from the start she has exercised control and Stammo is getting irritated with her. "Terry's body was mutilated," he says. "Whoever killed him carved a five pointed star, a pentacle, on his skin. I see that over your front door is a picture covered with pentacles and moons. Is the pentacle a symbol connected to your religion?"

She is not in the least fazed by this question. A smile plays on her lips. "That disk hanging above the front door is a picture done by the child of one of our parishioners. It represents the sky with moons and stars in it. Nothing more, Detective Stammo."

At one level, I admire her deft handling of Stammo's clumsy questions but her slickness bothers me. Stammo seems unable to get control of the interview so it is my turn. I know he will be pissed off if I leap in with a question, so I just stand up, turn away and wander over to the pictures on the walls. I head for the closest one that is framed by a pair of the black drapes and, just as I get close to it, I turn and look at the Reverend Harris. For the first time I detect an uneasy expression on her face which she immediately banishes with a smile.

"If you would like, detective, I could show you those pictures at some time and explain their significance," she says. "Unfortunately, I have to prepare for the service which *must* start at six, sharp. But if you would like to come back at another time..." She raises her eyebrows, her invitation coquettish.

"It's OK," I assure her, "I'll just take a look at these while you are talking to Detective Stammo." I turn back toward the strange picture and examine the details.

Behind me, I hear her remonstrate, "I am afraid that's not possible. I really must prepare. I will have to ask you both to leave now. We are in the phone book. Please call and make an appointment for a more convenient time."

Her self-assurance of minutes ago has slipped and Stammo takes advantage of it. "Why don't we stay for the service? You're free, right Rogan?"

Her tinkling laugh now sounds forced. "Although we welcome new members to our little church, this evening's service is restricted to established followers of the Masters. It would be forbidden for you to attend."

We have her off-balance now. "That's OK," I say, without turning away from the picture. "Nick, come and take a look at this."

I hear the creak of the chair as Stammo stands; the sound of his shoes on the hardwood floor; and, just before he reaches me, the deep rumbling growl that we heard as we approached the front door.

I turn to see a tableau, stranger than the picture I was examining.

Two paces from me is Stammo, facing me, frozen, eyes like saucers. Morgan Harris is looking at us with the smile returned to her face. Behind her, the black curtains have been drawn back, revealing a door—it must open onto the backyard of the house—which frames a tall man restraining the biggest dog I have ever seen. He looks like a cross between an Irish wolfhound and a pit bull, having the size of the former and the disposition of the latter. He isn't slavering but the baleful look he is giving me could be a precursor. I have never been frightened by dogs and consequently have never been bothered by one, but I can see some room here to make an exception.

Stammo, however, is rooted to the spot. He and I may have had our issues and although I have little respect for his powers of detection, I know for a fact that he can be fearless and has received many commendations for bravery. But right now he is paralyzed.

There is only one thing to do.

I let go of the tension that has crept into my shoulders and walk calmly past Stammo and the Reverend Harris toward the dog who is still emitting a quiet rumble. "Boy, he's beautiful," I say. "OK if I stroke him?"

The man pulls back on the leash wrapped tightly round his left hand but it is an unnecessary action. The dog is making no aggressive movements; he is just focused on my face and the growling has stopped… for the moment. I come to within a pace of him and crouch down so that we are eye to eye. "What's his name?" I ask, looking up at his handler. With a shock, I realize that the man's face is familiar; he is someone I know well, but I just cannot place him. It feels like meeting someone out of context, like when you run into a checker from your local supermarket in a cinema line up: you know that you know them but you can't remember from where.

The man is not pleased. "BL," he says. It's a strange name for a dog; I wonder what it stands for.

I open my hand and move the flattened palm toward the dog's nose. "Good boy, BL. What a handsome boy you are." He sniffs my hand and his brow ridges soften. I can see a slight twitch in his tail. I smile at him and advance my hand toward his face and rub his cheek then let my hand rub under and behind his ear until his tail is in full swing.

Still fussing him I stand up and say, "We'll let you get on with the preparations for your service now." I turn back toward Morgan Harris, who looks relieved. "However, we will be back to talk some more soon."

I glance over toward Stammo. He has managed to turn round but he has a patina of perspiration on his face and a very pasty look to him. I take a couple of steps up the aisle toward the front door and turn back, just like Lieutenant Columbo used to do in that old TV show. "Before we go, just one more question. What does O – B – O – E mean to you?"

I'd bet dollars to donuts that the mystification on her face is genuine. I look at BL's minder and his face is a blank. Then out of nowhere, another question leaps into my mind, a question stunning in its total irrelevance to the Terry Wright investigation.

"How long was Mrs. Marguerite Varga a member here?"

Out of the corner of my eye, I see a reaction from Stammo but my focus is on Morgan Harris. This time her face shows guile, not mystification. I sense she is weighing options. Her right hand reaches up and she tugs gently on her right ear, her forefinger caressing the diamond stud she is wearing.

Then she realizes that she has paused for too long.

She opts for: "I'm sorry detective, but the names of our parishioners are confidential."

Not to a court order, I think but refrain from saying it lest she take the advice of the Mayor of York: *My lords, we were forewarned of your coming, And shut the gates for safety of ourselves.*

"Thank you Reverend Harris," I say and head for the door with Stammo close on my heels.

There are a number of other questions we could have asked but they are all insignificant compared to what I saw on that wall.

11

SAM

Cal, or should I say Rocky, didn't give me much warning and now that the time is here, a big part of me wants to delay until we meet on Friday. But the better part of me wants to do this away from the public eyes of a restaurant. With Ellie at her BFF's house for a Valentine's Day party, I can tell him the news in private. Just the two of us.

I take courage from the medallion in my hand with its inscription, *To thine own self be true.* My father's five year chip always gives me the courage to do what's right and not to give up. Cal may feel a bit hurt but it is better to—

The doorbell curtails my thoughts and increases my heart rate.

I reach for my cane. But, no. I don't want to feel

weak... or look weak. I can detect the roll in my walk but I've learned to minimize it... or so I tell myself.

Through the fish-eye lens of the peephole, he is the one who looks distorted, like a flashback to his distorted years on the streets. I see him reach for the doorbell and I open the door.

"Hey." We say it simultaneously and laugh.

"Come in."

He steps into the hallway and slips off his loafers. They are new. Nice.

"Let's go into the living room." I take his arm as a means to cover any possibility of a stumble and then immediately regret it. It's sending the wrong message. I look at him and the tender smile he gives me confirms it.

He takes a seat on the couch and I take the chance to put some space between us and sit in my favourite armchair.

"Where's Ells-bells?" His new nickname for Ellie. She always pretends that she doesn't like it.

"She's at Sarah's house for a Valentine's Day party. She'll be home pretty soon."

"Oh, good."

That's not like him. "So what was it that you wanted to talk to me about?" I can hear the suspicion in my voice. And so can he. For a moment he looks confused.

"It's a case I'm working on," he says. "You took some photos of a Marguerite and Harold Varga?"

Relief! "Oh yes. Sure, I remember them well. It was a couple of months ago. They were really good subjects. How did you—" Then it washes over me with a cold caress. "Has something happened to one of them?"

"Mrs. Varga was killed by a pickup truck on Monday night. We're pretty sure it was murder."

"Oh, that poor man." I can see how they looked through the camera lens. It always shows the truth. And their truth was that they really loved each other.

"Whenever a woman is murdered and no drugs are involved, the husband comes under the microscope as the prime suspect. When I interviewed him he—"

"There's no way," I tell him.

"No way what?" He is irritated that I cut him off.

"There is no way that Harold Varga was involved in his wife's murder. He was completely in love with her."

"I have difficulty imagining that pompous drone in love with anyone other than himself." His voice has gone up a decibel or two.

Cal's radar is usually right-on about people. I am amazed that... "Wait a minute. Are we talking about the same man. Harold Varga who's a VP at Toronto National Bank?"

"Yes."

"He's one of the nicest clients I have ever had," I tell him. "I don't know where you get that pompous crap but I really liked him. Truth to tell, I didn't particularly like Marguerite Varga. She was a bit distant, maybe a bit of a snob too. But Harold was a lovely man."

"Well he sure fooled you," Cal is at his most patronizing. It's infuriating. "When Nick and I met him in his office, most of the time he was arrogant and dismissive."

"First, he did *not* fool me." He wilts a little under my stare. "When you look at someone through the lens of a camera, you are focused on them one hundred percent. All extraneous objects disappear from view and you see the subject as they really are. I am telling you that Harold Varga is a nice, warm, personable man who really loves, I mean loved, his wife. *That's* the truth of Harold Varga."

"Well that's not the man I interviewed today," he grumps.

"My second point. Maybe what you call pomposity was his reaction to a couple of cops coming into his office and insinuating that he killed his wife."

"We didn't—" He stops himself and takes a deep

breath. "I wanted to get your opinion of him, and of them as a couple. It's just that when I got it, it wasn't the one I was looking for." He smiles ruefully.

"So that was what you wanted to talk to me about? My opinion of Harold Varga?" I can't help chuckling.

His face becomes serious for a second and then he gives me his big, goofy Cal smile. "There was something else I wanted to talk to you about."

We are approaching the moment of truth. "Good," I say. "Because there's something I want to talk to you about too."

He looks at me and I see a glimmer in his eye that I think is hope. Then I know what it is that he wants to tell me and it is not what I want to hear. Worse, what I have to tell him is what he definitely does not want to hear. I've got to head him off at the pass.

"Ca— Rocky, I need to—"

"Sam, I love you. I've never stopped loving you. I want to be with you. You, me and Ellie. A family again."

Oh, Cal. No. Damn you Cal! Why did you have to say this now? Now, whatever I say, it's going to hurt you. Unless... But I can't.

The doorbell springs into life. Someone is beating a tattoo on it.

Ellie!

"Cal, I need some time to process this. Please don't ask me to respond right away. Let's talk again at the end of the week."

I push myself to my feet and struggle over to the front door. I open it and Ellie is there with Sarah and her dad, Adam.

"Hi guys. Come in, come in."

I'm opting for safety in numbers. What a coward I am.

12

CAL

WEDNESDAY

As I walk into the room, several flat, neutral stares are directed at me. For a moment I freeze and the longer I stand here, the more eyes are turned toward me. I cannot get Stammo's words out of my mind: *Why risk having a junkie back in the department is what they're saying. People feel they can't trust you.* Is that what I'm seeing in the eyes of my colleagues? Do they want me out and are they all itching to find a reason for the junkie to be let go? Is it just that I'm four minutes late for the meeting or is it the resentment of me being four months back in the department? Maybe I'm just being paranoid.

"Thanks for joining us Rocky." Steve's voice gives no overt indication of the sarcasm that I know is there. Since he was promoted to sergeant, he has initiated twice-a-week meetings to discuss the cases that he is responsible for solving. "Sit down. Nick was just updating us on the Varga murder."

As I pick my way through the room to the one remaining chair, Stammo is saying, "Anyway, it looks like it was a contract hit and the husband is the most likely suspect. However, Rogan turned up what may be an interesting coincidence but we can get to that later."

"OK. What about Terry Wright?" Steve asks.

Stammo gives a detailed run down of the investigation so far: no useful forensics at the scene and nothing of interest on Terry's computer. This is a blow. I had been hoping that Terry might have left something that would lead us to his killer. To my irritation, Stammo makes a point of leaving out any reference to Michael Chan's repeated spelling of the word *oboe*. However, through the irritation, I have to admit that it causes me to question whether it has any relevance to the case. I am sure that it meant nothing to the Reverend Harris or to the dog minder but something in Mark Wright's complete lack of reaction to the word has caused an itch in my mind, an itch I have to scratch. Terry's friend Michael said, 'O – B – O – E ssshhhh!' like it was a secret, something that he shouldn't be talking about. I need to talk to him again but this time without Stammo. He'll be pissed and so will Steve, if he finds out, but probably not enough to fire me. Probably not. I think the boy might talk to me more openly without my minder hovering in the background.

"So tell 'em, Rogan." Stammo's voice pulls me out of my thoughts and back into the room. I zoned out there, I have *no* idea what he is asking about. I take a sip from a cup of the department's excellent coffee while I try to collect my thoughts.

Nothing.

"Sorry Nick, what?"

"On the wall."

I can feel myself flushing and I wonder if Stammo is doing this on purpose. "What wall?" The question comes out too aggressively drawing a couple of sniggers from the assembly.

"Tell 'em what you saw on the wall... at the church. You know the paintings."

"Oh, right. There were these paintings all around the walls of the church. I looked at one of them. It was definitely strange. It was like a painting done by..." I stop myself from saying the name of Hieronymus Bosch. In my sensitized state about how my colleagues feel about me, I don't want anyone to think that I am talking down to them. Now I feel guilty about *that* thought; the people in the room are a pretty smart bunch. "...I dunno, a mad artist," I finish lamely. "It was like an image of hell. There were dogs gnawing the intestines of people and birds pecking out eyes but in the foreground, on an earthy patch of land, was the body of a man. His eyes were empty sockets and there was an X carved over his mouth with lines of blood running down his chin. It was just like what was done to Terry Wright. Made the hair on the back of my neck stand up, I can tell you."

The revelation sends a murmur through the room, although Steve shows no surprise so I expect that Stammo has already briefed him without me.

"Eric," Steve says to one of the other detectives, "what did you find out about similar murders elsewhere?"

"Not a lot really." Detective Eric Street is a bright young guy recently transferred from Special Investigations. He has a reputation for thoroughness. "There have been—"

He is interrupted by the door opening. Superintendent Cathcart, the senior detective in the Vancouver Police Department, walks into the room. He was very unhappy at being forced by the Deputy Chief to take me back into the department. My paranoid part thinks that he has come here to fire me publicly. I think of Harold Varga making the point that Cathcart is his friend; maybe Varga has pressured him.

He closes the door but stays standing. "Sorry to interrupt. Carry on," he says.

"Go on Eric," Steve says.

Eric Street straightens up, clearly keen to make a good impression on his boss's boss's boss. "We were discussing the Terry Wright murder sir," he says. "There have been other murders where pentacles have been scrawled on the walls using the victims' blood and there have been numerous murders where the victims' eyes have been mutilated. There were five cases in the western States where pentacles had been drawn on the body, not carved, but in all five cases they caught the guys who did them and they are all either in jail or in hell depending on which State they were in. There was nothing I could find where an X was carved across the mouth."

I throw a quick glance in Superintendent Cathcart's direction. He is standing very still, with no expression on his face. He is dressed immaculately but revealed in the light from the window beside him, I can see a long white hair growing out of his right ear.

Steve nods and thinks for a moment. "This religious angle is tricky. We can't just go barging into a church with guns blazing but we do have to investigate the minister and that guy with the dog... him especially. Also we need to get a list of their members and see if there's anyone of interest on the list." He thinks some more. "Anyone got experience with odd religions, Satan worshipers, stuff like that?" he asks.

Suddenly an image from the past leaps into my mind. "Not personally," I say, "but I do know one guy who was really into all that stuff. He's a bit weird but very knowledgeable."

"Can you trust the guy?" Steve asks. I nod. Yes, I can certainly trust Damien Crotty. "OK. Check him out for any criminal record and if he's clean, tell him about the murder and your visit to the church and see if he has any ideas."

Steve turns back to Stammo. "Anything else, Nick?"

"Yeah. I told you how Mrs. Varga was on her way to a church on Oak Street when she was hit by the truck. Well, when we were at the church investigating Terry Wright's death, Rogan asks out of the blue if Marguerite Varga was a member and the minister kinda froze for a second and then gave us the 'membership lists are confidential' line. Both Rogan and I thought that she was holding back. It might be nothing, or it might be a big coincidence or there may be a connection. I dunno, but I think it's worth spending some time on." He stops speaking and thinks for a moment. "This is a bit off the wall, but what if the church is a front for a professional group of hit-men."

This comment gets a few chuckles and someone

jokes, "Our Lady of the Blessed Assassination." I have difficulty suppressing a grin and I notice Superintendent Cathcart trying to hide a smile.

"Yeah, well you can joke," says a ruffled Stammo, "but stranger things have happened." He glances at Cathcart to gauge his reaction; he does not like to have fun made of him in the presence of a senior officer.

Steve brings the meeting to order. "OK, OK. Is there anything else?" The hubbub dies down and no-one offers anything else. "Right. Eric, I want you to widen your search for similar murder cases to cover all of the US but first I want you to do some research into this 'Church of the Transcended Masters' and if there are other branches or affiliates, I want you to focus on similar murders in their areas.

"I'm gonna talk to the Crown Prosecutor's office and see what are the chances of getting a court order for their membership list. I've got a feeling that we may run into a problem with our beloved Canadian Charter of Rights but I'll give it a go anyway. OK, anything else on this or the Varga case before we go on to the next one?"

Something that bothered me all last night starts to resolve itself.

"On the Varga case," I say. "I did some checking on him and the feedback I got was that he's a really nice, pleasant guy. It didn't fit with how he was during our interview. But when I think back, he only got snotty with us twice. Once when I asked about his wife's church and then when I asked whether she had any enemies..." I realize I have been thinking out loud and I don't have a coherent conclusion or point to make. I should have thought this through before opening my mouth.

"Who did you check him out with?" asks Steve.

I really should have kept my mouth shut.

"Sam, my wife. She took some photographs of the Varga's."

I hear another snigger.

"Due respect to your ex," Stammo chimes in, "but sitting for your portrait, of course you're gonna be all smiles."

I shake off my annoyance at Stammo for re-minding me that Sam is in fact my ex-wife and has been for four long years.

"But there is one thing," Stammo says with a grin on his face. "Rogan, you remember the guy with the dog? Did he look familiar to you?"

"Yes, he did. I'm sure I've seen him before, some-where. D'you know who he is?"

"No, but I bet you saw him when you were shaving this morning. Take a look in the mirror. He looks just like you; he could be your brother. You don't have a brother do you?"

He's right! That's why he was so familiar. But

what bothers me comes from Stammo's question: the thought of having a brother.

Superintendent Cathcart interrupts my thoughts. "I just came down here to say something about Harold Varga. I know the man socially." Out of the corner of my eye, I catch Stammo nodding. "I very much doubt that he has done anything wrong but I want you all to know that you don't need to worry that I might put any pressure on you because I know him. Your ex is right Rogan. He is a nice enough guy but if he uses my name, you can ignore it."

I can see why Cathcart rose to such a senior position. Not only was he a great cop but he is very smooth with a cultured voice, ideal for wowing the brass and the politicians.

"Thank you sir. We appreciate it," Steve says.

Cathcart nods and leaves.

So much for Harold Varga's big claim of being buddies with the top dog. I turn to Stammo with a smile on my face but he is not smiling. He looks like he is bottling up some sort of rage.

13

CAL

"That's a Chaos Star," I said. "Cool."

His surprise overcame his hallmark demeanour and he did the totally unexpected. He smiled.

"How d'*you* know that?" he asked, reaching up to touch, or rather caress, the earring that had caught my eye.

"I just finished reading *The Eternal Champion*," I said.

"All three books?" I nodded. His look was long and appraising. "What's your name?"

"Cal Rogan."

He extended a hand from his voluminous black velvet sleeve, palm down, dark purple nails extended. "Damien Crotty."

We shook hands and built that rarest of structures, a bridge between two universes in the high school multiverse: the nerds and the goths.

During our years at Magee High School on two different occasions we each went way beyond the normal bonds of friendship to extricate the other from a bad situation.

As I listen to his phone ringing, I can see him as he was then: my height but rake thin; jet black hair with a long red streak; black, five buckle boots; all the requisite chains and leather and that eight-pointed Chaos Star stud.

"Damien Crotty." Despite the passage of time I recognize the voice, mellowed perhaps, but still with his hallmark intensity.

"Hi Damien, it's Cal from Magee High School."

"Cal? Cal Rogan, right?"

"Yeah. How're you doing?"

"Great. But I'm at the airport. I'm just stepping on a plane to New York, then on to Frankfurt."

"That's a bummer. I wanted to meet with you and talk to you about something."

"No prob, it's just a business trip. I'll be back in a few days."

A goth on a business trip seems like a contradiction, but who knows what he might be into now. "OK, good. Let me just ask you something now."

"Sure but you'd better be quick, they're gonna make me switch off the phone any moment."

"Right. I don't know if you knew, I'm in the Vancouver Police Department now."

"Oh, right... No, I didn't know. But go on."

There is a change in his voice. It's not altogether surprising given our history but I'm hoping that the reason for the call will allay his former antipathy toward the forces of the law. "I'm investigating a murder, the murder of a ten year old kid. There were some symbols carved on his body and I'd like to get your take on it."

"Oh. I thought you were going to ask me... uh, something else entirely." He laughs. *"Sure. Why not? But I'm not exactly a symbologist like that Robert Langdon guy in the Da Vinci Code."* He chuckles but the sound is cut off by an announcement in the background. I get the feeling that I am not going to be able to ask him everything I need to know. When the announcement finishes, he continues. *"I can still remember a few things, though. I should charge you a consulting fee. Fire away."*

I hope he is joking about the fee; the Department gets really uptight about its detectives incurring unauthorized expenses. I ignore the rumbling in my gut and I tell him about the mutilations to Terry's body and about the visit to the Church of the Transcended Masters.

"Jeez, what type of freak would do that to a kid?" he asks.

"I was hoping you might have some ideas about that," I say and then immediately want to retract the words. I remember that his little group of goths was referred to as freaks by most of the rest of the school.

Except for some background noise, there is silence on the line. *Shit!* My clumsy wording has pissed him off.

"Damien, are you there?"

More background noise. At least he hasn't hung up on me.

Yet.

Then, *"Hi, Cal. Sorry about that. Just had to stow my carry on. Listen, they're gonna make me switch the phone off in a minute. Can you email me photos of the mutilations and I'll get back to you?"*

I guess it is the best I'm going to get. "Sure. What's your address?" I scribble it down. "Just one last thing..."

"You'd better be quick."

"Does O – B – O – E mean anything to you? Could it be significant."

"O – B – O – E, like oboe, the instrument?"

"Yeah."

I hear a female voice, then Damien. *"Sure. OK Miss, no prob,"* then, *"Cal, I gotta turn this thing off. I'll think about it and email you."* He chuckles. *"The only thing I can think of right now is that oboe is a hex word. Send me the photos. See ya."* Then he's gone.

A chill slithers down my spine.

Hex. It rings in my head, taking me back to every fantasy novel I ever read. It means a curse or an evil spell; it can also mean a witch or witchcraft. It is a word that Shakespeare would have loved, had his birth not predated it by about three centuries. Heart pounding, I call Michael Chan's mother and make an appointment to meet with her and Michael after school today. I just have to work out how to give Stammo the slip so that I can do it alone.

14

DEBBIE

Not even Mrs. Crabbe can spoil my day. She sits at my desk going through her purse and mumbling angry words under her breath. Boy, her name like *totally* fits her personality. I snatch a quick look out the window at the blue sky and can't wait for my lunch break. Only fifteen minutes. And tonight my lovely Tony is taking me to the third Canucks game against LA. Woo-hoo! Best boyfriend *ever*.

"Here it is," she says, all happy with herself... well at least as happy as *she* can ever get.

I put on my sweet smile that I use on all the old bats. "What seems to be the problem Mrs. Crabbe?"

"Young lady," she says, "there doesn't *seem* to be a problem, there *is* a problem. Look at this statement." She smooths out the crumpled paper on my desk. She smells of that old lady smell. "See right there." A polished red nail darts out and points to the first entry in the withdrawal column. "Right there, you see, nine thousand eight hundred and seventeen dollars were withdrawn from my account and I want to know why." I look at the balance of the account; it's over seven times what the bank pays me in a year.

"Let me just look in the computer," I say.

"You can look in the computer all you like, my dear. But before I leave here I want my money back, with interest." She is one snotty old bitch.

I tap in her account number and look at the account activity. It all looks pretty normal. The withdrawal is a transfer to another account done by internet banking. "Do you have another account with us?" I ask.

"I don't see how that is any of *your* business," she says.

Gotta keep my smile in place. I gotta keep my smile in place. "It's just that the transfer was made to—"

She raises her eyes and sighs, then catches sight of the boss. "Oh, Mr. Varga," she calls. "Might I trouble you for a moment?" Just what he needs, poor man, what with his wife just dying. But he just comes over anyway and shakes her hand like she was the Queen or somebody totally important. He's so nice.

"Perhaps *you* could sort this out for me," says the old Crabbe, all sweet now.

I explain the situation to him and he looks at my computer, taps a few keys and takes the statement that comes out of my printer. I look up at him. He looks pale and there is a thin layer of sweat on his forehead. I hope he's not getting sick.

"I really must apologize Mrs. Crabbe. It was a bank error. This is a copy of your previous month's statement." He places it in front of her. "See here, on the last day of the month, there is a deposit for the same amount made at this bank. Did you deposit that amount?"

"No, of course not. I was in New Zealand visiting my daughter, although why she wants to live so far away, I'll never understand." I just manage to stop myself from saying 'I know why'.

"You see it was our mistake," Mr. Varga says smoothly. "We deposited the money in error last month and then transferred it out this month. We sent you an advice of the error by email and internet banking."

"Oh, I don't *do* email," she says, all snooty.

"Anyway, you were paid interest on the amount for the time that it was in your account, so perhaps you would accept that with our most sincere apologies for the error."

She's like all smiles now. "Thank you for sorting it out so quickly, Mr. Varga."

"It's my pleasure Mrs. Crabbe." He turns to me and checks his watch. "Debbie, why don't you walk Mrs. Crabbe to the elevator and you might as well take an early lunch too."

"Thank you Mr. Varga."

When I get back, I must ask him about that transaction because what he told the old bat didn't make much sense to me. Still he's the VP so I guess he knows what he's doing.

15

CAL

I t's time for my weekly humiliation. I never know when it's going to come but come it always does and it falls to Steve, as my boss, to do the job.

"It's that time, Rocky." Always the same words.

I put down the coffee, my new addiction, get up from my desk and follow him out into the corridor.

"Do you think it was Varga put the hit on his wife?" he asks, probably as much to fill the awkward silence as anything.

"He's the logical suspect but my gut says he didn't do it. But I am sure he knows more than he's telling us. Trouble is, guys like that, you put a bit of pressure on them and it's lawyer time."

"Don't worry. You and Nick'll work it out."

We're there. He pushes the door open and walks

in. I follow. There's no-one else in here, thank God. It always increases the humiliation by orders of magnitude when there are other cops present.

He hands me the plastic cup and I unscrew the orange lid. He has to witness me giving the sample but at least he allows me to turn and face the urinal. I fill the cup and replace the lid tightly.

Steve holds open the brown evidence bag and I drop the specimen inside. He seals it, signs it and takes off without another word, leaving me to wash up. Condition four of my reentry into the department is completed for this week.

Stammo walks in and marches over to the urinal I just used. "So what do we do next on the Varga murder?" he asks.

"Nothing on the truck?"

"No, we're never gonna see that sucker." As if to emphasize the point, he farts.

"I'd like to find out if she really was a member of the Reverend Harris' flock. If she was, it's just too much of a coincidence that she's killed the day after the son of another church member is found dead."

"Steve tried but we're not gonna get a warrant for the church's membership without a lot more evidence." Stammo makes a big operation of shaking.

I take a breath and mentally cross my fingers.

"Why don't I go and talk to her, one-on-one, see if I can wheedle it out of her?" I suggest.

He shakes his head, using his supervisory pre-rogative to turn me down. He zips up and heads for the door but stops.

Long look.

I don't think I'm going to like what's coming.

Wrong again.

"Sure. Why not? Give it a try. I wanna spend some time digging into Varga's background, maybe talk to the financial crimes guys, see if he's on their radar." He leaves while I'm still drying my hands.

As I walk back down the corridor, I pull out my cell phone; it looks like from here on, I'm going to have a Stammo-free day.

16

CAL

The unexpected brilliance of the February day does nothing to improve the aura of the Church of the Transcended Masters. With tall trees on three sides, not a scintilla of sunlight falls upon the building and it projects the same dismal aspect that it did last night.

Except for one thing.

Standing in the open doorway, framed in the light from inside, she is wearing the same hooded white robe from last night or one that is identical. It gives her an ethereal look which I suspect she cultivates. As I approach, she extends her hand for me to shake. It is slender, dry and the grip is firm beyond my expectation.

"Thank you for seeing me at such short notice, Reverend Harris," I say.

She draws me inside and closes the doors. Again the room is illuminated by candle light: a psychological ploy of some sort, perhaps. Or am I just being too suspicious?

"Let's go to my study." She smiles at me and I experience the tightening in my chest that most men would feel in proximity to so beautiful a woman. She leads me up the stairs and I see that her feet are bare. I can't help noticing the sway of her hips as she ascends and I am tantalized by the thought that the robe might be her sole item of clothing, which inevitably leads me to imagining what her slender body would look like without it. As my body reacts, she turns and looks back at me; her smile intimates she knows my thoughts... and perhaps approves of them.

Pull yourself together, Rocky. I am letting my imagination carry me to places not compatible with my reasons for being here. My libido returns with unexpected strength at random, and inconvenient, times. I wonder if it would have been better to come here with Stammo after all?

At the top of the stairs, there is an open area with three rooms leading off it and more stairs that lead up to another floor. Her study is a small room with a desk and a couch under the window but I am drawn toward the wall to the right of the door. It is a floor-to-ceiling bookcase containing books on a variety of religious subjects, representing a variety of religions. Apart from the Bible, the Qur'an and the Torah, there are a number of Indian texts including the Bhagavad Gita and even the Karma Sutra. As I scan the titles, I see *The Book of the Law* by Aleister Crowley and *The Golden Bough*.

"Please sit down, detective Rogan." She has perched on the arm of the sofa with her feet on the cushion, indicating for me to sit at the other end. But for this meeting I want to control the agenda so I sit on the corner of her desk, my back to the door, hemming her in. I look down at her.

"May I ask what your religion believes in, Reverend Harris?" I ask.

She gives her tinkling laugh, showing small white teeth. She is very beautiful yet the laugh makes her beauty less intimidating and more inviting. I have a sudden intuition that she knows this and uses her sexuality, with careful calculation, on both men and women. The knowledge deflates the attraction that I felt just moments ago.

"That is way too large a conversation to be having now. Suffice to say that we revere the Masters from many religions and philosophies and follow the path that is common to all." She fixes her gaze on me. "You should come to one of our open houses on Friday evenings," she ends in a flirtatious tone.

I lead with a lie. "We now know that Marguerite Varga was a member of your congregation."

"When you called to arrange this appointment you said that it was to talk about the murder of Terry Wright." The smile is no longer on her face nor is it in her voice, not in itself an admission.

"Yes, we'll come to that. For now I would like to talk about Mrs. Varga. I understand that her husband didn't approve of her attendance here?"

"I don't think that man approves of anything not related to that damn bank of his." I'll take that as an admission; good bluff. "He came to the church just once, with Marguerite, and sat through a two hour open house with a sour face and not once did he ask a question or share in any way. It was like Marguerite had forced him to come here. Rather than talk to anyone, he just snooped about the house."

"When was this?" I ask.

"A few months ago. September maybe. I could check the guest book if you'd like."

"Maybe later. Were there problems between them, do you think?"

"I counselled Marguerite, detective Rogan. I have to respect the confidentiality of our conversations."

"I appreciate that, Reverend Harris, but Mrs. Varga is dead, murdered. If your silence prevents me from catching her murderer..." I leave it hanging.

After weighing my comment for a moment, she volunteers, "Marguerite was a wonderful, vibrant woman who recently had been largely ignored by her husband. He's completely absorbed in his work and when he wasn't at work he was out—" she catches herself... or is it a ruse?

"Out doing what?" I ask.

"Just out."

I look down at her and hold her gaze. She smiles but her charms hold no power over me now; I just look. For a moment it's a staring contest then she breaks eye contact.

"He used to gamble. He would spend a lot of time out gambling. Marguerite didn't approve."

"Was his gambling causing them financial difficulties?"

"I honestly don't know and I don't think Marguerite would have known either. He makes a great deal of money at the bank but Marguerite was not privy to the details of their finances. He just transferred money into her account every month, like she was an employee... or something." I wonder what that *something* might be.

"Were either of them having an affair?"

"Marguerite or Harold?" she asks redundantly. "No, I uh... No."

"Are you sure?"

"Absolutely sure." She's telling the truth but not

the whole truth and I don't know what she's hiding, so I don't know what to ask.

Time to change tack. "Let's go downstairs. I want to ask you something."

The hairs on the back of my neck come to a bristling attention at the quiet noise behind me. I force myself to turn slowly; rapid movement is not a good idea. The dog is standing in the doorway, a growl rumbling in his throat. This time he is not leashed and his handler is nowhere in sight.

"Hello boy," I say. What the hell's his name? It was two letters. BJ? No. It was B something. But what? I skip mentally through the alphabet until I get it. "Hi BL, how are you, boy?" Making no sudden movement, I stand and extend my flattened hand to him. This time there is no sniffing, no tail movement, no softening of his brow ridges. Just the steady rumble.

We face each other down and I wonder why Morgan Harris doesn't intervene. Then I feel her arm slip inside mine. She is standing to my right and slightly back and I can feel the shape of her breast through the robe pressing on my bicep. I look down at her and see the same expression that I saw on Stammo yesterday: naked fear. The dog is reacting to that fear in true canine fashion by maintaining his guard. I tense my muscles as I wait for him to move.

"BL!"

My eyes follow the sound of the voice and I see the dog's minder coming up the stairs onto the landing.

"BL! Come!"

The man ignores us and continues up the stairs to the floor above. I watch him and can see how closely his face resembles my own. Stammo was right about that. It's very weird. Given my family history it is more than conceivable that I could have a half-brother. If I do, I don't want it to be him.

With a look of reluctance, the dog turns and follows and I feel Morgan Harris relax against me with a sigh. But she does not let go of my arm. "Let's go downstairs now." Her voice is no more than a whisper and once again she looks like a teenager, a small, frightened teenager at that.

She hangs on to my arm as we make our way down and, despite my new found belief that she uses her sexuality as a tool, I let myself enjoy the sensation of her nearness.

As we reach the main floor, there is a single bark from above, making her shudder and tighten the grip on my arm.

"If you're frightened of the dog why do you have it here?" I ask.

"I'm only frightened when he is allowed to run

free. Seth normally keeps him in the back yard and almost always has him leashed when he's indoors."

Seth. So the dog minder has a name.

"Why do you have him here at all?"

"When my father died, I took over the church and about fifteen months ago Seth came to live here. He's my brother. He insisted on bringing BL with him."

"Is Seth a Minister too?"

"Seth?" She laughs. It is not the playful, tinkling laugh that she affected earlier; it is of a much more cynical strain. "Hardly."

So why is he here, I wonder?

I lead her to the picture I saw last night and take the time to examine it in detail. It is disturbing. In addition to its resemblance to Bosch, there are elements redolent of Hogarth's *Four Stages of Cruelty*. The figure in the foreground reminds me of Terry's mutilated face and my stomach churns; I am picturing Ellie disfigured like that and the fear and horror she would have felt. I won't be able to live with myself if I don't bring this monster to justice.

I cannot keep the outrage from my voice. "Why would you have *this* in a church?" I ask her.

"The way the pictures alternate, it reminds us that we must always strive to do good in the midst of evil." Her response is calm, aggravating my anger, but she releases her grip on my arm.

Without taking my eyes from her face, I point to the figure in the foreground. "Why does this person have his eyes put out and a cross carved over his mouth?"

"This picture depicts the evils of lying," she says evenly, "it reminds us that every time we lie, we blind ourselves to the truths of the Masters."

"Did you know that Terry Wright's body was disfigured in exactly the same way?"

The shock is palpable. Her body stiffens and she draws away from me. She glances at my face, perhaps to verify that I am telling the truth, then turns and looks toward the staircase we so recently descended.

"Noooooo," she moans. She looks back at me. "No."

I stay silent.

"How could he—?" Her voice chokes off in midsentence.

"How could who?" My body is tingling. The next words out of her mouth may give me the name of Terry's killer and I have a gut feel about whose name it will be.

She doesn't answer my question.

"How could *who*, Reverend Harris?"

She is breathing heavily, trying to gain control.

"Terry," she says. "How could he have died like that? Whoever would do that to an innocent child?"

Did I jump to the wrong conclusion or has she just covered a slip?

"Do you have any idea who might have killed Terry?" I ask.

"No, of course not."

I decide to go with my gut.

"Where was your brother between five-thirty and eight-thirty on Sunday night?"

"Here with me. All evening." She either misses or is not worried by the implication of the question. "We don't have services after the midday one on Sundays so Seth helps me with the accounts and we have a meal together."

"Was anyone else here with you or did anyone visit?"

"No it was just the two of us."

If I had more than just a gut feel, I would haul Morgan and Seth Harris in and interrogate them separately to see if I could break her alibi for him. But I have nothing. It's out of the question.

My Blackberry buzzes. It's a text from Damien Crotty. *Looked at your gruesome pix. It's not a pentacle. The X on lips and eye damage familiar but I can't place it. Just getting on plane from NY to Frankfurt. Will email from there. DC.*

It's not a pentacle was not what I wanted to hear and there's no mention of oboe.

I want to text him back but my next question is

too important. Maybe my next call with Damien will shed some light on the latter.

I have just one more thing for Reverend Harris before I go. I move eight feet to my left and look at the next picture shrouded by black curtains. It is similar to the previous one but has no mutilated person in the foreground. I continue around the room stopping and examining each picture. In the eighth one I find what I am looking for: to one side there is a group of musicians. They are dressed in formal jackets with top hats but below the waist they have animal legs with cloven hoofs.

"Reverend Harris, would you come and explain this picture to me, please?"

She is still standing by the first picture and does not walk over but elects to speak to me from the other side of the room. "It depicts the evils of our 'eat, drink and be merry' society. If we listen to music other than the music which is inside us, we will lose our way to the house of the great ones."

I point to one of the musicians. "Is this one playing an oboe?" I ask.

"No. They are playing flutes, pipes and drums. Simpler instruments from simpler times, Detective Rogan." For a second time she has shown no reaction to the word.

And for some reason her complete lack of visible reaction increases my suspicion of this church, her and her brother.

I make a vow to myself that if they are involved with Terry's death, even peripherally, I will find a way to take them down, even though right now, I don't have a clue how to do it.

17

CAL

I cannot even begin to imagine how I would handle it if Ellie were like this. Michael is a lovely little kid but he seems somehow cut off from the world. At the moment he is sitting cross-legged in the Chan's living room applying his full concentration to a glittery purple car in his hand. It is radio-controlled but he is just holding it up and watching the rear wheels spin. The sunlight from the window is shining on the wheels and reflecting off the turning hubs. He is swaying back and forth, as if in time to slow, gentle music that only he can hear.

I turn my attention to his mother. She is looking with love at her son but I can see the sadness underneath.

"Thank you for seeing me so quickly, Mrs. Chan.

When I was here before, with Detective Stammo, Michael was repeating the letters O – B – O – E. We have reason to believe that this may have some relevance to what happened to Terry and I'd like to ask him about it."

"Of course," she smiles and I can see that a great well of kindness lives inside her. "If you ask me the questions, I'll do my best to get Michael to answer them." She gets up, takes a piece of paper from the coffee table and crouches beside her son. She puts the paper in his line of sight.

"Remember what we agreed, Michael?" She points to a picture on the paper, like the first frame in a comic strip. "First, you play with your car." Her finger moves to the second frame. "Then we talk to the detective." Her finger moves on. "Then you have two chocolate chip cookies." She takes the car from his hand, switches off the motor and puts it down. Then she scoops him up in her arms and sits back on the couch. He does not venture a look at me but pulls the sleeve of his sweater over his hand and starts rubbing it on the tip of his nose.

Grace Chan looks at me and nods.

"I'd like Michael to tell me what O – B – O – E means."

Before his mother can say anything he pipes up, "Ssshhhh! It's a secret. Terry's my friend."

"Yes, darling. I know it's a secret and it's important to keep secrets," she says, "but we talked about this. We shouldn't keep secrets from our parents or from policemen. Do you remember?"

He nods. "Oboe is blood."

"Oboe is blood? What does that mean, Michael?" I ask.

"I mustn't say." He is rubbing his nose faster.

"Why can't you tell me, Michael?"

He is starting to rock again. "It's a secret. They'll hurt Terry if I tell."

"Who will hurt Terry?" I ask.

"They will, the bad people. They'll hurt him if we say the whole thing."

"Who are these bad people, Michael?"

"I don't know. Ask Terry." Now his foot is flicking toward me.

"OK, Michael, that's OK. You don't have to tell me who they are," I say. "I only have one more question, OK?"

"OK." His voice is muffled by his hand which is now rubbing both his nose and his lips.

"You said that they'll hurt Terry if you say the whole thing. Is 'oboe is blood' the beginning of something?"

"Yes."

"Like a rhyme or a story?" I ask.

He looks at me for an instant, his little face distorted with anger, then diverts his gaze to the floor.

"You said 'one more question', not 'two more questions'," he says.

"I promise you that nobody can hurt Terry now. I just need to know what 'oboe is blood' means."

His voice is louder. "I don't want them to hurt Terry. He's my friend." He buries his face in his mother's sweater.

Grace Chan looks at me and I can see moisture in her eyes. She shakes her head. "No more." She mouths at me.

"I just wanted to ask—" the glare she snaps at me cuts me off.

"You were very good Michael," she says. "It's cookie time now." His foot stops flicking and his body slumps a little.

I look at her and mouth the words, "Does he know Terry's dead?"

She shakes her head again.

"OK, Michael," I say. "You were very good. Thank you very much for helping me."

Scooping her son up in her arms, she stands. "Please wait a minute, Detective. I'm going to give Michael his cookies." She carries him through the living area and into the kitchen.

Oboe is blood. What could that mean? If Damien Crotty is correct and oboe is a hex, perhaps 'oboe is blood' is the beginning of some sort of incantation or spell or maybe a curse. As a kid I was always terrified of the occult ever since sneaking into the movie *The* Exorcist. But as an adult surely I've evolved beyond such silly superstition... haven't I?

So why does the thought of an incantation run prickles along my spine?

I pull out my Blackberry and send Damien an email. *What did you mean when you said it's not a pentacle and does 'oboe is blood' mean anything to you? Cheers, Cal.* He'll still be in the plane to Frankfurt so I won't get a reply until tomorrow morning.

While I have the Blackberry open, I Google 'oboe is blood' and Google tells me that there are twenty-six and a half million results. I scroll through and see references to the links between blood pressure and playing the oboe and a bunch of other stuff. I remember a Google trick someone taught me and I put the words in quotes. This time it says *No results found for "oboe is blood".* Maybe Google's not up to date on the black arts. I chuckle at the ridiculousness of *that* thought.

Maybe the truth is that this oboe thing is a huge red herring. Terry died three days ago and we don't have much. His mother was a member of a weird church and he was autistic. Not much at all really. Perhaps we need to concentrate more on the parents.

And who were the 'bad people' to whom Michael referred? People from the church perhaps?

"Milk and cookies." Grace Chan is placing a tray on the coffee table; it holds two glasses of milk and two plates each holding two chocolate chocolate-chip cookies. "Would you like some, Detective Rogan?"

"Yes, thanks. It's very kind of you."

They are home-made and delicious. They are similar to the one's my mother baked most Sundays when I was growing up.

"I'm sorry if I upset Michael," I say.

"He was very close to losing it just then. You have to be very careful when you push autistic children to do something they don't want to do; you can end up with a major meltdown."

That's the same word that Mark Wright used about Terry.

"Does it happen often?"

She sighs and nods. I feel a wave of sympathy for her. My lovely Ellie can get angry on occasion but I have never seen her react with what could be referred to as a meltdown, like the way Michael reacted yesterday morning when I was here with Stammo.

"It must be tough," I say.

"You don't know the half of it, detective." She gives me a wan smile.

"How did Terry's parents handle it?"

"Good. Yes. I think it's been harder since Mark lost

his job. It must be what... three years ago now. They lost their house, everything. It was really tough. They were no longer able to afford therapy for Terry. Elizabeth had to go back to work at the hospital. Mark hasn't been able to get a full time position. He's doing some consulting work, but... Anyway they both adore Terry." She realizes what she has just said. "I guess I should say adored." She looks upwards and blinks.

I remember the expensive looking computer equipment on the Wright's dining-room table. "Is he a computer techie?"

"Yes. I'm not quite sure exactly what it is he does. It's very technical, mathematical in some way."

I think back over my visit to the Wrights and one little fact becomes an itch that needs scratching. It still bothers me that Terry was able to climb out of the window of his bedroom without his father hearing at least something.

"I hate to have to ask this question, but we need to explore all possibilities."

She nods.

"Does Mark drink? You know, more than normal. Or maybe take drugs?"

She blushes. "You're putting me in a very difficult position. There's stuff that Elizabeth has told me in confidence."

I nod encouragement. I hope.

Long pause. An uncomfortable cough. Another pause.

"I guess if I've told my son that he has to tell the truth to the police, I'd better do the same." She takes a deep breath. "Definitely no drugs. Mark never drinks at home, you realize. He would never do that; you know, not put Terry at risk. But lately Elizabeth says that he has been hanging around with a client. They go out a lot and Mark often comes home drunk. She says that she met the client once and took an instant dislike to him; she actually felt frightened by him. But she can't say anything to Mark about it. He gets angry. He says it's his only client and they need the income to pay their bills. I'm sure it's nothing. Why would it be relevant to what happened to Terry?"

The thought of Mark Wright having a client who frightened his wife makes me think about Michael's reference to 'the bad people.'

"It's probably not," I tell her truthfully. "It just helps to understand what's going on in the family. Neither of the Wrights will ever know we had this conversation by the way."

"Thank you." She looks relieved.

I stand up. "Thank *you* for your candour And for the milk and cookies; they were great. If Michael says any more about oboe will you call me right away and let me know?" I hand her my card and she shows me to the door.

It's four o'clock. From here it's less than ten minutes to Ellie's school but I have to drive across Vancouver in rush hour, drop off the car, stow my gun and then drive back. I rarely take my gun home, never when Ellie's going to be there.

As I walk down the garden path toward the car, my happiness at the thought of seeing my daughter is marred by the feeling that I have accomplished little here other than upsetting the Chan's son.

Stammo would say that this oboe stuff means nothing, get on with the real police work. Maybe he's right. I am on what Shakespeare called *a sleeveless errand*.

So why can't I leave it alone?

18

ELLIE

I like it at Daddy's; he's very fun. Except when he asks me that question, "How was school today?"

"Good." That's a fib. I hate St. Cecelia's, except for gym and recess. Oh, and music class.

"Do you want some more ice cream, sweetie?" he asks.

"Please." Mommy's strict about fruit and vegetables but Daddy isn't.

"Do you still have the hamster in your class?"

"I'm in fourth grade, Daddy." I wish we did have a hamster. I like them. When I'm grown up and have a pet shop, I'll have lots of hamsters. And dogs, *lots* of dogs.

He's looking at me and I just know he's going to ask another question about dumb school.

"How's Mommy?" At least it's not a question about school. He worries about Mommy's MS.

"Fine."

"Was she doing something special tonight?"

I'm not supposed to tell Daddy the secret Mommy told me. But I'm not supposed to lie to Mommy or Daddy. I already told Daddy one fib just now.

"Yes," I tell him.

"That's nice. What's she doing?" he asks.

I wish I didn't have to keep secrets. Especially when I don't like the secret.

"Nothing," I say.

He just looks at me. It's not fair! I'm not supposed to keep secrets from Mommy or Daddy. I eat some of my ice cream. It's coffee. I love coffee ice cream; Daddy always gets it for me. I have another spoonful.

"Sweetie?" He says it like a question. He's good at asking questions. He asks bad people questions and then when they tell lies he puts them in prison.

"She's having a date." I feel bad for Mommy that I've told. But she shouldn't go on a date when she's got Daddy and she shouldn't make me not tell.

"Oh," he says. "Who with?"

"Don't know." She's been out with him a couple of times but I've never seen him.

Daddy looks sad. "Have you...?"

"What Daddy?"

He has that look on his face like Mommy has when she's shopping and she can't decide which blouse to buy. He has a couple of grey hairs, just above his ear. I never saw them before.

"It doesn't matter, sweetie." Now he looks very sad. I'm a little bit mad at Mommy for making Daddy sad. If she could see him like this, she would just want to marry him again for sure.

Poor Daddy. I want to make him laugh. "Knock, knock!" I yell.

"Who's there?"

"Tom Sawyer."

"Tom Sawyer who?"

"Tom saw yer underwear."

He's laughing but I can see he's still a little bit sad. He comes around the table and picks me up out of my seat and hugs me. "I love you, my little sweetie," he says.

I hug him super tight. "I love you too, Daddy."

He carries me into the living room and sits in his favourite chair with me on his lap. He kisses me on the top of my head. I like it when he does that.

"In your class at school do you have any kids with special needs?"

"Yes. Justin. He has a helper."

"Are you his friend?" he asks.

"Kind of. I like Justin but he's a bit weird."

"Will you do something for me?" he asks and I nod. "I want you always to be extra nice to Justin. Invite him to play with you. Talk to him if you think he's lonely."

"Sometimes he doesn't want to play."

"That's OK. I just want you to be a friend to him. That's all."

"OK, Daddy." I think about what happened in class today. "Justin remembers stuff," I say.

"How do you mean sweetie?"

"Well, Ms. Ormond was reading from a book in English class this morning and at recess, I was standing talking to Emily—Emily thinks she's my friend but I don't really like her—anyway, I heard Justin and he was saying the words from the book. He remembered everything in the story."

"Wow." He's quiet for a moment. "Were the words exactly the same as when Ms. Ormond read it?"

"I think. It sounded the same."

He's thinking. I look at his face; it looks so serious. He's thinking about being a policeman. That's so better than thinking about Mommy on a date. I give him a big kiss on the cheek and he gives me a big Daddy smile. "Knock, knock," he says.

"Who's there?"

"Justin."

"Justin who?"

"Just in time to do the dishes."

He's funny. He picks me up and takes me to the kitchen. "You fetch me the dishes and I'll put them into the dishwasher," he says.

He's not sad anymore. He's probably forgotten that Mommy's on a date.

19

CAL

THURSDAY

"*Pentacles are almost always circumscribed with one, usually two circles.*" Damien always was a precise kind of guy. "*What you've got there is just a star. The damaged eyes and the cross on the lips are from a painting, I'm trying to remember the details. Oboe is blood. Definitely hex. LOL. Be back on Saturday, talk to you then. DC.*"

His email was written while I was asleep. It's straightforward enough except for the LOL. What makes 'oboe is blood', or the fact that it is a hex, funny? I've tried calling him but his phone is switched off. I hope he checks for messages.

I think twice before ringing the Wright's doorbell. I didn't tell Stammo that I was going to come here before going in to work. It could be interpreted as insubordination and jeopardize my official return to the department. I just need to do it, so I'm hoping it's better to ask for forgiveness later than being denied permission now.

Out of the corner of my eye I see the living room curtains twitch. It reminds me of a nosy neighbour I once interviewed. Seconds later, the front door flies open and I am shocked by what I see.

Elizabeth Wright is transformed from the woman I interviewed earlier this week. The bags are gone from under her eyes, her hair is loose and looks great. She is dressed in fashionable gym gear. But what shocks me is her expression.

This is not the face of a woman who has just lost a child.

Overjoyed is an understatement, yet the joy is somehow tinged with fear and I feel the same spark arc between us as on Monday in Terry's bedroom.

It all lasts but a second; she focuses on my face and everything disappears, leaving me with a feeling akin to loss.

And in a flash, I know what just happened; it makes me modify my plan for this interview.

"May I speak with you for a few minutes Mrs. Wright?"

"Uh, yes, of course." She is flustered now. "Come in Detective, uh…"

"Rogan," I supply. "Rocky Rogan."

She leads me into the living room and I sense

that something is different but cannot decide what. I look around; the furniture is the same and most of the dining room table is still taken up with Mark Wright's expensive computer monitors. There are even left over breakfast things on the far end of the table.

She folds herself into an armchair. The movement is both elegant and sensual. She extends her hand indicating that I should sit, so I do.

"Is your husband in?" I ask.

"No. He's at a breakfast meeting. I don't know when he'll be back."

"I visited your church." I say. When Stammo and I left here on Tuesday, she and her husband had refused to give us the name of the church yet there is no surprise in her face. She already knows.

"I was disturbed by something I saw there. There is a picture on the wall of a man lying dead—"

"Mutilated like Terry," she says in a flat tone, expressionless eyes focused on me.

I deliver the understatement of the year. "It seems too much of a coincidence to me."

I don't yet comment on the fact that she was able to finish my sentence with such precision. How did she know to which picture I was referring? Unless someone told her of my visit and I'm pretty sure I know who that someone might be.

I leave my statement hanging, like a question, but she does not take the bait; she just looks at me in silence. "Does it seem like a coincidence to you Mrs. Wright?" I ask in as gentle a tone as I can summon.

She looks away from me, toward the door, and shrugs. In profile she is even more beautiful... vulnerable. Tears are welling in her eyes, making me want to go over and comfort her. Not a good idea.

"Do you think it is possible that someone in your church may have had a reason for wanting to kill Terry?"

She shakes her head and the tears are now flowing down her cheeks. "Mrs. Wright, I think you need to talk to me. Tell me everything you know." She's sobbing now and I wait. Finally, she manages to calm herself. She looks at me. She's going to talk. I can feel a small tremble in my gut at the expectation; I smell a revelation coming.

But my Blackberry buzzes. I slide it out of my pocket. Damn! The caller is Stammo. Almost certainly about to ask me where I am and why I'm not a work yet. I wrestle with the options for a few seconds... then decide: I might as well be hung for a sheep as for a lamb so I send him to voicemail, immediately regretting it.

His call disturbed the flow of my interrogation. "What were you going to tell me Mrs. Wright?" I ask.

But Elizabeth Wright has used the moment to collect herself. Instead of talking to me she stands and takes one step over to a bookcase. She takes a CD from a pile and inserts it into a tiny player. The sounds of *a capella* female voices fill the room, singing a haunting chant.

"Hildegard von Bingen," she says above the music as she returns to her seat.

"I'm sorry?" I don't know the reference.

"This is her music. She was a Christian mystic who lived nine hundred years ago. She is one of the Transcended Masters we hope to emulate."

The ancient music is beautiful, somehow overflowing simultaneously with both sadness and joy. It makes the hair stand up on the back of my neck.

"I can't explain it, detective." Her voice is calm and controlled. I am not going to get the revelation that I would have got if I'd ignored my Blackberry. "No-one at the church would have any reason to hurt Terry and even if they did, they would not profane his body by using an image from one of the black pictures. They represent the evil aspects of humanity which we must all guard against." She is using the speech patterns and tones typical of people who are members of cults. Ten or so years ago, Steve and I busted a so-called church that was bilking its members and their wealthy families out of thousands of dollars. Even when their leaders' mendacity was revealed, the followers still spoke of the church, it's leaders and it's members in hushed terms of respect.

"How many members are there?" I ask.

"Over a hundred true followers," she says with some pride.

"So you knew Mrs. Marguerite Varga?"

"Of course. Not well, but I knew her. So tragic that she died on her way to worship."

"Don't you think it's strange that she died the day after Terry?"

"Everything happens for a reason detective. Maybe Marguerite was chosen to help Terry in the afterlife." True believers explain everything within the context of their belief systems—come to think of it, we all do—however, she is giving none of the signs of dissembling.

"What about Seth, the Reverend Harris' brother? Is he a true follower?"

Her smile confirms my earlier conjecture. "Seth is still learning The Ways." Her voice is gentle. "He is new to the Church. He joined after the death of his father, the former Reverend Harris. In time he will be a wonderfully strong follower of the Masters."

Her glowing endorsement of Seth does not jibe with my feelings about the taciturn dog handler. Nor do they quite align with the Reverend Morgan

Harris' demeanour toward her brother and his dog.

Elizabeth is a true believer and I know I am not going to get any unbiased information on the church from this meeting. Time to focus on other areas. I want to follow up on something Elizabeth said last time I was here with Stammo; it was triggered in my mind by Grace Chan yesterday afternoon.

"Tell me about your husband's business?"

The pleasant, almost dreamy look disappears. "Why do you want to know?" she asks.

"It must be very interesting work if..." I start but cannot finish. I feel guilty about the reason I was going to give; it will only help to drive a wedge between them. Mark Wright was engrossed in his work to the extent that Michael was able to sneak out of the house unnoticed.

I'll take the higher road and tell the truth.

"When I was here with Detective Stammo on Tuesday you said something like, *'If Terry was killed by someone wishing to hurt us, ask my husband about that.'* What exactly did you mean?"

She blushes, wipes a wisp of errant hair from her face and tucks it behind her ear. The gesture reminds me of Sam and last night's conversation with Ellie comes rushing back to me. I can't bear the thought of Sam out on a date with another man. I'd thought, wanted, hoped that she would be considering the possibility of a reconciliation. I try to push the thoughts out of my mind and refocus on Elizabeth Wright.

"You must understand that I was distraught. I wasn't thinking straight," she says.

"Is there anyone your husband knows who would want to hurt him or pressure him in some way? A competitor, a former colleague," I pause, "a client or someone?"

She flinches on the word client but says nothing.

I pause. The ethereal voices continue their chants.

"What does he do?" I ask.

"He's a security expert. He helps his clients keep their computers secure. Keep out hackers. That sort of thing."

"So if he made a mistake and a client's security was breached, that client might be very angry at your husband."

"Well, I suppose. But be realistic, detective. Business people don't go around killing children to make a point."

I would agree with her, were it not for the fact that the most important case of my life was a murder committed for business reasons. I don't see how a child's murder could possibly be connected with business... which makes it a line of questioning worth following.

"So why did you say that I should *ask your husband about that*?"

"As I said, I was distraught."

She smiles at me in a way that I find subtly seductive. The hair she tucked behind her ear escapes and falls forward over her eye. She ignores it.

"Are you sure there's no-one your husband knows who might be in some way involved in Terry's death?"

"No. No, of course not." And I know to a certainty that she is covering something up. I look hard into her eyes and she repeats, "No."

Without breaking eye contact, I change tack again, "Oboe is blood. What does that mean to you Mrs. Wright."

"Nothing. It was just something that Terry had been saying before he..." Her voice peters out. "He kept repeating it and a bunch of other gibberish. It annoyed Mark which just made Terry do it all the more."

"What sort of gibberish?" If Elizabeth remembers, I will have more of the hex. Maybe enough for Damien to shed some light on this bizarre murder.

"Oh it was just letters and numbers like he was spelling something out, with the odd word thrown in."

"Do you remember any of it?"

"No." She is becoming irritated. "It was just gibberish."

"What was gibberish?" Mark Wright's voice cuts through the chanting coming from the CD player.

He is standing in the doorway. The volume of the music must have covered the sounds of his return. He is wearing a nicely tailored suit and is carrying an expensive-looking leather satchel. It looks heavy and I'm guessing that it carries a laptop computer. If they are living in this tiny little house with its shabby furniture because of some financial setback, I wonder where the money for all this computer equipment comes from.

"What was gibberish?" he repeats.

"You know," replies his wife, "that *oboe* thing that Terry used to say."

"Oh, that," he says dismissively setting my antennae twitching.

I stand. "Mr. Wright, when I was here on Tuesday afternoon, I asked you if O – B – O – E meant anything to you. You said no. That wasn't true was it."

He literally squirms for a moment. "Well, I didn't make the connection," his voice has an angry ring to it. "I mean it was the day after I learned my son had been murdered. I wasn't thinking straight. I didn't know..."

"His friend Michael said 'Oboe is blood.' Please tell me what that means," I ask.

"Nothing. It was all part of their fantasy game playing." He takes a deep breath to calm himself. "I assure you detective, it has no relevance to Terry's death."

Now I *know* it does.

"Tell me about your business, Mr. Wright."

It is like a sobering slap in the face. He goes pale and his face becomes a blank.

"Detective, my wife and I are the victims here. If you want to interrogate me about my business, you can wait until I get my lawyer involved. So, unless you have any other questions, I suggest you leave right now."

I hold his gaze for a good five seconds before saying. "Thank you, Mr. Wright, Mrs. Wright."

I turn and go.

This has been a frustrating interview in many ways. I have gained no new insights into the Church of the Transcended Masters nor into the meaning of 'oboe is blood' except that it is in some way relevant to Terry's death.

However, I may have gained something far more valuable: a viable theory of the crime.

20

CAL

Stammo is not a happy camper. "I said you could go and interview the chick in the church by yourself. Not the Chinese kid and Elizabeth Wright. What the hell were you thinking?"

I want to tell him that I got some information that I would not have got if he had been with me. But I keep my counsel, knowing, like Benvolio, *if he hear thee, thou wilt anger him.*

"I'm sorry Nick. I just thought—"

"Well don't. And when I call you, you fucking answer, OK?"

There is a tiny fleck of saliva on the corner of his mouth, a tiny perfect sphere.

"Yeah, Nick. I'm sorry about that."

"I don't know how to write this up," he mutters, as much to himself as to me.

He gets up from his desk, exhales loudly and walks to the window.

And then it clicks with me. Stammo is as unhappy about his being my minder as I am. In a strange way it creates a bond between us. Now I feel guilty doing the interviews without him.

"I really am sorry, Nick," I repeat.

He nods without turning back.

After a long pause, "What did you get?"

I tell him about my visits to the church, the Chan family and Elizabeth Wright and the ideas that are forming around them. He focuses on the one item I knew he would.

"So your buddy from school, the Goth guy, says that 'oboe is blood' is a hex. That's like a curse, right?" He ponders this. "So Terry and his friend are going around repeating this curse and Terry gets killed for it, maybe by someone from the church."

"It's a bit of a stretch, Nick."

"Stranger things have happened." He looks ruffled. "Some of those churches down Oak Street can be pretty weird."

"What I find more interesting is Elizabeth's reaction this morning after she peeked through the curtain and then came to the door. For a moment, her face was all lit up until she saw it was me. I'm sure that through the curtains she mistook me for Seth, the brother of the minister."

"So you think she might be having an affair with this Seth character?"

"Yeah. And I don't trust that guy at all. When I saw him yesterday, I got a really bad vibe from him and when I mentioned Terry's mutilations, the minister said 'How could he?' I thought that Seth might have killed Terry. She was his only alibi."

"Why would he kill the kid, other than for repeating the hex?"

"What if he is having an affair with Elizabeth and wants her to leave her husband but she won't, because of Terry. So Seth kills Terry to take away that excuse."

"That's a bit of a stretch too… but not impossible. Either way, the Church of the Transcended Masters could do with another visit."

"I'd like to take along a little prop that might get her talking," I say. When I tell him what it is, his smile is feral.

———

ON THE WAY HERE, we talked about the fact that Marguerite Varga, our hit and run victim, was a member of the church. There is no logical connection between the cases and Stammo thinks it is a coincidence but my gut tells me that there is a link, though for the life of me, I cannot fathom what it might be.

Morgan Harris opens the door to us with a look of annoyance on her face. She is dressed in a tight angora sweater and blue jeans and I wonder if her irritation is due to the fact that we have arrived unannounced and that she was unable to greet us in her white surplice. Again, I feel the stirrings of attraction and she catches my gaze and gives me a disconcerting look that tells me she knows what is going on in my mind.

"Miss Harris," says Stammo, now back in charge, "we would like a moment of your time."

"Unfortunately, this is not a very convenient time for me." Her voice is brittle. "And it's *Reverend* Harris."

"Well *Reverend* Harris, let me remind you that two members of your *church* have been murdered in the last seven days. I would have thought that you would want to help us find out who killed them."

She wilts under Stammo's barrage. "I'm sorry. Come in please." She leads us through a door to the right of the church's main room and into a kitchen. "I was having some tea. Can I offer you a cup."

"No thanks," Stammo answers for both of us. "Is your brother here?"

"Uh, no." She was not expecting the question.

"We wanted to ask him about his affair with Elizabeth Wright."

For a beat, she does a pretty good imitation of a goldfish. Just long enough to invalidate any denial that she might have considered. Stammo and I stay silent, waiting for her to speak.

Five seconds... ten seconds... "Well, I, uh, really can't comment."

"Is it serious?"

"You'd have to ask him."

"We will. Where is he right now."

"I'm not sure."

I remember my meeting with Elizabeth earlier this morning: how she was dressed and the look in her eyes. "He's with her now, isn't he?" I ask.

"No... I don't know..." She looks from me to Stammo and back. Then she sighs. "Yes," she capitulates.

"How serious is it?" Stammo's voice has an unaccustomed gentleness to it.

"For her, it is very serious."

"And for him?"

"Oh, I don't know..." She casts about with her eyes. "Seth is a charismatic man, women are drawn to him. I think many see an element of danger in him that they find attractive. But he is not... well, a one-woman man."

This weakens the already-slim theory that Seth

killed Terry to break her link to her husband, leaving room for a much more unpleasant thought. Two of them, in fact.

"Does her husband know?" I ask. Husbands have been known to kill their own children to punish their wives; although I must say, Mark Wright doesn't look the type.

"I don't know but please promise me you won't tell him." I wonder if the look of horror on her face is for the hurt that would be caused to Mark Wright or the damage that a scandal might do to her church.

Stammo uses her reaction. "If you are completely forthcoming with us, we may not need to discuss the matter with Mr. Wright."

During Stammo's questioning, my eyes have been sweeping the kitchen and on the counter I see a dog collar. It is studded like the collar of a goth might wear and has an engraved nameplate. I walk over and pick it up, which gets a reaction from Morgan Harris. She is about to say something to me when Stammo snaps, "Reverend Harris?"

"Oh, uh... yes. I'll tell you anything I can." She keeps her eyes on me.

"What was the connection between Mrs. Wright and Mrs. Marguerite Varga?" Stammo asks.

She is caught by the change of subject. "Well nothing really. They knew each other of course but they were not particularly close. They were from quite different backgrounds. I guess the only thing they had in common was the fact that their husbands both came to the church once and then never came back a second time."

"Did their husbands come on the same day?" I ask.

"No, months apart."

Stammo looks at me and nods.

I put the dog's collar back on the counter. "Would you come with me please, Reverend Harris," I say as I lead her out of the kitchen and into the main hall. I head for the black-draped picture on the far wall, the one I looked at on our first visit. I turn and wait for her to catch up to me and notice that Stammo is not behind her. I point to the mutilated body in the foreground and take the prop from my pocket: a five-by-seven photo of Terry's face, taken by the pathologist. "Wouldn't you say that it is more than likely that one of your parishioners, someone familiar with this painting, killed Terry?"

She is transfixed by the horror of the photo. "It can't be," she whispers.

"What can't be?" I ask quietly. I sense Stammo moving up behind me.

"None of our members could do this to a child."

"Well I want you to think about who might have done this? Who apart from your members or their guests might have seen this picture and carved up Terry's face?"

"No-one!" she sobs. "The black pictures are covered when we have guests at our open houses, so it couldn't be a guest and none of our members would do such a thing."

"Reverend Harris, I would like you to think long and hard about this and contact me if you have any information that might lead us to Terry's killer. Any information at all." I put the photo and my business card into her hand.

As per our plan for this interview, we head toward the front door.

On the way to the car, I tell him my speculation about the significance of the three letters engraved on the dog's collar lying on the kitchen counter.

"I told you," he says with his feral smile.

21

CAL

No, no. Not that one," he snaps. "That's mine. The Mac was hers." His tone implies that he regards his late wife's computer as a lesser life form. He really is a pompous ass. Yet Sam's opinion of him keeps coming to mind. Sam is rarely wrong about people; is his attitude the result of some feelings of guilt?

Stammo and I are here to pick up Marguerite Varga's computer. Normally someone from Forensic Services would do this but Steve got some pressure from his boss, Inspector Vance. Varga complained to Superintendent Cathcart that not enough was being done to find his wife's killer, so we need to be 'more visible.' Cathcart's name again gives me that familiar sinking feeling.

Now that we are here, in the study at Varga's

home, we intend to make good use of the visit. As I unplug the Mac from a power bar under the desk, Stammo asks, "Do you think your wife's death could be connected to your gambling, sir?"

There is a tiny pause and I am furious at Stammo for asking the question while I am on my hands and knees under the desk and cannot scrutinize Varga's face.

"I *beg* your pardon, Detective Stammo," he says, his tone acerbic, "*what* did you just ask me?" He is playing for time.

Stammo surprises me. He is usually deferential toward people who have influence with the department's brass but not now that Cathcart has given us the all clear signal. "I think you heard me, sir," he says evenly.

This time the pause is longer and gives me time to get to my feet. I notice that the study walls are covered in photos of Marguerite and Harold Varga: in formal wear; on the beach; sitting at a table in a Mexican restaurant with big glasses of Sangria in their hands and bigger grins on their faces. I remember the photo that he gave us in his office, the one that Sam took, they looked happy in that one too.

"As you know, *Detective* Stammo, gambling is legal in Vancouver. Are you inferring that I am somehow mixed up with criminals because I like to place the occasional wager?" His tone makes me want to take him down a peg by pointing out his misuse of the word *infer* but then the thought makes me feel small-minded and petty.

"I wasn't saying that, sir," Stammo replies.

"Then what were you saying?"

"So where do you gamble, sir?" I interject.

Varga pauses again.

"Well... not that it's any of your business but I usually go to either the Edgewater or the River Rock." The casinos he has named are the largest ones within a twenty minute drive from this house. It's an obvious answer and I don't believe it.

Nor does Stammo. "Do you have any gambling debts, sir?" he asks.

Varga is angry now and that anger is covering something. I'm sure of it.

"Casinos do not let people run up debts, Detective. *You* should know that. One buys chips with a credit card." The condescension in his voice drips everywhere.

I make him regret what he has said with, "Could we see your credit card statements then sir?" the innocence of the question writ large on my face.

For a second his eyes seek a way out. He knows those credit card statements are going to reveal a side of him that he wants to keep secret. Then, with a supreme effort, he takes a deep breath and calms down. I am convinced that his gambling is connected to his wife's death and that he knows it. I know first-hand the guilt that comes when a loved one dies because of one's own actions. I know how that pain can be masked by anger and, out of nowhere, I feel a great empathy for the pompous Harold Varga and the pain he must be feeling. I regret the question I just asked.

"Thank you for your time Mr. Varga," I say quietly. "We are very sorry for your loss."

He looks at me for a moment and nods. I see a tear forming in the corner of his eye.

"Just a couple of other things." There is a hard edge of anger in Stammo's voice now.

"No, Detective. No more. Not now."

The glare I get from Stammo is a harbinger of his wrath. It takes me all my control not to squirm physically.

22

CAL

I am still stinging from the apoplectic tongue-lashing I got from Stammo for curtailing the interview with Varga. He was right of course. I shouldn't have let my own guilt from my recent past have clouded my judgment but I did. He was so mad he made me single-handedly load Marguerite Varga's computer and three boxes of files into the back of the Crown Vic.

Once he calmed down, we talked about the interview and Varga's reactions. His gambling is almost certainly connected to his wife's death. Despite the legalization of gambling, there are still a number of high stakes, illegal games and bookies in town. Stammo and I agreed that he probably owes a ton of money to some underworld character. Stammo figures either he killed her for the insurance money to pay off his debts or his creditors killed her as a lesson to him.

But, as I think about it now, something about those photos in his study—combined with Sam's opinion of Varga—tells me that he was in love with his wife and that he wouldn't kill her. And if he was in debt to some illegal gambling operation, they wouldn't kill his wife. That would just encourage him to go to the police. Anyway, gambling operations aren't like drug gangs, they don't kill people at the drop of a hat. The connection between his wife's death and his gambling has got to be a lot more subtle than I can yet fathom but I know it's there. Somewhere.

I turn the Healey into the parking garage of my condo. The automatic security gate is open. I drive through and stop. Condo rules say that you have to wait for the gate to close behind you.

It doesn't.

Then I see why.

The garage lights are out. Must be a power failure.

The garage looks strangely unfamiliar, lit only by the Healey's headlights. The reflection of the lights off the fire-resistant coating on the ceiling makes it feel like I am driving deep into an ice cave.

As I go down to the next level, the thin light from the open security door is no longer visible.

Apart from my headlights, the only other light source is from the red exit signs over the doors into the elevator lobby.

I can see my parking spot between the hulking shapes of two SUVs. I always worry that the doors of those SUVs are one day going to ding my beautiful British racing-green paintwork.

Three stalls down I see an unfamiliar white van parked at an angle. It looks like a BC Hydro truck but its lights are off and there is no sign of any electrician.

I reverse into my spot making sure to leave an equal distance between myself and the behemoths on either side. I turn off the engine and headlights.

Darkness and silence. No voices, just the ticking of the engine as it cools.

I cannot see the red exit sign to guide me to the elevator which gives me an unpleasant feeling of disorientation. The darkness feels oppressive. Creepy even.

I am going to have to feel my way out of here, like a kid playing blind man's buff.

Then I remember the flashlight in the trunk.

I get out of the car and locate the trunk release by feel, insert the key and unlock the trunk. It opens with a squeak which I had never noticed before; I must remember to oil the hinges. The squeak is the only sound in the blackness.

I have that feeling you sometimes get in a darkened room. The irrational feeling that someone is
standing behind you. I can feel the goose-bumps at
the thought.

I feel hastily around the floor of the trunk, my
hand coming into contact with the jack, the rubber
hammer for releasing the hubs for the wire wheels,
three emergency flares held together with an elastic
band which feel like sticks of dynamite. No
flashlight.

I whisper an expletive.

It sounds loud.

Then there is another, softer sound but I cannot
tell if it is close or far away. No cause for panic.

As I reach further back, my fingers come into
contact with the Maglite.

"Gotcha."

I click the switch and the interior of the trunk is
bathed in bright LED light.

I have a great feeling of relief and I cannot help
chuckling at my momentary primal fear of the dark.
I straighten up and shine the light at the cars parked
across from mine.

There is a scuffling sound.

It's close.

It's behind me.

As I turn, hard hands grab my biceps and a

damp cloth is clamped across my face. There must be two of them, at least.

The one holding my biceps is directly behind me, so I take three hard steps back and hear the whoosh of his breath as my momentum slams him into the garage wall. His hold on me is lessened and I try to wriggle out of his grip but I am too weak. The cloth is still over my face. The acrid smell makes me want to cough. I know I only have a very few seconds to fight my way out of this.

The flashlight is jerked out of my hand and shone into my face.

Someone jabs me hard in the stomach expelling the oxygen from my lungs, making me take in deep breaths.

One chance. I lift my foot and stamp down hard on the instep of the man behind me. He shouts out in pain and one of my arms is free. I reach across myself to grab his other arm but I have no strength in my hand.

My head is forced back and I am looking directly into the flashlight. No. It can't be a flashlight because it's getting smaller and smaller, like a space ship accelerating into the cosmos.

Smaller and smaller until it flashes into warp-drive and is gone.

23

CAL

I can breathe. With difficulty. My face hurts. Something feels rough. I can smell coffee. *Wake up and smell the coffee.* I ease my eyes open. The world is sepia. Something is on my face: brown, meshed and miserly in its allowance of light. In the dim, all I can hear is my breathing: lungs forcing air through sackcloth.

I experiment with movement. I can roll my head but not without pain. I cannot raise my hand to my face. I try the other. Pinned. I feel thin wire cut into my wrists and my ankles.

The panic hits. *Where the hell am I?*

I move my fingers. Blanket. I try to sit up and bed springs groan. I groan. A hand on my chest easily returns me to the horizontal.

Silence. The silence increases my feeling of impotence.

"Hello." *Inane thing to say.*

Still silence.

Questions rush to my mind but I suppress them all. Speaking now would be pointless... and show weakness. Breathe deeply. Calm the rising waters. You're OK. You can get out of this.

A door clicks closed.

There is a new level of silence, in some way more ominous. I try to sit up and this time there is no resisting hand. My bound wrists hold me to a semi sit-up so I slump back. I deep breathe. Right into my belly. Ten breaths.

Think, Rocky.

What was my last memory before being here? I'm not sure. Thursday evening. Parking my car, the garage darkened. Then what?

I need to know more about where I am.

I push my head up. I strain my eyes to see through the sack. The light in the room is artificial. It's nighttime. That's all I can see.

The smell of coffee is from the sackcloth. It masks everything else: no clues from that department.

I grit my teeth and try to work my hands free of the wires binding them until I feel blood dripping from my wrists.

I quiet my breathing and listen. There is a hissing sound, vaguely familiar but I cannot identify it. There is a faint traffic hum. It tells me nothing.

Time passes and I strain for a clue, any clue.

Then the fear seeps in. Slowly at first.

I think back a year or so to the drug gang that tried to kidnap me. Kill me. But they are all in prison or dead. So who has got me now? Another gang? But why? The maniac who brutally murdered Terry Wright? Or maniacs.

I cannot control the rising heart rate, pumping fear through my body.

I must be here because I am nearer to solving Terry's murder than I thought.

Every cop knows that the simplest hypothesis is the most likely. The most likely suspect is Seth Harris. The man with the dog. Was it his hand on my chest? Is he Terry's killer? His only alibi is his sister.

What is he going to do? Carve me up like Terry and leave me in the woods?

The door opens.

Two sets of footsteps. One in shoes, one in runners. Seth and Morgan Harris together? Maybe I'm in the basement of their church.

A hand grabs my right wrist. Are they going to cut me now?

I feel my bowels loosening and clench against the ultimate humiliation.

But instead of baring my chest for the fatal blow, the sleeve of my jacket is pulled up and something is tied around my right bicep. My heart starts a frenetic pounding at the familiar feel.

"God no. Please no. I'll tell you anything..."

Not that. Anything but that.

The alcohol smell cuts through the mask and the wire cuts into my wrists as I try to pull my arms free. The pain becomes excruciating.

"NOOOOOO." I scream. "HELP ME! HELP ME!" Maybe someone passing on Oak Street will hear me.

My struggles are suppressed by a hand on my face and knees on my chest.

I struggle to buck off my assailant. If I can't stop this, in seconds, everything that I have gained in the last fifteen months will be flushed away. Sam, Ellie, my return to the VPD will all be gone.

I shake my head to loosen the grip and clamp my jaws onto the hand. With a grunt the hand is jerked away.

"Please don't do this." I am not above begging. "Please... Anything..."

And in a tiny corner of my soul, the Beast, so long suppressed, paraphrases Shakespeare. *The gentleman doth protest too much, methinks.* And I know it. This is what the Beast has been craving, for every minute of every day for one year, three months and six days, since the hour when Sam dropped me off at rehab. My skin crawls at the knowledge that a part of me wants this. Wants this more than anything.

"Please..." I am sobbing with anguish... or is it desire?

Or both.

I hardly feel the pinprick in my arm, I just feel the throbbing where the wire has shredded my wrists.

The ultimate cruelty: they are going to get me hooked again and they are going to let me enjoy it.

The surgical elastic is removed from my arm with a snap.

Three... two... one...

Oooh.

Ooooooooooooooooooooh.

24

CAL

FRIDAY

It's morning. I can tell from the quality of the light filtering through the coffee sack covering my head. I have been here for over twelve hours.

They shot me up some time during the early hours. It was the fourth time. They are as regular as clockwork; before I feel any withdrawal, they inject me again.

They do it in silence, but for the hissing sound.

About every four hours. Always in my right arm.

All attempts at communication are ignored except for my request for water; a corner of the sacking was rolled back and a straw thrust into my mouth. The water was warm and tasted of chlorine; from a tap but not recently.

Something is different. But what? I strain for a

sound, any sound. The hum of the traffic is there but the hissing has stopped. What was that hissing? It seemed familiar but from the past, from my childhood. Outdoors...

That's it! The hissing was a Coleman lantern. We are not in the church on Oak, we are in a building with no electricity; probably an abandoned building with no running water.

Between brief moments of sleep, I have had a lot of thinking time and somehow the euphoria induced by the heroin has relaxed my mind and sharpened my thinking processes... I think.

I have two theories.

The more I think about it something feels so wrong at the Church of the Transcended Masters. Am I getting too close to something? If I am, it must be huge because criminals don't kidnap cops; the consequences are just too dire. But the big negative in this theory is that there is no way that Seth and Morgan Harris could know that heroin is my Achilles heel?

It now makes less sense than my second theory.

Most of the gang that we busted last year may be in jail but their leader is still a powerful man with a long reach. We never found where he keeps his money but, at a conservative estimate, he must have amassed over two hundred million dollars. He has enough to pay for a professional kidnapping. To see me a junkie again would be the perfect revenge for me ruining him. It would be sweeter even than killing me, to know that I will lose everything: Sam, Ellie, the job, everything.

But where is this going? How long are they going to keep me?

With a shock I realize they have to let me go today. I am meeting Sam and Ellie for dinner tonight and it's my weekend to have Ellie. Although part of me dreads it, I need to ask Sam about who she was on a date with and if it's serious. The thought of her with someone is more painful than the cuts on my wrists.

The door opens.

One person this time. I have to try and negotiate my way out of this.

"Hi," I say. "Listen, if you want to get me hooked, you've succeeded. Giving me more is not going to make a difference."

My right sleeve is pushed up for what, the fifth time now?

"You could let me go now."

The surgical tape ties off the blood flow.

"I have to see my daughter tonight. You under—"

My plea is cut off by a blow to the side of my head.

I smell the alcohol.

My right arm. I'm right-handed, I always shot up in my left arm. I try to picture him shooting me up. Dr. Marcus said that Terry's fatal blow was delivered either from the front by a lefty or from behind by a righty.

Before I can make sense of it, I feel the prick of the needle.

It is time to feed the Beast.

25

ELLIE

I can tell Mommy's mad at Daddy; she says she's not but I know she is.

It started in the restaurant. She kept calling his cell phone and leaving a message and I could tell she was getting angry. She ordered my dinner but didn't order anything for herself and while I was eating she called her boyfriend. She gets angry when I call him that. 'He's just a friend, Ellie,' she always says. She kept saying things like, 'No, it's not like that,' and 'I really want to as much as you do,' and 'I'll call you as soon as he arrives, I promise.'

But Daddy didn't arrive and now we are back home and it's eight-thirty. I'm scared for him. Maybe he's in a car accident. When I tell Mommy this she looks worried.

"Why don't you call the hospital and ask if he's there, Mommy?"

"Don't worry sweetie," she says. "Daddy will be OK. If he was in an accident the police would call me."

She thinks for a moment and then makes a phone call.

"Hi," she says, "This is Samantha Rogan. Is my husband still there?" She never uses Daddy's and my name anymore; she always says she's Samantha Cullen. She called Daddy her husband. I wonder if that means that we are all going to live together again. I really, really, really hope so.

I can hear whoever she is talking to but I can't tell what they are saying. "Not since Thursday? Are you sure?" she says. She listens some more then, "OK, thanks."

Now she looks worried like me. I don't like it when she looks worried.

"Pleeeeaase, Mommy. Pleeeeease call the hospital. I want to see Daddy." I can feel tears starting.

"Ellie, for god's sake!" she yells at me.

She's made me start crying. She didn't have to shout like that.

"Oh, sweetie, I'm sorry," she says and puts her arm round me. I squirm away from her and cross my arms. Now I'm really crying a lot and I want Daddy. I want him now.

The door-bell rings.

OMG. I made Daddy come to the door. I'm like Hermione in Harry Potter. I turn to Mommy and give her a big smile then run so fast to the door.

"Ellie wait—" Mommy says as I pull open the door.

"Daddeeeeeeeeeeeee—"

But it's not Daddy. It's a stranger. I'm not allowed to talk to strangers. He looks—

"You must be Ellie," he says and smiles at me. I don't like how he smiles.

Mummy's right beside me. "Hi," she says. I look up at her and she is smiling at him in a funny way. I look at him and he is smiling at her just the same. I've seen that look before... on the face of a boy on Hannah Montana... Ooooh. No way! He's Mommy's boyfriend.

"Ell, sweetie, would you go to your room for a moment. I need to talk in private."

"NO."

She looks at me and she's mad at me. "OK," she says and steps outside pulling the door closed behind her.

I'm a little bit worried that she will go somewhere with him but she wouldn't leave me here, not without Daddy or a babysitter, even that horrible Roxanne. I can hear them talking.

"You shouldn't have come but I'm so glad you did," she kind of whispers.

"I just really wanted to see you."

Then they stop talking... It's quiet... For like a minute... Maybe I should just open the door and check if...

As soon as I think it, the door opens. I am definitely like Hermione.

Mommy comes back in and brings him with her.

"Ell, honey, this is my friend that I was telling you about. He's just going to come in for a moment."

"Hi Ellie," he smiles at me. *Now* I can see why Mommy likes him. He puts out his hand for me to shake. He tells me his name but I don't want to hear it. He's not my Daddy. I don't want him here.

26

CAL

SUNDAY

It's morning again. I have been here since Thursday night, tied to this bed. They have given me only water for the last sixty-something hours. And heroin every four hours, up until yesterday evening. Then they stopped.

It must be ten or twelve hours since the last fix and the agony of withdrawal is in full force. It's the worst it has ever been. My muscles keep knotting into unbearable cramps and I cannot suppress the screams that bubble up. My bowels and bladder have voided repeatedly and even the stench of that hurts. Pain knifes through every joint and every muscle of my back. Every spasm makes the bonds at my wrists and ankles cut deeper into the flesh. Even the touch of the sackcloth on my face is excruciating. Maybe they have abandoned me, left me to die. I hope it will be quick.

Without warning something cold and wet falls across my face. There is a strong chemical smell and then I am suffocating. It ratchets up as a hand pushes down over my mouth and nose. They are killing me. The fear lancing through me eclipses even the pain. That's...

———

I'M at the bottom of a well. I'm cold and wet and far, far above me is the sky. As I drift upwards, the throbbing in my head gets worse. But there is no other pain. No withdrawal. As I float out of the well, I open my eyes. I am lying on my side, on the floor. The walls are grey concrete and the windows, high up, are encrusted in grime with arachnid-lace curtains which occlude the watery winter sunshine. I look down at my body and the reason for the lack of withdrawal symptoms is revealed: a hypodermic hanging from a vein in my right arm. I reach over with my left hand—which is covered in blood from the cuts in my wrist—withdraw it with care and then fling it into a corner of the room.

The effort intensifies the throbbing in my head.

There is nothing in the room. No bed, no sack, no drug paraphernalia. Nothing.

I pull myself to my feet, fighting a wave of nausea.

The room is old, it smells of mildew and I can hear dripping; the sound tells me how thirsty I am.

The dark green paint of the door is flaking. The brass handle feels slimy and I have to grip hard to turn it. The door won't open. I'm locked in. I have to work hard to suppress the desire to scream for help. Why did they put me through the ordeal with the heroin in order to let me die of thirst in a locked room? I must think.

Unbidden, Iago's words rescue me from my rising panic: *but we have reason to cool our raging motions*. Reason. I must apply reason. No-one would go to the trouble of shooting me full of heroin to leave me here to die. Either someone is going to come and unlock the door or...

I turn the handle and pull harder. With great complaint, the warps in the door surrender and it opens. This is not the room I was held in. People came and went in that room without noise.

It is dim in the hallway. I hear movement and strain to see where it comes from. Are my captors still here, watching... waiting. Before me are vertical bars. Cells. Inside the cell in front of me is a hospital style bed with restraints. I'm on Shutter Island. The laugh that escapes at the thought sounds maniacal. Breathe deeply, Rocky.

There is a scuffing sound behind me. Electricity charges up my spine and I spin, raising my hands to ward off the inevitable blow. There is a blur below me and I shudder as the rat runs past my foot.

I do more deep breathing.

At the end of the hall is another green door, a painted exit sign above it. I walk quickly toward it, keen to get off this floor but trepidatious of what may be on other floors. The door opens easily and reveals stairs going down. Wherever I am, I'm on the top floor. I try the doors to each floor on the way down. Every floor is deserted, abandoned and as dank as the one above. At the top of the last flight of stairs, which I surmise leads to a basement, I go to the door and walk through. This floor is brighter and seems dryer and less forbidding. There are no cells and the windows are of normal height. Through the windows I can see some skeletal trees and a wall of dark red brick that runs perpendicular to the windows. To my left is a large black door which I open.

Complete disconnect!

In front of me is tarmacked pavement. Sitting in the middle is my car, the winter sun glinting off the British racing-green paint and the chrome-spoked wheels. Behind it is an expanse of green, rising to a crest topped with dark evergreen bushes. Beyond the bushes are brick buildings that look like they belong to an ivy league college and in a flash, I know where I am.

Riverview Mental Hospital.

The building where I was held is the notorious cell block for the criminally insane, long abandoned and now used only as a movie set for made-in-Vancouver films.

The surrealism of the last few days dissipates and I feel a wave of determination to discover who did this to me and why.

27

CAL

I must *walk alone, like one that has the pestilence.* I desperately want to talk to someone about what has just happened to me but there is no-one I can turn to.

My first thought is to call my boss and former partner, Steve, and tell him; but what if he thinks I am inventing the whole thing to cover up the fact that I have heroin in my blood stream? He administers the random urine test on me once a week. The presence of morphine in the urine can be detected up to forty-eight hours after using heroin, so if I am not tested before midday on Tuesday, I should be OK. Should be. It depends on how much heroin they gave me.

I toy with the idea that I tell him about the kidnapping but leave out any reference to being shot full of drugs. But what do I say happened? I was locked up, blindfolded, tied up for the weekend? Why would anyone do that?

Arnold? He is a man of many resources who manages the trust fund I have from Mr. Wallace but I can't confide in him because a condition of the trust fund, is that I stay clean.

In the old days, I could have talked to Roy; I could tell him just about anything. The thought brings a wave of sorrow.

Whoever kidnapped me was considerate enough to leave my cellphone in my car. Sam was the first person I called. I couldn't tell Sam the truth. There was no telling what her reaction might be. If she knew I had used, she would probably cut me off from Ellie, regardless of the reason. I lied to her. I told her that I had had to go undercover on a case over the weekend but somehow she knew it was a lie. She didn't confront me with it, she just said, "Sure, Cal. No problem." The tone of her voice said it all. She hung up and did not answer when I called her back.

I must resign myself to the fact that I cannot tell anyone. As Hamlet said, *The players can not keep counsel; they'll tell all.*

And so here I am in my car, parked outside the Met pub, just three blocks from the Main Street police station feeling sorry for myself and trying to decide. Within a couple of hours, I am going to go into the physical agony of withdrawal that only heroin can assuage. Can I face going cold turkey? If I do, how bad will it be? The week I spent in detox fifteen months ago was unbearable but was that because I was recovering from years of using? Will it be easier this time? If it's bad, how will I cover up at work tomorrow?

Then I see him. The steer. He's scouring the streets for customers. If I just make one buy, I can stave off the worst of the withdrawal with small hits, just enough to take the edge off. In a few days I can wean myself off. So long as Steve doesn't test me for a few days... But I know it is the Beast talking. The Beast: that part of me that craves the high, craves the impossible dream of recapturing the bliss of my first hit.

The steer is two cars away from me. My hand, unbidden, goes to the door handle but does not open it... yet.

I am on the razor's edge.

28

CAL

MONDAY

So where the fuck were you on Friday?" Stammo asks.

I repeat the lie I told to Steve, "I had the flu that's been going around. I would have called in but my battery was dead and I don't have a land line at home. I still feel like crap." The last sentence is true anyway. The flu story covers the fact that I am sniffing and moving slowly because of my aching joints. I had to use one flap of heroin last night just so that I could sleep but I am cold turkey today. I feel terrified that my absence will cause Steve to think the worst and test me immediately. I just hope he holds off until Wednesday, by which time my urine should be clean. That's assuming that I don't need to use again, just to keep the pains at bay.

Stammo can be sympathetic at times, "Thanks

so much for coming in and sharing your flu germs," he grunts. This is obviously not one of those times.

The keen, young Eric Street joins us in the room. "Hi guys," he grins.

Stammo grunts from habit; I grunt from pain.

I hope no-one notices as I pull down on my sleeves. I don't want anyone to see the cuts on my wrists from the wire restraints.

"I widened the search for murders similar to Terry Wright's but couldn't find anything. Also, there are no other churches by the name of 'Church of the Transcended Masters' and there is nothing in criminal records, either here or in the US, on Morgan or Seth Harris; I googled them too but didn't get anything."

"Thanks a bunch." Stammo is not a happy camper. His usual odour of cigarette is overlaid with another familiar smell. I suspect that he is also suffering from the flu but in his case, it's the 26-ounce flu, as Roy used to call it. The *legal* type of phony flu.

But Eric is not phased by Stammo. "I do have something on your other case: info on Varga's gambling. I've got a good buddy who works at the River Rock. I sent him Varga's photo. He's a regular there. He drops about five grand a month at the blackjack tables. He's not a great player so he rarely wins."

"That's sixty grand a year." Stammo's math skills and interest are both aroused.

"Yeah and that's not all. My buddy texted Varga's pic to a buddy of his at the Edgewater. Varga drops a similar amount there too. Also, some of the other punters he hangs with at the Edgewater are a bit suspect."

"Do you have any names?" I ask.

"No, but the casinos like to be seen to be cooperating with the police, so he is going to get me copies of their surveillance videos the next time Varga is in there, which will likely be tomorrow."

"Good work, Eric."

"Yeah," Stammo grunts.

My almost four year hiatus from the department has left me a bit behind in the information technology area so I ask Eric, "If Varga is losing over a hundred grand a year at the tables it's not such a big deal if he's earning a ton of money from the bank. Any chance that you could find out what he earns?"

Eric smiles a secret smile. "I'll see what I can do," he says with a Marxist flick of his eyebrows. He starts tapping at his laptop's keyboard as my phone starts to ring.

"Detective Rogan."

"Hello, Detective. This is Grace Chan, Michael's mother."

"Oh, hi." This is unexpected.

"You know that thing that Michael kept repeating, 'oboe is blood'? Well he is now repeating a whole lot of

other stuff that I can't make sense of, but I thought I should tell you."

"Do you think we could come over and talk to him?" I ask.

"Yes... OK... but could I ask you to back off quickly if he gets upset?"

"Absolutely. Could we come over today?"

"He'll be home from school at three-thirty. You could come then."

"Thanks, we'll see you then."

I fill Stammo in on the phone call, hoping that he will say I can visit the Chan's by myself.

"OK," he says, "let's go over there this afternoon then." He's back in supervisory mode.

As we head out, I say "See you Eric," and almost run into Steve.

My face drops and I feel my blood run cold... not at the near collision but at Steve or, more precisely, at what I see in Steve's hand. A small brown evidence bag that I know contains a plastic bottle with an orange lid. Why today? Last week he tested me on Wednesday. For an instant I think that he knows about what happened to me in Riverview but that's crazy, the truth is he just didn't buy my story about the flu. He thinks that I was out getting high.

"It's that time, Rocky," he says.

"I've been taking medication for the flu, Steve, it

might screw up the results." It's all I can think to say in order to try and delay the inevitable.

"Write down the drugs you've been taking and I'll submit them with the sample and let the lab decide."

My mind races to find another excuse, any excuse that will delay the test. I look at Steve and then at Stammo. Both have grim looks on their faces.

Stammo steps forward and takes the bag from Steve. He gives his feral smile. "I gotta take a piss and I need to talk to Rogan about an interview we're doing today." He strides down the hallway toward the can. "I'll make sure he fills the bottle. I'll bring it to you right after, OK?"

Steve shrugs and I follow Stammo.

I might, just might, have been able to find a way to get Steve to delay the urine test. He and I go back a long way and we were good friends before my spiral into addiction. Stammo, however, has never liked me and I've spent a lot of time taking the piss out of him to his face. Now he's going to take the piss out of me... literally.

There's got to be a way out of this.

We are steps from the washroom door.

It opens and Superintendent Cathcart exits and steps aside to let us pass.

"How are things going on the investigation into Marguerite Varga's murder?" he asks.

Maybe I can find a way of getting out of this drug test.

I don't want to tell him that we have very little, that we have been focusing on our other case. "There may be a connection with the murder of the boy, Terry Wright, sir," I say.

"Yes that's a bad one... ritualistic," he says. I cannot read what he is feeling about Terry's murder but it is certainly not the outrage that Nick and I have been experiencing. "What sort of connection?" he asks.

"Both the boy's mother and Mrs. Varga attended the same church. Also it seems that Varga was a big gambler." Suddenly, I see an opening. "You know Varga, sir. Could you spare us some time to answer a few questions about him?"

His eyes drill into me. *Please say yes. Invite us up to your office right now. Anything to get me out of this test.*

"No point. I hardly know the man. I met him at a charity function," he says. "Anyway I have a meeting to go to right now. If I think of anything about Varga that might be of interest, I'll let you know." He turns and walks off.

"Came off as a bit of a brown-nose there Rogan," says Stammo.

He walks into the washroom and, after a fleeting

thought of fleeing, I follow. One of the uniformed old timers, Sarge, is drying his hands.

Instead of handing me the bottle, Stammo taps the evidence bag against his leg and asks, "So you think this 'oboe is blood' thing is important? What did you call it, a hex?" There is a slight smile on his face. It is like he is taunting me, knowing that I am worried about this test.

"Yes, I do." My mind is racing. Should I tell Stammo what happened to me? Maybe he would give me a break here.

But that wouldn't work, Steve would just make me take it again and maybe a blood test too. *Oboe is blood*.

Sarge throws the paper towel in the bin, nods at us and leaves.

Stammo takes the plastic bottle out of the bag and unscrews the top.

He nods at a urinal. "Take a piss, Rogan."

There's no way out now. In twenty four hours I'll be on suspension at best, summarily dismissed at worst.

Bowing to the inevitable, I walk to the porcelain, unzip and put my hand out for the bottle... but he doesn't hand it to me.

He steps up to the urinal at the far end and looks down. "I told you to take a piss," he says.

What is happening here? In my confusion, I can't go.

After about a minute, he steps back. In his hand is the specimen bottle, three quarters full of dark yellow. He screws on the orange cap, drops it in the evidence bag and directs a stare at me.

"Just this once," he says. "And we *never* talk about this. It never happened, OK? Never."

I nod blankly as he walks out.

29

BIKER

I fuckin' hate doing this job. Havin' to dress up like some geek and stand in line for half an hour with a bunch of old farts who want to talk to a teller 'cause they don't know how to use the fuckin' bank machines. This is only the second drop of the day. Eight more to go. It's a few hours before I'll be dressed in my colours and downing a few beers.

I gotta remember the positions of all the cameras. Keep my head down and hope the Canuck's cap covers my face. Not that it really matters but it don't hurt to be careful, eh?

"Can I help the next person in line?" Well, at least I got the cute little blonde. She's wearing a white shirt, open just enough to get a peek at what's inside. Makes me want to lean over the counter and grab hold of them luscious—

"How can I help you, sir?" Cold as ice. It's like the snotty little bitch read my mind. Man, I'd like to catch her alone one night. I'd show her some things she's never seen before. I feel the old stirring. I could wait around near the bank at closing time, follow her home... I lick my lips. Nah. No chance of that; gotta stay with the plan; too much at stake.

"I'd like to deposit this into my aunt's account please." I get that moment of panic I always get when I say them words, or something like 'em. What if she knows the old biddy. It's not very likely, she lives on the other side of town fer Chrissake. But I always worry about it when I push the piece of paper across the counter. She looks at the paper and taps at her keyboard for what seems like a long time. What if something's wrong? Maybe the old bitch has popped off and they're gonna wonder why her nephew don't know about it.

Finally, she turns back to me. "How much would you like to deposit, sir?" She says the last word with a sneer in her voice.

"Nine thousand, seven hundred and thirty dollars." I push the envelope to her. It's always less than ten grand but more than nine. Never the exact same amount.

While she's counting it, I think of the things I

could do for her. I can just picture her naked right now. Man, I'd like to do her but it's out of the question. I gotta start thinking about something else before what I am thinking starts to show. It'd give the old biddies in the line up a bit of a thrill though.

The little cutie puts a slip of paper and the money in a plastic baggie with a ziplock. I wonder if the guy who invented those knew how much they would be used in the drug trade? She hands me another slip of paper. I give her a big smile and she knows what I'm thinking. I turn to go and then remember.

"Can I have the envelope please, Miss?"

I almost forgot about it, thinking about doin' her.

Can't forget the details.

If something happened, my fingerprints are on that envelope.

Anyways, I'll phone this one in and then on to the next one.

30

CAL

I've turned it over and over in my mind and can only come up with one explanation.

Stammo knows that I was kidnapped and shot full of heroin and for some reason he feels badly about it and wants to give me a break. But how could he know? Is he somehow connected with whomever kidnapped me. I have ruled out the Church of the Transcended Masters as the kidnappers. Not that I don't think that Seth character could do it, I'm pretty sure he could, but how would they know about my addiction. It's more likely it was the remnants of the old drug gang but what connection does Stammo have with them?

We are sitting opposite the Chan residence. Each in our own vehicles. Stammo insisted we come separately, probably to avoid being in a confined space with me where I might try and quiz him. Or maybe he just wants his own car there so that he can take off early right after this interview. Knowing what he knows about me, he is not going to let me do any interviews alone for as long as I'm on probation.

I look at his SUV, parked ten feet in front of me. It's a top of the line Buick Enclave with all the bells and whistles, including all-wheel drive; it must have set him back more than fifty grand. Not out of the question on a cop's salary but he mentioned that he has a couple of kids; if he is paying child support and maybe alimony too, a grand a month for a vehicle is a bit much, not to mention the cost of maintenance, insurance and all the gas it guzzles.

I don't like what is forming in my mind. No-one wants to discover a colleague is dirty. But nevertheless, I am going to run a search on his license plate and find out if he owns the car outright or has it leased. If he bought it outright, where did he get the cash to do that?

Even if he is dirty, why would he cut me a break by doing the urine test for me?

The withdrawal pain is bad now. Maybe it's clouding my judgment, maybe I'm missing something.

My train of thought is broken by the arrival of Grace Chen's minivan, back from school with

Michael. She pulls into her driveway and I reach for my door handle but something stops me from opening the door. I glance ahead and see that Stammo is still sitting motionless in his seat.

Grace Chen parks the car in front of the garage, comes around to the passenger side and slides open the back door.

In the quiet of the street, I hear the sound of a car starting: the crank of the starter and a blip of the gas pedal that gives the engine a throaty growl. A black Cadillac Escalade pulls out of a parking spot three cars up from the Chan house. It passes the house, stops and backs up into the driveway.

The hair on the back of my neck rises as my senses go on alert.

Grace Chen looks up at the SUV as Michael jumps down from the minivan. She smiles un-certainly.

Michael says something and his mother tousles his hair, crouches down and speaks to him. She seems to be reassuring him about something. She is completely focused on her son.

Whoever is in the Caddy stays there. My unease increases.

Then everything changes.

The driver and passenger, both women, both wearing smiles, get out of the vehicle at the same time. They are conservatively dressed; with a sigh of relief, I guess they might be social workers or therapists of some sort, there for Michael.

Michael flashes a momentary, but intense, look at them and then focuses on their car. His mother smiles and walks toward the driver.

She says something.

The passenger saunters around the back of the Escalade and passes between it and the minivan. She crouches down and speaks to Michael, who stares furiously at the tarmac of the driveway. I remember from my previous visits that he does not like to make eye contact.

I glance at the clock on the Healey's dash: three-thirty. Time for our appointment with Grace and Michael. Either the visit from the social workers is unscheduled or Grace Chan has double-booked.

I get out of my car and look ahead at Stammo. He is still in his seat. I walk forward and as I get next to his door, I can hear the sounds of Art Blakey; Stammo's head is back on the headrest nodding to the beat, eyes closed, hands flopped over the bottom of the steering wheel. A part of me wants to thump on his door and shock him into the real world but then I remember what he did for me this morning. He saved my job for me... but why?

I hear a gasp and turn to see Grace Chan as she doubles over, staggers and falls sideways on to the driveway behind the Caddy, her hands clamped over her stomach.

A shock wave runs through me. *I'm an idiot!* Social workers don't drive ninety thousand dollar SUVs.

The passenger scoops up Michael and clamps a hand over his mouth. Both women are dashing back to their vehicle, the passenger hampered by Michael who is kicking and struggling furiously.

I pound on Stammo's door and shout "Stop! Police!" as I break into a dash.

Then I feel myself spin and hit the pavement. *What the...*

A screech of breaks.

I look up. There is a car in the middle of the road. I must have run into the side of it. Why didn't I see it, or at least hear it?

I push myself to my feet.

Ignoring the electric car and the shocked young man who is getting out of it. I sprint toward the Caddy. In the ten seconds I just lost, the driver has got back in but Michael's furious struggles are hampering the passenger. She is trying to hold on to the writhing child, keep a hand clamped over his mouth and open the SUV's rear door, all at the same time. A tactical error. She should have opened the door before she approached the boy.

She is the obvious target.

With every ounce of my strength, I dash for the Caddy, my eyes focused on the struggle at its rear.

I hear the driver start the engine.

With an impressive effort, in one motion, the passenger gets the back door open, and flings Michael inside, just as I come up to the vehicle.

Fortunately, my obvious target was also obvious to the driver. She does not expect my next move.

I pull open the driver's door, grab the front of her coat and, with the aid of every microgram of adrenaline flooding my muscles, I yank her out of her seat and throw her across the driveway and on to the lawn. I hear the snapping noise of breaking bone and a scream, but she's lucky: if she had been a man, I would have smashed him, head first, into the surface of the driveway.

Now for the obvious target.

I am looking down the barrel of what looks like a Beretta semi-automatic. She has it trained at my chest. A pro. I guess *I'm* the obvious target now.

She glances to her left. Michael is scrambling out of the back door of the SUV. I can see the indecision in her eyes. If she tries to grab him, she may give me an opening. Self-preservation wins out. She lets Michael run to his mother, who is back on her feet, though unsteady.

Keeping the gun trained on me, the would-be kidnapper climbs into the back of the Escalade.

I hear the driver's door close. Damn! I should have smashed her into the driveway. Almost simultaneously, I hear Stammo yell, "Police! Stop!"

He is standing at the bottom of the driveway, twenty feet in front of the Caddy, with his gun trained on the windshield.

But I can see the indecision in *his* eyes now.

Michael and his mother are directly behind the Caddy. If he shoots at the driver, his bullet could go straight through the windshield and the back window and find an innocent target.

Even as I think this, I am pulling my Sig from its holster. Bullets in the tires will stop any chance of escape. I am not as good a shot as Stammo but if I'm quick enough...

Before I can aim, the driver floors the gas and the Escalade spears forward. In a fraction of a second, Stammo makes his decision and aims downward at the engine.

His gun barks twice.

I take a shot at the driver but miss, shattering a rear window.

Stammo leaps to one side in good time to avoid the two-and-a-half tons of metal bearing down on him but the driver anticipates his move and steers into him; the impact sends his skinny frame spinning toward the road where a tree stops his progress with a sickening thud. He flops to the floor like a rag doll.

The Escalade squeals onto the street and roars off. I dare not take another shot; there are row houses on the other side of the vehicle.

A quick glance reveals that Michael and his mother are OK. Pulling out my radio, I run to Stammo's motionless body. I call it in while I check the pulse in his neck. It's there, but feeble.

And it's all my fault. I should have dealt with the driver properly. If anything happens to Stammo, I will have to live with this error for the rest of my life.

My whole body feels cold. A wave of nausea passes through me as the withdrawal pains, temporarily held in check by the adrenaline surge, flood back into my body.

31

CAL

TUESDAY

The turmoil inside me matches the turmoil that has been visited upon the Chan family.

Their lives have been turned upside down. Yesterday they were normal parents coping with a son with some challenges. Now their son is a kidnap target and they have a policewoman living in their house.

My turmoil is different. Last night, I was at the office until close to midnight, being interviewed by Steve and his boss, Inspector Vance. He is a highly respected officer and is regarded as a 'cop's cop'; I like him a lot, despite his frog-like appearance. Vance is mad. Any attack on his officers he takes personally, very personally. After the interviews I had what seemed like endless hours of paperwork relating to firing my weapon. It was made all the more tense by my need to keep pulling my shirt cuffs down to cover my wrists, still red from the wires used to bind me in Riverview. At one point I caught Vance looking strangely at me.

After a visit to VGH, where I was not allowed to see Stammo, I finally got home, full of guilt at what happened to my partner just because I didn't take the time to deal with the driver of the Escalade.

The events of the day combined with the withdrawal pains were my rationalization for taking just one small hit of heroin, just enough to let me sleep.

And this morning... just one more little hit to help me get through the day. Steve tested me yesterday, he's not going to test me again until next week.

I can rationalize it however I like but I know the Beast is starting to take control and I can see my life slipping away. I know where this path leads. Tonight I will have finished the last of the heroin I bought on Sunday then no more. *No more.*

"Do you know who it was tried to kidnap Michael?" Dave Chan asks.

"No sir," Steve answers before I can, "I'm afraid we didn't even get the license plate of the vehicle." He gives me a hard look; another screw up on my part. "But we—"

"1564 SYL"

All eyes turn to Michael who sits waggling the fingers of both hands while staring at them with all his attention.

"Was that the license plate of the black car yesterday Michael?" I ask.

"SUV not car. Cadillac Escalalde ESV, AWD, Black Ice metallic, 1564 SYL."

Steve whips out his cell phone and dials. He walks into the hall and I can hear him repeating the details that Michael gave us.

The eyes of Dave and Grace Chan turn on me.

"It is too much of a coincidence," I say, "for Terry's death and Michael's attempted kidnapping to be unrelated and I believe that there may be a connection with these hex words they were both repeating."

"Hex words?" Grace looks confused.

"Yes, Michael was repeating the phrase *oboe is blood*. We have reason to believe that that is some sort of hex..." Blank looks from the Chans. "You know... a curse or incantation?"

They nod, unsure, but I see something in Grace Chan's eyes. She knows something.

"You said that Michael had said some more words?" I ask.

Grace glances at her son. "Yes. It was mainly just

letters and numbers with the odd word thrown in here and there."

"Could you ask Michael to repeat it?"

Michael's finger wagging intensifies and his brows furrow.

"He is still upset by what happened yesterday. I don't think he will be much help."

As if to underscore his mother's words, Michael pivots away from me.

"Maybe I can help," his father offers. "I can remember some of the words. *Obsess* was one and *bell* was another."

I write them in my notebook.

Grace chimes in, "*Face* and *able* and *flee* were some of the others but it was mainly just letters and numbers."

"And you think that these are curses or incantations?" Dave Chan cannot mask the incredulity in his voice; or is it sarcasm?

"Oh, and *stab* was another." Grace says and then gasps in realization at what she has just said.

In the silence, we are all thinking the same thing: how Terry died. Grace Chan is worrying the corner of a cushion with her fingers.

I get a flash of intuition, or so I think, "Mrs. Chan," I say gently, "may I ask what's on your mind?"

She looks at her husband, who just looks confused, then at Michael and finally at me. "I told you that Elizabeth, Terry's Mom, invited me to that church she goes to."

I nod.

"Well, part of their service was called 'Incantations to the Masters' and it was a bit weird, with lots of strange words that didn't really make much sense." I can feel the hair on the back of my neck. "I wonder if there is some connection to these, what did you call them... hex words."

Before I can answer, Steve has returned and chimes in. "It's possible and we are looking into it. But if I could change the subject... Mrs. Chan, did either of the women who tried to take Michael look familiar to you?"

Steve takes over the questioning and asks all the right, standard questions. He is a great interviewer and interrogator and I just leave him and kind of zone out. It's now pretty clear that the Church of the Transcended Masters is connected to Terry's death and Michael's attempted kidnapping. I burn to get to the bottom of it. When we first talked to Michael about *oboe is blood* he talked about the bad people hurting Terry. What bad people did he mean? The people in the Church? The Reverend Harris' brother Seth, perhaps?

Steve has wrapped up his questions. He stands to

go and I follow him to the door. When we are out of Michael's hearing, I say, "Mrs. Chan, I would really like to talk to Michael about all these words, where he and Terry got them from and about the 'bad people' he referred to before. When do you think I could do that?"

She gives a slight sigh. "Call me tomorrow and we'll see how he feels."

I thank her and turn to follow Steve down the steps to the driveway when an odd thought pops into my head.

I turn.

"Mrs. Chan, when you visited the church with Elizabeth Wright, did you by any chance meet a Mrs. Marguerite Varga?" Why the name of our other murder victim comes to mind I don't know.

"No," she wrinkles her brow. "I don't think so, but the name is familiar."

She turns to her husband who looks off into the distance for a moment. "Yes... Varga..." he says, "That was the name of Mark Wright's boss when he worked at the bank. I remember, because although Varga terminated him, Mark seemed to think he was a really good guy and I couldn't quite figure out why he would be so friendly with the person who fired him."

The shock of this revelation has stopped Steve in his tracks. The vague connection between our two murder cases has become a lot less vague and that so-called church is in the centre of it.

And my next interview is going to answer a key question in this investigation; maybe *the* key question.

32

CAL

Now I can't get over my second shock of the day.

No purple nails. No red streak in dyed black hair. Not even the chaos star earring has survived the transformation. Damien Crotty, the king of the Magee High School goths, has become a Harry Rosen ad in pinstriped Zegna suit, rep tie and Salvatore Ferragamos.

The entire change of persona makes me suspicious and I am starting to doubt my previous assertion that I can trust this man completely.

We've done the hi-how-are-you-it's-been-a-while-what-are-you-doing-now thing and are in the airport Starbucks.

"So Cal, how can I help you with this murder investigation?"

I sniff. The first sign of withdrawal. I am not the same person I was in high school either. Maybe it's Damien who should not trust me completely.

"Well, you saw the crime-scene photos of the victim. I thought the wounds, each one at the apex of a five-pointed star, made the shape of a pentacle but in your email you said that it wasn't."

He runs his fingers, still skeletal, through his grey-flecked, brown hair. "It's a while since I took an interest in this stuff but I can tell you that a pentacle is always circumscribed by two circles. If you're thinking the wounds are meant to be a pentacle, then they were done by someone who doesn't really know what they're doing."

"Yeah, but what about the hex words?" I ask. "You said that *oboe is blood* is a hex, plus I have some others: *stab, obsess, bell, face, flee*, what about those."

He chuckles. "Oh, yes. They're all definitely hex words."

I wonder why he finds this funny?

"So what sort of curse or incantation would they be used in?" I can hear the eagerness in my own words. I want to connect this unequivocally with the Church of the Transcended Masters; maybe I should take Damien there to look at the pictures on their walls to see if he can spot something.

He is looking at me with one eyebrow raised and

then suddenly he erupts into peals of uncontrol-lable laughter.

"What?" I sniff again. Something tells me the withdrawal is going to be bad when it hits.

Tears are rolling down his face and he is trying to catch his breath. What have I said that is so funny? I can feel my irritation rising *for mirth doth search the bottom of annoy.* But I keep it in check... with some difficulty. I know that my anger is really for the people who got me hooked. Whoever they are, I am going to find them.

He wipes his eyes on a monogrammed cotton handkerchief. "I'm sorry, Cal. Wrong sort of hex." He chuckles again but avoids a return to the hyster-ics. "It's hex as in hexadecimal."

"What's that?"

"Computer code."

"*Oboe is blood* is computer code?"

"Well, yeah." He perceives my perplexity. "Do you know what a byte is?"

"A computer character?"

"Right. In computer terms, each byte is de-scribed by two hexadecimal characters." As he is speaking, he pulls a laptop out of his briefcase and starts it up. It is obviously a lot better than my com-puter at home because it starts up almost instantly and the desktop looks different. Damien sees my look. "Linux," he says, which means nothing to me.

He opens a document. "OK," he says. "A byte is often expressed using two hexadecimal characters. Hexadecimal means sixteen. So each hexadecimal character has a value between zero and fifteen, which is expressed by the numbers 0 through 9 and the letters 'a' through 'f'. So look at this."

He types the letters and numbers 0b0e15b100d into the document.

"Look at the first four hex characters, zero b zero e. If you treat the zeros as the letter o. it spells 'oboe'. Now the next two characters are 1 and 5. If you treat the 1 as an I and the 5 as an S, the 15 becomes 'IS'. Now in the next five characters if you treat the number 1 as the letter 'L', b one zero zero d becomes 'blood'." He types in spaces. "oboe 15 b100d says 'oboe is blood'. It's the same for all the other words you mentioned."

I digest this for a while. "What about *stab*?" I ask.

He types in 57ab. "It's a bit of a stretch but the 5 is the s and the 7 is like a 'T', kind of. I didn't make these things up; they are just fun for us geeks. My favourite is 0b5e55, obsess."

"So what does *oboe is blood* actually mean then?" I ask.

"I dunno. It's just describing a string of bytes. It might be a large number or a code of some sort. I'd need to know the context."

"How about I give you a lift home and I'll explain on the way."

Damien may have dashed my hope of a connection between the rituals of the church and the hex words but something else is forming in my mind and I'm not quite sure what it means.

33

CAL

"It's definitely relevant, Steve." I can feel the rush. Something in this case is breaking and I'm sure we are getting closer to the truth of what happened to Terry Wright and Elizabeth Varga. Unfortunately the excitement I feel does not blunt the withdrawal symptoms that are ramping up fiercely. "They made a big mistake trying to kidnap Michael Chan."

A random thought runs through my head. *Could the people who tried to kidnap Michael be the same people who kidnapped me?*

"Why?" the keen, young Eric Street asks.

"Because this *oboe is blood* thing is the connection between Terry and Michael. They must have wanted to kidnap Michael so that he couldn't tell us the whole code. The code must be the key to Terry's murder. If we can find out what it means everything will fall into place."

I know that the significance of *oboe is blood* has taken us closer to solving this crime but has it put me in more danger from *my* kidnappers?

Steve nods. "Also, if we can find the would-be kidnappers we can sweat them. The license plate the kid gave us was from a stolen Mini Cooper but his description was real precise: an Escalade ESV, All Wheel Drive, black ice metallic. Eric's contacted all the Cadillac dealers in Western Canada to see who bought one in the last year or so. Maybe we can track them down that way."

Something about the Cadillac's description is bothering me but the pain in my bones is too distracting for me to focus.

"I haven't got anything back yet but it should be fairly soon." Eric has a big smile on his face.

"So, Cal," Steve asks, "What d'you think should be the next step?"

This is the first time since I've been back in the Department that Steve has asked my opinion. I've been pretty much treated like a rookie, kept under Stammo's wing. It feels good for a moment until I remember why Stammo is not here to supervise me.

"I think the first thing is to try and get the full code from Michael. I'll get it to my buddy Damien and we'll see if he can decipher it, then I—"

"Who?" Steve interjects, "the witchcraft expert?"

"Yeah, I forgot to tell you, a couple of years after he left high school he dropped all that goth stuff and got into computers. He consults to organizations like CSIS and the CIA. He was in Germany helping track down a hacker who had got into their government's most secure email server."

Steve shrugs. "OK, but you've gotta give it to our own forensic crime unit too."

"Sure, of course. Anyway," I continue, "I also want to talk to Mark Wright. In his living room, he's got a big computer setup. Terry may have got the code from him."

"Good, go for it." Eric and I both get up.

"One other thing," Steve says, "I contacted the Crown Prosecutor's office. They agreed that Elizabeth being a member of that church and having an affair with the minister's brother, combined with the picture of the mutilations just like Terry's, might be enough cause to get a warrant and go search the church's premises."

Oh, this is definitely turning out to be a good day. By this time tomorrow we may have made an arrest. I can't keep the big, stupid grin from my face.

On top of this, I feel that my relationship with Steve is moving back to the way it was years ago before I was started on heroin. We were a real team then. It feels good.

Eric leads the way out of Steve's office.

"Oh, Rocky, before you go..."

I turn back with a smile only to see Steve take a bag out of his desk.

A brown evidence bag.

He shakes it and I hear the plastic bottle rattle around inside. "It's that time again."

34

CAL

"DO IT. DO IT NOW" My body screams at me.

"Why not, Cal. You're busted anyway," whispers the Beast, who is so much more subtle. "Tomorrow or the day after, the lab results will be back and you'll be fired. Makes no difference if you take this little hit now. It'll take the pain away; all the pain. Tomorrow you can work on giving up."

The items are laid out before me on the kitchen table: alcohol swab, surgical elastic, spoon, eye dropper, sterile water, lighter, tiny cotton-ball filter, needle and that last precious bag of white powder.

My hand reaches out and takes the baggie. I open it and pour the contents onto the spoon.

From nowhere, the image of Terry Wright's

body, forlorn in the forest, comes to mind. In this image I can see the quasi-pentacle. His face changes and it becomes Ellie's face. My subconscious is telling me something. If the people who killed Terry are the same people who kidnapped me, then they will not think twice about hurting Ellie or Sam. I shudder. I have to solve this crime.

The Beast laughs. "Come on Rocky," he whispers, "taking it will stop that picture in your mind. Just use it to ease the pain now. In the morning you'll feel stronger. You can take charge and go cold turkey. But there's no point in wasting this last hit."

The Beast is right. It can't make matters worse. Maybe with the pains gone, I can better focus on the details of the crime.

I feel weak.

Out of nowhere, I think of Sam. Whenever she feels weak she takes out her father's five year AA chip; it reminds her what happens when you give up. He gave up, started drinking again and six weeks later he killed himself. Sam never gives up.

The spoon vibrates; my Blackberry is ringing. I glance at it lying on the other end of the table. Coincidence?

I press the talk button. "Sam?"

"Hi, Daddy. Guess what?" Ellie's enthusiasm explodes out of the phone and my heart melts. Even

when I was living on the streets of the downtown east side, I kept my relationship with Ellie intact.

"Hold on just a minute, Sweetie. There's something I need to do first."

"OK, Daddy. But be quick."

I sniff. "I'll be as quick as I can, my little love." I put down the phone.

Do it now and do it fast.

I take the spoon, get up from the table and step to the sink. Tap on. Spoon under tap. The white powder is carried away and disappears down the drain. I grab the spray and swoosh away any last remnants.

"Stupid," sneers the Beast. "Now you'll have to buy more." My body joins in with a fierce pain in my leg. I force myself to ignore them both and grab a bottle of Extra Strength Tylenol from the end of the counter.

I pick up the phone. "Hi, Sweetie. I'm back."

She prattles on about her day at school, her voice is the sound of a fountain in a peaceful garden. I concentrate on the victories and defeats of her day to keep away the screams of the Beast and the pains of the withdrawal.

"Daddy." Her voice has changed to a whisper. *"I think Mommy still loves you."*

The lump in my throat imprisons my reply.

Maybe telling her I still love her has got through to her.

"Do you know why?" she asks.

"No, Sweetie," I manage to croak.

"It's her new boyfriend."

I feel like a voyeur. Like Ellie has become a spy for me. It feels wrong. I should stop Ellie talking like this.

I fill the silence. "What about him?"

"Well he's not a policeman or anything—"

Decency wins out for once. "Ell, I don't think you should be talking to me about Mommy's friend. I don't think Mommy would like it, do you?"

"No, but—"

"OK. So let's talk about what we are going to do tomorrow night, when you're with me." *And Sam is with...* The Beast chuckles at my thoughts.

"OK, Daddy," begrudgingly,*"I want to go for dinner at Cactus Club and then..."*

As she talks, her old enthusiasm returns but the thought of Sam with another man sits uncomfortably in my stomach and spoils my enjoyment of it.

After we say goodnight and make kissy noises over the phone, I hang up and the demands of the Beast tell me where I need to go and what I need to do next.

WHILE I'M WAITING, I tune out the droning voice and think about the events of the day.

After my urine test, which I took in silence—no questioning why on consecutive days, no attempts to avoid or delay—I visited the Chans and Michael was amazing. While I held the digital recorder he recited the code. It was hundreds of characters long yet something tells me that he recalled it perfectly. I sent the recording to our Forensic Unit and uploaded it to a URL given to me by Damien. Hopefully one of them will tell us what it means.

Another voice takes over, opening with the familiar words. Its drone is less but I tune it out too and take a sip of coffee, not very good coffee at that. The cup is polystyrene. Only here. Everywhere else the cups are made of paper.

The Wrights were not at home when I went there. The Rocky part of me was glad because the withdrawal pains were bad; the Cal part really wanted to know where Terry got the code from.

If he got the code from his father's computer, what was in the code that made it worth killing him and trying to kidnap Michael? Who would overhear one of them reciting the code and know its importance? Anyone hearing them say *oboe is blood* would just assume it was gibberish. I turn the possibilities over in my mind... and then I have it. In a flash it becomes crystal clear... and I do not like it one bit.

"Cal." The voice cuts through my speculations. "Would you like to share?"

I get up and walk to the front. After one more sip, I put down the polystyrene cup.

"Hi. My name's Rocky and I'm an addict."

35

CAL

WEDNESDAY

I have got to solve this case today because tomorrow I'm a dead man. The results of the urine test will be in Steve's hands by tomorrow morning at the latest and I'll be out.

The withdrawal pains are just bearable. Maybe the four Extra Strength Tylenol I took?

I'm going to get some answers from Mark Wright. It's seven AM, too early for him to have left the house for the day.

As I reach up for the bell, the shattered wood is obvious. The door is partially open; it has been forced. I pull my Sig from its holster and push the door open. It is quiet in the house. There is a metallic smell in the still air.

I look across the tiny entranceway into the living

room. The dining-room table is in my line of sight. The three computer monitors are still there but dark, powered off. There is a mousepad and a mouse with its cable hanging off the edge of the table, connected to nothing. The expensive looking computers under the table are gone.

"Mrs. Wright."

No reply.

I step into the living room, sweeping it with my gaze and my gun. She is slouched on the sofa in a silk robe, eyes staring at me; one long, elegant leg is uncovered, which makes me catch my breath.

She is motionless.

"Mrs. Wright?" I hear fear in my voice.

But it is unfounded.

"Gone." Her voice is flat, her body motionless.

"Is there anyone else in the house?"

"Gone." She repeats. Is she referring to Mark or to whomever broke in?

I cross the room and push open the kitchen door. Empty. Through the kitchen, into the hallway. The bathroom smells of her perfume; it reminds me of being in Terry's bedroom with her and I feel a tightness in my chest. Terry's room is exactly as I remember it. Along the hall, I check the master bedroom. Empty.

As I turn, I startle. Elizabeth Wright is standing,

silent, behind me; her eyes wild. And again I feel the catch in my throat.

She brushes slowly past me, placing one hand on my chest as she does so. One lapel of her robe brushes my jacket and pulls back to reveal the silky rise of her breast. She walks round the foot of the bed and stands across from me and I feel myself breathing faster. I need to get this back on a business footing.

I cough away the catch in my throat. "Mrs. Wright, what happened here?"

"Gone," she says.

"Who is gone, Mrs. Wright?" I get a strong sense that I might be dealing with a mad woman. I know I should call for immediate backup, including a female officer. I don't like my reason for not wanting to do so.

"Terry is gone. Mark is gone. Seth is gone."

She fixes her eyes on me as she undoes the belt of her robe.

"Where is Mark?" The catch is back in my throat.

She lets her robe fall open, revealing white skin from her throat to below her navel.

I try to say something... anything.

She shrugs the robe from her shoulders. She is naked beneath it.

I have not been with a woman in five years. My libido, long suppressed, is now in full flight.

She kneels on the bed and I cannot take my eyes from her perfect body. I want this woman so badly. I've felt it from the first moment I saw her.

"Help me to forget... for just a moment." A tear rolls down her cheek. "Please." She reaches out a hand to me. "Please."

I know I mustn't do this. It betrays my feelings for Sam. It betrays Elizabeth's fragile mental state. It betrays my honour as a police officer.

Steeling myself, I turn around.

And close the bedroom door.

———

IT WAS FAST, passionate, with an animal, almost feral intensity and an unbelievable, explosive conclusion. A release we both so desperately needed.

"Thank you." She whispers.

I kiss the top of her head, resting on my chest; my tenderness toward her is counterbalanced by my self-loathing for taking advantage of her.

"I don't want to spoil the moment but I do need to ask you some questions." The cop in me trying to assuage the guilt.

"That's OK," she sighs. "I feel safe for now."

"You remember we talked about Terry repeating *oboe is blood* and how it annoyed Mark?"

"Sure."

"We have reason to believe that it was part of some sort of computer code which he may have got from Mark's computer, something important. Mark may have been angry with him for repeating the code, not just a father irritated because his son keeps chanting nonsense."

"Step-father. Mark was Terry's step-father."

Ah-hah. That adds strength to my theory.

"What do you know about Mark's client?"

In the silence I feel the movement of her jaws against my chest. She is grinding her teeth. It's something Sam used to do. I feel a grinding in my gut.

"Not much. I only met him once. I didn't like him, he scared me. Mark wouldn't talk about his work; he said it was confidential, secret. But I didn't like what it was doing to him. He became very erratic, nervous. He kept saying that it was going to make us a lot of money."

"Did he know about your affair with Seth Harris?"

She shows no reaction at my knowing.

"I told him about it on Sunday. Told him I wanted to leave him and be with Seth. He stormed out of the house. I was sure he would come back but

I haven't seen him since. I was worried that he would go to Seth and confront him, so I called Seth. He was angry with me for telling Mark." She is crying, I can feel her tears on my skin. "Seth hasn't returned my calls after that, so I went to see him yesterday evening at the church. He wouldn't let me in..." The tears become sobs. "Just told me... that he... never... wanted to see me again."

I hold her and stroke her hair until she calms. Her talking seems to be cathartic, or so I tell myself.

"Did Mark take his computers with him when he left on Sunday."

"No. That was why I was sure he'd be back."

"So where are they?"

"Early this morning, about five o'clock, two men smashed open the front door and took them."

Oh my god, the front door. Anyone could just walk into the house and find us here.

"Why didn't you call the police."

"They said if I did, they'd know and that they'd come back and kill me."

"Did you get a good look at them?"

"No, they were wearing ski masks."

I am starting to worry about that unlocked front door.

"We should get up," I say.

Elizabeth lifts her head off my chest and kisses me.

She gently runs her nails down my neck, chest, stomach...

———

A TEAM from the Forensic Unit is on its way. They will be trying to lift prints or otherwise identify the people who stole Mark Wright's computers. I got Elizabeth to change the bed and put the sheets into the washing machine. In the unlikely event that the techs get too ambitious, I don't want them finding my DNA.

She has given me a description of Mark's client and agreed to work with a technician using software to create a picture of him.

Although she has tried to remember, her description of the thieves is little more than useless.

The theft of the computers has dashed any hope that I had of discovering the importance of the oboe code quickly, before the lab results come back. Then I remember the last time I saw Mark Wright. When he arrived while I was questioning Elizabeth about the phrase *oboe is blood,* he was carrying an expensive-looking leather satchel.

"Did the thieves take Mark's laptop?" I ask.

"No, he took it with him when he left. He never goes anywhere without that thing."

Another hope dashed.

"They didn't take the blades, of course," she adds.

"The blades?"

"Well that was what Mark called them. They were his pride and joy." There is some bitterness in her words.

"What are they?"

She gets up and I follow her into the kitchen. The sway of her hips eliciting from me equal parts of desire and guilt. She opens a door, to what I had assumed was a pantry. Steps lead down to a basement. We descend. It is hot in here. The room is unfinished with bare heating ducts and electric wires stapled to wooden beams across the low ceiling. A washing machine is swishing away the evidence of our morning. There are boxes of toys and books, a couple of bikes and a tool bench. It has the musty smell of the normal family basement.

But that is where normalcy stops.

In the middle of the room is a floor-to-ceiling rack made of angle-iron. Bolted into the rack are two cabinets that remind me of air conditioning units... No, they are more like bookcases holding rows of identical metal books. On the top shelf of each unit I can see fans turning behind a metal grid. The air coming from the fans is warm.

I look at Elizabeth. "Blades?"

"That's what he calls them. They're computers of some sort."

I count the metal 'books'. There are ten to a shelf, three shelves to a cabinet. That's sixty computers.

I need Damien to see these. I'll call him right after I take another handful of Tylenol.

36

CAL

I step through the door like a man stepping down from a tumbril: this is the end. Inspector Vance, head of the Major Crimes under Superintendent Cathcart, is sitting at his desk, his face unreadable.

I wouldn't have been sent here by a very angry Steve if the results of the urine test were not yet back. This is the one man firing squad.

"Sit down." Vance nods toward a chair.

I comply. Nothing I can say now will make any difference; I am gone. I have already decided to tell them about my kidnapping. It won't change anyone's mind but I need to do it. I'm sorry it's Vance that has to do this. He's one of the good guys.

Maybe I should just tell him I know about the test and make it easier all round. I'll just say that I know what the results are and that I accept that he needs to fire me. Vance is a good cop; if it is easier for him, I will be happy to resign.

"If it's easier, I could resign."

Vance looks puzzled.

"What?"

Oh, my god. I am not here to be fired. What have I just said?

"What the hell do you mean, Cal?" Vance asks.

I'm hit by a wave of panic. Now what do I say? A big part of me longs to come clean about the drug test; a bigger part of me wants just one more day to wrap up this case and nail the bastard who killed Terry Wright. The bigger part wins out. But what do I *say*? Then, in a flash, I remember the previous conversation I had with Vance and I use it.

"When we talked on Monday night about Stammo getting run down by those women, you said that there would be a formal investigation. Isn't this a follow up from that meeting?"

"No," Vance says, doing nothing to keep the irritation from his voice. "I want you to brief me on the Wright and the Varga killings. These cases seem to be going nowhere, so I've decided to become more hands-on." A wave of relief sweeps through me. So *that's* why Steve was mad; his boss is taking over the cases personally. They haven't got the results of the second drug test back yet.

I've got to switch my thought to the cases at hand. Vance has a mind like a steel trap and cannot tolerate sloppiness.

"On the Terry Wright murder, I think that it was the father. Terry's mother says that he has been missing since Sunday. I think he's run." I tell him about the *oboe* code and the computer equipment in the basement. "He was working for someone, a client, who Elizabeth Wright says was 'scary'. I believe Mark was doing something criminal and that if his 'client' knew that Terry was repeating this code he would be in a lot of trouble. He killed Terry to shut him up."

"Killed his own son? This *oboe* code must be pretty important to kill a kid." Vance asks, skeptical.

"Elizabeth Wright told me that he was Terry's step-father." I don't tell him that she told me this in bed, a mere ninety minutes ago.

"I think his client is part of a criminal gang of some sort. When they found out about Terry's friend Michael parroting the code, they decided to get rid of him too."

Vance jumps on this. "How would they get to know that?"

"If Mark Wright killed his own step-son, he wouldn't have any qualms about tipping off his 'client' about Michael." My stomach drops as I see how illogical that is. If Mark killed Terry to stop the gang finding out him chanting the *oboe* code, why would he then tell them that Michael was repeating it? Are the handfuls of Tylenol blunting my mind as well as the pains in my body? Vance's sharp mind is sure to spot the error and he's going to come down hard on me for sloppy thinking.

He looks off into the space behind my right shoulder. Gathering his thoughts for the tongue lashing he's going to give me.

But he doesn't.

Why not? He must have spotted the error in my argument. Maybe he's...

"Why do you think he mutilated the kid?" He fires the question at me.

"The wife goes to this odd church. In one of the pictures they have on display, there is a body mutilated in the same way. I think Wright did it to implicate the church in the killing." I feel a bit uneasy about this. I remember Reverend Harris saying that Mark came as a guest and during guest meetings, the dark pictures were covered up. However, at some point, he could easily have sneaked a look.

"Why would he do that?"

"His wife was having an affair with the brother of the pastor. Maybe he wanted to point the finger at him." Again that feeling of unease. Elizabeth said she told Mark about the affair on Sunday, a week after Terry's death. I keep this from Vance, rationalizing that Mark Wright could easily have found out about the affair long before his wife told him.

I buttress my theory. "It would give him another reason to kill Terry: to punish his wife for the affair."

He thinks this over for a moment. "What is this *oboe* code?" he asks.

"I don't know. I sent it to Forensics and they haven't got back to me yet."

"Who'd you send it to?"

"Sally Wilkes."

"Good."

He looks hard at me and I feel like I am being interrogated. I can see why Vance was one hell of a good detective. I feel a need to fill the silence and I want to tell him that I also sent the code to Damien but Inspector Vance is territorial in the extreme; he would haul me over the coals if he knew I have involved an outsider. I'm hoping that Steve will be too ticked off at Vance for taking over his cases and won't offer up this info.

Or maybe he already has. Maybe Vance is waiting for me to tell him.

A cold drip of sweat trickles down my spine.

"So, what about the Varga killing?"

My relief at the change of subject is short lived. I'm pretty sure that I'm going to get blasted on this one.

"We're not much further ahead. We can't find

the truck that killed her. We've had patrols checking every blue Ford F150 they run into but, so far, nothing. The husband gambles a lot and it's rumoured that he hangs around with suspect characters in the casinos, which we are checking into. The angle I want to follow up is the link between the two cases."

"Yeah, Steve mentioned that." His voice is skeptical. "Explain it to me."

I need to be convincing.

"Marguerite Varga used to go to the same church as Elizabeth Wright; they knew each other but not well. Both husbands attended one guest service there, though not at the same time. But the bigger connection is that Mark Wright used to work for Harold Varga at the bank."

"Not much of a connection, is it?" There is more than a little sarcasm in his voice.

He raises his eyebrows a hair's breadth, waiting for my response.

"No sir."

"OK," he says. "Here's what you're gonna do." This is going to be an order, not a suggestion. "Find Mark Wright and grill him. I want to be kept up to date on this, so make sure I know as soon as you've tracked him down. We'll need to either get a confession or exonerate him. Forget trying to rely on a connection between the two cases. On the Varga case, find the damn truck and track down the killer.

It's over a week since she was killed and you've got fuck all, so get to it. Steve's asked for more man-power on the case and I've authorized it. He said he wants someone else working the attempted kidnap-ping to the Chan kid. He'll let you know who."

Before I can object, he picks up his phone and swivels his chair away from me.

I am dismissed.

37

CAL

One more day. Tomorrow I will probably no longer be a member of the VPD, so a little insubordination now is no biggie.

One more day to find a killer and right now, I feel stretched in many directions at once.

The ostensible reason for being here is to interrogate Elizabeth and try and find Mark's whereabouts.

However, I am just as interested in what Damien might find out from those computers in the basement. He's down there now, clacking away at his laptop which he has plugged into the 'blades'. He has to be quick. Inspector Vance wants a VPD Forensics team here to do the same thing; they are probably en route right now. I want his opinion first but I don't want to have to tell Forensics who this person is and why he is here.

Also Elizabeth is sitting too close to me on the couch. I desperately need to find Mark and question him, so I need her to be... I don't know what I need her to be.

I stand and walk into the kitchen. There are dirty breakfast things in the sink. If this house had a logo, it would be an egg stained dish. "How's it going Damien?" I call down.

He can detect the agitation in my voice. "It's OK Cal, I'll only be a few more moments." That's good but in my limited experience computer people do not have a realistic sense of time.

I pace back into the living room and sit in the chair opposite the couch.

"Can you think of anywhere Mark might be?" I ask her for the second time.

"I DON'T KNOW CAL, I really don't," Elizabeth says. She gets up and kneels at my feet, her hand on my thigh. Way too close. Damien could come upstairs at any moment.

I cannot get a handle on my feelings for Elizabeth. Is it more than lust? I want it to be; or is that just my feeling of guilt that I have taken advantage of her in a moment of weakness? I know I love Sam but is she a goal forever unattainable? Is my past an immovable barrier to our reconciliation? Is this new man in her life going to be permanent?

I hear a car stop outside the house. Forensics! Damn. I'll have to get Damien out the back way fast before he's had a chance to really investigate those computers. I stand and look out the window. The car is a Lexus, definitely not VPD issue.

I look back down and see the tenderness in Elizabeth's eyes; it is overwhelming. I do not want to hurt this fragile woman who has lost so much in the last ten days.

"Do you have a cabin or a boat?" I force myself to sit down and get back on track.

"No. Since Mark lost his job at the bank, we have lost everything."

She straightens up and kisses me gently on the side of the mouth. The effect is—

"They were wiped—"

Damien is standing in the doorway with a shocked look on his face. He must have seen the kiss and the red glow now suffusing my cheeks.

I stand up, looking guiltier than if I had remained seated.

Damien recovers his professional tone "The servers. Everything's been deleted."

"But you can recover stuff right?"

His smile is rueful. "'Fraid not. After he deleted

everything, he copied a file to every sector of every disk. Whatever was on there is gone. Unless he had it backed up somewhere."

"Ffff..." I hold back on the expletive as a nasty thought hits me. Can I really trust Damien? We are both a long way from high school and I don't really know what he might be into these days. What if there was something valuable on those computers, something that Damien could use. Would he be above copying it onto that fancy laptop of his and then deleting it from the computers downstairs? I hope that I'm wrong because it's too late to do anything about it now.

I have to face the fact that I might have screwed up big time here.

"I'm sorry I dragged you all the way here for nothing," I say.

"It may not have been for nothing." His smile is broad now. "While I was down there I was wondering why he would need all that computer power. I think I know what the *oboe* code is?"

"What is it?" I can't keep the catch from my voice.

"I need to go back to the office to verify it before I commit myself. I'll call you in a couple of hours if I'm right." He heads for the front door.

I glance nervously out the window. I really don't want Forensics reporting back that they saw a man with a laptop leaving the house right before they discovered that the computers had been wiped clean.

But there is only the Lexus outside. My sigh is just audible.

"Wait. Tell me what you suspect, at least."

He cuts a glance at Elizabeth. "Let me check it out first."

As much as it frustrates me, he is right. Despite my feelings for her, I don't know how much Elizabeth may have been involved in her husband's activities. Plus I need Damien out of here.

"I'm sorry I kissed you in front of him," she says as soon as the front door closes.

I ignore the stew of conflicting emotions. "We can talk about that later. Right now I need to find your husband."

"I don't have any ideas."

Simultaneously, I hear the solid clunk of a car door closing and the sound of a starter motor.

"What's his cellphone number?"

"He has two." While I write the numbers in my notebook, she rests her hand on my forearm.

"Was there somewhere you went on vacation or for long weekends that Mark liked a lot?"

"Cal, please." She takes my face in her hands and gives me a tantalizing kiss on the lips.

My body betrays my resolve and I return the

kiss. She runs her hand up the inside of my thigh and finds the evidence of my desire.

She stands up and I know that I am powerless to resist. Taking my hand she leads me to the hallway and the doorbell rings.

She leans into me. "Let's leave it," she whispers. Her breath in my ear sends a tsunami of sensation through every nerve in my body. I hear a voice through the door as she draws me toward the bedroom.

I glance back.

Whoever is at the door could be relevant to the case. It could conceivably be Mark Wright.

She has opened the bedroom door and stepped inside. I turn back to her. With one lithe movement, she reaches down to the hem of her dress, lifts it up over her head and drops it to the floor. She is naked beneath it.

She makes my decision for me. I hope that it is a permanent decision.

I close the bedroom door.

Taking my Sig from its holster, I open the front door.

"Hey, Rocky." Staff Sergeant Sally Wilkes of the Forensic Unit is new to VPD so knows me only as Rocky. She walks in. "I've come to look at those computers, orders of Inspector Vance. This is Sarah," she introduces her companion. They look like the odd couple: Sally is in a conservative suit and has a flowing mane of auburn hair, Sarah has a very short brush cut and is dressed in a steampunk style.

I return my gun to its home and lead them down the hallway into the kitchen, glad that my back is to them. Damien left the door to the basement open. "They're down there. I'm leaving now, call me as soon as you know anything. Mrs. Wright is in her bedroom."

I return to the bedroom door and knock. "Mrs. Wright," I say loudly enough to be heard below. I turn the handle but the door is locked. "Our forensics people are here, so I'm leaving now."

No response.

I leave, feeling like a jerk. But a jerk with the image of Elizabeth's naked body permanently tattooed into my neurons.

As I head down the path I notice that the white Lexus is gone.

38

CAL

Both Mark Wright's cellphones are switched off but Forensics are monitoring them for any activity. They are also looking into his financial records for any payments that might pinpoint his location. Meanwhile, I am sitting on my thumbs in the plush reception area, waiting for Harold Varga to grant me an audience.

There still is no trace of the truck that killed Marguerite Varga and despite Inspector Vance's skepticism about the connection between the cases, it is all I have to go on.

"Detective Rogan." He is standing there in another expensive suit. "I can only spare you fifteen minutes as I have a lunch appointment. Follow me." Without offering his hand, he turns and stalks down the corridor to his office.

Instead of offering me a seat on the leather chairs in the corner of the office, he points to one of the guest chairs at his desk. When he sits, I notice that his chair is adjusted so that his eye level is above mine.

"Mr. Varga, who might have known that your wife was going to be on the way to her church on the evening she was killed?"

"People from the church I suppose... and me. No-one else that I can think of."

"What about Mark Wright?"

I watch his face like a hawk. Dropping Mark's name into the conversation, completely out of context, has the desired effect. I see shock, then consternation, or is it fear? Then it is replaced by anger.

"What the hell do you mean by that?"

"I mean, did Mark Wright know that your wife went to the church every Sunday night?"

"No of course not, unless Elizabeth told him. But Mark couldn't possibly have had anything to do with my wife's murder. He was—"

"He was what, sir?" I ask.

"He was... uh, distraught over his son being missing. He would have been waiting at home for any news."

I love it when a plan comes together. "So you and Mark have been in frequent contact with each other."

He sees the trap he has fallen into and I see light refracting through a tiny bead of perspiration on his forehead. "Well, I uh, wouldn't say frequent but we talked from time to time."

"Frequent enough that you knew the details of his son's disappearance and subsequent murder."

"Well... yes."

Now for the long shot. "What do you know about the *oboe is blood* code?"

Home run. All the blood drains from his face.

"The what?" he asks.

"Mr. Varga, I think it is about time for you to come clean. We know what the code means."

He stares at me and I can see the conflicts wrestling behind his eyes. Then his face calms. The bluff worked; he is going to tell all.

"OK, Detective Rogan. I have had about enough of this. I am going to ask you to leave right now. I will be putting a call through to my good friend Superintendent Cathcart to complain about your inept handling of this investigation. Kindly leave now."

So much for that bluff working.

He stands. I don't.

I just look at him. Maybe the first bluff did not work but in a minute, I will ask him to accompany me to the police station.

My phone vibrates. Without breaking eye contact, I take it from my pocket and press the green talk button.

"Rogan."

The five words I hear change everything.

39

CAL

At last the frustration is over; we are going in now.

For over ninety minutes, I sat in the car a block from the Golden Motel waiting for backup from Tactical Support and worrying that at any moment he could decide to run. The only thing that kept me from disobeying Steve's order to stay out of sight and not go in alone, was the slim chance that Mark Wright may be armed. A one-on-one armed confrontation runs the risk of the suspect coming out on top and escaping, with his gun, into the world at large. And something else is scratching at my mind. I'm missing something; I can't put my finger on it but it feels like it's important.

At a whispered command, one officer swings the

ram and the door flies open, he steps back so that two of his colleagues and I can enter fast.

The first thing I see is the gun in Wright's hand, a Browning, identical to the one that I used to carry before the department changed over to the Sig Sauer, except it has a silencer. Where would a computer guy get a handgun with a silencer in Canada? The silencer is covered in blood. The headboard and the wall are spattered with the contents of Wright's cranium, forming an unholy halo.

I walk over and can smell the recently discharged weapon. The body is warm. He died while I was waiting outside.

———

THE CONGRATULATIONS of Steve and Inspector Vance feel hollow. I may have closed the Terry Wright case but, if I had disobeyed orders, I could have gone in before Mark killed himself and we would have the killer in custody. Now I have to face his wife, my new lover, and tell her that her husband is dead and that I could have saved him.

She opens the door and is looking stunning in the same dress that she wore earlier. She takes my hand and draws me inside. As soon as the door closes, she kisses me and I can feel the urgency in her body. She breaks the kiss. "Did you find Mark? Was he still there?"

"Yes." I lead her into the living room and sit her down. Before I tell her, I have questions that must be answered.

"Tell me exactly what was said in your phone call from Mark."

"He told me that some people were after him, criminals. He said he had enough money for him and me to get away together; that I should pack a bag and come to the Golden Motel. I told him that I would come as soon as I could. Then I hung up and called you."

"Did he say why these criminals were after him?"

"No. He just said that they were bad, very bad."

"How did he sound when you told him you would go with him?"

"Relieved. Excited, I suppose. He told me to hurry."

A worm of unease is slithering in my gut. There's something wrong with this story.

"How long were you on the phone to him?"

"I don't know. Two minutes maybe."

"Did Mark have a gun?"

She emits a harsh laugh. "A gun? Mark? No. Of course not." She sounds very sure. "Why?"

The worm becomes a viper.

It's time to come clean. I sit down beside her and take her hand in both of mine.

For the first time I notice that the haunting chants are playing on the CD player. Will her religious beliefs be strong enough to get her through this? "When we got to the motel, Mark was dead. It looks like suicide."

She is silent, motionless, just staring at the wall. Five seconds. Ten. A lone tear furrows her cheek. Then another. She extracts her hand from mine, covers her face with both hands and slumps forward, sobbing into her lap. I try to console her by gently rubbing her back. Through the dress, I can feel that she is not wearing a bra and feel ashamed at the excitement this generates in me.

"Why?" she sobs. "Whyyyyyy?"

"We have reason to believe that he may have killed Terry."

She continues sobbing but there is no denial.

40

STAMMO

I gotta stop myself getting bitter about it. Maybe the fuckin' doctors are wrong. I've been hurt before, shit, I was shot more'n once and I bounced back. There's no way I'm gonna spend the rest of my life in a wheelchair. No way!

But either way, the job's gone. Shit!

Shit! Shit! Shit!

I'm squeezing my hand so tight, I can feel the metal of the locket cutting into my palm.

"Can we come in?" It's Rogan. He's got his kid with him.

"Hi Nick, how are you feeling?" I can tell from his face he knows my prognosis.

"Hi Mr. Stammo," Ellie says with a shy little smile. It's the best thing I've seen all day... by far.

"Hi honey, how are you?"

"Good." She smiles again and I can't help smiling back.

She's holding a big bunch of flowers in a vase.

"Put them here El," Rogan guides her to the window, "where Mr. Stammo can see them."

Mr. Stammo. That's what people will be calling me from now on, not Detective Stammo. Not anymore. The thought's more painful than the pains in my body; the drugs keep those in check. For the first time in my life, I can see why people might take drugs to dull the pain in their mind. Is that what started Rogan on heroin all them years ago?

Ellie sits in the visitor chair with one of them electronic book things. Why would anyone take drugs when they've got a little angel like her to come home to?

"Tonight's my night with Ellie; I just picked her up from after-school care."

I nod. Seeing her reminds me of my own kids. I haven't seen them since... Now I'm going to have more time on my hands, maybe I'll go visit them in Toronto... wheelchair and all. Maybe.

Rogan breaks the silence. "Nick, I'm sorry. The driver, I should have put her out of commission, it's my fault you're..."

"Forget it, Rogan. It wasn't your fault. When you threw her outta the SUV, I could hear the bone snap from where I was." I look at Ellie, I hope she didn't hear that. She seems lost in her book but I better be careful I don't swear or say anything else that might upset her. "No-one would'a thought that she'd be able to get up again," I continue, "let alone get back in the driver's seat. You did the right thing to go after the one with the kid."

"Thanks, Nick, it's just…" He looks down at my legs, covered up by the blankets but I can see the relief wash over his face. "They're pulling out all the stops trying to find those women and that SUV. Michael Chan gave us the number plate but it was stolen. We're going to get them, Nick. I promise you."

The silence is awkward. We both know that's a promise it's gonna be difficult to keep. He looks at Ellie and a smile comes over his face for a moment. Then it changes. He's pumping up his courage to say something and I got a pretty good idea what it is.

"Why did you take that urine test for me, Nick?" His voice is very quiet. "How did you know?"

Maybe I should tell him. I got nothing to lose now. He deserves to know the truth, 'though I'm not too sure how he's gonna take it. He blows up real easy. But I want him to know that I didn't have anything to do with it, that I didn't find out about it until after. I think for a bit about how to explain it and I can tell he's getting impatient.

"It's like this, Rogan. I haven't always been the

straightest of cops. Over the years, I done some things I ain't too proud of but I want you to know that I would never—"

"I knew it." He cuts me off with a snarl. "You sold me out. You made it pretty clear that you didn't want me in the Department, so you sold me out to some drug gang so they could pump me full of dope and get me hooked again. How much did they pay you Nick?"

"What the f—" I cut myself off. I don't want to swear in front of little Ellie. "What the heck are you talking about, Rogan. If I'd sold you out why would I take the f—, why would I take the test for you."

"I don't know. Maybe because you felt guilty."

Screw him. Bastard thinks I've been taking money from some gang. Screw him! He can find out who did it himself.

I fix my eyes on him. "I think you'd better go now, Rogan."

He can see he's fucked it up. "I'm sorry, Nick," he says. "I shouldn't have accused you like that. It's just that I'm so angry about it. They gave me another test the day after. The results aren't back yet but when they are... "

So I did it for nothing. They got him anyway. He's going to go from Detective to Mr., just like me.

"Who was it, Nick? Who did it to me?"

I just shake my head and point at the door. "Now," I say.

He takes Ellie's hand and leads her out. She turns and waves and gives me a huge smile; it makes a tear spring to me eye. Shit, I haven't cried in years. I blink it away and stroke the locket in my palm.

41

CAL

THURSDAY

I can hardly contain my impatience. I am sitting on an expensive, soft leather couch in a room that takes up the whole floor. The desks are packed together and occupied by people, predominantly male, each with a bank of three computer monitors in front of him, deeply engrossed in work. The walls are exposed brick and the ancient beams are as they were when this was an industrial warehouse. In other words, it is a typical Gastown high tech company.

After dropping off Ellie at school, I am here at Damien's office in answer to his text: *I know what oboe means. It's HUGE.* Although I called him first, he refused to discuss it over the phone, saying it was too sensitive to discuss on a cell, so now I'm here on tenterhooks. A tattooed and leather-clad receptionist with red and green streaks in her jet black hair—reminiscent of Damien's past—has asked me to take a seat and wait.

I need to take another handful of Tylenol. The withdrawal pains are no longer crippling but are still painful. I look around and see that there is a large, glass-fronted coffee room behind me. I get up from the luxury of the couch and walk toward it.

I can smell coffee. I take in a deep breath and for a moment, I am transported back to my capture in the disused building in Riverview. It's the same coffee that permeated the sack which was placed over my head by my captors. It sends off a peal of warning bells.

I try and shake off the thought that Damien could have had anything to do with my kidnapping. It doesn't make sense. He was in Frankfurt when I was taken. And if it was Damien, how would Stammo know about it. No it just doesn't make any sense at all.

I enter the coffee room. On a counter there is a drip coffee pot, a Bodum French press, a vacuum flask and a very expensive looking espresso machine. These techies definitely like their coffee. To my surprise, at the end of the counter are two beer taps.

An intense and slightly forbidding looking woman is loading beans from what looks to be a five pound sack into a grinder. This close I can smell the coffee strongly. It *is* the same. And the sack could easily be a twin of the one that was placed over my head. It has *got* to be a coincidence. There must be thousands of people who drink this brand of coffee.

"Do you know where this coffee comes from?" I ask.

Her smile completely changes her face and it is captivating. "Yes, I do. It's quite unusual. It comes from Guatemala, from a fair trade, family plantation. After Damien visited there last year, he brought some back and we have been buying it from a local importer ever since. It's very good. Would you like a cup?" So, there are not thousands of people drinking this brand.

At my yes, she pours a cup from the vacuum flask. She is right, it is good... and somehow familiar. I take another sip and I know where I have had this before. A chill envelopes me. I am happy that Damien was not involved—that it was indeed a co-incidence—but horrified at the truth. It takes all my will power not to leave and go back to VGH and make Stammo come clean.

"Hi, Cal. Sorry to keep you waiting. A conference call with a client in Germany. Good, you've got coffee, so come on through." Damien leads me along a narrow path between the desks and I try to force the thoughts of my capture behind me for the moment and start to wonder what all these people do. I had no idea that Damien's company was so big. There must be forty people on the floor.

We go into a sparsely furnished corner office and he closes the door. On his desk is one of those Newton's cradle executive toys. I feel like the middle ball, attacked from both sides and getting nowhere.

As I sit down I realize that I forgot to take the Tylenol but I'll tough it out for a while.

I can feel my excitement ramping up. When I get fired today—as I almost certainly will—at least I am going to go out in a blaze of glory for solving this element of the crime, the motive for Terry's death.

He waves his hand toward the people outside his office and says, "They're all what you would call hackers," he says. "Some of them have been to jail for hacking into governments' and corporations' computers and the others didn't go to jail because they were too smart to get caught."

"What are they doing here?" I have an uncomfortable feeling that I have walked into some huge illegal operation, the proverbial den of thieves.

He can read the look on my face and smiles. "Our clients pay us big bucks to try and break their security, hack into their servers, access their data, that kind of stuff. We are paid to pit our wits against the client's own IT staff to find and report weaknesses that criminal hackers could take advantage of."

Do companies really do that?

"You have enough clients paying you to hack their systems that you can employ what, forty people?"

"A hundred and thirty, we have the two floors below this one too." He smiles at my bemusement. "Who'd have thunk it eh?"

I shake my head but don't feel one hundred percent comfortable with the answer.

"Anyway," he says, "you didn't come here to learn about my business; you came here to learn about *oboe*."

"I'm all ears."

"What do you know about encryption?"

"Nothing really; it's how computers scramble information so that no-one can read it. Something like that?" I feel a bit embarrassed that I'm going to get out of my depth very quickly in this conversation. Three years on the streets left me a bit behind in the world of high tech.

"Well yes. When you log into your bank's computer to pay a bill you enter a user name and password and can get to all your financial records. Well, everyone who operates a secure system, like a bank, uses an encryption method called public key encryption. Your computer encrypts a message to the bank's computer using the bank's *public* key that is available to anyone who wants it. But the message can only be decrypted by the bank's *private* key, which is known only to the bank's computer.

"When you gave me the *oboe* code, I showed it to one of my guys and he agreed that it was probably a key. Well, public keys are available to anyone and have no intrinsic value, so I made a guess that maybe this was a private key and if it was, it could be very valuable."

"Valuable to whom?" I ask. I am only just getting this.

"If you had the private key of a bank *and* if you could access data going to the bank's computers on, say, an unsecured wireless network in a coffee shop or a library, you could find out the user name and password of every person who accessed the bank's computer on that network."

"So you'd have access to those people's accounts?"

"Yes. You could do anything they could do with internet banking. Pay bills, transfer money to other accounts at the same bank. Depending on the bank's system you might be able to wire money to accounts at other banks."

"But the bank's customers would find out pretty quickly if someone else had transferred money out of their account, wouldn't they?"

"Yes. When they logged in to their account, they would notice the transfer and complain to the bank. If the bank got complaints, they would know that they had been hacked and, among other things, would probably change their keys. That's what's so funny."

"Funny?" I ask.

He smiles at my puzzled expression. "Yeah. You see, I figured that it might be the private key of a bank or insurance company, so I did a little experiment. I wrote a program to get the public keys of all the major Canadian banks and insurance companies and then encrypted some data with the public keys and tried to decrypt it with the *oboe* code. And bingo, it turns out *oboe* is the current private key of one major Canadian bank."

"Toronto National Bank," I say. Varga's employer and Mark Wright's former employer.

Now it is Damien's turn to be puzzled. "How did you know that?"

"It's relevant to the case I'm working on." I don't need to share the details with him yet. "Why did you say 'funny' before?"

"Well if someone has got the private key of a bank, they are going to use it to steal money. As I said, customer's would notice, inform the bank and the bank would change the key. But they haven't. That's strange."

My coffee has cooled. I use it to wash down a handful of Tylenol. Damien gives me a strange look.

"Who in the bank would know the bank's private key?" I ask.

"Someone in the IT department and maybe one senior executive."

Varga! I can feel my antennae twitching.

"Could that be the VP of Private Banking?"

"Not a chance. It would be much higher up the chain."

So much for that theory. But another one leaps to the fore.

"What about a former IT guy?"

"No. The person in IT doesn't actually know the key, but he knows where to access it. If that person quit, all his access rights would be removed and anyway, they would probably change the key too."

"If a former employee did have the key, how might he have got it?"

Damien gives me a sly smile. "The guy with all those servers in his basement?"

I nod.

"I would *really* like to know how he did it, but all those servers were wiped clean. Still... I guess he must have found a way."

So Mark Wright had the key to hack into people's accounts, but he didn't use it because, if he had done, people would have complained and the bank would have changed the key. And there is another thing that doesn't make sense—

"Cal," Damien interrupts my chain of thought. "You realize we need to tell the bank that their private key has been stolen."

"Yes, I suppose so. Someone more senior than me in the department should contact them. I'll get on to that as soon as I get back; I'm going there now."

As I take my leave, I realize that although I now know what the *oboe* code is, I can't see how it fits into the puzzle of the deaths of Terry Wright and Marguerite Varga and the attempted kidnapping of Michael Chan.

Except that it strengthens the theory that they are all connected.

And I do know who kidnapped me and shot me to the moon. I never would have guessed.

42

CAL

Mark Wright didn't kill himself and I'm starting to doubt that he killed his step-son."

Inspector Vance takes the news without a reaction but Steve sighs. "Cal, the initial forensics point to suicide."

I level an eye at him. "Yes Steve, I remember another case where the forensics pointed to suicide but it turned out not to be." He looks uncomfortable; he knows the case I am talking about. "The point is, his wife says that he called her, asking her to meet up with him at the motel. His plan was to take off with her, disappear. He said he had enough money for them to go and live in another country."

Steve is irritated at me now, he does not like to

be contradicted in front of his boss. It hits me how much he has changed. When we were street cops together, he would follow every lead. I suspect he is becoming a politician now. "Maybe he wanted to punish her. Get her all excited about leaving and then come to the motel and find him dead." Even before he has finished, I can see a flush appear on his cheeks. He knows it's a flawed theory.

Vance cuts in. "If he was planning to run, that's a pretty good sign he was guilty of killing the kid. I still think we've got our killer. Mark Wright killed his step-son to punish his wife for having an affair with the guy at her church. He cut the kid up like a picture in the church to try and implicate the lover."

"There are a couple of things you don't know," I say, earning a sharp look from Steve. "One: it's un-likely that Mark Wright ever saw the mutilation pic-ture in the church, he was only a guest there once and the minister says that at guest meetings they keep the pictures covered. Two: his wife says he didn't know about her affair until after Terry was dead."

"Who's to say he didn't sneak a look at the pic-ture," Steve counters. "And the wife could be wrong about when the husband learned of the affair. No, Cal, I gotta believe Mark was the killer."

I grit my teeth but before I can say anything,

Vance chimes in, "I'm gonna wait until all the forensics are in on Wright's death *and* the autopsy's done before speculating whether it was murder or suicide. Then we'll decide the next step."

"About the *oboe* code..." I cut myself off. Vance doesn't know that I had Damien working on it and he wouldn't be happy if he found out.

"What about it?" he asks.

"Did, uh, Sally Wilkes in Forensics work out what it meant?" I cover.

"Not yet but it's probably nothing." For a second I toy with the idea of relating Harold Varga's reaction to the words *oboe is blood* but decide to wait. I'll go and see Sally Wilkes in Forensics right after this meeting and put the encryption key idea into her head. Then it can come from her, rather than from an outsider. *Then* I can bring up Varga's reaction.

"Steve, can you excuse us for a minute?" Vance requests.

Steve glances at me, gets up from his chair and leaves without a word.

I'd better come clean with Vance about the code. It is too important. It provides a strong motive for Terry's death and for Michael's kidnapping and I'm starting to think that the bank needs to be told. Damien says he showed it to one of his ex-con hackers, what if he starts making use of it?

"Sir, about the *oboe* code—"

"Cal, we need to talk."

He looks very uncomfortable.

I can feel a clamping in my stomach. I'd temporarily forgot about—

"The results came back," he says quietly. "Your last urine test showed positive for opiates. You've been using again, haven't you?"

"Yes sir, but there were extenuating circumstances." I can't let him fire me now. I need to find out the truth about this case, I need to find out who tried to kidnap Michael Chan and crippled Stammo in the process. If I tell him about my kidnapping and the drugs they pumped into me—

"Cal, I'm really sorry about this but I've got to ask you to give me your gun and your ID. You are suspended with pay from right now until your case is reviewed at a disciplinary hearing by the Police Board."

My heart is thumping in my chest. "You really need to hear—"

"I'm sorry Cal. You can bring it up with the Police Board. It's out of my hands. Steve is waiting outside the door to escort you off the premises. Someone from Human Resources will be contacting you." He holds out his hand.

Defeated, I take my gun from its holster and hand it over, then my ID.

Back in the Department for fewer than six months and now it is over.

Again.

———

I HAVE one thing I must do before I leave the building and I know how to manipulate Steve into helping me. He is standing silently over me while I take my few personal effects from my desk and put them in a box that was conveniently left on my chair.

The task done, I ask him the first thing that I need him to agree to. "Steve, this is embarrassing; can we go out the back way? Please."

He agrees. We make our way down the corridor to the back stairwell. Just before we get there I make my second request. I stop outside the lunch room. "Can I just have a quick drink of water please?"

He shrugs. "Sure."

I walk in, put my box on a table and go to the sink. I pour water into a paper cup and drink. Then throw the cup into the garbage can under the sink. While I am bent down, I reach over and open the adjoining cupboard.

There is the proof.

Sacks of coffee. That smell.

The humiliation of knowing that my own colleagues wanted me gone so badly that they were prepared to do this...

I look up at Steve. He holds my gaze for a moment but then looks away.

Et tu, Brute.

43

MIKE

One wrong card. One wrong card and I owe them over a hundred grand. 'Pay up,' the huge one said, 'or... do this one little job for us.' I'm between a rock and a hard place. If I don't keep doing it I'll have to sell off everything to pay 'em; if I do it and get caught, I'll get fired and lose my pension. Pat and the kids'll be long gone. I got no choice.

I connect a new set of cables to the device. Despite the heavy duty air conditioning in the network operations centre, I can feel the sweat running down my face. It only takes a few seconds but if—

"What you doing Mike?" My heart rate doubles.

I dare not turn round; he'll take one look at my face and know something's up. "Got a job ticket on this router," I tell him. "Looks like a faulty cable," I wave the cable in my hand. "Won't be long."

If he walks down the alley between the racks and sees what I'm doing, I'll be well and truly f—

"Soon as you're finished, let me know, I need your help installing the new gear we got in from Cisco."

"Couple of minutes."

Silence. I guess he's moved off. I look up at a router above my head and can just see the end of the alley out of the corner of my eye. No-one's there. He's gone.

I can't keep the trembling out of my hands while I connect the last of the cables. It seems to take forever. Take 'em one at a time, Mike. I force myself to do it.

Done.

Now all of Toronto National Bank's internet connections from their Calgary hub are also routed through it. God knows where the data's going. Who would want it anyway? It's all encrypted.

44

CAL

Steve knew. I can't bring myself to believe that he was one of them, but he knew. Knew that a bunch of our colleagues had taken me and pumped me full of smack. I could read it in his eyes when I opened the cupboard full of head-sized sacks of coffee.

It's why he made me take a second test, he knew something was wrong with the first one.

That's why I'm here.

To apologize.

He's asleep, so I sit down beside his bed. I don't know Stammo's age but it's around fifty I'm guessing; lying there in the bed, he looks gaunt and much older. He is gently snoring.

I can wait. The one thing I have now is time.

Despite the fact that Stammo and I have never

liked each other and probably never will, he is a fair cop. It's why he took the urine test for me. He wanted me out of the department as much as anyone, but not that way. And I repaid him by accusing him of selling out to some drug gang I thought had ordered my kidnapping.

So I'm going to wait here and think until he wakes up.

They can put me on suspension but they can't excise the cop from me. I am not going to let go. It may look like Mark Wright killed his step-son but there are just too many things nagging at me. Mark was working for someone, a client, what was it Grace Chan said? *Someone that Elizabeth took an instant dislike to.* I must ask Elizabeth more about him. Mark somehow used all those computers in his basement to get hold of the private key for the Toronto National Bank's computer systems. Maybe he got it so he could sell it to this 'client'. If the client knew that Terry and Michael knew the code and were repeating it, then he might have been responsible for killing Terry and attempting to kidnap Michael. But if someone other than Mark killed Terry, how did they get him out of the house under Mark's nose. Unless they did it with Mark's cooperation.

Wait a minute. Wait a minute, what if—

"What are you doing here Rogan?"

"Hi Nick. I came here to apologize."

"Uh-huh?" Non-committal.

"I know who kidnapped me and shot me full of heroin. It was some of our colleagues. I don't know who specifically and I don't really care. I just want to say that I'm grateful that you tried to help me out by taking the drug test for me and to say I'm sorry for what I said last night. I was waaaay out of line."

"Yeah... You were."

Silence.

"They put me on suspension."

"Who pulled the plug."

"Vance."

"Not Steve?"

"No."

He digests this.

"When?"

"An hour ago."

"When did they pull the second urine test on you?" Where's Stammo going with this?

"Tuesday afternoon about three."

His eyes narrow. "So why'd they wait 'til Thursday morning to fire you."

"Maybe the lab was backed up and—"

"No way. They turn those tests round right away. They're not like DNA. Steve knew the results Wednesday morning."

"Maybe the paperwork got delayed. It happens."

"Yeah." He's not convinced.

"What are you getting at Nick?"

He gives me a long, hard look. Something is going on behind his eyes but I can't read what it is. He opens his mouth, then closes it.

Finally. "Nothing."

"Come on Nick, what is it?"

"Time to check your dressings, Detective Stammo." She is blonde, cute and excessively perky.

"You'd better go."

I stand, "Yeah," and head for the door.

"Rogan."

I turn.

"Thanks for coming. And thanks for... you know."

"Thanks, Nick."

I turn again and walk through the door.

"Watch your back," he throws after me.

Why would I need to watch my back? I've already been fired.

45

CAL

I didn't need to show my VPD identification to get in here. I have a window of opportunity where I can interview people who will not know I've been suspended. While I wait in the reception area setting up my phone for this meeting, I mull over Stammo's words. Watch my back against whom? The members in the department who kidnapped me have achieved their goal: I'm gone from there. After the hearing by the Police Board, I'll be fired for sure. So who is it I have to watch out for? And if he's right about the speed of the drug test turnaround, why *did* they wait a day and a half before firing me?

"Mr. Varga will see you now, sir?"

I get up and follow the plush secretary through the bank's plush corridors into Varga's plush office. I can smell coffee and the leather of the chairs but am offered neither.

He doesn't get up from his desk nor does he look up from the document he is studying. "What do you want *now* Detective Rogan?"

One look at his demeanour and I know *Here is neither cheer, sir, nor welcome.*

"Mr. Varga, as you probably know, Mark Wright is dead."

He still doesn't meet my gaze. "Yes. Such a tragedy."

Man, this is like shooting fish in a barrel.

"How *did* you know, sir?"

Now he makes eye contact. "I beg your pardon."

"Who told you Mark Wright was dead?"

"It was on the news last night."

"Yes sir but Mark's name wasn't mentioned. It wasn't released to the media. So who told you?"

Rather than answer my question, Varga reverts to type. He takes a deep breath and leans back in his chair. "Why are you questioning me about a former employee, Detective? Should you not be trying to find the man who murdered my wife?"

I have nothing to lose now.

I walk to his walnut-burl executive desk, lean over him and plant my palms on the report he was reading. His arrogance morphs into fear. "Now listen to me you little worm. I know Mark Wright had the private key which would allow him to hack into people's transactions with your bank's computers. I want to know what you and he were up to and I want to know how your wife's murder factors into this. I'll ask you again. Who told you that Mark Wright was dead?"

The blood has drained from his face. He stares into my eyes, trying not to give away any indication of what is going on in his mind. He succeeds.

Then I realize it doesn't matter. I know who told him.

We maintain the tableau for ten seconds. Then he breaks it by leaning back and smiling.

"I don't know what you are talking about Detective Rogan and I don't think you do. If you want to, you can take me into custody and I'll have my lawyer meet us at the police station. So either do so or get out of my office." I thought slithers into my brain? Does he know I have been suspended?

"I thought so," he says.

I take out my phone and hold it up. If I were still a cop, I would be calling Steve about an arrest warrant but I'm not and the bitterness of that fact lances through me. In a strange way, it makes me more determined to take the smug smile from Varga's face.

But for now, I just take his photograph.

46

CAL

She flies into my arms and holds me tight, too tight. And too long. Again I am confused about my feelings for her or, more to the point, her feelings for me. Her son died a week and a half ago and her husband died yesterday, ostensibly by his own hand and yet her hug has an urgency demanding more than just consolation.

She draws me into the living room. "I'm so glad you're here, Cal."

"I've been suspended." The words come from my mouth of their own volition. I had no intention of telling her. Quite the opposite in fact. But there they are, out of the box.

"Oh Cal, I am so sorry."

But she is not. She's on her own agenda. The

news of my pending termination is a mere ripple on the surface of the crashing waves in her mind.

Her face lights up like a little girl's. "Let's go away," she says.

"I can't take a vacation now. Just because I've been suspended doesn't mean I'm going to stop investigating this case and there's Ellie—"

"I don't mean a vacation. I mean let's go and live somewhere. Mexico, Fiji or somewhere in Europe if you'd prefer."

I get the sense that she is going to spiral out of control. "Elizabeth," my voice is as calm as I can make it, "I can't leave Vancouver. What sort of job could I get in those countries?" It flashes through my mind that I don't know what sort of job I will be able to get here and, if Arnold hears the reason for my being fired, he will have the right to terminate payments from my trust fund. For the first time since Vance suspended me this morning, I feel fear. Fear of the cold hand of poverty reaching out to grab me and drag me back to the streets. And Ellie... "And you're forgetting—"

"You won't need to work." She cuts me off with a tinkle of laughter. "I have all the money we'll need." She grins at whatever she reads on my face. "Don't worry. Mark had a large life insurance policy and there's the money... We'll have lots." She is becoming more manic. The words tumble out of her mouth. "We can maybe have a cottage on a beach somewhere. Or imagine a cute little apartment somewhere in Paris, wouldn't that be lovely, Cal. Or London; I *love* London. We could spend our days—"

As she speaks my stomach knots.

"Elizabeth!" I have her shoulders gripped tightly in my hands and manage to resist the urge to shake her into silence. "Elizabeth, I can't. I can't leave Vancouver. I have my daughter here; I would *never* leave her. And my job. They may have suspended me and they are almost certainly going to fire me, but I'm not going to just give up. The Department thinks that Mark killed Terry but I'm not sure he did. I want to find the real killer. I have to. It's what I do for God's sake."

"OK, Cal. OK. I can understand that. We'll talk about it again later." She has not given up. More to the point, she has not reacted to the revelation of my uncertainty that Mark killed Terry.

Before I can say anything, she takes my face in her hands and places a whisper-light kiss on my lips. Then another. Then on my cheek and the back of my jawbone. Then she envelopes my ear with her mouth driving my body into overdrive.

I know I shouldn't be doing this. But I'm just too weak to resist and hate myself for it. All thoughts of

why I came here in the first place dissolve into noth-
ingness.

————

I AM EXHAUSTED but I cannot sleep. I stare at the
ceiling and listen to Elizabeth's steady breathing as
she sleeps, her head on my chest. Our lovemaking
was wild and wonderful and unlike anything I have
ever experienced. She has a wanton quality that is
intoxicating. It has left me physically drained but
mentally clear and sharp.

The elements of the case swirl through my head:
the deaths of Terry Wright and Marguerite Varga;
the Church of the Transcended Masters, the girl-
woman who is the pastor and her brother Seth, with
his dog BL. I remember the dog's collar lying on the
kitchen counter, engraved with the initials BLZ:
Bee-el-zee. Is that short for Beelzebub? A biblical
name for the devil. Is Elizabeth's church a cover for
something else or is it just Seth?

As I think about Elizabeth and Seth, she stirs in
her sleep. I don't want her to wake up just yet. I have
too much to think about in the quiet of her
bedroom.

Something bothers me about yesterday's meeting
with Inspector Vance: Steve wants to have different

detectives investigating the attempted kidnapping of Terry's friend Michael Chan. The two women who tried to snatch him were obviously professionals, maybe from out of town. Someone was prepared to pay big bucks to silence Michael, to stop him from repeating the *oboe* code. Mark Wright and Varga were obviously using the code to rip off the Toronto National Bank in some way. When Terry and Michael started to chant the code in public, it became a threat to their plans. A good reason for Mark to have killed Terry. My earlier doubts about Mark's complicity are no longer valid; they were based on his motive being Elizabeth's affair with Seth.

But the attempted kidnapping of Michael Chan doesn't fit with Mark Wright or Harold Varga. Neither a computer techie nor a banker have the connections to hire trained thugs, female ones at that, to plan and stage a kidnapping which would have worked like a well-oiled machine if Stammo and I hadn't been there. It must have been Mark's client, the one that Grace Chan said terrified Elizabeth. When Elizabeth wakes, I'm going to ask her about this 'client'.

It's obvious now I think of it. Harold Varga and Mark Wright were just cogs in a bigger machine run by this infamous 'client'. The murders of Mark's step-son and Varga's wife may have been to put pressure on them. Their scheme to rip off the bank was masterminded by someone else. This whole thing is starting to smell of organized crime.

Two things I need to find out: Who was Mark's client? What scam were Mark and Harold Varga perpetrating on the bank?

Elizabeth can help me with the first question but the second one is going to be more difficult.

An irritating buzz disturbs my thoughts. My Blackberry. When Inspector Vance took my gun and ID, he omitted to take the department issued cellphone. I lean over the bed and a pull it from the pocket of my pants, dropped in haste an hour ago.

I notice the time, 6:05, but the caller ID is blocked.

"Rogan."

"Hello Mr. Rogan. It's Clare here, from Ellie's after-school care."

My mind draws a picture of a plump blonde woman with a kind face and a nice smile. Why would she be calling me?

"Is Ellie OK?"

"Oh yes," she catches the fear in my voice. *"Ellie's fine. It's just that Sam hasn't arrived to pick her up yet. She's always here by five-thirty, six at the latest. It's when we close."*

"Have you called her cell phone?"

"Several times and left messages. Could you come

over and pick her up. We should have closed at six and I have to—"

"No problem. I can be there in ten minutes."

A cold worm of fear slithers through my gut. Sam is never late for anything.

47

CAL

The silence feels unnatural. It heightens the fear. With that sense which lies between feeling and hearing, I become aware of my rapid heart-beat.

The front door was not damaged. Sam's mother's spare key—given to me, somewhat begrudgingly, when I dropped Ellie off into the care of her and my ex-step-father-in-law—opened it silently.

The hallway is as I remember it from my last visit. All the pictures lining the walls are in perfect alignment. At the end of the hall the kitchen door is open. On the marble countertop beside the sink there is a coffee press, full, with the plunger up. I make my way there but there is no smell of the coffee to make the house feel somehow less deserted. The coffee is cold. Beside the press is a clean mug and a carton of half-and-half. I have a picture in my mind of Sam, curled up on the couch, savouring her beloved coffee. A little thing that reminds me how much I love her.

But Sam is not on the couch. The living/dining room is empty, silent, lifeless.

Lifeless.

With dread I climb the stairs, remembering a time, fifteen months ago, when I climbed another set of stairs to find a body drenched in blood.

I have to stop thinking like this.

The bathroom and Ellie's bedroom are clear.

I rest my hand on the handle of Sam's bedroom door. It is the only room in the house I have never been in... other than in fantasy. I steel myself, knowing what is to come. The door swings open silently. Peach and dark green are the predominant designer colours Typical of Sam, there is a place for everything and everything's in its place—another one of her little quirks that I love.

The room smells of Coco Chanel.

Feeling like a voyeur, I take a step inside.

And see it. The only thing out of place.

A bright neon-pink slipper, its colour clashing with the design of the rug, on its side with one bunny ear up and the other down. Ellie's favourite I pick it up and the fear melts away. The body, which my suspicious detective's mind expected to find, is not here.

I linger for the moment enjoying the illicit feeling of being here uninvited. Folded on her pillow, the right-hand pillow, is a men's XXL t-shirt, her preferred night attire. I picture her in it, a wanton look in her eye, like...

I shake my head, close Sam's bedroom door and cross the tiny hallway to Ellie's room. As I drop her bunny slipper on the floor beside her bed, I startle, the sound of my Blackberry making me jump in the silence.

The Caller ID says *Samantha Cullen*. Thank God, thank God. But my relief quickly turns to anger.

"Sam, where the hell are you?"

Silence.

"Sam?"

"Rogan. Back off. Stop your investigation and she won't be harmed. Understand?" The words are made more sinister by the sound of the voice distorter the caller is using. The shock-waves tingle through my body. A picture of a terrified Sam, head covered with a coffee sack and wired onto a gurney in a dank room in Riverview, forces its way into my mind. Il-logical, but no less disturbing.

"Who is this?" Stupid, amateur question.

"Do you understand?"

"Yes, sure. OK. But when will you let her go?"

Another stupid question a cop should never ask. With a wrench, my experience of adult kidnappings already knows the answer.

Never.

"Soon. Remember, you're not a cop anymore, so just stop digging. Keep digging and the kid's next."

"OK. No prob."

"Oh, and don't tell your former colleagues about this call. Just keep it between us and you'll see her back in no time." Liar. The caller's plan is that I never see Sam again.

He hangs up. From the maelstrom of emotions assailing me, one name emerges. One person whom I think I can trust to help me.

———

"SALLY?"

"Yeah?" The reception on my phone is not too good in here; I can hardly hear her.

"It's Rocky Rogan."

"Hey Rocky, what's up?" There is nothing in her voice to make me think she knows I'm no longer with the department.

"I need to track down the movements of a cell phone over the last couple of days."

"No problem. Just call my Unit. Charlie's on duty; he'll do it for you."

"The thing is, Sally, this is a very sensitive case. I need you to do it for me and keep it confidential."

"Which case?"

"The kid, Terry Wright."

There is silence on the line for a while.

"I didn't know that was a priority." She sounds wary and it rings an alarm bell. Why would Terry's case not be a priority?

"Well it is now. A high priority. What I need is the location of this cell phone and the calls it made over the last two days." Sam was last seen dropping Ellie off at school yesterday morning. She could have been taken any time since then. "The number is seven seven eight, nine one one, zero five four five."

She repeats the number back to me.

"OK. I'll call you as soon as I get the info,"

"Thanks, Sally. Remember to keep this quiet."

Stammo can read the concern on my face. "Don't worry Rogan, Sally Wilkes is one of the good ones. She'll get the movements of Sam's phone real fast *and* she'll keep her mouth shut."

I've already briefed Stammo about Sam's kidnapping. It was a difficult decision to involve him. Whoever called from Sam's phone told me not to talk to my ex-colleagues but I need to talk to someone. I'm not sure why I picked Nick but standing there in Sam's house, it just felt right.

As though reading my mind, he says, "You did the right thing to come to me. I think you're right about these murders being tied in with organized crime."

"The guy on the phone said not to talk to my *former* colleagues. He knew I'd been suspended. I'm thinking there might be a leak in the Department."

His eyes bore into me and he bites his lower lip, on the left side. He is weighing options, pondering a decision. There is a monitor in the next room. With rising agitation, I hear it beep seven times before he talks. He shifts his position in the wheelchair.

"It's more than a leak. There's a dirty cop in the department."

"How do you know?" I can't believe it.

He ponders this too. I expect he's wondering if he can trust Rocky, the junkie. The monitor next door continues its inexorable beeping. Five, ten, fifteen. I notice my mouth is hanging open. I close it and my teeth click together. Then he makes his decision.

"Over the last year, I worked two murders involving drugs. In the first one I had a guy dead to rights for the murder: witness, motive, forensics, the whole bit. But when I went to pick him up, he'd gone, vanished into thin air. We'd kept everything real quiet. I was sure that the witness wasn't the leak so I had this nasty feeling that someone in the department might have been.

"So in the next drug-related murder, I arrested the guy and brought him in without telling anyone first. It was another open-and-shut case except when it came to trial, all the DNA evidence went missing and the bastard was acquitted. Right after the trial, one of Sally Wilkes' guys resigned and word was that he had screwed up the evidence but I just didn't buy it. I went to the guy's home and questioned him about it. He was shit-scared. Wouldn't talk to me. Screamed at me to get the hell out of his house. I figure someone got to him. I'm pretty sure someone in the department is dirty."

"Any ideas who?"

"Nah! But whoever it was must have known I'd be suspicious. If there's one thing I hate, it's a dirty cop. I was gonna find out if it killed me." He looks down at his useless legs. "Being stuck in here has given me some thinking time."

He bites his lip again. "Those women, in the black Escalade; the driver swerved out of her way to hit me. Why would she do that? Her priority was to escape. Maybe she was told we might be there and she was to kill me, or maybe both of us, if she got the chance. I dunno, maybe I'm just being paranoid."

Stammo's story is ringing bells big time. "Both murders were related to drugs cases?"

He nods, "Yeah."

"So if the guy who called me on Sam's phone was tipped off by someone in the department that I had been put on suspension, and if that someone is a dirty cop in the pay of a drug gang, then that means *our* cases are drug related."

"Yeah, I guess."

Then, just like that: Click. A huge piece of the puzzle falls into place. I can feel a tingle in my spine.

"Nick, you know what this means? It means—"

I snatch my ringing Blackberry from my pocket.

"Cal, it's Sally Wilkes. I don't think you were a hundred percent straight with me. That cellphone was registered to your ex-wife."

I feel a cold knife in my gut. "I know, Sally. I'm sorry I didn't tell you. But it *is* connected with the case, I promise you."

"I'm not sure what to do here, Cal. Using Departmental resources on a personal matter is strictly forbidden. You could get fired for it; hell, you could get me fired for it. I can't risk my pension on your say-so. If I get the OK from someone higher up..."

I want to scream at her that Sam's life is in danger that I have to find her, find her and bring her home safe, but I rein in my frustration and say, "Sally, just hang on a minute."

I cover the mouthpiece and tell Stammo.

He grabs the phone from me. "Sally, Nick Stammo here... Yeah, hi... Listen, Rogan's being straight with you here. We believe that the same people who put me in the hospital have grabbed his wife. We need that information right now... Uh-huh... Uh-huh. Rogan, write this down." He starts repeating what Sally is telling him. "It was turned on at seven-ten this evening on the Lions Gate Bridge... one call to Rogan then turned off... prior to that it was used at her home at four... an incoming call from a phone booth... then at four forty-five it was switched off, still at her home. Uh-huh... OK. Sally email me and Rogan all the details of the calls. Thanks... Yeah, I will... Thanks, Sally."

For a moment, I am paralyzed. Sam's phone was turned on and off on the Lions Gate Bridge. What if they dumped her off the bridge. No-one could survive that. I can feel a panic rising in me.

Stammo reads my mind. "No way Rogan. They just dumped her phone off the bridge. Lions Gate is real busy at seven at night. No scum in his right mind is gonna dump someone off the bridge at that time."

He's right. My fear factor ratchets down a couple of points.

My Blackberry buzzes, so does Stammo's. It's the email from Sally Wilkes. In silence we view the caller and GPS data. Nothing out of the ordinary. The last entries show she gets a call at home from a phone booth in Kerrisdale; she stays at home and twenty minutes later she, or someone, switches off the phone. It stays off until the Lions Gate Bridge.

"Where do we go from here Nick?" I hear the pleading in my voice.

"We?" he asks.

He's right, why should he help? We have been enemies for most of the time we have known each other and, despite what he said before, he must have *some* resentment that I didn't take out the driver more permanently. But for that error, he wouldn't be here in the hospital in a wheelchair.

I shrug. "I'm sorry. I shouldn't have asked."

I'm going to have to go it alone. If there is a dirty cop in the VPD, I can't go to the former colleagues for help because if I do, the kidnappers will hear about it. Maybe Arnold can help. He's got a ton of contacts in the security industry. The only problem is that I'll have to tell him I've been fired from the Department and why. I'm not sure he'll buy the fact that I was kidnapped and pumped full of heroin by my former colleagues; that sounds way too much like junkie fantasy. If he knows I've been using again, he could use his power as a trustee to cut off payments from the trust fund that Mr. Wallace set up for me. When I'm fired with no salary coming in, I'm going to need that money.

I've got to find Sam but I have no clue how. I guess first I should interview her neighbours; see if anyone saw anything but if I strike out there...

I head for the door.

"Rogan, wait."

I turn.

"If I help you with this, there's a favour I want in return, OK?"

"Sure, anything. What is it?"

He looks embarrassed. "I'll tell you when we've found Sam."

I breathe a sigh of relief. "Thanks, Nick, I really appreciate it."

He nods. We look at each other for a second and I nod too.

"What did the caller say to you?"

"He said to back off, stop my investigation. He knew I wasn't a cop anymore and said that Sam would be returned soon if I co-operated and that Ellie would be next if I didn't."

Stammo ponders this for a moment. "First thing, you said *he* but if the caller used a voice distorter, it could have been a woman. It could have been one of the broads that tried to kidnap the Chan kid and tried kill me. It might explain why there was no sign of forced entry at Sam's place. She would be more likely to open the door to a stranger if it was a woman."

"True." It's a possibility for sure. "But it could have been anyone, the phone call that Sam got could have been from someone saying that they were going to deliver a parcel or something."

"The other thing is the call was made from a phone booth in Kerrisdale. You know who lives there? Harold Varga, that guy who works for the bank. It's a bit of a long shot but—"

"Maybe not such a long shot. If you're right and there's a dirty cop in the department, in the pay of some drug gang, then that means that these murders are probably drug related, right?"

He nods.

I take a minute to bring him up to date on the significance of the *oboe* code.

"So," I continue, "I figured that Harold Varga and Mark Wright were using the code to rip off the bank. What I couldn't figure is how. If they were siphoning money out of people's accounts, those people would complain as soon as they saw their bank statements and spotted the missing funds. But if this whole deal is about drugs, it's much more likely they're using the code to *launder* money. That means that Harold Varga is up to his ears in drug money. If he wanted to stop me in my tracks, kidnapping Sam would do it."

He nods again. "There's another thing," he says. "The caller said they kidnapped Sam to make you back off from your investigation, right?" I nod. "Well they suspended your ass this morning. That should have been enough to get you off the case. So who knew you were still—"

"Varga! After Vance fired me, I came here to apologize to you and then went to see Varga at lunchtime. You remember how he told us that he was big buddies with Superintendent Cathcart. What if he called Cathcart after my visit? What if Cathcart's the dirty cop? It explains something else too. When I was talking to Varga, he knew Mark Wright was dead. Someone in the department must have told him. Also, he acted like he knew I wouldn't arrest him or haul him in for questioning. Maybe he knew I'd been suspended. Cathcart may already have told him."

He digests this. "The two murder cases I was telling you about, it could easily have been Cathcart who screwed them up."

I open my mouth to respond but he holds up a finger for silence. I can almost hear the gears in his brain grinding. The monitor in the next room beeps another seven times before he speaks. "I knew it was cops who pumped you full of heroin. Young straight arrow, Eric Street, was one of them and he couldn't resist telling me. He knew there was no love lost between us, so he thought I'd want to know. Well, no matter how I might feel about you, that is no fuckin' way to treat a fellow member; that's why I took the test for you. I never figured they'd test you again the next day.

"I got to thinking why'd they do it. Sure, some of 'em didn't like an ex-junkie in the department, still... But now I think about it, what if Cathcart wanted you out?"

"But why?" I ask.

"You were the one who kept on about the *oboe* code. I didn't think it was important and nor did Steve. But you insisted that we follow it up, you became a pain in the ass about it. If Cathcart's the guy, he'd have known the importance of the code and that he needed to shut you up before you found out what it was about. If he just let Eric and some of the others know he wanted you out and that he sanctioned someone doing something..." He leaves it hanging.

I struggle to quash the feelings of anger and shame erupting from the knowledge that Eric Street and some of the other cops—the *young fry of treachery* as the Bard would have it—may have been manipulated into kidnapping me and awakening the Beast by pumping me full of heroin. Right now, I need to focus.

"But how do I get Sam back?" I ask.

"What about Ellie?" Stammo asks. "D'you think she might be in any danger?"

A chill runs through me. This case started with the murder of a child. The voice on Sam's phone said, 'Your kid's next.' With a chill, I recall the previous time that Ellie's life was threatened.

One phone call to my former in-laws verifies that she is OK, fast asleep in their spare bedroom. A second call to Arnold ensures that someone very hard and very resourceful will be at their house within an hour, no questions asked. Not yet anyway.

"While you were on the phone, I've been thinking it through. You can't approach Varga, he may have made the call to Sam but he's an office guy, he's not the type to get his hands dirty doing the actual abduction."

I disagree. "But I could wring the information out of him."

"Yeah, but what if he's not involved. Just because the call came from Kerrisdale doesn't mean it was him. If you go over there and rough him up and he's *not* involved he's gonna be calling Cathcart to complain and they'll know what you're up to. Then Sam's really gonna be at risk and so is Ellie."

Stammo's logic is irrefutable.

"OK, but I'm going to interview Sam's neighbours and see if anyone saw anything this afternoon."

"It's almost ten o'clock, Rogan."

"I don't give a flying..." I head for the door.

"Rogan!" I turn and face him. "Remember, we're partners in this. Keep me in the loop."

"Don't worry Nick, I will." I smile. "And thanks, I really appreciate it."

He gives a smile back. A rare visitor to his face, it looks out of place.

I'm glad he's on my side but I wonder what is the favour I am going to have to do in return for his co-operation.

48

CAL

My mind is having difficulty seeing Superintendent Cathcart as the dirty cop. It makes sense logically but a worm of doubt is slithering through my mind. I'm replaying my conversation with Stammo in my head. I know there's something I'm missing but my focus on Sam's kidnapping is blurring everything else.

I walk up the front path of Sam's fourplex and go down three steps to the door of the basement apartment below Sam's unit; it is inhabited by a sweet old lady with a penchant for cigarillos, the smell of which seeps up through the heating ducts and drives Sam mad. The lights are still on.

"Who is it?" she responds to my second ring.

"Mrs. Venes,"—I know her name from the

mailbox—"it's me Cal Rogan, Sam's ex-husband," I say through the door.

"It's late. I don't like opening the door after eight."

"I know. That's very wise. It's just that Sam is missing. I need to ask you some questions."

"You're a policeman, right?"

"Yes." My stomach clenches from the sadness that this may soon no longer be true.

The door opens and she peers at me over the security chain. "Hmmmm." The door closes and then opens wide. "Well you'd better come in. It's cold out there."

I enter directly into the living room, the smell of cigar smoke strong in the air. It is a museum of bric-a-brac: dolls; Hummel figurines; old china that I don't have time to look at.

"You say Sam's missing?" She looks like the thought frightens her.

"Yes. I need to ask you if you might have seen or heard anything earlier today, between four-thirty and five-thirty."

"No dear, I wasn't even here. I went out in the afternoon to have a coffee with my friend, Mabel. Then I went to the IGA to do my shopping. I didn't get back here until twenty past five."

"Did you see or hear anything out of the ordinary when you got home."

"Not really. It was getting dark..." she searches her memory. "Sam's lights were on. I remember that but nothing else. I was a bit angry you see, it distracted me."

Sam's lights were off when I was here before.

"Did you hear Sam leave?"

"No. I was listening to the last of the early news on TV while I made my dinner."

This feels like a dead end. I'm going to try the other two units.

"I really appreciate your help Mrs. Venes. I'm sorry to call so late."

"That's alright dear." She walks me to the door and ushers me out. She peers out into the night. "Of course, she couldn't have taken her car."

My antennae twitch. "Why do you say that?"

"Well, that's what I was so angry about, you see. There was this big truck parked right in the middle of the ramp into the underground parking. It was so inconsiderate. No-one could have got their car in or out of the parking."

"Can you describe it?"

"When I say truck, it was one of those big things people drive these days, half truck, half car. I don't know why people like them. In my day we were happy—"

"Do you remember the colour?"

"Yes it was black..." she thinks for a moment. "It

was a Cadillac. I remember I saw the crest on the back. My late husband Stanley always drove a Caddy. He said that it was better to buy quality where your family's safety was concerned."

My mind is full of the picture of the dark Escalade sending Stammo's skinny frame flying through the air. Almost trembling with hope, I ask her, "You didn't happen to see the license plate did you."

"As a matter of fact I did. I wrote it down when I got in. I was going to call a tow truck if it was still there at six o'clock. Would you like me to get it for you?"

"That would be wonderful." I can hardly keep the excitement from my voice.

She bustles through the living room and into what I assume is the kitchen and returns almost immediately.

"5163 TYK." She hands me the paper with the number.

"Did you hear or see it leave?"

"No, but after the local news finished at six, I went to check if it was still there but it was gone."

"Thank you so much Mrs. Venes, you have been extremely helpful."

"Any time, detective. I hope you find Sam. She is a lovely person. I'm very fond of her and Ellie."

She closes the door and after calling in the

number to Stammo, I make my way to the ad-joining basement suite. It is dark, quiet. On the third ring of the doorbell, the door of the suite above, next door to Sam's, opens. "What is it?" a voice calls down.

I look up and see a man looking over the rail of the porch to the upper units.

"Hi," I call up. "It's Detective Rogan. Sam Cullen's ex-husband. May I have word with you?"

"Sure." The voice sounds uncertain. "Come up."

I ascend the steps to the porch.

The door to the suite next to Sam's is open and the lights are on. The man is now standing in the doorway. To put him at his ease, I smile and extend my hand. "Hi I'm Rocky Rogan. I'm sorry to disturb you but Sam has gone missing and I'm trying to find out what happened to her."

Before the man can react, another man appears in the doorway behind him. He is tall, with a pleasant face and a shaved head.

"What's going on?" he asks.

"Says he's a cop. Sam's ex. Says she's gone miss-ing." He looks me in the eye. "Can I see some ID?" he asks.

My heart drops. These people may have some vital information but they are not going to give it to me unless I can prove who I am. I mentally kick my-self for introducing myself as 'Detective' Rogan.

Maybe I can bluff my way around this, though his face says he is not going to be easy to bluff.

I reach into my pocket and start searching for my non-existent ID.

"Wait a minute." The bald man has come out on to the porch. "Yes, I've seen you here before, bringing Ellie home or picking here up."

Both men relax and I almost collapse with relief.

"Come in. We'll help you any way we can."

They lead me into the hallway. It is the mirror of Sam's unit. In the living room, two women are sitting opposite each other at a table in the dining area. Cards are spread out in front of one of the women and there are small stacks of cards face down in the other three places at the table.

"Bridge night," the second man offers by way of explanation. "I'm Ed Hunt and that's my wife Cora about to go down in three no trumps doubled and vulnerable." He sighs and I smile as if I know what he's talking about.

His friend extends his hand. "I'm Pete MacAvoy and this is Alice. We live downstairs."

"So what's this about Sam?" Ed asks.

"I want you to keep this very confidential but we believe she has been abducted."

There is an indrawn breath from one of the ladies and an "Oh no!" from the other.

"I need to ask you if any of you saw or heard anything late afternoon or early today?"

"I was at work," Ed offers.

"Me too," from Pete.

All eyes go to the ladies.

Cora looks uncomfortable but says nothing. Alice furrows her brow. "I don't remember anything unusual."

I look at Cora but she maintains her silence. She is hiding something.

I let my eyes drill into her for a moment. "Did either of you see a black Cadillac SUV parked on the ramp down to the underground parking?"

"Black, no." It's Alice who answers. "But my brother's dark blue one was parked there at around five-thirty. He was dropping off some glasses we had lent him for a big party he had last Saturday. His fiftieth." She smiles.

With a feeling of hopelessness, I can feel my one clue starting to crumble. "Do you happen to know his license plate number." I'm clutching at straws.

"Not the numbers but the letters are TYK. I kid him that it's because he's a just an overgrown tyke."

So much for a connection with the women who almost killed Stammo.

"Was there anything else either of you could tell me?" Silence. "Cora?" I look directly at her again.

She looks down at the tablecloth. It's paisley and looks expensive.

"Sam is missing, I have to know."

She sighs. "Yes, of course. It's just that... well, you're not just a detective, you're her ex too. It's embarrassing." She is silent for a moment, then, "Her boyfriend was here. I saw him arrive at five o'clock. Ellen had just finished and it was starting to get dark, so I went to draw the curtains and I saw him coming up the steps."

"How did you know he was her boyfriend?"

"She introduced him to us on Saturday, didn't she Ed." Her husband nods.

"Do you know his name?" I ask.

"I knew you were going to ask that but I just can't remember. Can you Ed?"

"Not a clue."

"Did you see him leave?" I ask.

"No. I went straight into the kitchen to prepare tonight's dinner."

"Do you know what type of car he drives?"

They shake their heads.

"If you think of anything, please give me a call, especially if you can think of his name." I write my cellphone number on a page from my notepad and give it to Cora.

I know for sure whom I have to interrogate next.

49

CAL

Not even the throaty roar of the Healey's exhaust can smooth the convolutions of my mind. Things are coming to light but not a lot makes sense. If Sam's boyfriend is the kidnapper, then he is involved in the murders and in the probable money-laundering scheme. But how long has she known him? Terry Wright's murder was only discovered ten days ago. Why would someone befriend Sam on the off chance that they might have to kidnap her in order to shut me up? Anyway, *my* kidnapping last weekend should have taken me out of the loop.

I must be looking at this whole thing wrongly. At the centre of all this is a dirty cop. Because of his connection to Varga, Cathcart is the logical choice but—

Oh my god. I struggle to remember my conversation with Stammo. He said *Those women, in the black Escalade; the driver swerved out of her way to hit me. Why would she do that? Her priority was to escape. Maybe she was told we might be there and she was to kill me, or maybe both of us, if she got the chance.*

Driving with one hand and half an eye on the road, I dial VGH and get put through to Stammo's room.

"What?"

His voice is bleary.

"Nick, you reckon that those women were told to kill you if they got the chance?"

"Yeah."

"So who told them? We went to Michael Chan's house because I got a call from Grace Chan. Right?"

"Sure."

"So who knew we were going there?"

"That little weasel, Eric Street. He was working right there beside us when that call came in. D'you think he's the dirty one?"

"No, he's not senior enough to be our man."

"Maybe he's Cathcart's errand boy."

"Maybe, but someone else knew."

"Who?"

"Don't you remember, as we were leaving, Steve came in with the bottle for me to pee in. You took the bottle and said you needed to plan out an interview with me. Steve was right there with Eric. He might have asked Eric where we were going."

Stammo is silent for a moment. *"Are you saying Steve is our guy?"*

"It's possible. He's certainly senior enough to have altered the outcome of your two cases."

"But Steve!? We both worked with him for a bunch of years. I don't buy it."

"I just want you to think it through. We can talk about it later."

"OK, but my money's still on Cathcart."

I change the subject and fill him in on my interviews with Sam's neighbours, then tell him where I'm headed.

He asks a few questions and then says, *"Be real careful how you handle this next interview, OK. It is one you definitely do not want to blow."*

———

HE STEPS out of the shadows of a laurel hedge and he has the look. Hard. I've seen it so many times before but usually on the faces of career criminals. I don't see any sign of a weapon but I know one is there. If I were to make a false move, he would drop me like a rag doll.

"You're Rogan." Not a question. He has been briefed.

"Yeah."

"Just to double check, what is the name of the man who sent me here?" His voice has a strong English accent. A Londoner, I think.

"Arnold Young." I have known Arnold for over a quarter of a century but only learned his last name a year or so ago.

He nods and moves back into the shade of the hedge.

The door opens before the chimes complete their peal.

"Any news?" Sam's step-father looks ten years older than his three score and ten. His eyes are red-rimmed and his skin looks parchment-white.

The hope in his face collapses when I shake my head.

"I need to speak to Ellie."

His wife appears behind him. "It's almost mid-night Cal, she's fast asleep." All her years of dislike for me resonate in her voice. Her husband moves back to grant me ingress but she stands her ground.

"She may know where Sam is."

"How can she?" Her dismissive tone pushes all my buttons. "She was at school when Samantha went missing."

"Come in Cal." His arm gently encircles his wife. "Cal knows what he's doing, honey. Remember he's a detective." He moves her sideways. Her body moves but her scowl doesn't.

Without asking permission, I head upstairs to the spare bedroom and open the door.

"Is Mommy home?" a tiny voice asks.

"Not yet, sweetie." I sit on the bed and enfold her in my arms. I want us to be a family again. Ellie, Sam and me.

"I couldn't sleep. I kept thinking about Mommy. She has never missed picking me up from school. Never."

"I will find her, Ell. I promise you that. And you may be able to help me."

She looks up at me, her eyes trusting. "OK, Daddy, I'll try."

I cannot suppress the feeling that I am probably asking her to betray Sam's confidence. "Sweetie, the last time Mommy was seen, it was with her boyfriend." A tiny frown works its way onto her brow and her lips draw tighter. "I need to talk to him to ask him if he knows where Mommy is."

She looks down at her hands. "OK." The syllables are drawn out.

"Do you know his name?"

"Yes."

Silence.

"What is it, sweetie?"

More silence.

Then the flood gates burst.

"Daddy, I don't like him. He looks like you but he's not nice like you and he has this horrible dog. I love dogs but I'm afraid of *his* dog. I hate him. He thinks he's all nice but he's not. He's—"

A sliver of fear surfs my spine. "Ellie!" I grab her by the shoulders. "What's his name?"

She responds to the urgency in my voice. "It's Seth. I can't remember his last name."

The sliver of fear explodes into a thousand shards of electricity.

"Harris... Seth Harris." The whisper escapes my lips and Ellie nods.

My mind struggles to put this in context. Sam is dating the brother of Morgan Harris, the minister of the Church of the Transcended Masters. How can that be? I first learned that Sam had a boyfriend last Wednesday when Ellie was at my place. She told me Sam was out on a date. That was the day after Stammo and I made our first visit to the Church, two days after the discovery of Terry's body in the woods. Sam must have known him before... My mind snaps back to a phone conversation I had with Sam on the Monday night, the first day of the case. I clumsily asked her out for dinner and she kind of deflected my intent into a family dinner with Ellie.

"Ellie, how long has Mommy been dating Seth?"

She shrugs.

I need a date reference. "Do you remember Valentine's day? You stayed at my apartment that night and told me Mommy was on a date."

She nods.

"Was that her first date with Seth?"

"I don't know." Her brow crinkles. "I don't think so. The week before she had that horrible Roxanne come and babysit me and she wouldn't say where she was going."

If Ellie is right, Sam had been seeing Seth since before Terry Wright's death. That is either the biggest coincidence in the history of the world or something more sinister. I suddenly feel like I am being manipulated by forces beyond my ken. But now is not the time to speculate. I need to find Sam.

I kiss Ellie. "OK Sweetie, I'm going to go now and bring Mommy home." I know I'm writing a metaphorical cheque that I may not be able to cash. "You snuggle up and go to sleep and we'll be home soon."

She smiles. "I'm glad you're a policeman, Daddy." She does not know how much those words hurt. I smile back and leave, worrying about the impossible decision I have to make right now.

50

CAL

FRIDAY

I'm doing a hundred and twenty klicks along Oak. *Hold on Sam, I'm coming. I'll be there in five minutes. Just hold on, my love.*

Every instinct from my training tells me that I need to call in my former colleagues. Going single-handed and unarmed against a kidnapper is stupid. I want the strength of the VPD on my side but the kidnapper's words, during the call from Sam's cellphone, flap around in my skull. The caller knew I'm not a cop anymore. How did he or she know that unless someone in the department called them? Hell, I was only fired fourteen hours ago. I don't think I can put Sam at greater risk by involving anyone else. I have to go it alone... but I know I shouldn't. I need help here.

I press the button on my bluetooth headset.

"Call Nick Stammo." After three seconds I hear his phone ring. After three rings I check the clock in the Healey. After midnight. He's probably asleep.

"Yeah... what?" He was asleep.

I brief him on my talk with Ellie and my indecision.

"You're going up against that Seth character and his dog alone?" His voice is incredulous.

Frustration spills over. "Hell, Nick. Tell me who the fuck in the VPD I can trust with this."

He is silent, five seconds of silent.

"Yeah, OK. Point taken."

I hear a monitor beep in the background. *"You armed?"*

"No. They took my weapon when they canned me."

"What about a personal weapon? D'you have one?"

"No. It's illegal. We're in Vancouver not L.A."

He snorts. *"OK, you can be Mr. High and Mighty if you like but you need a weapon. You know my apartment building? Go there and wake up my landlady, Mrs. Van Vloten, she's in suite 103. Tell her to let you into my place. I'll call her and let her know you're coming. There's a Glock 17 in my bedside table, top drawer. Take it alright? If that dog so much as looks at you squirrely, double tap it's ugly great head."*

"Nick—"

"STFU, Rogan. Just do it. I'll call Mrs. V now. Remember, suite 103. Call me when you get to the Church."

He hangs up just as I pull up on the side street beside the Church of the Transcended Masters. I'm not going to take the fifteen minutes I need to go to Nick's apartment and back. I don't share his fear of BLZ and I don't want gunfire around Sam.

As I exit the Healey, I can feel the adrenaline. Not only am I going to rescue Sam but I am going to have a nice little chat with Mr. Seth Harris, without the shackles of the Charter of Rights and Freedoms. I'll start by *not* politely knocking on the front door. With that thought in mind I open the trunk of the Healey and remove a tire iron. It is a simple design: a two foot long bar, at one end a socket wrench for removing the nuts that secure a wheel, at the other end a screwdriver-like head for prying off hubcaps. It's of no use on the Healey, which has chrome knock-on wire wheels. I keep it in the trunk for other purposes.

The Church sits in a double lot, one house in from the side street. I walk into the alley that runs behind the houses and have a flashback to another alley in my former life—an alley in which I twice almost lost my life. I suppress a shudder.

Where the back of the lot borders on the alley, there are several trees and a labyrinthine tangle of bushes and shrubs dominated by wild blackberry thorns. I am grateful that it is winter, I doubt I could penetrate the cover in summer. Through the brush, I can see the back fence: seven feet high and topped by a tight coil of glittering razor wire. Beyond it, the house lies in shadows. No light escapes from any window. It has an abandoned aspect to it. I hate to think of Sam locked in there.

I scour the garden for any evidence of BLZ. In the cimmerian area behind the house I think I see a doghouse. In a moment I will know if it is occupied. Being as quiet as I can manage, I tread a path through the brush, crushing the plants beneath my shoes. Brambles cling to my pant legs and I hear an expensive-sounding tear. It is far less than the damage I am about to inflict on my leather jacket.

I reach the fence and examine it. There seems to be no sign of any security device. No terminals that might indicate electrification and no sign of cameras, bells or other telltales. It is close to freezing. I breathe out several times at different heights. The vapour of my breath shows no sign of any laser beams. Yet I can't be sure.

Holding my breath, I take off my jacket and drape it over the razor wire, lining side down, in the vain hope that not too much damage will show on the outside. No alarm sounds, which does not mean that no alarm has been tripped. I slide the tire iron into the back of my belt, praying that it will hold fast.

I climb the fence finding easy hand- and footholds in the chain links. The slight rattle of the fence is a scream in the still night. I freeze, waiting for the snuffle of a dog or the sound of an alarm.

Nothing.

Nothing that I can hear, anyway.

With my hands just below the level of the razor wire, I straighten up and curl forward so that my stomach is resting on my jacket. I feel the razor wire give under my weight.

Deep breath.

Again.

I roll forward and reach down with both hands, get a good grip on the chain link, and then flip my legs up and over the fence. I miss snagging a trouser leg on the razors but as I steady my dropping body, the fence rattles loudly. Way too loudly. I land, release my grip on the fence and drop into a crouch.

Silence.

Nothing moves but the steam from my breathing.

Am I doing the right thing here? Is Sam really in this house? Am I putting her more at risk by coming here? I smother twinges of regret that I didn't get some form of backup and that I didn't take the time to stop for Stammo's Glock.

Too late for any of that.

I make my way to the back door. As I get closer, I see a faint glimmer of light through a window to the right of the back door. Recalling the layout of the interior, I guess that the window is behind the black drapes that back the altar. On our first visit here, Seth and his dog appeared through those drapes and the back door was visible.

There are three wooden steps up to a tiny patio. In the dark, it is impossible to examine the condition of the steps. I put my foot on the first step and slowly transfer my weight onto it. It gives a little under my weight. Good sign: the wood feels rotten and less likely to creak.

One more silent step. I'm holding my breath. I let it out gently.

Two more silent steps and I am on the patio, the back door six feet away. I'm hoping that the wood around the back door is as rotten as the steps.

I reach behind me for the tire iron.

Creak!

The door opens and I'm flooded with light.

" Don't move an inch." I can just hear the woman's voice over the hammering of my heart.

As my eyes adjust to the powerful flashlight I see the silenced gun pointing at me. It's big, mat black, not your typical woman's gun. Her stance is professional.

"Put your hands behind your head."

I obey.

The flashlight and the gun move backwards,

"Follow me. Real slow."

She backs inside the house, away from the door and to my right.

I follow.

As I enter the house she backs away further to the right. We are behind the black drapes.

"Keep your hands on your head and close the door with your foot." She's definitely a pro.

I turn to my right, facing her. I don't want her to see the tire iron stuffed in the back of my belt. I hook my foot behind the door and push it closed.

The curtain to my left opens to reveal the inside of the Church. The woman holding the curtain open has her arm in a sling. The smile she gives is not pleasant.

"Go through," her partner with the gun commands.

I sidle into the room so that neither of them can see the tire iron.

The candles are not in use and in the harsh electric light, I see Sam.

She is sitting on one of the chairs, bound and gagged with duct tape.

She is not alone.

Two chairs away is another captive, also bound

and gagged. When I see who it is, everything is turned upside down as my mind races to integrate the new information.

"Step back."

I do as I'm told without taking my eyes off Sam. I smile what I hope is encouragement to her.

I take a good look at my captors. Both women are squat and hard-looking; they could be sisters. The one with the gun is slightly taller and has what looks like a knife scar on her right cheek, she places the flashlight on the floor and then carefully puts the gun in her partner's good hand; she smiles almost tenderly and rubs her partner's shoulder.

When she turns to me, her face hardens as she takes a plastic tie from her pocket.

"Slowly put your hands behind your back," she orders and I comply, trying not to show my glee at her stupidity for not checking if I have a weapon. My right hand takes a firm grip on the tire iron.

I weigh the odds. They are slim. The woman with the broken arm and the gun is ten feet away from me. My first thought is to throw the tire iron at the one with the gun, then grab her partner and, using her as a shield, propel her into the path of the gun. But a voice in my head, a voice with a Scottish accent, says, *Remember, Laddie, there's nae much moves faster than a bullet.* It's the voice of my old combat instructor at the Justice Institute—he's never let me down yet.

Throwing the tire iron is a non-starter; I need a better plan. Scarface starts to circle round to my right, if she gets behind me she will see my weapon. I rotate to my right, facing her, with my back to the other captives.

"Turn around!" she says but no sooner are the words out of her mouth than there is a crash from behind me. The woman with the gun turns toward the sound and as she turns, the gun pans away from me.

Instinct takes over.

In one motion, I pull the tire iron from my belt and take three fast strides toward her. Too late she turns back. Before she can level the gun, the tire iron descends and smashes into her right wrist. The sound of the gun spinning off across the hardwood floor is inaudible, masked by the woman's scream.

I spin toward her partner, she is exploding in the direction of the gun.

"You bastard!" she shrieks.

In a split second I can see that in a race for the gun, it is an even bet as to who will win. *When the odds are even, Laddie, do the unexpected.* I make a dash but hold back enough to let her get there first. When she bends down to pick it up, I will nail her with the tire iron.

But she senses my hesitation and reads my mind. She must have had the same instructor.

She turns fast and charges me, her face a mask of fury.

She's coming from my left.

There is no chance to get the tire iron into play.

My left fist snakes out and her nose runs right into it. In the second of extra time this gives me, I swing the tire iron hard and low and it makes contact with her knee. As she drops to the floor, I have all the time in the world... and I use it to summon up every ounce of strength to kick her in the head. She goes down like a rag doll.

I turn around to check on her partner.

She's gone.

A trickle of fear runs down my back. She was the one who drove Stammo down, despite having a broken arm.

I see a residual movement of fabric; she has disappeared behind the black drapes.

I quash the impulse to follow; she may have a broken arm and a smashed wrist but she may also have another weapon behind there.

I turn and take three paces toward the gun. It has come to rest under a chair in the second row. I kick the chairs out of the way and pick it up.

For the first time I glance toward Sam. The chair in which she has been tied is toppled over into the row behind her and several chairs are scattered around. She made the crash that distracted the woman with the gun. I burn to rush over and hug her but do not dare risk the time. I check the gun, a Smith and Wesson M&P 9mm; the safety is off—it's ready to rock and roll.

"OK, I'm armed now. You'd better come out." I shout the words. I am not going to enter the curtains to the right of the altar, through which she disappeared, but I need the flashlight that Scarface placed on the floor. I walk loudly across the hardwood floor to retrieve it. "If you don't come out I am going to start shooting through the curtains."

Silence.

I slip out of my loafers and stride soundlessly to the far left of the altar.

Deep breath.

In one motion, I sweep the curtains aside, step through and level both the flashlight and the gun down the corridor behind the altar. The woman is lying face down on the floor. I approach her and see that she is either unconscious or faking it. She is lying on the broken left arm and I can see that her right wrist has been badly damaged by my blow with the tire iron. If she wants to use a gun again, she will have to learn to shoot left-handed.

The instant of sympathy that I feel dissipates as I think of Stammo, at the hospital, sitting in his wheelchair, never to walk again. A desire for rough justice swells inside me. One bullet to the base of her spine would be a fair *quid pro quo*. I burn to do it. I can find a way to make the evidence support the use of the weapon. I move around her so that I am standing by her head. One bullet, fired at an angle passing downward through the spine will cause maximum damage without killing her.

Aim.

Breathe.

Hold.

We are all undone, unless the noble man have mercy.

The unbidden words deflate me and my burning anger dissolves in a flood of sanity. Like Stammo said, *You can't become a vigilante. It leaves you feeling too dirty.*

I take her by the scruff of her neck and drag her through the curtains into the main room. Her partner is stirring. Two quick strides and I kneel on her back. She is still holding the plastic tie. I snatch it from her hand and use it to bind her wrists behind her back. A search of her jacket pocket produces more ties. I use one to secure her ankles and another to secure her partner's ankles. I am loathe to secure the partner's injured hands but I remember the last time I counted her out; that error in judgment put Stammo in a wheelchair for life.

I take her injured wrist and bind it to the back of her leather belt. She groans as I do it but without regaining consciousness.

The scene is secured.

Now Sam is my priority.

As soon as I've released her. I will call 911. With a rush, I realize I've just solved three crimes. The attempted kidnapping of Michael Chan, the assault on Stammo and the kidnapping of Sam.

Although it is probably less than a minute since I entered the room, I am breathing like I have just finished a marathon. I go over to her and gently right Sam's chair. She is bound to it by plastic ties and is gagged with duct tape. I glance at her fellow captive and he is bound the same way... but to hell with him he can wait.

I look into Sam's eyes and instead of seeing relief I see fear.

"Mmmmmmm." She is trying to communicate, her eyes wide.

I reach forward to peel off the tape.

She shakes her head and looks past me.

"Mmmmmmm." She is frantic.

Electricity fires up my spine as I realize what she is trying to say.

I start to spin around and the world explodes in light.

51

STAMMO

Mrs V. is pissed at me.

"Detective Nick," it's what she always calls me, even when she's mad, "do you realize what time it is? It's nearly one o'clock and no, your friend has not been here yet. If he has any sense he is in bed, like we all should be. If he comes, I will call you OK?"

"OK, Mrs. V. Sorry to disturb you."

Fuck. Rogan can be such a smart ass sometimes; going into a situation like that without a gun is just plain stupid.

I phone him... no reply again.

Rogan's got to be onto something big. Kidnapping his wife to shut him up is a pretty big reaction. He's gotta be real close. That puts him in real danger. I gotta get him back-up.

But who? He's right, we can't trust anyone in the VPD. Anyone I might call could be the dirty cop. I hate to admit it but Rogan's right, it could even be Steve.

I wanna just go jump in my car and go after him. This fuckin' wheelchair. If only— Can't go there, a waste of energy.

What has Rogan unearthed with this *oboe* thing? He said the code could be used to steal people's bank account numbers and passwords.

If this whole thing is about drugs and banking then we are talking money-laundering... but how? The big problem for people laundering money is that if you deposit more than ten grand in cash into your bank account, the bank has to report it to the federal government. We've often wondered if some of the gangs might have opened hundreds of accounts and every day deposit just under ten grand into each of 'em but that would never work. For one thing, to open a bank account you need ID and an address for them to send statements to. On top of that, the bank's computers would spot all these accounts with cash going in every day. What you would need is thousands of accounts that you only used...

That's it!

Oh my God, that's it. You'd need thousands of accounts that you only use *once*.

They are using the *oboe* code to steal thousands of people's account numbers and passwords. Then every day someone goes and deposits just under ten grand in cash into a bunch of different people's accounts. As soon as the deposit is made, someone logs into that person's account using internet banking and immediately transfers the money out of the person's account and into the gang's account. If the bank's customer notices the transaction on their statement, they just assume that someone at the bank screwed up and deposited the money into the wrong account, then immediately corrected it and transferred it back out; no harm, no foul.

If they're doing this using just ten different accounts every day, that's just short of a hundred grand a day. That's thirty million a year. It's fuckin' brilliant is what it is.

I cannot wait to tell Rogan.

Man, I hope he's OK.

I try phoning him again.

52

CAL

I hear a moan... It's repeated. Not certain, but I'm pretty sure it's not me. "Cal?" I fight against the crazy glue holding my lids together and force open an eye.

Hardwood floor. Laminate.

"Cal... here."

Pain screams through me as I move my head.

I see feet.

Bound.

"Sam?"

I roll on my side. This time, the moan I hear *is* mine.

I look up at her. She is still tied in her chair but the side of her face and her clothes are drenched in blood. There is an ugly wound on her temple.

I struggle to sit up but my hand is impeded by

the gun in it. How did that get there? I remember having it but I don't remember dropping it. When I went to Sam, it was in my hand but I didn't have it when I was trying to remove the duct tape from her mouth.

Wait. She just spoke. I look at her face. Someone has removed the tape. I wonder why?

Gee, I am so tired.

I close my eyes.

"Cal! Stay awake."

Just five more minutes... please.

"CAL!" It is a shriek this time.

I am bolt upright now. The Smith and Wesson clatters on the floor.

I am infused with urgency and force myself to my feet.

Sirens. Just on the edge of hearing but getting close. Or is it just a buzzing in my head?

"Sam," I ask, "what happened?"

"I don't know," she falters. She looks around and horror fills her eyes.

I follow her gaze. She is looking at the other captive.

The sirens *are* getting closer. They are not in my head.

Seth Harris, Sam's kidnapper and erstwhile boyfriend, is still sitting, bound and gagged, three chairs away from Sam. But now he is different.

ROBERT P. FRENCH

"Sam, did Seth kidnap you and bring you here?"

"No... What? Kidnap? He didn't kidnap me. He brought me here but..."

The sirens are close. They're coming here. Thank God. VPD to the rescue.

I look at Seth. Three bullet wounds in his face have rendered him almost unrecognizable. Who would have killed him? I glance around. There is no sign of the women. Just Sam, Seth and me...

And my fingerprints on the gun.

"Sam. Who killed Seth?"

"I don't know. He wore a mask. He hit you first, then he hit me. That's all I remember."

The sirens wind down but through the frosted glass beside the front door, I see the strobe of red and blue lights. I look at Seth again and wonder why Sam and I are still alive. Why didn't the killer—

I hear the sirens of a second unit. Then a third.

And my fingerprints are on the gun.

If they follow procedure, one will take up a position at the back of the house.

In an instant I sum up the full import of what has happened here. My fingerprints are on the gun and I have fifteen seconds tops.

I go to Sam and take her by the shoulders.

"I was never here, Sam. Tell them everything that happened except for the fact that I was here. Do you understand?"

"But Cal, why sh—"

"Sam, listen. The VPD suspended me. My prints are on the gun."

I have no time to say more.

I grab the gun and stuff it in the back of my pants.

"Please Sam. I was never here."

I dash through the drapes, out the back door, down the steps in one jump and run to where my jacket is draped over the barbed wire. I grab the chain links but out of the corner of my eye, I see more red and blue strobing.

They are coming up the alley.

With a flick of the wrist, I flip my coat off the wire and cringe at the ripping of the expensive lining. Seven running strides take me to the south side of the fence, bordering on the next-door neighbour's back yard.

Gotta move fast.

Jacket over the wire.

As I put my foot up onto the chain link fence it catches something in the undergrowth. Something metal.

I hazard a quick look down.

It's a license plate. ZOA 1645. I mustn't leave prints. I lift it using only my palms on opposite edges and toss it toward the back steps where it will be seen by the uniforms when they check the back yard.

No more time. Climb the chain links. Lean over my jacket. Vault. Retrieve jacket. More ripping.

I run across the neighbour's yard and have no difficulty navigating the wooden fence that separates his property from the sidewalk.

Two deep breaths. Put on my jacket. Cross the street then saunter toward my car half a block away. Hands in pockets, playing the part of an insomniac local out for a late night stroll. As I cross the alley, I turn casual enquiring eyes toward the police car parked behind the church. I can't see whether either of the uniforms in the car is looking at me, maybe even recognizing me.

Both of the patrol officers get out of the car at the same time. One looks at me. I fight to suppress my flight reflex and just stand and watch for a moment.

He walks toward me as his partner turns his attention and his flashlight to the back of the church. If he recognizes me I am in real trouble.

He's young, probably fairly fresh out of the Institute. I don't know his face. He probably doesn't know mine.

"Can I help you sir?"

"No Officer. I was just out for a walk, couldn't sleep."

He just looks at me. He's good.

I do as he expects and fill the silence. "What's happening at the Church?"

"Are you a member sir?" there is suspicion in his voice.

For a moment I freeze. I assume he means am I a member of the Church but he could be asking if I'm a member of the VPD. Maybe he has recognized me.

"No Officer." True for option one and false for option two.

"OK sir," he says. "Probably safer if you carry on with your walk."

I nod. "Good night Officer."

I casually continue my stroll.

As I approach the Healey, I want to look back to check if he is still watching me, which will look suspicious to him. But getting into the car would give the lie to my out-for-a-walk story.

I turn and start to cross the road and, like a good pedestrian, I look both ways.

He has gone.

I spin back and get in the Healey.

I turn the key and press the starter button.

British cars built in 1964 don't like cold and damp. It doesn't start.

I pull out the choke about half way and try again. It doesn't start.

I check the mirror. The young patrol officer is standing at the entrance to the alley, looking at me.

I try again, resisting the impulse to floor the gas pedal and flood the ancient SU carburettors. It doesn't start.

I can feel the gun stuffed under my belt at the back, my fingerprints all over it.

The officer steps toward me.

Choke full out. Quick prayer to the sports car gods. Press the starter button.

It roars into life. The officer breaks into a run

I accelerate away hard, hoping that he can't read my license plate.

53

CAL

I'm sorry, sir. You can't go in there."

I'm in no mood for this but I respond with all the politeness I can muster. "I'm afraid I have to."

"Sir, it's two-thirty AM. Patients need their sleep. If you persist, I will have to call security."

"Do what you feel you have to, nurse. I have to see Detective Stammo on official police business."

She is clearly undecided, so I stalk off to Stammo's room.

Stammo is in bed but sits up as I enter the room. Either he was awake or he is the lightest sleeper with the fastest reactions that I have ever encountered.

"What happened?"

No foreplay, straight to business.

I tell him about the trip to the Church of the Transcended Masters. When I tell him about the two women being there he utters the one expletive that makes me cringe. His eyes narrow when I tell him that when I arrived, Seth Harris was a captive too. This turns to incredulity when I get to the part where I woke up and found Seth Harris dead.

"So did he kidnap Sam, or what?" he asks.

"Well, she said he didn't. She said he brought her there."

"So Seth could be an innocent bystander in all of this?"

"I thought that for a moment but as I was leaving through the back yard, I stumbled over a license plate. It was the license plate from the blue truck that killed Marguerite Varga. The plate that was stolen from the old couple in Langley. Seth has to be the one who hid it there. He was the only—"

Then it hits me.

Where was Morgan Harris?

Was she also being held as a captive in some other part of the house or is it possible that she was somehow in league with the two women? It's a long shot but...

I tell Stammo my thoughts.

He thinks for a moment then shakes his head. "It's possible but that means that she would have been in on killing her own brother. I don't really buy that."

I think back to my meetings with the Reverend Morgan Harris. Despite her childlike appearance she was certainly capable of manipulation. But it is a long step from manipulation to fratricide. Except...

"We only have her word that he was her brother. What if he's not? He certainly looks nothing like her."

Stammo chuckles. "No, if he looks like anyone, it's you. Maybe he's *your* brother."

I try to smile as I suppress the unpleasant feeling this gives me. Given my family background, nothing's impossible.

Nothing's impossible.

Maybe Morgan Harris *is* involved with the two women. Maybe it was *her* who knocked me out, after I put the women out of action. Sam said that it was a man but a man in a mask. Maybe she just assumed it was a man; I will need to talk to her some more about this. What if—

"Wait a minute, Rogan." Stammo breaks into my train of thought. "You just said that when you found the license plate, you were leaving through the back yard. Why the hell were you doing that?" His eyes narrow. "You didn't call it in?"

"I thought you called it in."

"Me? No."

"Someone did. Patrols were arriving as I left over the back fence."

"Then why the hell did you run?" I can see his anger rising.

I have been debating internally whether I should tell him about waking up with the silenced gun in my hand and Seth with three bullets in him. We have only been collaborating for little more than twenty-four hours; prior to that we were colleagues by circumstance, enemies, or at least rivals, by choice.

He sees my hesitation and his face reddens.

I decide.

I tell him everything.

"Where's the gun now?"

"Under the driver's seat of my car."

"What the... Geez, Rogan." He looks off, deep in thought, grinding his teeth. "You shouldn't'a run," he says. "You shoulda' stayed 'til the patrols got there. You may have had the gun in your hand but they would have swabbed you for GSR and found out it wasn't you that shot the gun." His anger at me is ratcheting up.

"What if whoever shot Seth, did it by putting the gun in my hand while I was unconscious? I'd have gunshot residue all over me."

He is close to shouting now. "That's no excuse—"

"Besides, I didn't have any time to think it all through. It was a split second decision. I just ran."

"No excuses, Rogan. You've gotta turn that gun in. It's evidence. Plus you're the only one who knows that those two were there."

"Sam knows. She'll have already told them."

He sighs in exasperation and the fact that I know he's in the right doesn't help.

"Yeah, but she doesn't know who they are. She doesn't know they're the ones that did this." He looks down at his useless legs under the blankets and uses the same expletive. "And don't go fucking around with the evidence, no wiping off your prints or scrubbing your hands."

He's right of course. It was a poor decision to run. I just have one question.

"Who should I go to? If I go to the one who's dirty... I mean it could be Superintendent Cathcart, or Steve, or anyone. There could be more than one."

"Just find out who's assigned to the case and go to him."

"OK, I'll go first thing in the morning."

"Not a good idea. What if they find evidence that you've been there or what if Sam tells them. Then you'll be on the defensive. You need to go to them now."

I don't know why I'm being so argumentative. "They won't and Sam won't."

Stammo lays back in the bed and rolls on his side facing away from me. He sighs and gives a dismissive gesture with his hand.

A great wave of tiredness washes through me.

And something else.

A cycle is in process, a cycle with which I am altogether too familiar. Everything I have done in the last twenty-four hours is wrong: when Inspector Vance suspended me, I should have stood up for myself and told him what happened, told him why my system was full of heroin; I feel guilty about spending yesterday afternoon in bed with Elizabeth Wright while Sam was being taken by Seth, kidnapped solely because she's my wife; guilty that I didn't contact VPD and get them involved when I guessed where Sam was being held; angry that I was too stubborn and stupid to accept Stammo's offer of his gun—if I had done so, Seth Harris would be alive and the women who crippled Stammo would be under arrest.

The Beast is calling me. He wants me to erase the memory of the last twenty-four hours. I may have licked the physical withdrawal with Tylenol but this need is greater than mere physical pain.

Just one little ten-dollar flap of heroin.

Just one.

"Sorry," I say as I turn and go. I don't know if I'm saying sorry to Stammo, or to Sam, or to Seth Harris or to myself and Ellie for what I am afraid I'm going to do next.

54

CAL

The eight items are all laid out neatly in front of me on the kitchen counter.

The night that surrounds me is quiet. There are no traffic sounds, no hints of music or TV seeping through the apartment walls. Quiet. Peace and quiet.

But inside me a screaming battle is raging.

I dissolve the powder on the spoon in the sterile water and the Beast screams his victory.

The cheap plastic butane lighter, neon green, plays its flame under the spoon, its soft roar a ripple in the silence. Inside, Ellie begs me not to do it, *don't go Daddy, I don't want to lose you,* she cries.

The liquid reaches boiling point and froths silently. *Cal, I want you back,* Sam's voice is seductive. *All you have to do is stop using.*

Don't worry, Rocky. You can have it all, roars the Beast.

I drop the little cotton filter into the spoon and put the needle into it, bevelled side down. As I draw the liquid up into the barrel, I see their faces: Stammo, Steve, Inspector Vance. They are silent. They just look, except for Stammo. He shakes his head and turns away.

And the Beast just laughs.

I tie the surgical elastic around my left bicep. A vein rises and I swab it with the alcohol wipe.

I know this is the point of no return. I know where this path leads. I don't care.

The voices inside stop.

Even the Beast—he knows he has won.

I take up the needle.

A face.

A child's face.

The eyes are bloody, damaged in some way, but I see the rebuke in them. It cuts into me. His mind reaches out to mine. He cannot speak, there is a cross carved over his mouth.

Please, his mind says, *please speak for me.*

"Noooooooooo!"

That voice was mine.

———

THE SOUND of the bell cuts through the labyrinth in which my dreams hold me captive.

I reach out and slam the alarm's snooze button.

But that's not it. The bell rings again.

I creak out of bed, pull on my pants, discarded on the floor last night, and go to the door.

The peephole shows Steve. What the—

I open the door and the other actors are revealed. Sarge and two patrol officers of the large variety. Definitely not Hotspur's *velvet-guards*.

"Would you come with us please, Cal?" It is not the request that the words imply.

Steve follows me back into my bedroom and stands silent while I get dressed. My mouth is screaming for a glass of water but I dare not go into the kitchen. If Steve follows me there, he will see my drug paraphernalia, left lying there last night after I somehow managed to squirt the precious liquid down the drain.

"What's this about, Steve?"

"Let's talk about it when we get to Gravely."

As we head back toward the front door, I go to grab my leather jacket from the hall closet but remember the state of the interior lining. Instead, I grab a black pea-jacket. Steve holds the door open for me. I walk through, relieved that he didn't want to look around, relieved that he did not see my drug gear, the jacket or...

But that's short-lived.

In addition to Sarge and his boys, the hallway now holds a three-man forensic team.

I look at Steve. He pulls a paper from his pocket and opens it. I have seen enough search warrants to recognize this as one.

Busted.

———

I HAVE BEEN SITTING HERE for almost three hours. It's par for the course. I was chartered and warned and asked to wait. Steve came in once with two bags of my clothes. "What items were you wearing last night?" he asked; I pointed them out and he left me alone with my water, and a Tim's donut, kindly supplied by the VPD.

Although I am itching to be gone so that I can track down the Reverend Harris, it has given my some thinking time and I know why I'm here. At first I thought that maybe Sam had told them but when I thought through every moment of my time at the Church, I remembered the flashlight, covered in my fingerprints... and the fingerprints of the woman who had the drop on me. And when I left the Church that fresh-faced young cop could have got my license plate. My arrest was inevitable.

Sitting here as an outsider, I wonder if I will ever

fit in again. Especially after what Stammo suspects: *My liege, beware; look to thyself; Thou hast a traitor in thy presence.* I could be in the same building as a dirty cop who is undermining the work of the department.

"Sorry to keep you waiting," he says as he walks in and takes a seat opposite me. I can see the reflection of his back in the two-way mirror; he has a bald spot taking over the crown of his head. I never noticed it before.

"I want you to tell me everything you did from about midday yesterday."

I'll start with a lie. Midday yesterday, I was paying a visit on Harold Varga. Let's see if *he* knows about it.

"After lunch, I went to see Elizabeth Wright—"

"What did you do at lunch time?" he asks.

"I had a sandwich at home."

His eyes narrow. "You didn't go and see Harold Varga?"

Gotcha. "Yes, but how did *you* know that, Steve?" I ask.

I watch him like a hawk. He doesn't answer immediately; he just looks at me but I can tell that options are being examined and decisions reached.

"I'll ask the questions here," he says.

Bad answer.

"OK, yeah. I did go see Varga."

"Why? You'd been suspended. You had no business going to see him."

I shrug. "I had a theory about Terry Wright's murder that I wanted to check out."

He doesn't ask me what my theory was. This is strange because Steve is a good interrogator; he rarely leaves stones unturned.

"I'm telling you right now, Cal, you are on suspension. Do not involve yourself in the Department's affairs anymore. Do you understand?"

"Sure, Steve, I understand." I understand the order but will ignore it. If Terry Wright can beg me to speak for him and can get me to resist the lure of heroin, I'm not about to abandon the investigation into his death just for the sake of the Department's standard operating procedures.

"So why'd you go and see Elizabeth Wright?"

Part of me wants to say, *"So we could screw each other's brains out,"* but good sense prevails.

"I wanted to talk to her about her husband's associates."

"What did she tell you?"

"Nothing of any use." Nothing at all in fact.

He looks at me long and hard. "OK, then what."

"Then I went home and thought about the case and that I'm probably going to be fired."

If they ask me to hand my Blackberry back, they are going to be able to check the GPS and find out that I was at Elizabeth's all afternoon. Thoughts of the afternoon stir my body.

"And you were home all evening?"

"No. At six o'clock I got a call from Ellie's after-school care to say that Sam hadn't shown up to collect Ellie."

I tell him everything that happened except for two things: my conversations with Stammo about there being a crooked cop in the VPD and having a gun in my hand when I woke up and found Seth Harris dead.

He takes it all in, asking the occasional question.

As I'm telling him about leaving through the back garden of the Church of the Transcended Masters, an officer from Forensics walks in with a report in a blue file folder. She hands it to him and leaves.

He scans it quickly and I can see disappointment on his face. I hope that he can't see the relief on mine.

"No GSR on my clothing, eh Steve?" I guess.

He neither confirms nor denies but I'm pretty sure I'm right.

"Why does Sam deny you were there?"

"I told her to."

"Why?"

"I didn't want you guys to know I was there."

"Why?"

"Sam was having an affair with Seth Harris. With Harris dead, it makes me a suspect."

"Yes, it does."

"Let's cut to the chase here, Steve. You know I didn't kill him. You also know that the search warrant didn't turn anything up... like a murder weapon." I feel the heat rising in my face as I think what the search warrant did show up: evidence of heroin which, ironically, I didn't use.

"Also, the flashlight on which you found my fingerprints had some other prints on it, didn't it?"

He nods.

"Whose?"

"I'm not at liberty to tell you that."

I blow up. "Come on Steve, you know and I know that it was one of the women who tried to kidnap Michael Chan, the women who put Nick Stammo in a wheelchair for the rest of his life. Who the fuck are they?"

"I'm sorry, Cal, that's sensitive information. I can't share it with you." He stops and thinks for a moment then continues, "One, because you're suspended and two because you are using again."

"It just happens that—" I start to protest, to tell him that I didn't in fact use last night... but what's the point?

I try to suppress a sigh. "OK, Steve. Either arrest me or let me go."

"I have other questions for you."

"You can ask my lawyer. Am I under arrest?"

He is silent.

"I thought not." I stand and leave the room but before I can close the door behind me he says, "Cal, wait."

I turn.

"There's a Police Board disciplinary hearing into your status with the Department at nine Monday morning at Gravely Street. Make sure you're there."

Hiding the turmoil, I hold his eyes for a moment. "See you around, Steve."

As I head down the corridor to the elevator, I pull out my Blackberry and make the call I would have made first thing this morning if I hadn't been rousted out of bed by Steve.

"Hi, this is the Cullen residence. May I ask who's speaking please?" Ellie's voice sounds very grown up.

"Hi Sweetie." I feel the glow that always comes from speaking with her.

"Hi Daddy." Her enthusiasm brings a huge grin onto my face. Her voice becomes muffled... *"It's OK Grandpa, it's my Daddy."* ...then back to normal. *"Where are you Daddy?"*

"I'm at the police station but I really need to talk to Mommy right now. Is she there?"

"Yes, I'll get her for you. Then we can talk after, OK?"

"You got it." I hear the sound of the phone being put down.

I enter the elevator and it takes me to the ground floor. As the doors open I see a uniformed female member trying to calm an irate citizen who is clearly not happy about something. Something about this tableau triggers a memory and Steve's words to me come rushing back, spawning an idea.

It's a crazy idea but something about it feels *so* right. I need to talk to Stammo and ask him if—

"Hi, Cal." Her voice sounds tentative.

"Hi Sam, are you OK?" I hear her mother's voice in the background. I can't hear the words but the tone is condemnatory.

"Ye-es." I'm pretty sure this means no. *"I need to speak to you Cal. Ellie and I are about to head home. Can you meet me there in half an hour?"* I hear a distinct grumble from Sam's mother in the background.

I check my watch.

"Sure, Sam. See you then."

I will have to wait to expound my theory to Stammo until after I have seen Sam.

55

SAM

It feels good to hold him so tightly. The three of us are hugging in the hallway in what Ellie calls an all-ee-in-together. "Thanks for finding me, Rocky," I say. I feel close to tears but I don't know if they are tears of gratitude for his rescue or tears of shame for what I have to do now.

"Thank you, thank you, thank you, Daddy," Ellie chimes in. "You said you'd bring Mommy home and you did."

We hug a little longer, all of us unwilling to break the spell... but I do.

"Ellie, honey, can you go upstairs and play in your room for a while so Daddy and I can have a talk?"

She looks at me... then at Rocky... then she

smiles. "Sure, OK, Mommy." She runs upstairs giggling.

I limp into the kitchen; the stress of the last twenty-four hours have aggravated my MS. Rocky follows and sits on one of the bar stools at the counter. "Thank you so much for rescuing me, Ca—, Rocky." I want to respect his desire to be called by his nickname but I don't always remember.

"Hey..." he leaves it hanging, embarrassed.

"We need to talk," I say and set about making coffee; it will allow me to speak without looking at him.

"Do we ever. First thing is when did you—"

"Wait!" I cut him off. "Me first."

He shrugs.

"Last night, after the police came, they took me to the Main Street station and I met with Steve. Among other things, he told me that you were suspended because you tested positive for heroin. Is that true?"

He stays silent until I turn and look at him. "Yes." He looks me straight in the eye. One word. No excuses. That's different.

"Are you still using?"

"No."

"Are you sure?"

He snorts. "You can't ever be sure, Sam."

This is very different. Where are the promises,

rationalizations and assurances which were so quick to his lips in the past?

A psychiatrist told me that the reason I was so drawn to Cal was a deep-seated need to cure him of his addiction as redemption for the fact that I couldn't cure my father of his. Am I grasping at straws?

I turn back to the counter, pour beans into the grinder and inhale the smell.

"What happened, Cal?" I can hear the break in my voice.

"I'll tell you everything," he says.

I listen intently to his story. As ridiculous as it seems to believe that his colleagues kidnapped him and shot him full of heroin, I know he is telling the truth; there is a quiet conviction in his voice that chips away at my resolve. When he tells me of how Ellie's phone call stopped him from using and how his need to speak out for the murdered boy stopped him again, I can feel the tears prickling my eyes and all my former resolve is gone. The two things that he loves, his daughter and his job, were what stopped him from using. I stop halfway through pouring boiling water into the coffee press, turn and throw my arms around him.

I am sobbing uncontrollably and I have no idea why. Since the day my father died, I hardly ever cry. I didn't even cry when I lost George. The last time I remember crying was in anger and frustration at Cal that time I thought he had put Ellie in danger.

He holds me tight and kisses the top of my head and I feel safe.

After what seems an age, my sobbing subsides. I look up and grin at him through my tears. He has tears in his eyes too and I feel myself melt. I look at his lips and know we are going to kiss. I want him so badly, right now. I slide my fingers into his hair and pull his head toward me. His eyes start to close... then snap open.

I feel his neck stiffen. His hands take my shoulders and gently push us apart.

There is a look of infinite sadness in his eyes.

"I need..." He clears his throat. "Sam, I need to ask you some questions."

I want to kiss away his sadness. "Later." I pull him back toward me.

He resists. "Not now, Sam!" His tone is like a slap in the face and I feel myself flinch. His rejection cuts into me.

"How long had you been seeing Seth Harris?" he asks.

Mention of Seth's name physically hurts me. The image of regaining consciousness and seeing his face, shattered by gun shots, bursts onto the screen of my mind, making my stomach churn. Why would he ask me this? My God he's jealous? I can feel the storm fuelling an anger in me.

"I don't see what business that is of yours." I step back from him and turn back to the coffee press. I feel overwhelmed by the hurt of his rejection and the horror of Seth's death. The hurt starts to turn into something else, something that I know I can't control.

"He's mixed up in the two murders I'm investigating. He kidnapped you to try and force me to back off. But the thing is, I think that you have been seeing him since before the first murder."

My amazement at his statements throws fuel on the fire.

"Seth is *not* a murderer, you idiot, and, for your information he did *not* kidnap me."

"Sam, you have to tell me what happened." It is delivered like an order.

"Matter of fact Cal, no, I don't," I yell. "I told the police everything yesterday. I don't have to tell *you* anything."

"Sam, please. They're going to blame Terry Wright's father for his murder and he may not have done it. I know it's—"

"Mummy why are you shouting at Daddy?"

Ellie is standing in the doorway holding her favourite Teddy bear. She only ever hugs him when she is upset or frightened. All my anger dissolves in an instant.

"It's OK, honey," I try to scoop her up in my arms but nearly lose my footing. Damn this MS. "I'm just a bit upset because of something. It's nothing for you to worry about."

"Mommy's right, sweetie," he steps in and picks her up. "Sometimes people speak loudly when they're upset." He gives her a big kiss on the cheek and she smiles and hugs him. "Just go and play for a bit longer so that Mommy and I can finish what we were taking about."

Oh, no. I am not in the mood to be interrogated right now.

"Actually, Cal," I say, "Ellie and I are going to have lunch now. Didn't you say that you had to get back to work? Let's talk another time."

He looks back and forth between Ellie and me.

"Sure," he says. "Hey, El, you know what day it is? It's Friday. So when I come back later to take you to my house, Mommy and I can talk again then."

Before I can check myself, the words come out of my mouth. "Ellie won't be going to your place this weekend. Not until you know for sure whether you're going to use again."

When I see the reactions on their faces, I hate myself for my cruelty.

56

CAL

The irritation that was in evidence during the early hours of the morning is gone. When I walk through the door of his room, he knows I'm on to something.

"What'cha got?" he asks.

I tell him about my arrest then try out my theory.

"One of the reasons they knew to pick me up was that my fingerprints were on a flashlight I used while I was at the Church but the person who used it before me was one of the women. So I asked Steve if they got a hit on her fingerprints. He didn't tell me that it was none of my business or that he was not prepared to discuss it, he said, 'that's sensitive information.' So I started to wonder what he meant by *sensitive*. What if those women are cops or maybe ex-cops that would certainly qualify as sensitive."

"You got a better look at them than me, did they look familiar to you?" he asks.

"No. But they would have been from out of town. They carried themselves like cops. The one who caught me on the back porch: she had the look and the way she handled the gun, her stance, everything said 'cop.'"

He nods. Then one of his rare smiles, more of a grimace really, steals slowly across his face. "If they were working under the direction of whoever in the Department is dirty, they gotta know each other pretty well. So you gotta ask the question *how* do they know each other. If these broads are from out of town and we can find out where, then all we gotta do is look at the history of the senior people in the department and find out who has worked in the place they're from. We'll have found our dirty cop."

"I like it," I say. "It's all a bit of a long shot. Lots of *ifs* but let's check it out."

He grabs his phone from the bedside table and dials.

"Hiya, Steve," he says. "How's it going, eh?"

They chat for a bit and I notice that he is playing with something in his right hand. I can see a slim gold chain and he is rubbing his fingers against whatever is attached to the chain.

When he has finished a not-wildly-hopeful up-date of his medical condition, he asks, "Any news on who the broads were who did this to me?" He winks at me but then all vestiges of humour wash out of his face. "No?... What'cha mean *no*?..." The hand holding the gold chain is clamped, the knuckles white. "So why did you tell Rogan that you knew who they were but that it was *sensitive* information?" I can imagine Steve on the other end of the line, backpedalling like mad. A look of dis-gust comes to Stammo's face. "Just 'cause I'm in a wheelchair, doesn't mean I need to be *protected* from the truth, Steve. Who the fuck were they?" he spits out.

He listens for a long moment. "You're kidding... What?... National fuckin' security? Are you kidding me?... Yeah... OK, OK, I won't... Right. See'ya, Steve."

He slams down the phone. "Cover up," he snorts at me.

"Yeah, but by whom?"

"Steve says when they ran the fingerprints, the computer said 'Access Denied'. He says he took it upstairs but nobody had the authority to override it, some national security bullshit. That's what he *says*, anyway." Skepticism is strong on his face. "You're right, Rogan, they're cops."

"Yeah but how do we find out who they are?"

"I dunno." He looks downhearted, not a very Stammo-like look.

Downhearted. That's a good description of how I feel. On the way here and all through our conversation, I have been repeating Sam's last words to me. Will she really keep Ellie from me?

I shake off the thoughts. "OK, Nick, why don't we go back to the basics, the murders of Terry Wright and Marguerite Varga. Let's go through what we know and what we suspect.

"Terry was killed on Sunday night, he was in the care of his step-father, Mark, but both parents agree that he likely climbed out the window of his bedroom. Terry had been repeating the *oboe* code and had taught it to his friend Michael who was also chanting it. The code is an encryption key that can be used to hack into people's internet banking. Terry probably got it from Mark's computer.

"Next day Marguerite Varga is killed in a hit and run. The stolen license plate from the truck which killed her was in the undergrowth behind the Church of the Transcended Masters. The killer could be either Seth Harris or even the Reverend Morgan Harris. The connection between the killings is that Mark Wright used to work for Harold Varga and their wives both went to the church.

"So there are at least two possible motives for the killings: Terry's murder might have been ritualistic, committed by a person or people connected to the church or it could have been to silence him from repeating the code and then made to look ritualistic to point the blame at the church."

"Or there could have been another reason," Stammo interjects. "Mark's wife Elizabeth was having an affair with Seth Harris. What if Mark Wright killed Terry to punish Elizabeth and then mutilated the body to look like one of the pictures in the church to point the finger at Seth."

"Or it could be a double motive," I add. "Mark was mad at Terry for spouting off about the code and killed him to shut him up *and* to punish Elizabeth and try and blame the boyfriend Seth." And as I say the words an alternative presents itself and erupts a queazy feeling in my stomach.

"Makes sense," Stammo nods. "Terry repeating the code must have been a problem; why else would those women try and kidnap Michael Chan too? They didn't want him repeating the code to us so that we could figure out what..." His voice trails off and I can see an ah-ha moment forming on his face. "Who knew that Michael was repeating the *oboe* code to us?" he asks.

"Apart from you and me, I asked Mark and Elizabeth Wright if they knew what O-B-O-E meant; they might have guessed that I got it from Michael. I don't think we ever mentioned it to Varga, until noon yesterday. On our second trip to the church, I looked at a picture that had some musicians in it and asked Morgan Harris if one of them was playing an oboe. Michael's parents would have known, they might have told someone that we were interested in the stuff that Michael was chanting."

"Call 'em and ask." Stammo's tone is urgent. I call Grace Chan and ask her; she tells me that she didn't mention it to anyone and is pretty sure that her husband didn't either. She promises to call be back if he did.

"Anyone else?" Stammo demands.

"No... Not that... oh, wait a minute. My buddy Damien. I emailed and texted him about the code as we were learning about it but he couldn't have anything to do with all this."

Stammo nods. "So... that just leaves you and me, Steve, Inspector Vance and Eric Street. And of course, Superintendent Cathcart would have heard about it from Steve or Vance. Unless Mark Wright worked out that you knew about the code from Michael Chan, the only people who could have known that Michael Chan was about to spill the beans on the *oboe* code are in the VPD and the only one to have a connection with this case is the Superintendent; every damn' time we talk to Varga he makes a point of telling us that he's friends with Cathcart. What if Cathcart's in this money-laundering scam with Varga and Wright. He was in the drug squad and organized crime before he got his promotion to Super. I'm guessing Cathcart ordered those women to kidnap Michael and get me off the case. If he was the one who got the guys to pump you full of drugs, he knew that he could have you fired at any time. With Michael out of the way and you and me off the case, the whole deal about *oboe* would just go away."

He's right. Cathcart is the logical choice. He was also one of the members of the senior staff who never wanted me back in the Department. Stammo's analysis is good, except...

"Sally Wilkes," I say.

"What about her?"

"When I got the *oboe* code in full from Michael I sent it to Damien Crotty and to Sally Wilkes in Forensics. If Damien figured it out in a few hours, surely Sally Wilkes or one of her guys would have done the same. So why did we never hear back from Sally about the code?"

Stammo's eyes narrow. He grabs his phone and dials. After a moment he frowns. "Hi Sally, this is Nick Stammo. That code that Rogan sent you, did you ever find out what it is? Give me a call back." He hangs up. "Voicemail," he grunts.

"OK, back to the original murders. The odds are that Terry was killed by Mark Wright to stop him repeating the code and maybe to punish his un-faithful wife into the bargain." Again I get the queazy feeling but ignore it and press on. "What about Marguerite Varga? Why was she killed? Let's assume that it was Seth Harris who drove the blue truck that killed—"

"Wait a minute." Stammo is holding up a finger. "Before we get on to that, here's a question. If the *oboe* code was being used for money-laundering, whose money was being laundered? You got Varga, a suit, and Wright, a computer geek. What did they do? Work out this money-laundering scheme and then go wandering around the streets to find a gang to sell the idea to? That doesn't make a lot of sense."

"What if it's like this?" I surmise. "We know Varga's a gambler. What if he's got a gambling problem and owes some money to some crook running an illegal operation. The crook tells him that he can work the debt off if he can use his po-sition at the bank to launder some money for him and some of his friends. Varga knows that he can only do that with the help of some IT expertise and contacts his former employee and IT whiz-kid, Mark Wright. Together they hatch up a plan to steal the *oboe* code and launder millions of dollars through the accounts of thousands of unsus-pecting bank customers. When Terry starts spouting the *oboe* code, Varga gets cold feet and tells them he wants out, so they kill his wife as a warning."

Stammo is silent for a while. When I attempt to speak some more, he holds up a finger. "You know what doesn't make sense to me is that anyone would care if Terry started reciting the *oboe* code. He was a ten year old kid with a mental handicap; who would take any notice of him? Who would ever know that the gibberish he was gabbling would be a secret bank code?"

He's right. Why would anyone care? And why would anyone care that Terry's friend Michael was also chanting the code and care enough to try and kidnap him?

We sit in silence. What is it about this case? Nothing makes sense.

The reminder on my phone beeps.

But before I leave the hospital I have to do one other thing: ask a question, the answer to which I dread hearing.

57

CAL

Please, please speak for me. The words refocused me onto my mission to speak for Terry Wright and bring his murderer to justice. They gave me the strength to resist, once more, the call of the Beast. I pray something gives me the strength to get me through this latest trial.

For the last four years, I have dreamed of getting back with Sam. Earlier, thoughts of Elizabeth made me pull back from her and, as the other William said, about a hundred years after the Bard, *Heaven has no rage like love to hatred turned, Nor hell a fury like a woman scorned.* I love Sam and I want her but, heaven help me, I have been sleeping with Elizabeth and I have feelings for her too... strong feelings. But what I've just learned needs to be resolved with her right now. I take a deep breath and relax my hold on the steering wheel. The speedometer tells me I'm doing ninety-five k's down Granville Street. I ease my foot off the gas; no need to kill myself on the way to see her. I need to—

There is a ping in my Bluetooth headset. I press the button. "Rogan."

"Detective Rogan, this is Morgan Harris."

All my senses go on alert.

"Hello, Reverend Harris, how may I help you?"

"I've been away for a couple of days. I just got back and there is crime scene tape over my front door. I had your card in my purse so I thought I should call you."

"Are you inside the building?" I ask.

"No. I didn't think I should cross the tape. I rang the doorbell several times but there was no-one in there."

Curiouser and curiouser, Alice. It is twelve hours since the murder of Seth Harris; the place should still be crawling with forensic techs. I check the dashboard clock. Twelve forty-five. I suppose they could be taking a lunch break, but not likely.

I am consumed with a desire to talk to the Reverend Harris. I need to find out if she is in league with the female ex-cops or just an innocent bystander. But I need to proceed with caution; this may be a trap.

"Where are you right now?" I ask.

"On the steps of the Church."

I need to get her away from there. If the forensic

team come back... Wait a minute, if this is a trap... OK, I can kill two birds with one stone.

"Do you know Max's Deli at Oak and 15th?"

"*Yes.*" She drags the word out, unsure.

"Meet me there in ten minutes," I say as I execute a U-turn on a busy Granville Street.

"*But I need to get into the Church, right now.*"

I have to head that off. "It's a crime scene, you can *not* go in there. If you do, you will be subject to arrest."

She is silent for a moment and I wonder if she is, in fact, already in the building.

"*OK. Ten minutes.*" She hangs up.

———

I PARKED the Healey on Montcalm Street, a block behind Max's, walked down the alley between 15th and 16th and entered the Sunrise Market through their back door. I stand looking through the front window onto Oak. Everything looks normal. No parked cars with occupants. No sign of a Cadillac SUV. Only one elderly lady with a Scottie dog in a carrier is standing at the bus stop and three high school kids in private school uniforms are sitting on the bench opposite; I wonder what they are doing out of school at one o'clock. No-one is loitering outside any of the shops.

Clear.

I hope.

I walk out of Sunrise and take six brisk steps north and check through Max's window. Morgan Harris is sitting alone at a table with a designer coffee in front of her. I go in.

It's busy, as always. There is no sign of the women I have come to think of as ex-cops. I scan the faces of the servers. None of them are showing any sign that something abnormal is going on, for example two tough-looking women hiding out in the kitchen.

I walk over to her table. Big smile, extend hand. "Reverend Harris, thank you so much for meeting me here."

Her smile seems genuine. It makes her look like a fifteen year old again.

She is wearing jeans and an angora sweater under a sheepskin jacket, with a matching angora beret perched on her head, a retro 1960s look. She looks stunning. For no reason at all, I think of Sam.

"Detective Rogan." She shakes my hand. "Why—"

I cut her off. She is sitting facing the front door. "Would you mind changing places with me?" I ask.

Her confusion seems genuine. "OK... Sure."

She gets up and sits in the chair opposite. Now I have a clear view of the front of the deli and across

Oak Street. In addition, she is shielding me from any bullet that an accomplice might fire through the window. Paranoia or self-preservation?

"Detective Rogan, why is there crime-scene tape at the Church?"

I have two goals for this interview: one, find out if Morgan is with the good guys or the bad guys and two, find out everything I can about her brother, Seth, if indeed he is her brother. And that's the place to start: the unexpected question.

I ignore her question. I still have what I hope is a pleasant smile on my face. "Reverend Harris, I need to ask you, is Seth really your brother?"

I watch her like a hawk. She frowns, looks askance at me and says, "Detective Rogan, there is crime-scene tape all over my Church. Instead of asking me silly questions would you please explain to me why." There is a mounting anger in her voice.

Time for some truth. "Yes, I will," I say, "but before I answer your question I need to ascertain whether you are involved in the crime that has been committed."

I give her my long, hard stare, honed over thirteen years as a detective and I see uncertainty in her eyes.

I press the advantage. "Is Seth really your brother?" I repeat.

"Yes, of course. Why would you ask that?" Unless I'm being fooled by those big blue eyes and little girl look—which is always a possibility—I am pretty sure that she is telling the truth.

"We have reason to believe that he is involved in some criminal activities."

There is a flicker in her eye but it is not surprise.

"What sort of activity?" she asks.

I bring out everything connected with the case, "money-laundering, assault," she flinches at that, "kidnapping, perhaps even murder."

Her eyes are wide, but from worry not incredulity. As I look at her, tears start to well up. She sniffs and looks up at the ceiling, blinking. She is breathing fast through her mouth, fighting for control. "What has he done now?" she asks.

"He's done things before, hasn't he?" I counter.

She nods.

"I think you had better tell me," I say as gently as I can muster.

She sits, looking at me, her expression temporarily unreadable... by me anyway. She looks away and bites her top lip then starts to nod slowly as she comes to some conclusion.

Across the street a number seventeen bus pulls away from the bus stop. The lady and her dog aboard. The high school kids are still there, laughing at something.

"He's my brother. I can't just..."

I go for the soft spot. "Reverend Harris," I say "we believe your brother has committed some crimes that may put your Church in a very bad light. The only way you can avoid the possible crushing publicity is by being truthful with me."

She is on a razor's edge and I have no idea which way she is going to tip.

"OK... OK, yes, it's time." She takes a tissue from her purse, wipes her eyes, blows her nose and takes a deep breath.

"You have to understand, it's not Seth's fault." She looks at me imploringly.

I want to tell her how many times I have heard that line from the family members of hardened criminals but instead, I smile encouragement and say, "Why is that?" It's often best to let a cooperative witness go at her own pace.

"Our father was a very strict man and he was very hard on Seth, abusive even. So Seth rebelled. He went against everything that my father stood for. As a teenager, he drank alcohol and took drugs—both of which are strictly against the teachings of our Church—and the more my father lectured him, the more he did it. Then he started hanging out with an old school friend of his, a guy named David. David was a charismatic kind of guy, dressed ex-tremely well, drove a very fancy Mercedes and al-ways seemed to have a lot of money to throw around. I never knew for sure, but I always suspected that David was involved in the drug business."

Her description sends an electric shock through me.

"Did this David have long, wavy, blond hair?" I ask.

"Yes. Why, do you know him?"

Blondie! Sidekick to my former nemesis and a man who once came very close to killing me. "Maybe. Sorry, go on."

"Anyway, Seth started working for David. I didn't see a lot of him during that time but when I did, he always had a lot of money and drove nice cars. I'm not sure if he worked for David in the drug business but he *was* involved in something illegal."

"How do you know that?" I ask.

"Our father died almost two years ago, leaving his ministry in my hands. I invited Seth to the funeral and to my surprise, he came, even though he and our father had not spoken to each other in several years. After the service, we had a reception in the Church and David turned up with two other men. One was very smooth, well dressed, polite, but I got a really bad vibe from him. I don't remember his name. The other was a slob with long greasy hair, bad teeth and a paunch."

This conversation is exceeding my expectations.

I have a pretty good idea who the smooth, well dressed one was. He's currently sitting in Millhaven prison.

"At one point during the reception, I was feeling a little overwhelmed, so I went through the curtains beside the altar. There is a door behind there that leads into the back yard, so I went out for some fresh air. When I came back, I was about to go back in through the curtains when I heard Seth's voice on the other side of them. He was having a conversation with the other three. I know I shouldn't have..." she looks at me and a gentle flush suffuses her cheeks, "...but I couldn't resist eavesdropping on them. The smooth one was saying something like, 'You've done well by us Seth. I want you to become my liaison with Dominic here. You'll bring his cash into our system and at the same time do any other little favours that he might ask of you.' Then they must have moved away from the curtain, because I couldn't pick out their conversation from the other voices in the hall. I'm sorry."

"Don't be," I reassure her. "It's very useful information." Understatement of the year! "What can you tell me about the one with the long greasy hair?"

"He was very creepy. I really wished that Seth hadn't brought him to the Church. I kept feeling that he was undressing me with his eyes. I couldn't work out how Seth, David and the smooth one could have anything to do with him."

"Was there anything else about him that you might have picked up, other than his name?"

She shakes her head.

"About how old was he?"

She shrugs. "Forty, forty-five?"

"Can you remember anything else distinctive about him?"

Again she shakes her head. I've got all I'm going to get about the fourth member of Seth's little cabal.

There is more I want to ask her but a little worm of guilt is slithering in my gut. I'm pretty sure that Morgan Harris is an innocent party and it is clear that she doesn't know that her brother is dead. I should tell her but there are some other things that I need to find out first.

"When did Seth come to live at the Church?"

"Not long after my father's funeral."

"You said that he always seemed to have a lot of money and drive expensive cars..." She nods at this statement. "So why would he need to come and live with you?" I ask.

"I asked him to. After my father's death, I was feeling a little nervous about being there by myself, so I asked Seth if he would come and live there." She gives a rueful smile. "I was also kind of hoping that he would take an interest in the spiritual life of the Church. In my heart, I knew that he is probably involved in the drug business and I wanted him to change. Becoming a church member could give him a whole new *raison d'être*..." She frowns and her eyes go to her left as she thinks. "I've just remembered something. The guy with greasy hair, Dominic, he spoke with a Québécois accent; he was French Canadian."

I file that away for later. "Go on with what you were saying," I invite her.

She shifts in her seat and looks hard at me. "Is my brother the reason that there is crime scene tape on the Church?" There is an assertiveness in her voice. "Do you have him in police custody?"

Feeling like a lowlife, I say, "No we don't have him in custody. But I need to know something about his relationships with women—"

"I'm not prepared to answer any more of your questions until you tell me what is going on." The assertiveness has become steely. I am going to have to come clean with her but not here in a crowded restaurant.

"Let's go." I stand. "I'll tell you everything but not in here."

I check the street outside as I open the door for her. The school kids are gone. Oak Street looks un-usually deserted. "Where are you parked?" I ask.

"Just round the corner on fifteenth."

As we turn the corner, she asks, "So, what *is* this all about, Detective?"

Before I can answer, I see it.

Adrenaline pumps into my system and I automatically reach for the gun that is no longer there.

I grab her shoulders and move her toward the curb where there is a green Subaru parked. "Crouch down beside this car and don't move until I say it's OK." My tone brooks no argument and she complies.

I strain to look through the windshield of the metallic grey Cadillac SUV, parked four vehicles ahead of us. As far as I can see it is empty. I scan the sidewalks on both sides of the street but there are no signs of the two female killers. It means nothing. They could be crouching behind a parked car. I look back toward Oak Street. Nothing.

"What's going on, Detective?" Morgan's voice has a distinct tremble in it.

"Wait here," I tell her as I crouch and run across the street. I stop behind a red van parked on the other side.

Taking a deep breath, I sneak a look along the sidewalk. Empty, except for an teenager walking a white Pomeranian.

I do another scan of the area before walking back to where the Reverend Harris is crouching.

"We have to get out of here fast," I tell her.

"Where are you parked?"

"There," she says, pointing. "The grey Escalade."

An electric shockwave passes through me. Have I made a huge mistake in my assumption of Morgan Harris' innocence? She owns the car that was used to try and kidnap Michael Chan and has put Stammo in a wheelchair for the rest of his life?

"That's *your* car?"

"Yes."

I reach down, take her arm and help her to her feet. Without letting go, I walk her to the Caddy. As we get closer, I can see there is a dent in the front fender on the driver's side and the headlight glass is mazed. The grill shows evidence of the predation of Stammo's bullets.

"How did that happen?" I ask, pointing to the damage.

"I don't know. Seth took the car earlier this week; he said that he damaged it parking."

"When specifically?"

"I don't know. Monday, I guess."

The day Stammo was injured.

"Did Seth often take the car?"

"Sometimes. It was my father's so Seth figured that he could use it anytime he wanted."

A thought hits me out of the blue.

"Did your father buy it new?"

"Yes, from a dealer in Richmond, a parishioner."

Why didn't Eric Street's inquiries to Cadillac dealerships turn up that juicy little fact? I file the thought away.

"Why did Seth take it on Monday?"

"His Jaguar was in the shop and he said he had a meeting and didn't want to go in his old pickup."

This is just getting better and better.

"What pickup?"

"He's got an old pickup that he's had forever. It was his first vehicle. He loves that truck."

"A blue Ford F150?"

"Yes. How did—"

"Where is it right now?"

"He keeps it in our neighbour's garage. But why do you—"

"Let's go." Gently leading her by the arm, I start along the street toward Montcalm, where the Healey is parked.

"What about my car?"

"You can't use it; it's evidence."

"Evi—"

"We'll take my car. Come on."

"I don't think I want to go with you." She tries to pull per arm out of my grip.

"Your choice. Either you come with me now or I arrest you formally and we wait for a paddy wagon to arrive and take you into custody." I take my phone from my pocket.

Now I am going to find out if she knows.

"Arrest me? ... Arrest me for *what*?"

She doesn't know I'm no longer an active-duty cop.

"For a start, accessory to grievous bodily harm. Your vehicle was used to cripple a police officer."

Her eyes widen in shock.

"So do you want to come with me now or take a ride in a paddy wagon?"

She looks like a little girl again. "Come with you."

As we walk to my car, I call Stammo and give him two tasks.

This has been some interview. Some of the pieces are clicking into place, but, yet again, for every answer there is a new question. Maybe our next stop will provide some clarity.

———

THERE IS a silence to the church. It's almost two o'clock. Time for any forensic team to be back from lunch. It confirms my suspicion: the team has been pulled back. By whom I wonder?

Morgan unlocks the front door and I peel back the yellow tape so that we can enter. I go in first. The scene is still similar to when I hightailed it out of here last night. The chairs around where Sam was held are still scattered everywhere, as is the chair in which Seth died: it is lying in a brown pool, the metallic tang of blood still noticeable.

I turn back to her. "When you come in, I want you to walk straight toward the stairs. Do not look toward the altar, is that understood?"

She nods. I refused to talk to her during the short drive here, which has fuelled an anger she does nothing to hide. However, she does follow the letter of what I asked. I follow her up the stairs to her little office on the floor above.

"Please sit down," I say with as much gentleness as I can muster.

She is about to refuse but detects the change of tone in my voice and expression. A look of worry crosses her face; she may have a glimmering of what's to come. She sits.

I take a deep breath and stare at the bookcases. She is probably going to need the comfort of her religious beliefs now.

"I'm sorry to have to tell you this but your brother was murdered last night."

I see the shock crash through her body. Her eyes are stricken and a strangled "No" escapes her lips, yet it is not a denial. She collapses forward, her head on her knees as sobs wrack her. I sit on the corner of her desk and leave her to her grief; I know that nothing I say or do can help her.

If what she told me is true—and I have no concrete reason to doubt her—on Monday, Seth took her car, switched the license plates and gave it to the women for the purpose of kidnapping Michael Chan and, incidentally, crippling Stammo. Then, four days later, the women tied up Seth in the Church and shot him, putting the gun in my hand. Then it hits me that it was probably them who called the police; they wanted me to be caught red handed. Nice try.

So what happened during the week that turned Seth and the women from collaborators to victim and killers? As I turn it over in my mind, a new idea emerges. The thing that gets most people killed in the drug business is gang rivalry. What if the man in Millhaven prison, who Seth clearly worked for, is not in collaboration with the dirty cop in the VPD. What if they have become rivals. If the dirty cop wants to take over control of the Vancouver drug trade, then killing Seth destroys the main link between my nemesis and the outside world.

My train of thought is broken by Morgan; she has stopped sobbing and is sitting back on the couch looking at me. "The wages of sin," she says. "Just as they are portrayed in the black pictures on our walls."

She reaches forward and takes a tissue from a box on the corner of her desk. A box probably put there for the use of troubled parishioners during counselling sessions. "Who killed him?" she asks as she dabs her eyes.

"We don't know yet," I lie. "Has he had any visitors here over the last week?"

"No."

"Have you had any new people at your services recently?"

"No."

Out of the blue, it hits me that I haven't asked one very obvious question. "Where were you yesterday evening?"

"Surrey. I was at a meeting of a group of independent churches. We met at the Sheraton in Guildford."

"When did you leave to go to this meeting?"

"Wednesday evening. I got back from Surrey an hour ago, when I called you."

"Can anyone corroborate that?" I ask.

"Yes," she says curtly. She pulls out her phone, checks the contact list and gives me three names with their phone numbers. "I was with them the entire time."

I write down the names and numbers.

"I would like to check on Seth's room, look through his stuff, see if there are any clues to who might have killed him. Is that OK with you?"

She nods.

Good. Her permission obviates the need for a search warrant. Not that I could get one. But if it comes to legal proceedings, I am still officially a cop and an agent of the Crown and, as such, I would need to be covered by a warrant if I did not have her consent.

"I'll show you his room."

She leads me up to the next floor.

On the landing, half way up, I find my nose wrinkling at a familiar smell. It gets stronger as we approach the closed door to Seth's room.

Morgan reaches out a hand to open the door but I gently take her wrist and stop her. Positioning myself between her and the door thus blocking her view of the room, I open the door.

The smell is stronger. It is accompanied by a buzzing.

Another question is answered.

Lying in the middle of the floor is the body of BLZ, Seth's giant dog. A small business of flies swarms around the bullet hole drilled between his eyes.

There is no sign that the forensics team was in the room. I wonder why? Whatever, I'll take advantage of it and do my own search first. Then I think we will go and take a look at Marguerite Varga's murder weapon in that neighbour's garage.

58

CAL

As I get out of the car, I scan the street and see him, sitting in a nondescript Honda Civic, strategically parked so that it provides him with the best view of the approaches to the building. His hard gaze catches my eye and he nods. Although I know they are *but attended by a simple guard*, I have complete faith in their safety.

My time with Morgan Harris took up all of the afternoon and I know I should be seeing Elizabeth right now, to ask the question that has been upsetting my stomach since seeing Stammo.

I did not call ahead for fear of rejection.

Sam opens the door a crack. "Rocky," she says. Neutral. Neither spurning nor welcoming.

"I need to explain a couple of things," I say, "and... well, apologize."

She steps back and opens the door wide.

She leads me into the kitchen. The house is quiet.

"Where's Ellie?"

"Out." Her tone is distant. "She's having a sleep-over at Sarah's house." She takes a breath and shakes her head. "I meant what I said. I can't risk having her with you if there is any chance... any chance at all of you still..."

She turns away from me.

What I hope are the right words form in my mind. "Sam—"

But the words are cut off by a cry that racks her body. I stand transfixed as she wraps her arms around her shoulders and gives herself over to her sobbing. I want to reach out and wrap her in my arms but fear she will draw away from me. *Thus conscience does make cowards of us all.*

No!

Too much of my recent relationship with Sam has been rooted in fear.

But no more.

I reach out, take her shoulders and, although I feel her tense, I gently turn her around. I wrap my arms around her and she sobs into my chest.

After what seems an age, her hands unlock from her shoulders and her arms envelop me. We stand, locked together in the middle of her kitchen, until the sobbing subsides.

We stand in the moment. Neither one of us wanting to speak, but eventually I must.

I know what I have to ask her; I just have to find a way to do it.

She looks up at me and I want to kiss her tear-stained face, kiss away the pain in her eyes. For the thousandth time, I kick myself for not kissing her when I was here earlier but the thought still gives me a stab of guilt as I think of Elizabeth.

"I love you," she whispers.

My heart skips at the words that I haven't heard from her lips since Ellie was eighteen months old, the words I have longed to hear for so long now. I want to shout, 'Oh God, Sam I love you so much.' Shout it at the top of my lungs. Logically, I now know that my relationship with Elizabeth is doomed but should I do the honourable thing and talk to her and end it first before recommitting myself to Sam?

My second of hesitation is translated in Sam's eyes, making the point moot. I feel her start to pull away.

"Sam, I *do* love you," it doesn't sound like I wanted it to sound.

"But...?" she asks.

Time for the truth. "But... I've been seeing someone."

"Oh." A single syllable overflowing with meaning. "Who?"

"Someone involved in the case."

"Oh."

"Sam, I love you. I've never loved anyone else. I just need time to break it off with her before I can..." The words sound callous, even in my ears.

She pulls away from me and sits down on a bar stool at the kitchen counter. "So why are you here?"

"To ask you some questions related to the case."

"I thought you were suspended."

"I am but I'm working the case with Nick Stammo. He believes that the investigation is being compromised by a dirty cop in the department." Her eyes widen in surprise. "You said that Seth Harris didn't kidnap you. What happened?"

At the mention of Seth's name her surprise turns to sadness.

"Seth called and came over to my place, he was going to take Ellie and me to dinner, only he had left his wallet at home. We went over to the creepy church where his sister is the minister and he went in. I was outside in his car. He took a long time. I was starting to get worried about picking up Ellie from after-school care, when I saw this woman come out of the front door. She came down to the car and crouched down by my window. I had never met Seth's sister, so I thought it might be her, but the woman pulled back her jacket and showed me that she had a gun in a holster. She signalled me to get out of the car, took my arm and lead me into the building. I'd never been in there before. Another woman, with her arm in a sling, was there and Seth was tied up in a chair, with a gag over his mouth. They did the same to me. Then the first woman went through my purse, took my cell and disappeared for a couple of hours. When she came back she had a man with her but I didn't see his face. They all went to another part of the house and I could hear talking. They were there for hours. They just left Seth and me tied up in the main room.

"I was starting to get really thirsty and then I heard a pinging noise. Suddenly the two women appeared and one went behind the curtains; next thing I know, you're coming into the room at gunpoint. You know the rest."

I wonder what it was that triggered the women to choose that moment to turn on Seth?

"Can you tell me anything about the man?" I ask.

"No. When he first came in, the woman with the broken arm grabbed my hair and told me to keep facing the curtains. Later when he came in and attacked you, he was wearing a ski mask."

"Was he tall... short...?"

"Average height really." She looks upward, reviewing the scene with her photographer's eyes. "His body shape was mesomorphic. He was very powerful looking. He hit you with a baseball bat; I was sure he'd killed you and then he came over to me. I was petrified. He laughed and hit me with the bat and that's all I remember until I came to and you were lying on the floor groaning and Seth was dead." The memory has drained the blood from her face.

"When did you meet Seth?" I ask as gently as I can.

She sighs. "Is that really relevant?" she asks.

"Yes, it is. I'm sorry to tell you this Sam, but Seth was involved in the drug trade."

"I can't belie—" She cuts herself short.

"How did you meet him?" I ask.

"He called me on my work number and said he wanted photographs of his dog. Said the dog was terminally ill and he wanted something special to remember him by. He came to my studio and after the session he invited me out for coffee. We had a few dates, nothing serious, and then..." her voice tails off.

"When did he first call you?"

"It was the last Wednesday in January. I remember because he called in the evening and Ellie was with you. We did the photo session with BL the next day."

More than two weeks before Terry Wright was killed.

I tell her the name of the man, locked up in Millhaven prison, upon whose orders Seth was operating.

When the initial shock wears off, I see the humiliation wash over her face. "He only dated me to get to you," she whispers.

"Not true, Sam. I think he dated you because he really liked you. It was those women who made use of the relationship to try and get to me." I don't really believe this but I can see that it makes Sam feel a lot better.

I seize the moment. "Sam, I love you. There's nothing I wouldn't do to get you back. All I want is to be a family again, with you and with Ellie."

She puts her arms around me. "I love you too. I want the same things that you want but now, twice, Ellie and I have faced real physical danger because of your job. I don't know if I can live with that. And I don't know if I could live with the constant fear that you may start using again."

Rationalizations crawl all over my mind like maggots on a corpse. I push them down and say, "I can't make any guarantees on either count."

"I know," she says and kisses me on the cheek. "Do you want to stay and have dinner?"

I can't think of anything I want more.

"I can't, Sam. There are two things I need to do first."

Both of them may yield missing pieces of the puzzle that is this case. One of them could do much more.

59

CAL

I have seen grizzly bears smaller than this guy and less tough looking, too. He fills the doorway. I wait for him to speak. He doesn't.

"I'm here to see Dominique Dufresne." I'm betting my looks are going to get me inside.

Nothing. No movement, word or deed.

"I'm Eli Harris." I decided to use a vaguely biblical first name.

Still nothing.

"Seth's brother."

His eyes narrow as he examines my face and there is a hint of recognition. I'd like to play poker with this guy but he doesn't play; he just guards the door.

"Seth's dead," he says.

News travels fast.

"I've been sent to see Mr. Dufresne by our mutual friend back east."

This is outside his very limited terms of reference.

He moves backwards enough to let me into the hallway. He closes the front door behind me.

The entranceway is large, more like a luxurious office lobby. There are expensive chairs along one wall; with a flick of his head he indicates that I should take one. I do.

Two doors lead into the interior of the house. He opens one to reveal a staircase going up, which he takes, closing the door behind him.

Opposite from where I am sitting is an expensive looking office desk made of what I suspect to be burled maple. On the desk are a keyboard and two expensive looking Apple computer monitors. Sitting behind the monitors is an expensive looking woman in an expensive looking navy blue suit.

She is drop dead gorgeous.

She ignores me utterly.

Sam's words, 'I love you,' keep running through my mind and I have replayed our time together this afternoon again and again. I am having difficulty focusing on anything else.

Stammo told me it took him about half an hour on his laptop, logged into the department's computers, to find an address for Dominique Dufresne, described by Morgan Harris as the greasy-haired criminal, named Dominic, with a French-Canadian accent. He has a criminal record in Québec for illegal gambling and is listed in the land-titles database as the owner of this large house nestled among the high-rises of the West End. Stammo thinks I shouldn't be here.

The third door in the lobby bursts open and a well-dressed man of around fifty walks into the room. He does not look entirely happy and, unless I am missing the mark, is not entirely sober. He walks to the desk and the receptionist's face breaks into a smile that is the very picture of convent-girl innocence. His look of annoyance melts in her glow.

From his pockets he pulls handfuls of casino chips, red, green, yellow and white, which she takes from him and professionally sorts into different piles. As she takes the last handful, her hand grazes the back of his. He smiles broadly.

She counts the value of the chips out loud to him, seventeen thousand, three hundred and twenty-five dollars, and he nods. She taps a code into the keyboard and there is a discernible click as a drawer in the desk slides open. She withdraws eight bundles of notes, all of different sizes, and hands them over. He tells her about how great it would be if they could go out together sometime. She looks around, with a soupçon of fear in her eyes and tells him that she would love to but it is just not allowed by the management. Her regret at this injustice just oozes from every pore. He sighs and walks to the outside door. She examines the right hand monitor then taps another code into her keyboard and a clunk indicates that the door is unlocked. She gives him a flirtatious wave and a wink as he disappears.

"Big winner?" I say.

Her look changes fast and now has all the warmth of a penguin's buttocks. Her dismissive grunt says maybe that seventeen grand was not winnings at all but the remains of the much larger amount with which he entered. Still, she sent him away happy. Good marketing.

The volume of air in the lobby reduces as the muscle re-enters. Another flick of the head indicates that I should climb the stairs.

I do.

He follows.

I am met at the top by a badly-dressed man with a paunch and a head of long, straggling, greasy hair. Monsieur Dufresne, I assume. True to the ethos of the establishment, he says not a word but turns and leads me into an office, every bit as plush as Harold Varga's, but decidedly less tasteful. There is a huge grandfather clock behind a desk similar to, but larger than, the one below.

Dufresne slouches in his chair and puts his feet up on the desk. His shoes are new, the soles unscuffed.

There are no guest chairs so I just stand there like a kid in the principal's office.

He closes his hand across his stomach, interlacing the fingers. They look as soft as a woman's hands, the nails manicured and polished.

The door closes quietly and I don't know on which side of it his pet grizzly is positioned. I want to check over my shoulder but that would indicate nervousness; these guys can smell fear.

"Seth never said 'e 'ad a brother." His accent is definitely French-Canadian.

I smile knowingly. "I'm sure there are a lot of things that my brother kept from you."

"Yeah, well 'e's dead now, so I guess I never will know 'is little secrets."

I shrug.

He looks nervous. "So... your boss sent you." It is partway between a statement and a question.

Now I can play on his nervousness: I look at him long and hard then nod.

"Are you...? Does he...? I mean you don't expect our deal to be still in place, right?" he asks.

"Why wouldn't it be?"

He licks his lips and looks over my shoulder. I hear a deep breath being drawn behind me.

The grandfather clock chimes the quarter hour.

"Dese new guys... they've taken over. I mean even Varga's taking orders from them now. They killed your brother and 'is messenger boy. I gotta deal with them. All due respect to your boss, but 'e's in jail, so are most of 'is men, and will be for a while. You're the only one not in jail, right?"

"Am I now?" I smile. I need to keep him off balance.

I hear a creak in the floor boards behind me.

"Look," he says. "I'm caught in the middle 'ere. I got no complaints about what you guys did for me but dese new guys... I mean they sent one of those broads to my house. My home! She talked to my wife and kid, threatened them if I didn't cooperate. I gotta go along with them. Varga refused at first and look what happened to 'is wife. He hasn't been back 'ere to gamble since. I lost one of my best customers dere, I can tell you."

I try and keep the surprise off my face. It may have been Seth's blue truck that killed Marguerite Varga but maybe it wasn't him driving it.

But there's something else that doesn't ring true.

"Why do you care about the woman? It looks like you can take care of yourself." I use this as an excuse to turn and gesture toward grizzly. He is leaning against the door, cleaning his nails with a wicked looking knife. His eyes meet mine and I have a great deal of difficulty taking my attention off him to turn back to face Dufresne. I think about Stammo's Glock; it would feel pretty nice nestled under my arm right now.

"One of them's out of commission now anyway," I add.

He doesn't react to this news but I think it's a surprise.

He licks his lips again. "There's stuff you don't know," is all he says. I wonder what stuff he is talking about. It must be big if it scares him.

Again he looks over my shoulder at grizzly. I can feel the hair on the back of my neck but I know if I show weakness by turning round again, this interview will be over.

"Who does the pick ups?" I ask.

"What d'you mean?"

Uh-oh, have I said the wrong thing? Oh well, in for a penny in for a pound. Let's go for broke, "Who comes and picks up the money you want laundered?"

"One of the broads."

"How do you get in touch with them?"

"I don't. They come regular. Same as your brother did."

"What days?"

His eyes narrow with suspicion. I screwed up. If I were Seth's brother, I would know the days.

Another creak in the floorboards sets up a tingling in my spine.

He holds his silence for six ticks of the grandfather clock, then, "I've said too much already," he grunts. "Look, tell your boss I'm sorry, I really am. I liked working with you guys but there's nothing I can do. I think you'd better go now."

"Just one last question. How did they—"

"I'm not saying no more. Are you going to leave or...?" He nods toward the giant behind me.

I shrug.

"Thanks for your time," is all I say.

I feel a huge paw lock onto my arm.

I tense, my mind feeling the bite of the knife in his other hand.

"Let's go," he grunts, leading me toward the door.

He leads me down the stairs, across the lobby and out through the front door. The receptionist doesn't even look up from her computer monitors.

As I walk down the path, I rejoice in being out of there. I may not have got the answer to the last question I was about to ask but I'm pretty sure I know what it was.

However, there is now another question to which I don't have an answer.

60

CAL

I dread why I'm here. Apart from anything else, it's close to midnight and I am exhausted; I have had three hours sleep in the last forty. My mind is still spinning from my meeting with Stammo; we have put it all together, except for one thing, and that one thing is ostensibly why I'm here. Ostensibly. The other reason is too confusing to contemplate.

She hugs me tightly. Too tightly.

"It feels like an age since I saw you my love," she says.

My love? I might have felt good about the words before my time with Sam this afternoon but she's right... it does seem like an age since yesterday afternoon.

She takes my hand and pulls me toward the bedroom. When I resist, she looks at me, the hurt clear in her eyes.

"Elizabeth, I'm here in an official capacity." I feel like the lowest of the low.

"Oh." A single syllable carrying multiple meanings.

We go into the living room and sit together on the sofa.

"Do you remember the thing Terry was repeating, 'Oboe is blood'?"

"Yes, but they were just nonsense words."

"No they weren't. It was the start of a computer code called a private key. The code belonged to the Toronto National Bank where your husband used to work. We believe that he was using the code as part of a money-laundering scheme."

"Oh. So that—" She cuts herself off.

I wait for a moment then say, "Go on."

She bites her lip and avoids eye contact with me. She stares into the distance, looking like she is wrestling with a big decision. After a full minute, she shrugs and then sighs. "I was going to say 'so that's where the money came from.'"

"What money?"

More lip biting... then, "When Mark called me from the Golden Motel and asked me to go away with him, he said money would not be a problem anymore, he said he had lots of it. I didn't believe him but when I found out he was dead, I checked our bank account. There was over two million dollars in it. It's still there." Tears are forming in her eyes.

Two million dollars seems like a hell of a big fee for money-laundering, especially as he would have to share any profits with his partner, Harold Varga.

"Cal, we could take it and go away somewhere, like I said before." She is getting revved up with this idea. "Now that you're no longer with the police, there's nothing keeping you here. We could bring your daughter with us. We could be a family." The tears are starting to trickle down her cheeks.

An infinite sadness descends on me. I think that my feelings for Elizabeth are based on the fact that she is so broken. I feel a need to heal her of her wounds, comfort her for the loss of her son and her husband, make her whole again. I kiss her gently but she responds passionately. I take her by the shoulders and gently push us apart. "Wait."

Something is clawing at me through the swirl of emotion. Something important.

But I need to get back to my agenda; this is still an interrogation whether I like the idea or not.

"Elizabeth, we think this *oboe* code may be the reason Terry was murdered. To keep him from repeating it to anyone. I know this is difficult but do you think there is any possibility at all that Mark may have killed Terry to keep him quiet?"

She is clearly horrified at the thought. "No. No. Mark could never do that. He loved Terry. He loved Terry like he was his own. Mark would never have done anything to hurt Terry... or me. Never!" The tears are cascading down her cheeks as the words come tumbling out. "How could you think such a thing?" An anger is rising in her. "He was devastated when Terry was killed. He blamed himself for the fact that Terry was upset that day. He kept blaming himself over and over again for not hearing Terry sneak out through his bedroom window. He even blamed himself for the fact that the video surveillance cameras weren't—"

"What video surveillance cameras?" The hair on the back of my neck is standing to attention.

Her eyes dart around the room; she is thinking furiously, her breaths coming quickly... then she sighs and deflates.

My voice gentle, I ask, "You said Mark blamed himself for the fact that the video surveillance cameras weren't...?" I leave the question hanging.

"He said they weren't working properly the night Terry was killed." I can see that she believes this... but I don't.

"Mark was very security conscious," she says. "When he installed all that computer equipment in the basement, he installed security cameras all around the outside of the house. They were hooked up to motion sensors and spotlights. Some were infrared for nighttime use. He was terrified that someone would steal those 'blades' as he called them."

"Do you have the disks the cameras were recording on to?"

"I don't think they record to a disk. They're webcams. The images go to a website. Mark sometimes had a window open on his computer displaying the images."

"Do you know the website's URL?"

"No."

"Are any of Mark's computers still here at the house?"

"No."

"Are the webcams still in place?" I ask her. My heart rate increases at the thought that they will have images of the night Terry was killed and there may be a juicy little bonus in there too.

"Yes, of course."

"Show me."

She takes me outside. There are eight small cameras, all installed under the eaves of the roof. None of them have wires coming out of them and into the house. I'll get Forensics to check... Wait a minute, I can't. I feel a hit of sadness that I no longer have access to Forensics.

But I do have access to technical expertise.

"Can I take one of the cameras?"

She nods.

After five minutes with Elizabeth's step ladder and her late husband's tool kit, I have one of the cameras in my possession.

As we go back into the house, I ask her, "You remember you told me that you met the man who Terry worked for? The one who made you feel uncomfortable?"

She nods.

"Did you meet him here at the house?"

"Yes."

"If we could retrieve the surveillance recordings, would you be able to identify him from them?"

She shakes her head. "No. He was only here the one time and that was before Mark got the 'blades' and installed the cameras."

No juicy little bonus. "Damn."

"Rocky, no more questions. Let's go to bed, I need you right now."

My body betrays my feelings for Sam; it wants Elizabeth so much right now and I know, or at least rationalize, that if I refuse her she will be hurt yet again. Another part of me is screaming out against it. It's the cop part of me. I know I have to ask the question I came here to ask. The question I have been avoiding since I walked through the door.

"I was at VGH this morning, visiting my partner," I pause, not wanting to take the next step.

She looks at me, puzzled.

I have to go on. "After I left him, I went to the Human Resources Department."

I stop, hoping she will know where I am going with this and allay my fears. She doesn't.

"On the night Terry was killed, you left the hospital at four-thirty. You didn't finish your shift. You told me that you didn't get home from work until eight."

She doesn't move. She just looks at me. I cannot read any emotion on her face.

The silence extends. It is as though she is willing me to take the next step, to make the accusation.

"Where were you between four-thirty and eight o'clock, Elizabeth?"

She turns away and walks over to the bookcase. She takes a CD case off the shelf. It is the hauntingly beautiful music she played when I was here a week ago. She looks down at the cover then lifts it up to her lips. Her back is to me and I can see the tension in her shoulders. She looks up, as though to the heavens, and her shoulders slump.

"I was with Seth. We were making love."

With Seth dead, it is an alibi I can't corroborate. Unless...

"Where?"

Her voice is barely above a whisper, "The Golden Motel."

The place where her husband was murdered. Is that just a coincidence?

"Did anyone there see you?"

"I don't know. Seth—" She stops herself short as the implications of the question hit home; she turns to me. "I didn't kill my son, Rocky." Her voice is calm... too calm. More calm than I have ever heard it. "I don't know how you could possibly think that."

Her denial does nothing to allay my suspicion.

She turns back to the bookcase. "I think you should go now."

But I can't. As much as I want to take that camera and have it yield its secrets, I have to stay and tell her that her former lover is dead.

61

STEVE
SATURDAY

I am not sure I am doing the right thing here. Stammo looks unsure of himself and Rogan—who arrived late saying that he had to drop something off to someone—is looking downright hostile.

"Why am I here guys?" I ask.

Rogan looks at Stammo and shrugs, then nods.

Stammo speaks first, "Steve, there's a dirty cop in the department, someone senior."

His words fire through me like a high tension electrical current and I ask the question I dread.

"Who?"

It comes out more like a squeak than a word.

"We're not sure but we think it might be Super-intendent Cathcart."

I regain my composure. "Cathcart? He's the original Mr. Clean," I say. "What evidence do you have?"

"First thing," Stammo says, "you remember those drug cases I had cold, how they both went south."

I know them only too well. "Yeah, on one of them, when you went to arrest the perp, he'd already run; on the other, the key forensic evidence went missing."

"Yeah, well I thought about it a lot and I figured that a dirty cop in a senior position in the department could easily have tipped off the first guy and arranged for that forensic tech to screw up the evidence for the second one."

Never underestimate Stammo.

"Ok, but why Cathcart?"

This time Stammo looks at Rogan and nods.

"We've got nothing specific against Cathcart," says Rogan, "except that he's good friends with Harold Varga."

"Varga?" That might work.

"You better tell him the whole thing Rogan," Stammo says.

Rogan is still not a happy camper but he nods. "OK Steve, you remember that thing that Terry Wright and his friend Michael Chan were chanting? We called it the *oboe* code."

I nod.

"Well I had a friend look at it and he discovered that it is a computer encryption key that Toronto National Bank use. Anyone with the key, who can eavesdrop on people logging into their internet banking at TNB, can steal their passwords. Mark Wright was a former techie from the bank and he and Varga were using the code to launder money."

"How?"

"They use the code to find out the passwords of thousands of different bank customers. Then they take the cash of the people they are laundering for and deposit it, in amounts each smaller than ten thousand dollars, in the accounts of the people whose password they have. Immediately, they transfer the money back out of the customer's account into an account of their own. When the customers see their bank statements they see a deposit followed immediately by a transfer out. They assume that the bank made an error and corrected it immediately, no harm no foul."

"How did you work it out?" I ask.

"My buddy who worked out the significance of the *oboe* code put the idea in my head and Nick worked it."

"So you think they killed the Wright kid to stop him repeating the code?" I ask.

Rogan looks uncomfortable. "I dunno," he says. "Terry Wright was autistic. If he was repeating something that sounded like gibberish no-one would take any notice of him. Who could possibly guess that it was a bank code being used for money-laundering? I don't really see that it was a motive for killing Terry. But it *was* a motive for the attempted kidnapping of Michael Chan."

"How come?"

"With Terry dead, Michael was now repeating the code. Suddenly someone is taking notice, that someone being the police. Michael had to be stopped."

Smart deduction. Let's see what else that clever mind of his has worked out. "So why was Terry killed and why was Varga's wife killed?" I ask.

"We're not sure yet," Stammo answers, "but here's what we think is going on. You remember how last year, Rogan was investigating his buddy's murder and we put that big drug dealer away. Well, it turns out that Seth Harris, the guy who was killed at the weirdo church, was working for Mr. Big. His sister, the minister, told Rogan about it. Harris was running his drug business for him. But Mr. Big's money-laundering scheme was shut down when we put him away, so he needed a new way to launder their drug money. Well, Seth is living at the Church with his sister and he has access to all the Church records. Rogan found a bunch of copies of all sorts of stuff in Seth's room, including two very interesting documents. One was a copy of his sister's notes on her counselling sessions with Varga's wife. She talks about the fact that her husband was a big gambler and that he was deep in debt to what she called an illegal casino. Another was the notes on the minister's counselling sessions with Elizabeth Wright. Seth found out that Mark Wright was a genius-level techie who was out of work but that he used to work for Varga's bank.

"So here's what we think happened. We know that Mr. Big's organization had been laundering money from his drug businesses and also for a number of illegal gambling joints, so Seth makes a couple of calls and finds out that Varga is in hock to this one guy Dominique Dufresne. Seth approaches Mark Wright and offers him the chance to make a lot of money. He simultaneously approaches Varga and tells him that if he will work with Mark Wright on setting up some form of money-laundering scheme, he will see that his gambling debt is written off; if he doesn't cooperate, Seth will tell the Bank that their Senior VP of Private Banking is on the hook to a crooked gambler. Varga and Wright agree and they work out this money-laundering scheme. Seth uses Mr. Big's money to buy Mark a bunch of computer equipment and somehow they get hold of the encryption key and put the plan into action.

"Now Mr. Big, although he's locked up in Millhaven, is back in business money-laundering and Seth is his front man, rebuilding the drug business and laundering the money through Varga's bank."

For some reason, Stammo seems to be trying too hard to sell me on this. "How much of this do you have evidence for and how much is just guesswork?" I ask.

Rogan jumps in with the answer. "I searched Seth's room at the church yesterday afternoon and found all his documents. Seth's sister confirmed that they were her counselling notes. She also confirmed that Seth, Dufresne and Mr. Big were buddies. I was at Dufresne's gambling joint last night and confirmed that Varga was in hock to him and that Seth was doing his money-laundering."

"How the hell did you get him to admit that?" I ask. Rogan may be a good interrogator but that's crazy.

He laughs. "You remember Nick saying in our meeting ten days ago, after our first visit to the Church, that Seth looked like me. When I went to see Dufresne, I pretended to be Seth's brother. Dufresne bought it."

I've got to hand it to Rogan, he is one inventive SOB. But we are not at the heart of the matter yet, not by a long shot. I need to find out what they know and what they are guessing. "So where does this supposed dirty cop come in?" I ask.

Rogan and Stammo exchange looks but I can't read them. Rogan turns to me and looks hard into my eyes for what seems like a long time. I get it. He is wondering if *I* am the dirty cop. I just look straight back at him but inside, I'm tense. Rogan and I were friends. We worked together for a lot of years and despite all the drugs and shit that's gone down recently, for some reason his good opinion still matters to me.

He seems to come to some conclusion. "Here's the thing," he says. "We think Cathcart has been doing this for a while. Nick has been doing some research and there have been instances of drug cases going sideways for years. The one big drug case we won last year could not have been influenced by him, because it was being pursued from outside the department, by me. It ended up with Mr. Big in prison.

"So Cathcart sees an opportunity. Maybe he can take over Mr. Big's operation. He cozies up to Seth and finds out all about the money-laundering scheme, but when Terry Wright is killed, he sees his chance. He tells Seth that Michael Chan is repeating the *oboe* code to the police and uses that as an excuse to bring in some muscle from out of town, the two women who tried to kidnap Michael and who put Nick in that chair. Seth even helped the woman by lending them his sister's SUV, only to be killed by them for his trouble. With Seth dead, Mr. Big is out of business."

Rogan stops again and looks long and hard at me. "So who are these women, Steve?" he asks "and don't give me any of that national security BS."

I can feel the colour rising in my cheeks. "Listen, Cal. I'm just a sergeant. If my boss tells me that his boss tells him that their identity is a national security issue, then I've gotta leave it at that.

"So it was Cathcart who played the national security card?" says Stammo.

I nod.

"It's crap, Steve." Stammo's voice has risen a decibel or two. "Those women are hired killers and we're sure they're cops or ex-cops. Cathcart is your dirty cop and those women work for him."

"You know what you can do here Steve," Rogan chimes in, "check the prints on the SUV. Once you eliminate Morgan and Seth Harris' prints, whatever's left belongs to those women. It is evidence that they have committed attempted kidnapping and assault, then you can force the issue—"

"What SUV?" I ask.

"The Caddy that was used to try and kidnap Michael Chan and that put me in this." Stammo expresses his anger by shaking the arms of his wheelchair.

I feel like I've stepped into another reality. "Where is this SUV?"

Stammo's eyes narrow. "Forensics have got it." There is exasperation in his voice. "When Rogan found it, he called me and I called it in. I phoned you but you weren't there, so I spoke to young Eric Street and told him. He said he'd get it towed in. Are you saying he didn't tell you?" His voice has a suspicious edge to it.

"Yeah, Nick, that's exactly what I'm saying." My tone sounds defensive even to me.

Stammo looks hard at Cal. "Tell him Rogan. Tell him what happened to you."

Rogan looks uncomfortable. "I don't think it's—" He stops himself in mid-sentence. "OK," he says and then blows my mind with the story of his kidnapping by fellow VPD members. Stammo completes the picture with, "Eric Street was one of them, he admitted it to me."

Why didn't I know about this? Someone wanted Cal out of the Department more than I did and it scares me that they went to such lengths. Who would condone...

"Are you thinking he might be tied in with Cathcart?" I ask.

"I am now."

I pull out my Blackberry. He answers on the first ring. "Eric, it's Steve. Did Nick Stammo call you yesterday about an SUV that needed to be pulled in by Forensics?" I can see Stammo bristling out of the corner of my eye.

"Yes, I sent them out but when they got there, the vehicle was gone. We figured that either Nick got it wrong or the owner drove it off."

Stammo is waving his hand in my face. I put Eric Street on hold.

"Ask him about the Blue F150, I called it in about an hour later."

I do.

"Yeah, we've got that but it had been wiped clean of prints."

I hang up and tell them.

After their expletives have subsided, Rogan smiles. "That proves that either Eric Street or someone in Forensics is dirty. I saw that truck in the neighbour's garage when I was at the church. There were fingerprints all over it that I could see with the naked eye. Someone wiped them clean."

Now it's me that feels uncomfortable; the thought of people I work with every day being criminals turns in my gut. I ask, "Who do you think these women are?"

Rogan looks me in the eye. "Steve," he says, "I think they are rogue cops or ex-cops, certainly from out of town. The way they handle themselves and their weapons makes me think so."

Stammo starts to say something but I wave him quiet. I need to process all this. I'm having a real problem coming to terms with the idea that Superintendent Cathcart, the most senior detective on the force, is dirty. And if he is, what do I do? Go to the Deputy Chief in charge of Investigations Division and tell him. If I'm wrong it's a definite career killer.

Rogan's phone rings.

"Hey, Damien," he says. "That was fast... Yeah... That's great... You're kidding... Yeah, text it to me. Thanks man, I owe you big time."

He looks back and forward between Stammo and me with a big grin on his face.

"What?" asks a frustrated looking Stammo.

"Wanna find out what happened to Terry Wright?" Rogan asks.

62

CAL

As I type the URL into Stammo's computer, I tell them about the video cameras installed around the Wright's house.

"They were tiny. He'd installed them under the gutters. They were Wi-Fi and connected through Wright's network to an internet server. I gave one of them to my buddy Damien—the guy who cracked the *oboe* code for me—and he found out the URL of the server where the videos are stored." I hit Return and there is a window asking me for a username and password.

"Oh, shit," Stammo grunts.

I enter the username *cal* and password *rogan*. I am presented with a list of dates.

"How did you know the password?" Steve asks.

"Damien texted the URL to one of his employees. It took him about fifteen minutes to hack into the site and create an account for me."

"So much for Mark Wright, the computer security expert," Stammo chuckles. "He spent his career helping other people with their security but didn't follow his own advice."

I scroll down the list of dates and click on the eleventh, the day that Terry was killed.

There are thumbnails of over a hundred mpeg videos.

"So where do we start?" Steve asks.

I study the screen for a while before I spot the pattern.

"Look at the file names," I tell him. "Each one has the date, then a time, then a two-digit number that I'm guessing is the number of the camera. Terry and Mark got home at five-thirty and Elizabeth Wright got home at eight and found Terry gone. We should look at the videos for that time."

There are twelve videos with the time 18:00 in the filename. I download them to Stammo's laptop and open the first one, for camera 01; it is two hours long. With twelve cameras, we've got twenty-four hours of video to look through and if they yield nothing, we'll have to look through the twelve videos for the previous two hours which cover the time period from five-thirty until six.

"Let's do it!" says Stammo.

———

IT LOOKS LIKE MISSION CONTROL. Set up around Stammo's bed are six laptops: his, mine and Ellie's and three that Steve has scrounged up from VPD. They are all using QuickTime's fast forwarding feature to speed through half of the videos from the twelve cameras, at four times normal speed. We have been doing this for two hours and it is deadly boring, but we dare not take our eyes from the screens for a moment for fear of missing something. A nurse who came in to check on Stammo was politely asked to leave.

Without moving his eyes from the screens he is watching, Stammo says, "You know what? We're not going to find anything. If there was anything on any of these cameras, Mark Wright would have seen it and told us. Shit, we're wasting our time."

"Not if he was the one who killed Terry," counters Steve.

"If he was, he would have erased any video evidence for sure. So we are still wasting our time."

"You're right," Steve says and slumps back in his chair.

"Keep watching," I say and out of the corner of my eye, I see Steve respond to the urgency in my voice. Stammo has triggered a thought in my mind. I can think of a reason why Mark Wright might witness his step-son's murder on video and not report it to to the police. The thought leads to another. If I am right, we have solved Terry's murder but at what cost? As much as I want to solve Terry's murder, I don't want it to be this.

"There!" Stammo shouts. He is pointing at the right hand laptop of the two he is monitoring. It shows a section of the garden and the path that leads to the front door. The only movement is in the top right hand corner of the screen, which shows a section of the road. Two cars flash by.

I pause the videos running on mine and Ellie's laptops and Steve does the same on his. Stammo has paused the video and is taking it back three minutes. He clicks Play and the video recommences at normal speed.

Nothing moves.

A car goes by.

I am holding my breath, dreading what I know I'm going to see.

Nothing.

Don't let it be, I pray silently.

"I was sure I saw something." Stammo's voice has a defensive ring to it.

I check the time display. One hour and twenty-three minutes into the video and we must be close the the point where Stammo stopped it.

Then someone enters the frame.

It's a man.

I let all the air out of my lungs in a long, silent sigh of relief.

Thanks to the excellent quality of the video, I can see that he is dressed in what looks like a black coat and a scarf wrapped twice around his neck, obscuring the lower half of his face. He is wearing a fedora and is studiously keeping his head down; he knows about the cameras. I can feel the adrenaline flooding my system; it can only be one of three people. As I think about it I eliminate two of them.

The man's head swings to the right and he turns and steps off the path, vanishing off camera. In all, he was only on the screen for a total of about four seconds—one second at four times fast forwarding.

"Nicely spotted, Nick." Steve claps Stammo on the back and I give him a broad grin. Stammo just nods but I know he's pleased.

We turn our attention back to the video; nothing moves for ten minutes so I lean forward and pause it. "Let's look at the other cameras for that time period," I suggest.

One after the other, we set the other videos to one hour and twenty three minutes and click play.

Six pairs of eyes drill into the screens for ten minutes. Nothing.

I'm about to curse when I remember that there are six other videos from the other six cameras. I grab Stammo's laptop and set up the first one to one hour and twenty-three minutes in. It is a view of the west side of the house and sitting on a thin strip of grass, his back to the neighbour's fence and looking straight up at the camera is Terry Wright. I drag the time control to the left, moving back in time, until he is no longer in the frame, then click play.

After a couple of seconds Terry walks into the frame; he is wearing a yellow winter jacket and grey sweat pants, haunting me with the picture of his dead body stretched out in the Endowment Lands. "This is the west side of the house. Terry's bedroom was on this side. It looks like he did climb out his bedroom window," I say.

Terry walks over to the chain-link fence. He kneels down and starts zig-zagging his fingers down the wire strands. He does this for several minutes then stops suddenly, turns round, sits down and draws his knees up to his chest. He wraps his arms around his shins and hugs his legs tightly to his chest then looks directly at the camera and starts saying or mouthing something, his head nodding in time to each syllable. This goes on for several minutes and with a flash of intuition, I say, "He's reciting the *oboe* code."

Before anyone can comment, Terry glances up and to his left then snaps his head forward so that he is staring fixedly at the wall of the house. He is continuing to mouth what I am now sure is the code but he is saying it faster and rocking his whole body back and forth in time to each syllable. He starts moving his head to the right while his eyes keep flicking to his left, as into the frame walks the man in the fedora.

Due to the camera angle, we are looking down at the back of the man's head. He crouches on Terry's left and the boy moves his head to his right, studiously avoiding eye contact. From the slight movements of the man's head, I infer that he is talking to the boy although Terry's mouth keeps moving faster and he is turning his head further away from the man. The speed of his rocking is increasing.

My mind flashes back to Michael Chan repeating 'O—B—O—E Shhhh!' his volume increasing with every iteration.

The man is gesticulating at Terry; he seems agitated. Suddenly his hand, encased in a leather glove, strikes out and clamps over Terry's mouth. The boy attempts to squirm away but the man's other hand grabs the scruff of his neck and drags him to his feet.

His arm snakes around Terry's body hugging the boy to his chest, and, keeping his back to the camera, he steps backward toward the wall of the house, until he vanishes out of the bottom of the frame.

We all inhale and I know that, like me, my colleagues have been holding their breath as we watched the opening scene of the murder of Terry Wright.

————

WE HAVE SCOURED all of the tapes for further footage of Terry's captor but, as I expected, have found nothing. It lends credence to my theory.

"Whoever it was knew the location and positioning of all of the cameras," Stammo snorts in frustration.

"It was Mark Wright," breaths Steve, barely above a whisper. "He killed his own kid. That was why he committed suicide."

"Killing your own kid is a bit extreme, Steve," Stammo objects.

"Terry was his step kid," Steve counters.

"It wasn't Mark," I tell them. "Apart from the fact that Elizabeth assured me he truly loved Terry, if he *had* done it, first thing he would have done is delete the videos for that time slot and replace then with videos from a different day at the same time."

They grunt acknowledgement of the logic. But Stammo spotted that I called Elizabeth by her first name, I saw the look he cut me.

Stammo scratches his head and says, "It could have been that nasty piece of work Seth Harris or maybe Cathcart."

"No, they're professionals." I say. "If they had caught Terry repeating the *oboe* code, they wouldn't have panicked and killed him. They'd have taken him into the house and had Mark deal with him."

Stammo can see the look on my face. "Well?" he asks.

"Thanks to you Nick, I've got a good idea of who it was."

He looks askance. "What did I say?"

"You said that after Terry went missing, Mark Wright must have checked the videos and found what we've just seen. So why didn't he contact the police straight away?"

I leave the question hanging.

Stammo shrugs but I see a glint in Steve's eye. "Harold Varga," he says.

"Exactly. The man in the video knew about the cameras. Apart from Mark Wright, there's Seth Harris, Cathcart and Varga but Varga's not a pro. He hears Terry repeating the *oboe* code and he panics and tries to silence Terry. When Terry goes missing, Wright checks the videos and recognizes Varga. But he and Varga are up to their ears in this money-laundering scheme. If Mark accuses Varga and we arrest him, it's all going to come out: if he tells us, he's screwed."

"So what *does* he do?" asks Steve.

"He goes to Seth Harris. Under the orders of our buddy in Millhaven prison, Seth is the one who got Varga and Wright working together, so Wright is gonna go to him."

"And Harris pops Varga's wife to teach him a lesson," Stammo says.

"No, I don't think so. But let's stick with Varga for a moment," I say. "What actual evidence do we have?"

"None," Steve grunts.

"A search of his place might turn up the clothes he was wearing in the video," says Stammo.

"We'd never get a warrant," I can hear the exasperation in Steve's voice. "And even if we did, chances are Varga has got rid of those clothes and if he hasn't, he would say that anyone could have the same clothes."

"So what did Varga do after he walked out of that video frame?" I ask.

"Take Terry to his car?" Stammo suggests.

I nod. "If we discount the possibility that Varga took Terry into the house and that Mark Wright was in on the murder, I think that's exactly what he would do. But what route did he take? He doesn't appear on any of the other tapes, so his choice of routes would be very limited. Steve, if you sent a forensic team with a laptop displaying the feeds from all the cameras, they could plot out all of the possible routes that Varga took without being caught by a camera. Then they could examine those routes for any trace evidence."

"I could do that," Steve says.

"If Varga took Terry in his car, there would almost certainly be evidence in the car, so, if we could get a warrant..." Stammo leaves the sentence hanging.

"So Varga gets off the Wright's property without being seen again by the cameras," Steve says. "He takes Terry to his car and drives off to the Endowment Lands to kill him. So where does he get the knife? Does he go home first and take one from the kitchen? Did he have one in the car and, if so, why? Did he stop and buy one from a store?"

"For that matter, when did he decide to make it look like a ritual killing?" I ask. "Varga's a banker, whatever would give him the idea to—"

Oh.

I just asked the right question.

One after the other, the pieces click into place until I have it.

Stammo and Steve are silent, somehow they can sense that something is going on.

As my mind wanders through the facts, the murders of Terry Wright, Marguerite Varga, Mark Wright and Seth Harris all make complete sense.

But to prove it, Steve is going to have to take one hell of a risk. I wonder how willing he is going to be to take it.

63

CAL

SUNDAY

I've got to admit that Steve has guts. He has put his whole career on the line based on a theory with no really compelling evidence. He's compounded matters by having Stammo and me here: I am still suspended and Stammo is on sick leave. The hospital promised dire consequences too, but Nick told them in no uncertain terms that it would take more than his nurses to keep him there.

We are letting Varga stew.

He is sitting in the interview room, alone. He is angry, for sure, but there is something else in his demeanour that I cannot quite read. Confidence? Whatever it is, it does not feel good to me.

The fact that it is Sunday morning is working in our favour There are not a lot of people in and none of the brass. I don't want to run into any of my colleagues. I know that if I do, I will be asking myself, 'Are you one of the bastards who kidnapped me, took me to Riverview and shot me up to the moon, just to get rid of me.' I feel my cheeks glowing at the humiliation. If, against all odds, I am reinstated tomorrow morning, will I ever be able to face them, let alone work with them?

We are gathered around the monitor connected to the interview-room camera, agreeing our strategy. In addition to Steve, Stammo and me, there are two people whom we all agree we can trust. I think it is the first time I have seen Sarge out of uniform; he went with Steve to pick up Varga and he is going to play a big part in our little charade, although, for his own protection, we have not informed him of all the issues in this case. The other is Hank King from the Crown Prosecutor's office: grey-haired, hawk-like and with a mind like a steel trap; we have told him everything that we have learned or that we suspect.

"OK. Let's do it." Steve stands, adjusts the tiny earpiece and walks out of the room. Within fifteen seconds, we see him on the monitor entering the interview room.

Immediately, Varga stands. "Sergeant Waters, have you contacted my good friend Superintendent Cathcart as I demanded?" He has lost none of his pomposity.

"Yes sir, I did. He said that he is unable to come right now," Steve lies.

It is like a slap in the face. Varga visibly flinches but does not deflate as I expected he would. "Then I..." He stops himself. I think he is about to ask to have a lawyer present.

"Yes sir?"

He is undecided for a moment, then says, "Then I suggest you ask all your questions now so that I can go."

He sits down and Steve follows suit.

Varga has been told that he is needed to answer some questions regarding his wife's death, so Steve's first question is going to throw him. I find myself smiling in anticipation and flash a glance at Stammo. He is wearing his wolf's grin. I'm glad he's had my back the last few days.

"Mr. Varga, for how long were you and Mark Wright running your money-laundering operation?"

A look of panic springs into Varga's eyes. It lasts for less than a second, replaced by a look of puzzlement. It fools no-one; his face has turned several shades whiter. If he is going to ask for his lawyer, now would be a good time.

"If Superintendent Cathcart is not available, I insist upon seeing someone more senior than a mere sergeant." He stands and glares down at Steve.

"Sit down please sir." Steve's voice is measured. "Or I will have to have you handcuffed to the table."

This time, Varga deflates as he sits. It's a perfect state of mind for him to be in as Steve delivers the next blow.

"So when you discovered that Mark had stolen two million dollars of the money you were laundering, you murdered him?"

"NO! I didn't even know he'd taken the money until—" Too late he stops himself. Steve broke him in under ninety seconds by accusing him of a murder we know he didn't commit.

Beside me, I hear Hank King murmur *"Prima facie."* Admitting to his involvement in the money-laundering operation will give him a motive for murdering Terry, which in turn gives us grounds for a search warrant.

Sarge gets up to go but Hank holds up a finger, signalling him to wait.

In the monitor, we see Steve shift his posture to mirror Varga's.

"Mr. Varga," he says quietly. "We have some sympathy for your situation."

Varga looks up, hope daring to break through the defeat on his face.

"Your only sin was gambling in the wrong place. We know they blackmailed you into taking part in the money-laundering scheme."

"That's right." Varga sits up straighter and leans forward and I smile as I watch Steve do the same. "They threatened to expose me at the Bank, I couldn't allow that could I?" Steve nods and pats Varga's forearm and the VP of one of the country's biggest banks recites a lengthy justification of his actions ending in, "...and so none of our clients lost any money as a result."

"Good enough," Hank says into the microphone and we see Steve nod his acknowledgement. Hank, in turn, nods to Sarge, who picks up the paperwork for the warrant and heads out to go see the on-duty judge.

In the interview room, Steve says, "I understand completely Mr. Varga and I think we can go very lightly on you... if you can help us with just one thing."

"Absolutely Sergeant Waters, anything." I smile at the fact that Steve is no longer a 'mere' sergeant.

"I want you to tell me about the police officer who has been involved in this whole operation."

The fawning expression is replaced by one of naked fear. Varga is unconsciously shaking his head. The video camera's resolution is not good enough to show it but I am betting that a cold sweat is beading its way on to Varga's forehead.

Steve's voice is soothing. "Sir, if you are prepared to testify in court about Superintendent Cathcart's involvement, we can offer you protection and we will grant you *full* immunity for your part in the money-laundering operation. I have a prosecutor waiting outside, willing to sign a confidential letter with your lawyer guaranteeing not to charge you with money-laundering in return for your co-operation."

The look passing over Varga's face makes me think of the Bard: *The offender's sorrow lends but weak relief, to him that bears the strong offence's cross.* But there is something else. Confusion perhaps. He is silent for a long time, then, "Alright, in return for full immunity, I will give evidence about Superintendent Cathcart's ah... complicity."

"Why don't I leave you to call your lawyer. When he gets here we'll sign the documents," Steve says and leaves the room.

Varga pulls out his cellphone. The wait for his lawyer to arrive will give us the time we need.

———

WE ARE PLAYING a game against time. We need to get some proof of Varga's guilt in Terry Wright's murder before the immunity letter gets signed with his lawyer. The forensic team at the Wright house has worked out the routes by which Varga could have left the property and the members have combed the areas in detail. They have found two slivers of material caught in a fence. One has been matched to a tear in the green t-shirt that Terry was wearing when he was killed.

The good news is: Varga's lawyer, named Sigmund Rice, a corporate type with an expensive suit and a pot belly, was difficult to contact; when Varga first called him, he was in church with his cell off. It took several calls followed by a two hour wait before he arrived. Steve showed him the footage of his client admitting to money-laundering and left them together for a while.

The bad news is: by the time Sarge got the on-duty judge to sign the search warrant, allowing the second forensic team to enter Varga's property—and the third team to examine his car, parked below this building—over an hour has passed.

Steve has badgered the forensic teams and, so far, we do not have everything we need.

Now Steve, Stammo and I are watching the monitor. Stammo is biting his nails

There is a letter on the table between Hank King and Sigmund Rice.

"This *seems* straightforward," says Rice. "You are giving my client immunity from prosecution on charges of money-laundering, *if* he assists you in your inquiries into corruption in the Police Department."

"Correct," King says.

"Hmmm... I think you need to amend this," Rice gives a creepy smile.

"How?"

"I want you to extend it to immunity from charges of money-laundering *and* all other activities arising therefrom."

I feel myself holding my breath and note the concern on the faces of my colleagues. If Varga suspects that we know about Terry's murder and has communicated his suspicions to Rice, they are going to want blanket immunity to cover that too.

"Why would I do that? It's far too vague," says King with a snort.

"Firstly, the police made mention of my client being involved in illegal gambling and secondly, they accused him of murdering his colleague, Mark Wright, which he patently did not do. I want those specific things covered in the letter."

King makes a play of thinking about this, then gets up, looks up at the video camera and leaves the room.

Varga is about to say something to his lawyer, but the latter points to the camera. And signals *Sshhh.*

Within seconds, King enters our room. "Have you got it yet?"

"No."

"Crap! I guess I can stall for a bit." He waits a few minutes then leaves and reappears on the monitor as he enters the interview room.

"My bosses are OK with those changes. Give me a moment to write them up," he says and leaves again. Varga and Rice sit silently, not wanting to talk in front of the camera. I take some small pleasure in the fact that the silence is costing Varga five hundred bucks an hour in legal fees.

Before King reenters our room, Steve's phone rings. "Yeah... OK... How long? ... OK, as fast as you can."

He hits the end button. "We might just make it," he sighs.

———

"TELL us about your money-laundering activities please, Mr. Varga." Steve is relaxed and friendly and both Varga and his lawyer seem to be the same.

"I was in debt to a gambling operation, not out of control you understand, but I needed a little time to pay. The man I owed the money to—"

"That would be Dominique Dufresne?" Steve interrupts.

"Yes. He threatened me. I had to do as he asked."

"And what was that?"

"Back in June of last year, Seth Harris, from my

wife's church," the last word comes out as a sneer, "had enlisted the help of Mark Wright who said that he could hack into the bank's computers if there was someone on the inside to handle the money once it had been through the clients' accounts. They forced me to go along with it, otherwise I would have been exposed to the Bank as a gambler."

Beside me, Stammo shakes his head. "Slime ball," he grunts.

"Was Mark being pressured too?" Steve asks.

"No," the distaste in Varga's voice is strong. "He just did it for the money."

"Do you know who was behind the money-laundering?"

"Yes, some criminal in jail back east. I don't know his name but Seth worked for him and so did... the police officer you want to expose."

"Superintendent Cathcart?"

Varga looks at his lawyer who nods.

"Yes."

"So how did the money-laundering operation work?" Steve is switching between subjects to try and catch Varga off guard.

"Mark cracked the bank's encryption in October. Seth had bribed or blackmailed someone at the phone company to connect a device to the lines into the bank's internet banking network. It recorded people's banking transactions and routed them through to computers in Mark's house. Mark's computers decrypted the transactions and got the account numbers, usernames and passwords of thousands of customers.

"Seth worked with the drug dealers. He would give them a list of names and account numbers and the dealers would have someone deposit cash into the accounts. It was always under ten thousand dollars, to avoid the bank having to report the transaction to the federal government. Then he would log on to the clients' accounts and transfer the money out of the clients' accounts into an account which I controlled. I transferred eighty-five percent of the monies deposited to offshore accounts. The other fifteen percent was the fee for doing the transaction which went into an account controlled by your Superintendent."

"How much money were you laundering?" Steve asks.

Varga smiles. He almost looks proud. "We were processing money for drug dealers and gamblers throughout Western Canada. Last month we processed just over fifteen million dollars."

"Holy shit," I hear Stammo gasp.

In the interview room, Steve doesn't miss a beat. "So your fee last month was two and a quarter million dollars. How much of that did you get?"

"Mark and I both received a hundred thousand dollars for our services."

By using words like *fee*, *processing* and *services*, Varga is trying to add an air of legitimacy to what he has done.

Then Steve asks Varga the question that I was thinking. "How much of the fee did Seth Harris receive for his services?" Steve is using Varga's own language patterns to maintain the sense of rapport with him.

"I don't know, you would have to ask him."

Interesting, Varga doesn't know Seth has been murdered. I wonder if Steve is going to tell him.

"So what went wrong?" Steve asks.

"What do you mean?"

"What do I mean?" Steve has raised his voice; he is changing tactics, switching from good cop to bad cop. "There you all were making money hand-over-fist, then Terry Wright and your wife get murdered within less than two days of each other. Something went wrong wouldn't you say?"

Varga looks down at the floor. He is fiddling with his wedding ring.

"Well Mr. Varga," Steve stands up. "What went wrong?"

Varga mumbles something and his lawyer tells him to be quiet.

"The only way you're free from prosecution is if

you're completely straight with us." Steve's voice is quieter.

Varga's lawyer leans over and whispers something in his ear. Varga nods and looks up at Steve. "It may have been my fault," he says. "I told Seth that I wanted out. I told him that the bank would eventually start to ask questions about the account all the money was passing through. I told him that I couldn't go on; that I wouldn't."

"When was this?"

"Two days before Terry passed away." The euphemism angers me.

"How did Seth react?" Steve asks.

"He exploded. He got physically violent with me. He hit me repeatedly in the stomach and back. I can show you the bruises. *He's* someone you should be arresting. He told me I had to go on and that I didn't understand the people I was dealing with. He said that he couldn't guarantee what would happen if I tried to back out." Varga thinks for a moment. "But it was strange now that I think back on it. He was angry, sure, but I think he was also frightened of what might happen to him if I backed out." He stares off into the distance.

"Did you ever speak to your friend Superintendent Cathcart about your wanting out?"

"No, why would I?" he says distractedly. For some reason, his response jars me. There is something that doesn't feel right. Steve seems not to notice anything; maybe I'm imagining things.

"So after you told Seth that you wanted out, what happened next?"

"The next evening, two women came to my house and demanded to see me. Ugly, brutish women they were. My wife answered the door, they quite frightened her. I met with them in my study and they told me that if I tried to get out now that I would regret it. They were very menacing. After they had gone, I spoke to Mark and he said that he had met them and that they worked for Inspector Cathcart. He sounded frightened." Varga looks Steve in the face. "Sergeant Waters, I believe that Seth Harris killed Terry Wright and those women murdered my Marguerite in order to keep Mark and I in line." He seems so sincere that I am getting a new respect for his ability to tell a bald-faced lie. I wonder if other parts of his story may be less than truthful and I wonder...

Steve drops his bombshell. "We believe that they are complicit in Seth Harris' murder, too."

Varga's eyes go like saucers and he sways in his seat. Rice, his lawyer has to steady him. Varga's eyes snap upwards toward the camera and it feels like he is looking straight at me. "Sergeant Waters, you must protect me," he says. But it feels like he is pleading with me, not Steve, and just what is he trying to tell me?

My mind is drawn away from the question by the ringing of Steve's phone on the desk in front of me. As agreed, Stammo picks it up, listens for a while and a rare smile crosses his face.

"Gotcha!" he says.

64

CAL

He looks each of us over. "If I had been asked to guess who was knocking on my door at three o'clock on Sunday after-noon, I would never have guessed you three. I suppose it must be important, so come in."

Inspector Vance's apartment is in a modern building in Yaletown.

Steve leads and I wheel Stammo into the living room.

I really appreciate that Steve has brought me to this meeting. Vance will be at my disciplinary hearing tomorrow and it will help that he sees what I have been doing... I hope.

After enquiring about Stammo's health, he asks, "So what can I do for you three?"

Steve takes the lead. "Thanks to some excellent

work by Cal and Nick, we have solved the Terry Wright case."

A big smile spreads over his frog-like face. "You're kidding, who was it?"

Steve tells Vance about the case including all the forensic evidence we got while Varga was being interrogated. "At the scene, we found evidence of Terry's clothing, with some other material that we matched to Varga's coat, which is definitely the coat that we saw in the video. But the real clincher was that we found blood on a pair of Varga's shoes. It has been sent for DNA matching which I have asked for quickly; it's O-negative which was Terry's blood type. In addition, we found a tiny piece of Lego in the trunk of Varga's car. It had a partial print of Terry's on it. When we presented him with the evidence, he confessed."

"Was it a clean confession?" It's the question that is always asked.

"Very clean. His lawyer was present and although he tried to stop him, Varga just kept talking."

"You got him at 275 Cordova?"

"Yes."

Vance mulls it over. "That's good work guys but you didn't come to my apartment on a Sunday afternoon to tell me this did you?"

"No sir. I'll come straight to the point. There's a

senior member in the department who is up to his ears in this money-laundering scheme."

Vance's finger's tighten over the arm of his chair. "Steve, before you go any further, are you sure?"

Steve nods.

"You have evidence?"

"Yes."

Inspector Vance's face does not give much away, but I can see wheels turning within wheels.

A very unpleasant smile morphs on to his face. "Cathcart?"

There is a look of amazement in Steve's eyes. "How did you know?"

"I've suspected for a while." He sighs and shakes his head. "What's your evidence?"

We give him a full briefing, starting with the very first interview when Varga made a big point of being friends with Cathcart and Cathcart's coming to our meeting to deny any closeness to Varga. He ends his pitch by handing over the transcript of his interview with Varga, signed by Varga immediately before we arrested him for Terry's murder.

Vance gets up from his chair and walks to the window. He looks South over False Creek and stands silent for several minutes.

He turns. "Not a word of this to anyone." He looks into the eyes of each of us. It's a hard look, one which, over the years, has frightened a lot of criminals into confessing their crimes. "Steve we'll talk about this tomorrow."

He walks us to the door, pats Stammo on the shoulder and shakes my hand. "Rogan, you can't mention this at your hearing tomorrow, but whatever the result, I will see that the right people get to know about your excellent work on this. Good luck tomorrow."

"Thank you, Inspector," I smile.

My words evoke a memory, an itch I have to scratch.

65

CAL

MONDAY

I should be feeling euphoric. I have been reinstated.

The meeting was surreal, like Kafka's *Trial* but in reverse. It was held in a bright meeting room at Gravely Street and everyone was positive and smiling, almost jolly. Superintendent Cathcart was noticeable by his absence. Everyone nodded with understanding at my story of being kidnapped and force-fed heroin and the testimony of Steve and Stammo—the latter looked very tired and uncomfortable in his wheelchair—was accepted without question. The board endorsed, by acclamation, Inspector Vance's recommendation of reinstatement.

Despite my enthusiastic thanks to them all, inside, the thought of returning to duty makes me feel... well, I don't really know what it makes me feel but it is not what I expected it would be.

Immediately after the review, Inspector Vance gave me back my gun and my ID and suddenly there I was: Detective Rogan again. As I left his office, I saw a very tense Detective Eric Street sitting on a chair outside. I resisted the desire to beat the snot out of the little fuck and instead enjoyed the *schadenfreude* which enveloped me as I threw him a big smile. But that dissolved when I remembered that there were at least two other VPD members involved in my kidnapping. Will I spend the rest of my career wondering which of my colleagues did this to me and which of them knew about it and did nothing? I try to shake off the feeling.

I can't.

Superintendent Cathcart is missing. His wife says that he received a phone call last night and left the house saying that he had to go in to work. No-one has seen him since, triggering a country-wide manhunt operation by the RCMP. A team of detectives are combing records of his history in an attempt to establish the identity of the women whom we are sure killed Varga's wife, Mark Wright and Seth Harris.

Inspector Vance, with his usual efficiency, has teams working on various aspects of the cases. He has sped up the DNA testing and it has just been confirmed that the blood on Varga's shoe is from Terry Wright, making the case against him fairly tight. Everything seems to be coming together, so why do I feel that something is so very wrong?

It's why I'm here at the Vancouver Jail on Cordova Street. I feel a burning need to turn over every stone no matter how seemingly irrelevant.

He walks into the room, a little unsteady on his feet, and I remember talking with Stammo about taking Terry's killer and a couple of baseball bats into an alley. It would feel good.

"Good afternoon, Detective Rogan," he says. "I am afraid that without my lawyer present, I am not prepared to answer any questions."

Despite the fact that he has exchanged his two thousand dollar suits for prison garb, his demeanour has turned one hundred and eighty degrees and he projects his old confidence and pomposity. It is as though he never confessed to the murder of Terry Wright. I get an unpleasant twinge that maybe his lawyer has found an error in our search warrant or the way in which we obtained his confession.

Well, there's always the baseball bat option.

I push the thoughts down and project my own feeling of confidence.

"Thank you for seeing me Mr. Varga," I say. Not that he had any option but I want to project a more subservient role right now. "May I ask how long have you known Cathcart?"

He looks at me, weighing options, and decides there is no harm in answering this question. His eyes go up and to his right. "About two years ago, in October. The Superintendent and I met at a charity dinner sponsored by my bank." Unbelievable! He is speaking like he will be out of here tomorrow and back to work. And his answer fuels my unease; it just does not fit with the slip of the tongue he made when Steve was interviewing him.

"You said that Seth Harris blackmailed you into getting involved in this money-laundering scheme. When did you first become aware that Superintendent Cathcart was involved?"

His eyes go up and to his left; he is constructing a lie. After a moment his eyes lock on mine. "No more questions without my lawyer present." His confidence of a moment ago has slipped.

"When you need to contact him, do you just call him at the office?"

Varga is clearly uncomfortable with my line of questioning. He folds his arms and looks away from me. There is a fine patina of perspiration on his brow. He swallows, twice.

"Come on Mr. Varga. None of these questions are connected with Terry Wright's murder."

He looks paler than when he entered the room.

He swallows again. "None the less…"

"There is no need to be afraid anymore. Superintendent Cathcart has gone missing and is the subject of a nationwide manhunt."

"Oh my God." He tries to stand up, grabs the table for support and flops back down into his seat. "Oh my God, no."

On the face of it his reaction is puzzling. He should feel better knowing that Cathcart is on the run.

He reaches out to me. "You have to…" His breathing is heavy. This is more than just fear.

He tips forward off the chair and does a face plant onto the linoleum floor.

"Guard!" I shout. "Medical emergency here."

I kneel down beside him.

His body is taken by a fit of trembling.

He looks up at me. "He promised," he croaks.

He grabs the sleeve of my jacket and tries to draw me closer.

"He promised. He said… said that… I… I would… be ex—"

A gout of blood spills from his mouth.

"GUARD!" I yell at the top of my lungs.

His eyes flutter.

"Who?" I ask him. "Who did this to you?"

His front teeth bite down on his lower lip but before he can say anything, a second larger flood escapes and spreads red across the floor.

His trembling increases.

Then stops.

66

CAL

Five hours of paperwork and interviews regarding Varga's death are more tiring than a week of investigation.

It's all over and all I can feel is let down. So many people dead or hurt because one crooked cop attempted to take over a large chunk of the Vancouver drug and money-laundering businesses.

First Varga, in a frenzy about his role in the money-laundering scheme and desperately wanting out, goes to see Mark Wright but stumbles across Terry Wright repeating the *oboe* code. In a moment of panic, he kills Terry to shut him up. Mutilating his body was an afterthought, an amateur's attempt to deflect suspicion from himself, a staid banker, and implicate Seth—in revenge for the beating he had received from Seth—by using an image that Varga had seen snooping about on his one and only visit to the Church of the Transcended Masters.

On Cathcart's orders, his female enforcers kill Varga's wife to frighten Varga into staying the course.

Then little Michael Chan, Terry's friend, starts spouting the *oboe* code to me. When Cathcart hears about this, he knows that I will do everything I can to get to the bottom of it. So he takes a two-pronged approach: he gets Eric Street and some of his buddies to take me out of the picture by shooting me full of heroin and he gets his hit squad to eliminate Michael. Stammo's good deed in taking the urine test for me delays me being suspended for just long enough to foil Michael's kidnapping but also puts Stammo in a wheelchair for the rest of his life.

Mark Wright, knowing it's all falling apart, uses his computer skills to steal two million dollars of the money-laundering profits and has the misfortune to ask his wife to run away with him; she rats him out to me, poor bastard. Somehow, Cathcart managed to hear about it—probably from Eric Street—and sent in his female hit squad ahead of the Tactical Support team. They staged Mark's death as a suicide.

With his women providing the muscle, Cathcart

had no need for Seth, who was the one link between the Vancouver drug business and its former kingpin in Millhaven Prison. Seth is killed right in front of Sam, an innocent bystander.

And last of all: Varga. His death from a virulent poison makes no sense to me. Cathcart is in the wind. He and his millions—and probably his female enforcers—are long gone. Why would he want to kill Harold Varga? Maybe to tie up loose ends. Maybe as insurance against a time when he may make a mistake and get caught; without Varga as a witness, there's little to tie him into all this. He could say he ran away because the pressure of the job got to be too much for him.

Everything is tied up nicely with a bow on it.

So why does something feel so wrong to me?

———

ELIZABETH IS SITTING in the passenger seat, close to the front door. I look at her and hate myself for my weakness. When I told her about Seth's murder, she broke down. I stayed to comfort her and—although it now feels twisted and abhorrent to me—as part of the comforting, we ended up making love. I don't think I will ever be able to look Sam in the face. With one act, I have ruined everything that might have been.

I cross the sidewalk and slide behind the wheel of the Healey.

"How did it go?" she asks me.

For a moment I am nonplussed, wondering how she knew about Varga's death until I realize that she is talking about the disciplinary hearing with the Police Board.

"They reinstated me. I'm a cop again."

It's not the answer she was hoping for. It is another roadblock in her plan to get me to go away with her. She doesn't yet know that the two million dollars that Mark took will be seized by the government as the proceeds of criminal activities.

"Congratulations," she says but her tone is empty.

"Thanks." Also empty.

She looks away and I don't know what to say to her.

"I don't know how I feel about going back."

She looks back at me, new hope in her eyes. "Does this mean—"

"I don't know," I say. But I do know. And I know what I have to tell her. But not here. "Let's go back to your place and talk about it."

She smiles and the look in her eyes makes me feel cold. It's the look of victory. I try to smile back.

She puts her hand over mine which is resting on

the gear shift. There is a dreamy, little-girl look in her eyes as she looks out the window.

I turn the key and press the starter button. As I shift into first, Elizabeth's hand clamps down over my wrist, the grip firm; I feel a tremble pass through her. It makes me uncomfortable. I don't want passion right now.

I check the wing mirror and start to pull out of the parking spot.

"It's him," she says, her voice a whisper.

"Who?"

"Him. Mark's client. The one you asked me about. The one that frightened me. Oh my God it's him."

I hit the brakes and the engine stalls. I turn in my seat to look at her.

She is looking toward the door I just came through. Did Cathcart just go into the Gravely police station? Is he giving himself up?

Steve is still standing there; it couldn't have been Cathcart. Steve is looking at us, his face expressionless.

Steve? Steve is partnered with Cathcart? Steve, to whom Stammo and I have told everything we know? No wonder Cathcart is in the wind. Steve must have tipped him off, probably before our meeting with Inspector Vance last night. Why is it always the people that I am close to who turn out to be the bad guys?

"The tall guy in the brown jacket?" I ask. I can hear the catch in my throat.

"What? No," she says, "the other one. The one who just went inside."

A wave of relief passes through me followed by one of frustration that I can't see through the glass doors.

I leap out of the car, feeling the elation of the hunt mixed with the relief that it's not Steve. He has turned to go back into the building. I call his name and he turns toward me.

"Who just went in?" I ask.

"What?"

"Just now, who just went into the building?"

He reacts to the urgency in my voice. "What's going on, Cal?"

I grab him by the shoulders; its all I can do not to shake it out of him. "For heaven's sake, Steve. Who just went in?"

But I know the answer. Varga gave it to Steve in his interview. From the moment that Stammo and I first met Varga, he was very keen to remind us that he was friends with Superintendent Cathcart. He took pains to emphasize the exalted rank. Yet when Steve was questioning him, at one point he said 'Inspector Cathcart.'

"Who just went in Steve?" my voice is calmer.

"Inspector Vance. Why?" I was right.

"Wait here," I tell him, "don't move an inch."

I cross the sidewalk again, crouch down and open the passenger door. "When you saw him, did he see you?" I ask Elizabeth.

"No, I don't think so. Maybe. I don't know." There is panic in her voice.

"OK, don't worry. You're going to be the safest person in Vancouver."

I take out my phone and dial.

"*Yes, Mr. Rogan.*"

"Arnold, are you at home?"

"*I am.*"

"In a about twenty minutes a woman named Elizabeth Wright is going to knock on your door. I want you to keep her safe."

Silence on the line, then, "*Very well. How long for?*"

"A few hours. I'll come and pick her up from you."

"*Good. I'll expect her; if she doesn't show up within half an hour, I'll call you.*"

"Thank you Arnold."

I give Elizabeth Arnold's address. "You'll be completely safe there," I squeeze her arm, "I promise you."

She leans out of the car and kisses me then

scrambles over the centre console into the driver's seat and straps herself in.

"Drive safely," I say and close the passenger door, unable to suppress a twinge that someone other than me is driving my beloved Healey.

Already a plan is falling into place. I turn back to Steve with a grim smile on my face.

67

CAL

Steve is cautious. He wants more proof than Elizabeth's identification of Inspector Vance as her late husband's client and he wants it before we make the next move. I was frustrated by this at first but a quick call to Stammo gave me the answer.

We are in the Forensics Unit. "Sally, before Cal went on leave, he gave you a code to analyze. What can you tell us about it?" Steve asks.

Sally Wilkes runs her fingers through her mane of auburn hair. "I gave it to Sarah to work on." She looks uncomfortable.

"And..."

"Well, she worked out what it was pretty quickly but..."

"But what Sally?" Steve looks at me. We know what's coming.

She doesn't speak.

"Sally, I know that it's a private key." I'm trying to make it easier for her.

It works. She sighs. "Well if you know, that's OK then."

"So why didn't you tell Cal about it?" Steve asks. "Cal tells me that Nick Stammo also called you about it and you never got back to him. Why, Sally?"

"Orders. I was told not to divulge any information. That it was a highly sensitive matter."

"Who gave you those orders?"

She is silent, looking downward, an internal debate waging.

The good guys win the debate. "My boss, but they came from your boss, Inspector Vance. I was told to sit on all the evidence." Again she is silent for a moment. When she speaks again, her voice is softer, she is embarrassed. "I was told that if any new evidence came in, I was to send it to Inspector Vance only. I didn't like it; it's not standard procedure."

"Oh my God," I say.

They both give me a questioning look.

"Mark Wright's supposed suicide. He called his wife from the motel. Your people were monitoring his cellphone, right Sally?"

"Yes." Her expression says it all. "We traced the location and informed Vance immediately."

"Vance knew Mark's location before I did. Before anyone."

We are silent. Steve knows the implication of this and Sally Wilkes is a smart woman, she must be putting two and two together fast.

Steve and I turn to go but I remember one other thing.

"Sally, what about the fingerprints on the flashlight from the murder scene at the church on Oak Street. Were you told to sit on those too?"

"No." She looks puzzled. "When we ran those we got an 'access denied' message from the system."

Steve looks at me and a silent communication takes place. We've got the first thing we wanted.

———

STEVE'S RANK is enough to get us a look at the log. It's right there. Midnight. Prisoner: Harold Varga. Visitor: Inspector C. Vance.

"Were you on duty last night?" Steve asks the guard.

"Yeah. Same as tonight. Four to midnight. Why?"

Steve points to the entry in the log. "Do you remember Inspector Vance's visit?"

He scratches his unkempt head. "Sure.Yeah. He stayed about half an hour."

"Did anything unusual happen?" I ask.

He shrugs. "Not really."

"What does that mean?" Steve asks, a definite edge in his tone.

"Well, he took the guy in a bottle of water, the expensive French stuff, eh. That's not what you'd call usual."

"Is it even allowed?" I ask.

"Not usually, but, hell, he's an Inspector. I'm not going to argue with him am I? Anyway he took it back out with him when he left."

I'll just bet he did.

"Is his cell occupied now?" Steve asks.

"No, but we've got—"

"It's a crime scene. Seal it off. Nothing goes in, nothing goes out, until a forensics team gets here. Got that?"

I won't let myself get too hopeful. Vance is far too smart to leave any evidence that the poison which killed Varga came from him. All we've got is Elizabeth's identification and Sally Wilkes' statement that Vance asked her to hold back details of the *oboe* code.

I AM amazed at Steve's willingness to put his career on the line again with such circumstantial evidence but here we are in the Deputy Chief's office.

The last time I saw the Deputy Chief was in his car as we raced to arrest the man who is now in Millhaven. I remember in great detail him cogently expressing the view, a controversial view shared by many senior police officers, that drugs should be legalized. I have a great respect for the man.

He knows that Steve is going over the heads of two levels of management to talk to him. "How can I help you, Steve?" he asks.

"Well sir, there are some fingerprints connected with the case we have been working on. The computer recognizes them but we get an access denied message. According to Inspector Vance, Superintendent Cathcart said that the identities were being withheld for reasons of national security. Could you verify that for us please sir?" Steve hands the file across the desk to the Deputy.

He ignores the file. "Why are you asking me, Steve? A request like this should come through Inspector Vance."

"I understand that sir."

Silence.

Steve doesn't try to justify going over Vance's head.

The Deputy's eyes hold Steve for a while. He is

assessing the ramifications of breaking protocol and doing as Steve asks.

His eyes turn to me then back to Steve.

"OK."

He opens the file and turns to the monitor on his desk. He angles it so that neither of us can see it.

He enters the file number into his keyboard. After a moment, the computer gives a familiar beep; he just got the 'access denied' message. He enters another code which he types quickly.

He stares at the screen, pondering whatever it is he sees there.

He looks back at the paper file on his desk and repeats the process with the computer.

He sighs.

"OK Steve. You were right. There is no national security hold on the files of these women. You got the 'access denied' message because they are the prints of two female RCMP members based in Ottawa."

"Currently serving?" Steve asks.

He nods. His face tells me that he doubts he is going to enjoy what he is about to hear but nonetheless he asks, "What's this all about Steve?"

Steve takes a big breath and starts to speak.

68

CAL

FRIDAY

I t's an odd taste but kind of nice, though unfamiliar to my palette which is more used to craft-brewed beers. I don't usually drink this early in the afternoon but it's been one hell of a week since Steve and I met with the Deputy Chief on Monday. Also it's Stammo's first day back in his own apartment, so he wanted to celebrate with a shot of bourbon or, as he calls it, his buddy Jim. But he didn't want to see me just to drink; I know *why* I'm here but *not* what it's going to cost me. He's holding off from bringing the subject up until I have briefed him on the details of the cases.

Though fraught with inter-jurisdictional nightmares, Vance's female hit-squad were quietly arrested in the Ottawa RCMP headquarters on Wednesday and, in separate interviews, both rolled on each other and on Vance. The latter was arrested this morning and, for starters, was charged with money-laundering, murder and conspiracy to commit murder. The women denied having anything to do with Superintendent Cathcart's disappearance both being back in Ottawa at the time. Vance is exercising his right to remain silent.

When the two million dollars in Mark and Elizabeth Wright's bank account was seized as the earnings from a criminal enterprise and she learned that I had told the appropriate authorities about the money, she spent five long minutes screaming at me and wishing me a long and painful death. Despite her invective, I could not help feeling sorry for her and have asked Arnold to buy a money order with funds from my trust account and deliver it to her; it's not a fortune but it will help her bury her husband and son and then live for a few months until she is ready to go back to work as a nurse at VGH.

Stammo savours another sip and says, "I'm sorry it was Vance, I liked the guy. Go figure eh?" I nod in agreement. He thinks for a bit. "But it does answer another question." He smiles at my questioning look, "You remember after you had the second drug test, you had a meeting with him and you thought he was gonna fire you but he didn't. What he did do was tell you to track down Mark Wright. He must have figured you had the best chance of tracking him down and you did, even if Sally Wilkes boys did beat you to it. As soon as Wright was dead, you were fired."

Another piece of the puzzle dealt with.

Stammo pours us each another shot. "No news of Superintendent Cathcart?" he asks.

"No. We're guessing he and Varga were Vance's last victims."

"You're lucky he didn't kill you when he had you unconscious at that church, Sam too for that matter."

"I figure he didn't want to raise the storm of attention that goes with a cop killing."

Stammo nods and raises his glass to me. Here it comes.

"So Rogan," he says. "When I offered to help you find your wife, I asked for a favour in return."

"Yes, Nick. It's the real reason I'm here this afternoon isn't it?"

"Yeah. Well you're off the hook for now, eh," he grunts.

He looks embarrassed, an odd condition for Stammo.

"Come on Nick, what was it you wanted?"

"I doesn't matter now. It wouldn't be fair to ask."

I don't like owing favours, so I should be happy to just let it go. I should leave now and go pick up Ellie from after-school care—we could make an early start on our weekend together—but something pushes me to say, "Ask anyway."

He looks out the window at the darkening street. "Well... at the time, you were on suspension from the department and it didn't look like you were ever going back. And there was me in this thing," he thumps the armrest of his wheelchair, "knowing that if I went back into the department, all I'd be able to do was desk work. So I got to thinking, maybe I should go into business as a private investigator."

"That's a great idea Nick."

"Yeah, well... maybe. Thing is..." he looks at me and looks away again. "I was hoping that if the Department didn't take you back, that maybe you could join me, you know, be partners."

The surprise is written large upon my face. For some reason I had thought the favour would be something to do with his kids from whom he is estranged. Not this. A whole bunch of conflicting emotions writhe across my mind: how can I face my colleagues on a daily basis, never knowing who was involved in my kidnapping? Will my job jeopardize any reconciliation with Sam? Can I live without the badge?

And somehow the conflicts resolve themselves.

Stammo misreads the smile that I can't keep from my lips. The annoyance sweeps over his face.

"Look, forget I said it. You've got your job back with the department. You love it. Why would you want to throw it away? I should'n'a said anything."

My laugh is long, loud and restoring; then the words tumble out of my mouth in a rush.

AFTERWORD

Thank you so much for reading *Oboe*, my second novel featuring Cal Rogan. If you enjoyed it I would really appreciate a review; reviews make a huge difference for an independently published author. You can review it at the website of the retailer from whom you purchased it. It can also be reviewed on Goodreads, which is always welcome.

Other books in the series are *Junkie*, *Lockstep*, *Three*, *Cabal*, *Captive* and the latest one *Jailed*. They are all available as large print paperbacks from Amazon.

ABOUT THE AUTHOR

Hi. I am a former software developer, turned actor, turned author. The Cal Rogan mysteries are set in Vancouver Canada and, I hope, reflect the best and worst of the city. If you would like to know more about my views on the drug scene, publishing and writing, or would like to contact me:

My website: robertpfrench.com.

Facebook: facebook.com/robertpfrenchauthor

Twitter: @robertpfrench

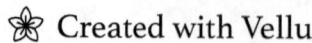